CW01499730

IN'

Locked room mysteries and other stories about seemingly impossible crimes have come in and out of vogue for the best part of two hundred years. I discussed some aspects of their impressive pedigree in my introduction to a previous British Library Crime Classics anthology, *Miraculous Mysteries*, and in more detail in *The Life of Crime*.

During the Golden Age of detective fiction between the two world wars, a host of writers published intricate locked room mysteries. Sometimes they tested their readers' suspension of disbelief to the limit; in skilled hands, however, this is a type of story that can provide wonderful light entertainment. An audacious and brilliant example is *The Hollow Man*, aka *The Three Coffins* (1935) in which John Dickson Carr's Great Detective, Dr. Gideon Fell, breaks the fourth wall to address the reader with a lecture about "the general mechanics and development of the situation which is known in detective fiction as the 'hermetically sealed chamber'". He adds that "All those opposing can skip this chapter", but those who do so will miss a delightful discussion.

Yet there have been times when good judges have been ready to write the obituary of this tantalising branch of detective fiction. Only seven years after *The Hollow Man* was first published, in his history of the genre *Murder for Pleasure*, the American commentator Howard Haycraft gave this blunt advice to aspiring crime writers: "Avoid the Locked Room puzzle. Only a genius can invest it with novelty or interest today."

Locked room mysteries continued to be written, however, mostly with limited commercial success. One outstanding practitioner, the American John Sladek, produced two dazzling locked room mystery novels, *Black Aura* and *Invisible Green*, in the 1970s, before retiring from the field to concentrate on more lucrative work, notably science fiction. In an interview with David Langford in 1982, he said: "I'm sure more people have read my two little detective puzzles because of the SF connection. Those two novels suffered mainly from being written about 50 years after the fashion for puzzles of detection. I enjoyed writing them, planning the absurd crimes and clues, but I found I was turning out a product the supermarket didn't need any more—stove polish or yellow cakes of laundry soap. One could starve very quickly writing locked-room mysteries like those. SF has much more glamour and glitter attached to it, in these high-tech days."

Nevertheless, some enthusiasts for the traditional puzzle mystery, writers and readers alike, kept the flag flying for the locked room puzzle. The American short story specialist, Edward D. Hoch, was a particularly adept and prolific exponent of the form, while Robert Adey published the first edition of his superb study *Locked Room Murders* in 1979. In France, Paul Halter launched a long career as a locked room specialist in 1987 with *The Fourth Door*; only in recent times, however, has this novel been available in English transla- tion. Another straw in the wind came with the publication in 1995 of Douglas G. Greene's *John Dickson Carr: The Man Who Explained Miracles*, an exemplary biography especially notable for its insight into Carr's writing techniques. Bob Adey's book, which has been revised and updated twice (once posthumously, by John Pugmire and Brian Skupin) was my prime source of information about stories that might be suitable for inclusion in this anthology. Like Doug Greene's biography, it is required reading for anyone fascinated by this branch of popular fiction.

AS IF BY MAGIC

AS IF BY MAGIC

*Locked Room Mysteries and
Other Miraculous Crimes*

edited by
MARTIN EDWARDS

This collection first published in 2025 by
The British Library
96 Euston Road
London NW1 2DB
bl.uk

1 3 5 7 9 10 8 6 4 2

Introduction, selection and notes © 2025 Martin Edwards
Volume copyright © 2025 The British Library Board

"The Wrong Problem" © 1936 John Dickson Carr; "The House in Goblin Wood"
© 1947 Carter Dickson. Reproduced by permission of David Higham Associates
on behalf of the estate of the author; "The Ordinary Hairpins" © 1916 E. C.
Bentley; "The Coulman Handicap" © 1958 The estate of Michael Gilbert; "As If
By Magic" © 1961 Julian Symons. Reproduced with permission of Curtis Brown
Ltd, London, on behalf of the Beneficiaries of the Estates of the authors; "The
Vanishing House" © 1924 The Estate of Will Scott; "The Border-Line Case" © 1936
Margery Allingham from *The Allingham Case-Book* reprinted by permission of
Peters Fraser & Dunlop (www.petersfraserdunlop.com) on behalf of Worldwrites
Holdings Limited; "The Shot that Waited" © 1934 The Estate of Vincent Corner;
"The Gold of Tso-Fu" © 1926 The Estate of Robert McNair Wilson; "The Two
Flaws" © 1934 The Estate of Harry Leigh Pink; "Murder Game" © 1968 Christianna
Brand. Reproduced by permission of A M Heath & Co. Ltd, Authors' Agents;
"Too Many Motives" © 1930 James Ronald; "The Case of the Man Who Was Too
Clever" © 1943 Ernest Dudley. Reproduced by permission of Cosmos Literary
Agency; "The Broadcast Body" © 1936 The Estate of Grenville Robbins; "The
Last Meeting of the Butlers Club" © 1980 The Estate of Geoffrey Bush.

Every effort has been made to trace copyright holders and to obtain their
permission for the use of copyright material. The publisher apologises
for any errors or omissions and would be pleased to be notified of any
corrections to be incorporated in reprints or future editions.

Represented in the EU by Authorised Rep Compliance Ltd., Ground Floor,
71 Lower Baggot Street, Dublin, D02 P593, Ireland. arccompliance.com

Cataloguing in Publication Data
A catalogue record for this publication is available from the British Library

ISBN 978 0 7123 5563 6
e-ISBN 978 0 7123 6869 8

Front cover image © NRM Pictorial Collection/Science Museum Group
Text design and typesetting by Tetragon, London
Printed in England by CPI Group (UK) Ltd, Croydon, CRO 4YY

MIX
Paper | Supporting
responsible forestry
FSC® C013604

CONTENTS

If I had to identify one specific moment which proved to be a turning point in the fortunes of the locked room mystery, I would pick the first series of the BBC TV series *Jonathan Creek*, written by David Renwick, which aired in 1997. Renwick, a long-time fan of impossible crime mysteries in general and Carr's work in particular, demonstrated that it was possible for a skilled writer to bring this sub-genre up to date, blending intricate plots with witty dialogue and appealing characterisation. Further popular television series, including *Monk*, *Death in Paradise*, *Ludwig*, and most recently *Patience*, have helped to reinvigorate the locked room mystery to an extent that would have amazed Haycraft and Sladek.

As a consequence, publishers no longer look askance at locked room mystery novels and short stories. Indeed, the wheel of fashion has turned so decisively that book publicists often use the term "locked room mysteries" to misdescribe stories that are merely "closed circle" mysteries. The difference is simple: a closed circle mystery is one in which the culprit is one of a defined group of suspects, whereas a locked room mystery is one where there is some element of apparent impossibility about the crime. There is no need for an actual locked room to feature in a locked room mystery, as long as there is some element of apparent impossibility. So, to take well-known examples from Agatha Christie's oeuvre, *Hercule Poirot's Christmas* is a locked room mystery but *The Mysterious Affair at Styles* is not: the latter is, like so many of her books, a closed circle mystery. Is this a distinction that matters only to purists? Perhaps, but many lovers of detective fiction are purists; happily, some of them also have first-rate blogs, such as Jim Noy's *The Invisible Event*, Steve Barge's *In Search of the Classic Mystery Novel*, Nicholas Fuller's *The Grandest Game in the World*, and Kate Jackson's *Cross-Examining Crime*, which discuss traditional mysteries with insight and enthusiasm.

Since *Miraculous Mysteries* appeared eight years ago, the British Library has reprinted numerous locked room mystery novels in the Crime Classics series, including *Suddenly at His Residence* and *Death of Jezebel* by Christianna Brand, and several titles by John Dickson Carr, either under his own name or writing as Carter Dickson. Judging by readers' reaction to these books, the time is ripe for another collection of short stories themed around the art of the impossible.

This book takes its title from a story by Julian Symons; even though he is often regarded as a scourge of Golden Age detective fiction, three of his mysteries merit inclusion in Bob Adey's book. There are contributions from a number of the "usual suspects" such as Christianna Brand and Margery Allingham, as well as some less familiar names, notably Grenville Robbins and Geoffrey Bush. It seemed fitting for this book to start and end with a story by John Dickson Carr. The second appeared under the Carter Dickson name and featured Sir Henry Merrivale; it also happens to be my favourite short locked room mystery.

As always, I'd like to express my thanks to everyone who helped me to track down obscure stories, notably Jamie Sturgeon and Nigel Moss, while Phil Stephensen-Payne's online index to crime stories in magazines has again proved an invaluable resource; thanks are also due to the publishing team at the British Library. And I'm particularly grateful to all those readers from around the world who get in touch with me regularly to let me know how much they enjoy rediscovering long-neglected short stories through this series of anthologies. Rest assured, there are more to come...

MARTIN EDWARDS
www.martinedwardsbooks.com

A NOTE FROM THE PUBLISHER

The original novels and short stories reprinted in the British Library Crime Classics series were written and published in a period ranging, for the most part, from the 1890s to the 1960s. There are many elements of these stories which continue to entertain modern readers; however, in some cases there are also uses of language, instances of stereotyping and some attitudes expressed by narrators or characters which may not be endorsed by the publishing standards of today. We acknowledge therefore that some elements in the works selected for reprinting may continue to make uncomfortable reading for some of our audience. With this series British Library Publishing aims to offer a new readership a chance to read some of the rare books of the British Library's collections in an affordable paperback format, to enjoy their merits and to look back into the world of the twentieth century as portrayed by its writers. It is not possible to separate these stories from the history of their writing and therefore the following novel is presented as it was originally published with one edit to the text, and minor edits made for consistency of style and sense. We welcome feedback from our readers, which can be sent to the following address:

British Library Publishing
The British Library
96 Euston Road
London, NW1 2DB
United Kingdom

THE WRONG PROBLEM

John Dickson Carr

John Dickson Carr (1906–77) is generally regarded as the supreme exponent of the locked room mystery. He was born in Uniontown, Pennsylvania, and I think it's fair to say that many of the finest locked room mysteries have been written by American authors. What was unusual about Carr—apart from the ingenious way in which he was able to ring so many variations on the locked room theme—was that he was an Anglophile who spent much of his life, including the years when he was at his creative peak, living in Britain. Three of his major series characters, Dr. Gideon Fell, Sir Henry Merrivale, and Colonel March of Scotland Yard, were British and many of his finest novels and short stories were set in England.

This was the first short story to feature Fell, whom Carr based on G. K. Chesterton, a writer whom he much admired, and another lover of stories about impossible crimes. When the *Evening Standard* asked Dorothy L. Sayers to arrange a series of stories about "Great Detectives", Carr was one of the friends to whom she turned for a story. She had got to know him through his membership of the Detection Club, and he refers in the story to a fictional version of the Club. The title alludes to Chesterton's Father Brown story "The Wrong Shape" and Carr's biographer Douglas G. Greene says it is "Chestertonian in its telling". The story first appeared in the *Evening Standard* on 14 August 1936, just two months after Chesterton's death.

A T THE DETECTIVES' CLUB IT IS STILL TOLD HOW DR. FELL went down into the valley in Somerset that evening and of the man with whom he talked in the twilight by the lake, and of murder that came up as though from the lake itself. The truth about the crime has long been known, but one question must always be asked at the end of it.

The village of Grayling Dene lay a mile away toward the sunset. And the rear windows of the house looked out toward it. This was a long gabled house of red brick, lying in a hollow of the shaggy hills, and its bricks had darkened like an old painting. No lights showed inside, although the lawns were in good order and the hedges trimmed.

Behind the house there was a long gleam of water in the sunset, for the ornamental lake—some fifty yards across—stretched almost to the windows. In the middle of the lake, on an artificial island, stood a summer-house. A faint breeze had begun to stir, despite the heat, and the valley was alive with a conference of leaves.

The last light showed that all the windows of the house, except one, had little lozenge-shaped panes. The one exception was a window high up in a gable, the highest in the house, looking out over the road to Grayling Dene. It was barred.

Dusk had almost become darkness when two men came down over the crest of the hill. One was large and lean. The other, who wore a shovel hat, was large and immensely stout, and he loomed even more vast against the skyline by reason of the great dark cloak billowing out behind him. Even at that distance you might hear the chuckles that animated his several chins and ran down the ridges of his waistcoat. The two travellers were engaged (as usual) in a violent argument. At intervals the larger one would stop and hold forth oratorically for some minutes, flourishing his cane. But, as they came down past the lake and the blind house, both of them stopped.

"There's an example," said Superintendent Hadley. "Say what you like, it's a bit too lonely for me. Give me the town—"

"We are not alone," said Dr. Fell.

The whole place had seemed so deserted that Hadley felt a slight start when he saw a man standing at the edge of the lake. Against the reddish glow on the water they could make out that it was a small man in neat dark clothes and a white linen hat. He seemed to be stooping forward, peering out across the water. The wind went rustling again, and the man turned round.

"I don't see any swans," he said. "Can you see any swans?" The quiet water was empty.

"No," said Dr. Fell, with the same gravity. "Should there be any?"

"There should be one," answered the little man, nodding. "Dead. With blood on its neck. Floating there."

"Killed?" asked Dr. Fell, after a pause. He has said afterward that it seemed a foolish thing to say; but that it seemed appropriate to that time between the lights of the day and the brain.

"Oh, yes," replied the little man, nodding again. "Killed, like others—human beings. Eye, ear and throat. Or perhaps I should say ear, eye and throat to get them in order."

Hadley spoke with some sharpness.

"I hope we're not trespassing. We knew the land was enclosed, of course, but they told us that the owners were away and wouldn't mind if we took a short cut. Fell, don't you think we'd better—?"

"I beg your pardon," said the little man, in a voice of such cool sanity that Hadley turned round again. From what they could see in the gloom, he had a good face, a quiet face, a somewhat ascetic face; and he was smiling. "I beg your pardon," he repeated in a curiously apologetic tone. "I should not have said that. You see, I have been far too long with it. I have been trying to find the real answer for thirty years. As for the trespassing, myself, I do not own this land, although I lived here once. There is, or used to be, a bench here somewhere. Can I detain you for a little while?"

Hadley never quite realised afterward how it came about. But such was the spell of the hour, or of the place, or the sincere, serious little man in the white linen hat, that it seemed no time at all before the little man was sitting on a rusty iron chair beside the darkening lake, speaking as though to his fingers.

"I am Joseph Lessing," he said in the same apologetic tone. "If you have not heard of me, I don't suppose you will have heard of my stepfather. But at one time he was rather famous as an eye, ear and throat specialist. Dr. Harvey Lessing, his name was.

"In those days we—I mean the family—always came down here to spend our summer holidays. It is rather difficult to make biographical details clear. Perhaps I had better do it with dates, as though the matter were really important, like a history book. There were four children. Three of them were Dr. Lessing's children by his first wife, who died in 1899. I was the stepson. He married my mother when I was seventeen, in 1901. I regret to say that *she* died three years later. Dr. Lessing was a kindly man, but he was very unfortunate in the choice of his wives."

The little man appeared to be smiling sadly.

"We were an ordinary, contented and happy group, in spite of Brownrigg's cynicism. Brownrigg was the eldest. Eye, ear and throat pursued us: he was a dentist. I think he is dead now. He was a stout man, smiling a good deal, and his face had a shine like pale butter. He was an athlete run to seed; he used to claim that he could draw teeth with his fingers. By the way, he was very fond of walnuts. I always seem to remember him sitting between two silver candlesticks at the table, smiling, with a heap of shells in front of him and a little sharp nutpick in his hand.

"Harvey Junior was the next. They were right to call him Junior; he was of the striding sort, brisk and high-coloured and likeable. He never sat down in a chair without first turning it the wrong way round. He always said 'Ho, my lads!' when he came into a room, and never went out of it without leaving the door open so that he could come back in again. Above everything, he was nearly always on the water. We had a skiff and a punt for our little lake—would you believe that it is ten feet deep? Junior always dressed for the part as solemnly as though he had been on the Thames, wearing a red-and-white striped blazer and a straw hat of the sort that used to be called a boater. I say he was nearly always on the water: but not, of course, after tea. That was when Dr. Lessing went to take his afternoon nap in the summer-house."

The summer-house, in its sheath of vines, was almost invisible now. But they all looked at it, very suggestive in the middle of the lake.

"The third child was the girl, Martha. She was almost my own age, and I was very fond of her."

Joseph Lessing pressed his hands together.

"I am not going to introduce an unnecessary love story, gentlemen," he said, "As a matter of fact, Martha was engaged to a young man who had a commission in a line regiment, and she was expecting him down here any day when—the things happened. Arthur Somers, his name was. I knew him well; I was his confidant in the family.

"I want to emphasise what a hot, pleasant summer it was. The place looked then much as it does now, except that I think it was greener then. I was glad to get away from the city. In accordance with Dr. Lessing's passion for 'useful employment', I had been put to work in the optical department of a jeweller's. I was always skilful with my hands. I dare say I was a spindly, snappish, suspicious lad, but they were all very good to me after my mother died: except butter-faced Brownrigg, perhaps. But for me that summer centres round Martha, with her brown hair piled up on the top of her head, in a white dress with puffed shoulders, playing croquet on a green lawn and laughing. I told you it was a long while ago.

"On the afternoon of the fifteenth of August we had all intended to be out. Even Brownrigg had intended to go out after a sort of lunch-tea that we had at two o'clock in the afternoon. Look to your right, gentlemen. You see that bow window in the middle of the house, overhanging the lake? There was where the table was set.

"Dr. Lessing was the first to leave the table. He was going out early for his nap in the summer-house. It was a very hot afternoon, as drowsy as the sound of a lawn-mower. The sun baked the old bricks and made a flat blaze on the water. Junior had knocked together a sort of miniature landing-stage at the side of the lake—it was just about where we are sitting now—and the punt and the rowboat were lying there.

"From the open windows we could all see Dr. Lessing going down to the landing-stage with the sun on his bald spot. He had a pillow in one hand and a book in the other. He took the rowboat; he could never manage the punt properly, and it irritated a man of his dignity to try.

"Martha was the next to leave. She laughed and ran away, as she always did. Then Junior said, 'Cheerio, chaps'—or whatever the expression was then—and strode out leaving the door open. I went shortly afterward. Junior had asked Brownrigg whether he intended to go out, and Brownrigg had said yes. But he remained, being lazy, with a pile of walnut shells in front of him. Though he moved back from the table to get out of the glare, he lounged there all afternoon in view of the lake.

"Oh course, what Brownrigg said or thought might not have been important. But it happened that a gardener named Robinson had taken it into his head to trim some hedges on this side of the house. He had a full view of the lake. And all that afternoon nothing stirred. The summer-house, as you can see, has two doors: one facing toward the house, the other in the opposite direction. These openings were closed by sun-blinds, striped red and white like Junior's blazer, so that you could not see inside. But all the afternoon the summer-house remained dead, showing up against the fiery water and that clump of trees at the far side of the lake. No boat put out. No one went in to swim. There was not so much as a ripple, any more than might have been caused by the swans (we had two of them), or by the spring that fed the lake.

"By six o'clock we were all back in the house. When there began to be a few shadows, I think something in the *emptiness* of the afternoon alarmed us. Dr. Lessing should have been there, demanding something. He was not there. We hallooed for him, but he did not answer. The rowboat remained tied up by the summer-house. Then Brownrigg, in his cool fetch-and-run fashion, told me to go out and wake up the old party. I pointed out that there was only the punt, and that I was a rotten hand at punting, and that whenever I tried it I only went round in circles or upset the boat. But Junior said, 'Come-along-old-chap-you-shall-improve-your-punting-I'll-give-you-a-hand.'

"I have never forgotten how long it took us to get out there while I staggered at the punt pole, and Junior lent a hand.

"Dr. Lessing lay easily on his left side, almost on his stomach, on a long wicker settee. His face was very nearly into the pillow, so that you could not see much except a wisp of sandy side whisker. His right hand hung down to the floor, the fingers trailing into the pages of *Three Men in a Boat*.

"We first noticed that there seemed to be some—that is, something that had come out of his ear. More we did not know, except that he was dead, and in fact the weapon has never been found. He died in his sleep. The doctor later told us that the wound had been made by some round sharp-pointed instrument, thicker than a hatpin but not so thick as a lead pencil, which had been driven through the right ear into the brain."

Joseph Lessing paused. A mighty swish of wind uprose in the trees beyond the lake, and their tops ruffled under clear starlight. The little man sat nodding to himself in the iron chair. They could see his white hat move.

"Yes?" prompted Dr. Fell in an almost casual tone. Dr. Fell was sitting back, a great bandit shape in a cloak and shovel hat. He seemed to be blinking curiously at Lessing over his eyeglasses. "And whom did they suspect?"

"They suspected me," said the little man.

"You see," he went on, in the same apologetic tone, "I was the only one in the group who could swim. It was my one accomplishment. It is too dark to show you now but I won a little medal by it, and I have kept it on my watch-chain ever since I received it as a boy."

"But you said," cried Hadley, "that nobody..."

"I will explain," said the other, "if you do not interrupt me. Of course, the police believed that the motive must have been money. Dr. Lessing was a wealthy man, and his money was divided almost equally among us. I told you he was always very good to me.

"First they tried to find out where everyone had been in the afternoon. Brownrigg had been sitting, or said he had been sitting, in the dining-room. But there was the gardener to prove that not

he or anyone else had gone out on the lake. Martha (it was foolish, of course, but they investigated even Martha) had been with
a friend of hers—I forget her name now—who had come for her
in the phaeton and took her away to play croquet. Junior had no
alibi, since he had been for a country walk. But," said Lessing, quite
simply, "everybody knew *he* would never do a thing like that. I was
the changeling, or perhaps I mean ugly duckling, and I admit I was
an unpleasant, sarcastic lad.

"This is how Inspector Deering thought I had committed the
murder. First, he thought, I had made sure everybody would be
away from the house that afternoon. Thus, later, when the crime
was discovered, it would be assumed by everyone that the murderer
had simply gone out in the punt and come back again. Everybody
knew that I could not possibly manage a punt alone. You see?"

"Next, the inspector thought, I had come down to the clump of
trees across the lake, in line with the summer-house and the dining-
room windows. It is shallow there, and there are reeds. He thought
that I had taken off my clothes over a bathing-suit. He thought that
I had crept into the water under cover of the reeds, and that I had
simply swum out to the summer-house under water.

"Twenty-odd yards under water, I admit, are not much to a good
swimmer. They thought that Brownrigg could not see me come up
out of the water, because the thickness of the summer-house was
between. Robinson had a full view of the lake, but he could not see
that one part at the back of the summer-house. Nor, on the other
hand, could I see them. They thought that I had crawled under the
sun-blind with the weapon in the breast of my bathing-suit. Any
wetness I might have left would soon be dried by the intense heat.
That, I think, was how they believed I had killed the old man who
befriended me."

The little man's voice grew petulant and dazed.

"I told them I did not do it," he said with a hopeful air. "Over and over again I told them I did not do it. But I do not think they believed me. That is why for all these years I have wondered—

"It was Brownrigg's idea. They had me before a sort of family council in the library, as though I had stolen jam. Martha was weeping, but I think she was weeping with plain fear. She never stood up well in a crisis, Martha didn't; she turned pettish and even looked softer. All the same, it is not pleasant to think of a murderer coming up to you as you doze in the afternoon heat. Junior, the good fellow, attempted to take my side and call for fair play; but I could see the idea in his face. Brownrigg presided silkily, and smiled down his nose.

"'We have either got to believe you killed him,' Brownrigg said, 'or believe in the supernatural. Is the lake haunted? No; I think we may safely discard that.' He pointed his finger at me. 'You damned young snake, you are lazy and wanted that money.'

"But, you see, I had one very strong hold over them—and I used it. I admit it was unscrupulous, but I was trying to demonstrate my innocence and we are told that the devil must be fought with fire. At mention of this hold, even Brownrigg's jowls shook. Brownrigg was a dentist, Harvey was studying medicine. What hold? That is the whole point. Nevertheless, it was not what the family thought I had to fear: it was what Inspector Deering thought.

"They did not arrest me yet, because there was not enough evidence, but every night I feared it would come the next day. Those days after the funeral were too warm; and suspicion acted like woollen underwear under the heat. Martha's tantrums got on even Junior's nerves. Once I thought Brownrigg was going to hit her. She very badly needed her fiancé, Arthur Somers; but, though he wrote that he might be there any day, he still could not get leave of absence from his colonel.

"And then the lake got more food.

"Look at the house, gentlemen. I wonder if the light is strong enough for you to see it from here? Look at the house—the highest window there—under the gable. You see?"

There was a pause, filled with the tumult of the leaves.

"It's got bars," said Hadley.

"Yes," assented the little man. "I must describe the room. It is a little square room. It has one door and one window. At the time I speak of, there was no furniture at all in it. The furniture had been taken out some years before, because it was rather a special kind of furniture. Since then it had been locked up. The key was kept in a box in Dr. Lessing's room; but, of course, nobody ever went up there. One of Dr. Lessing's wives had died there in a certain condition. I told you he had bad luck with his wives. They had not even dared to have a glass window."

Sharply, the little man struck a match. The brief flame seemed to bring his face up toward them out of the dark. They saw that he had a pipe in his left hand. But the flame showed little except the gentle upturn of his eyes, and the fact that his whitish hair (of such coarse texture that it seemed whitewashed) was worn rather long.

"On the afternoon of the twenty-second of August, we had an unexpected visit from the family solicitor. There was no one to receive him except myself. Brownrigg had locked himself up in his room at the front with a bottle of whisky; he was drunk or said he was drunk. Junior was out. We had been trying to occupy our minds for the past week, but Junior could not have his boating or I my workshop; this was thought not decent. I believe it was thought that the most decent thing was to get drunk. For some days Martha had been ailing. She was not ill enough to go to bed, but she was lying on a long chair in her bedroom.

"I looked into the room just before I went downstairs to see the solicitor. The room was muffled up with shutters and velvet curtains, as all the rooms decently were. You may imagine that it was very hot in there. Martha was lying back in the chair with a smelling-bottle, and there was a white-globed lamp burning on a little round table beside her. I remember that her white dress looked starchy; her hair was piled up on top of her head and she wore a little gold watch on her breast. Also, her eyelids were so puffed that they seemed almost oriental. When I asked her how she was, she began to cry and concluded by throwing a book at me.

"So I went on downstairs. I was talking to the solicitor when it took place. We were in the library, which is at the front of the house, and in consequence we could not hear distinctly. But we heard something. That was why we went upstairs—and even the solicitor ran. Martha was not in her own bedroom. We found out where she was from the fact that the door to the garret stairs was open.

"It was even more intolerably hot up under the roof. The door to the barred room stood halfway open. Just outside stood a housemaid (her name, I think, was Jane Dawson) leaning against the jamb and shaking like the ribbons on her cap. All sound had dried up in her throat, but she pointed inside.

"I told you it was a little, bare, dirty-brown room. The low sun made a blaze through the window, and made shadows of the bars across Martha's white dress. Martha lay nearly in the middle of the room, with her heel twisted under her as though she had turned round before she fell. I lifted her up and tried to talk to her; but a rounded sharp-pointed thing, somewhat thicker than a hatpin, had been driven through the right eye into the brain.

"Yet there was nobody else in the room.

"The maid told a straight story. She had seen Martha come out of Dr. Lessing's bedroom downstairs. Martha was running, running as well as she could in those skirts; once she stumbled, and the maid thought that she was sobbing. Jane Dawson said that Martha made for the garret door as though the devil were after her. Jane Dawson, wishing anything rather than to be alone in the dark hall, followed her. She saw Martha come up here and unlock the door of the little brown room. When Martha ran inside the maid thought that she did not attempt to close the door; but that it appeared to swing shut after her. You see?

"Whatever had frightened Martha, Jane Dawson did not dare follow her in—for a few seconds, at least, and afterward it was too late. The maid could never afterward describe exactly the sort of sound Martha made. It was something that startled the birds out of the vines and set the swans flapping on the lake. But the maid presently saw straight enough to push the door with one finger and peep round the edge.

"Except for Martha, the room was empty.

"Hence the three of us now looked at each other. The maid's story was not to be shaken in any way, and we all knew she was a truthful witness. Even the police did not doubt her. She said she had seen Martha go into that room, but that she had seen nobody come out of it. She never took her eyes off the door—it was not likely that she would. But when she peeped in to see what had happened, there was nobody except Martha in the room. That was easily established, because there was no place where any one could have been. Could she have been blinded by the light? No. Could anyone have slipped past her? No. She almost shook her hair loose by her vehemence on this point.

"The window, I need scarcely tell you, was inaccessible. Its bars were firmly set, no farther apart than the breadth of your hand, and in any case the window could not have been reached. There was no way out of the room except the door or the window; and no—what is the word I want?—no mechanical device in it. Our friend Inspector Deering made certain of that. One thing I suppose I should mention.

Despite the condition of the walls and ceiling, the floor of the room was swept clean. Martha's white dress with the puffed shoulders had scarcely any dirt when she lay there; it was as white as her face.

"This murder was incredible. I do not mean merely that it was incredible with regard to its physical circumstances, but also that there was Martha dead—on a holiday. Possibly she seemed all the more dead because we had never known her well when she was alive. She was (to me, at least) a laugh, a few coquetries, a pair of brown eyes. You felt her absence more than you would have felt that of a more vital person. And—on a holiday with that warm sun, and the tennis net ready to be put up.

"That evening I walked with Junior here in the dusk by the lake. He was trying to express some of this. He appeared dazed. He did not know why Martha had gone up to that little brown room, and he kept endlessly asking why. He could not even seem to accustom himself to the idea that our holidays were interrupted, much less interrupted by the murders of his father and his sister.

"There was a reddish light on the lake; the trees stood up against it like black lace, and we were walking near that clump by the reeds. The thing I remember most vividly is Junior's face. He had his hat on the back of his head, as he usually did. He was staring down past the reeds, where the water lapped faintly, as though the lake itself were the evil genius and kept its secret. When he spoke I hardly recognised his voice.

"'God,' he said, 'but it's in the air!'

"There was something white floating by the reeds, very slowly turning round with a snaky discoloured talon coming out from it along the water; the talon was the head of a swan, and the swan was dead of a gash across the neck that had very nearly severed it."

"We fished it out with a boat-hook," explained the little man as though with an afterthought. And then he was silent.

On the long iron bench Dr. Fell's cape shifted a little; Hadley could hear him wheezing with quiet anger, like a boiling kettle.

"I thought so," rumbled Dr. Fell. He added more sharply: "Look here, this tomfoolery has got to stop."

"I beg your pardon?" said Joseph Lessing, evidently startled.

"With your kind permission," said Dr. Fell, and Hadley has later said that he was never more glad to see that cane flourished or hear that common-sense voice grow fiery with controversy: "with your kind permission, I should like to ask you a question. Will you swear to me by anything you hold sacred (if you have anything, which I rather doubt) that you do not know the real answer?"

"Yes," replied the other seriously, and nodded.

For a little space, Dr. Fell was silent. Then he spoke argumentatively. "I will ask you another question, then. Did you ever shoot an arrow into the air?"

Hadley turned round. "I hear the call of Mumbo-Jumbo," said Hadley with grim feeling. "Hold on, now! You don't think that girl was killed by somebody shooting an arrow into the air, do you?"

"Oh, no," said Dr. Fell in a more meditative tone. He looked at Lessing. "I mean it figuratively—like the boy in the verse. Did you ever throw a stone when you were a boy? Did you ever throw a stone, not to hit anything, but for the sheer joy of firing it? Did you ever climb trees? Did you ever like to play pirate and dress up and wave a sword? I don't think so. That's why you live in a dreary, rarefied light; that's why you dislike romance and sentiment and good whisky and all the noblest things of this world; and it is also why you do not see the unreasonableness of several things in this case.

"To begin with, birds do not commonly rise up in a great cloud from the vines because some one cries out. With the hopping and always-whooping Junior about the premises, I should imagine the birds were used to it. Still less do swans leap up out of the water

and flap their wings because of a cry from far away; swans are
not so sensitive. Did you ever see a boy throw a stone at a wall?
Did you ever see a boy throw a stone at the water? Birds and
swans would have been outraged only if something had *struck* both
the wall and the water: something, in short which fell from the
barred window.

"Now, frightened women do not in their terror rush up to a
garret, especially a garret with such associations. They go downstairs
where there is protection. Martha Lessing was not frightened. She
went up to that room for some purpose. What purpose? She could
not have been going to get anything, for there was nothing in the
room to be got. What could have been on her mind? The only thing
we know to have been on her mind was a frantic wish for her fiancé
to get there. She had been expecting him for weeks. It is a singular
thing about that room: but its window is the highest in the house,
and commands the only clear view of the road to the village.

"Now suppose someone had told her that he thought, he rather
thought, he had glimpsed Arthur Somers coming up the road from
the village. It was a long way off, of course, and the someone admitted he might have been mistaken in thinking so...

"H'm yes. The trap was all set, you see. Martha Lessing waited
only long enough to get the key out of the box in her father's room,
and she sobbed with relief. But, when she got to the room, there was
a strong sun pouring through the bars straight into her face: and the
road to the village is a long way off. That, I believe, was the trap. For
on the window-ledge of that room (which nobody ever used, and
which someone had swept so that there should be no footprints) this
someone conveniently placed a pair of—eh, Hadley?"

"Field glasses," said Hadley, and got up in the gloom.

"Still," argued Dr. Fell, wheezing argumentatively, "there would
be one nuisance. Take a pair of field glasses, and try to use them in

a window where the bars are set more closely than the breadth of your hand. The bars get in the way: wherever you turn you bump into them; they confuse sight and irritate you; and, in addition, there is a strong sun to complicate matters. In your impatience, I think you would turn the glasses sideways and pass them out through the bars. Then, holding them firmly against one bar with your hands through the bars on either side, you would look through the eyepieces.

"But," said Dr. Fell, with a ferocious geniality, "those were no ordinary glasses. Martha Lessing had noticed before that the lenses were blurred. Now they were in position, she tried to adjust the focus by turning the little wheel in the middle. And as she turned the wheel, like the trigger of a pistol it released the spring mechanism and a sharp steel point shot out from the right-hand lens into her eye. She dropped the glasses, which were outside the window. The weight of them tore the point from her eye; and it was this object, falling, which gashed and broke the neck of the swan just before it disappeared into the water below."

He paused. He had taken out a cigar, but he did not light it.

"Busy solicitors do not usually come to a house 'unexpectedly'. They are summoned. Brownrigg was drunk and Junior absent; there was no one at the back of the house to see the glasses fall. For this time the murderer had to have a respectable alibi. Young Martha, the only one who could have been gulled into such a trap, had to be sacrificed—to avert the arrest which had been threatening someone ever since the police found out how Dr. Lessing really had been murdered.

"There was only one man who admittedly did speak with Martha Lessing only a few minutes before she was murdered. There was only one man who was employed as optician at a jeweller's, and admits he had his 'workshop' here. There was only one man skilful enough with his hands—" Dr. Fell paused, wheezing, and turned to Lessing. "I wonder they didn't arrest you."

"They did," said the little man, nodding. "You see, I was released from Broadmoor only a month ago."

There was a sudden rasp and crackle as he struck another match.

"You—" bellowed Hadley, and stopped. "So it was your mother who died in that room? Then what the hell do you mean by keeping us here with this pack of nightmares?"

"No," said the other peevishly. "You do not understand. I never wanted to know who killed Dr. Lessing or poor Martha. You have got hold of the wrong problem. And yet I tried to tell you what the problem was.

"You see, it was not *my* mother who died mad. It was theirs—Brownrigg's and Harvey's and Martha's. That was why they were so desperately anxious to think I was guilty, for they could not face the alternative. Didn't I tell you I had a hold over them, a hold that made even Brownrigg shake, and that I used it? Do you think they wouldn't have had me clapped into jail straightaway if it had been *my* mother who was mad? Eh?

"Of course," he explained apologetically, "at the trial they had to swear it was my mother who was mad; for I threatened to tell the truth in open court if they didn't. Otherwise I should have been hanged, you see. Only Brownrigg and Junior were left. Brownrigg was a dentist, Junior was to be a doctor, and if it had been known—But that is not the point. That is not the problem. Their mother was mad, but they were harmless. I killed Dr. Lessing. I killed Martha. Yet, I am quite sane. Why did I do it, all those years ago? Why? Is there no rational pattern in the scheme of things, and no answer to the bedevilled of the earth?"

The match curled to a red ember, winked and went out. Clearest of all they remembered the coarse hair that was like whitewash on the black, the eyes, and the curiously suggestive hands. Then Joseph Lessing got up from the chair. The last they saw of him was his white hat bobbing and flickering across the lawn under the blowing trees.

THE WARDER OF THE DOOR

L. T. Meade and Robert Eustace

L. T. Meade (1844–1914), or to give her full name Elizabeth Thomasina Meade, was a highly prolific Irish author, renowned in her lifetime mainly for writing stories aimed at a young female readership but now perhaps better remembered for her detective fiction, including in particular her collaborations with Robert Eustace (1871–1943), a pen-name for Eustace Barton. Eustace was a doctor who supplied medical know-how for stories written by Meade and (in later years) Edgar Jepson and Dorothy L. Sayers.

One of their best-known works was *A Master of Mysteries* (1898) from which this story is taken. The tales in the book were narrated by the ghost-hunter John Bell, who introduced himself as follows: "It so happened that the circumstances of fate allowed me to follow my own bent in the choice of a profession. From my earliest youth the weird, the mysterious had an irresistible fascination for me. Having private means, I resolved to follow my unique inclinations, and I am now well known to all my friends as a professional exposer of ghosts, and one who can clear away the mysteries of most haunted houses… To explain, by the application of science, phenomena attributed to spiritual agencies has been the work of my life. I have, naturally, gone through strange difficulties in accomplishing my mission."

"IF YOU DON'T BELIEVE IT, YOU CAN READ IT FOR YOURSELF," said Allen Clinton, climbing up the steps and searching among the volumes on the top shelf.

I lay back in my chair. The beams from the sinking sun shone through the stained glass of the windows of the old library, and dyed the rows of black leather volumes with bands of red and yellow.

"Here, Bell!"

I took a musty volume from Allen Clinton, which he had unearthed from its resting-place.

"It is about the middle of the book," he continued eagerly. "You will see it in big, black, old English letters."

I turned over the pages containing the family tree and other archives of the Clintons till I came to the one I was seeking. It contained the curse which had rested on the family since 1400. Slowly and with difficulty I deciphered the words of this terrible denunciation.

"And in this cell its coffin lieth, the coffin which hath not human shape, for which reason no holy ground receiveth it. Here shall it rest to curse the family of ye Clyntons from generation to generation. And for this reason, as soon as the soul shall pass from the body of each first-born, which is the heir, it shall become the warder of the door by day and by night. Day and night shall his spirit stand by the door, to keep the door closed till the son shall release the spirit of the father from the watch and take his place, till his son in turn shall die. And whoso entereth into the cell shall be the prisoner of the soul that guardeth the door till it shall let him go."

"What a ghastly idea!" I said, glancing up at the young man who was watching me as I read. "But you say this cell has never been found. I should say its existence was a myth, and, of course, the curse on the soul of the first-born to keep the door shut as warder is absurd. Matter does not obey witchcraft."

"The odd part of it is," replied Allen, "that every other detail of the Abbey referred to in this record has been identified; but this cell with its horrible contents has never been found."

It certainly was a curious legend, and I allow it made some impression on me. I fancied, too, that somewhere I had heard something similar, but my memory failed to trace it.

I had come down to Clinton Abbey three days before for some pheasant shooting.

It was now Sunday afternoon. The family, with the exception of old Sir Henry, Allen, and myself, were at church. Sir Henry, now nearly eighty years of age and a chronic invalid, had retired to his room for his afternoon sleep. The younger Clinton and I had gone out for a stroll round the grounds, and since we returned our conversation had run upon the family history till it arrived at the legend of the family curse. Presently, the door of the library was slowly opened, and Sir Henry, in his black velvet coat, which formed such a striking contrast to his snowy white beard and hair, entered the room. I rose from my chair, and, giving him my arm, assisted him to his favourite couch. He sank down into its luxurious depths with a sigh, but as he did so his eyes caught the old volume which I had laid on the table beside it. He started forward, took the book in his hand, and looked across at his son.

"Did you take this book down?" he said sharply.

"Yes, father; I got it out to show it to Bell. He is interested in the history of the Abbey, and—"

"Then return it to its place at once," interrupted the old man, his black eyes blazing with sudden passion. "You know how I dislike having my books disarranged, and this one above all. Stay, give it to me."

He struggled up from the couch, and, taking the volume, locked it up in one of the drawers of his writing-table, and then sat back again on the sofa. His hands were trembling, as if some sudden fear had taken possession of him.

"Did you say that Phyllis Curzon is coming tomorrow?" asked the old man presently of his son in an irritable voice.

"Yes, father, of course; don't you remember? Mrs. Curzon and Phyllis are coming to stay for a fortnight; and, by the way," he added, starting to his feet as he spoke, "that reminds me I must go and tell Grace—"

The rest of the sentence was lost in the closing of the door. As soon as we were alone, Sir Henry looked across at me for a few moments without speaking. Then he said,—

"I am sorry I was so short just now. I am not myself. I do not know what is the matter with me. I feel all to pieces. I cannot sleep. I do not think my time is very long now, and I am worried about Allen. The fact is, I would give anything to stop this engagement. I wish he would not marry."

"I am sorry to hear you say that, sir," I answered. "I should have thought you would have been anxious to see your son happily married."

"Most men would," was the reply; "but I have my reasons for wishing things otherwise."

"What do you mean?" I could not help asking.

"I cannot explain myself; I wish I could. It would be best for Allen to let the old family die out. There, perhaps I am foolish about it, and of course I cannot really stop the marriage, but I am worried and troubled about many things."

"I wish I could help you, sir," I said impulsively. "If there is anything I can possibly do, you know you have only to ask me."

"Thank you, Bell, I know you would; but I cannot tell you. Some day I may. But there, I am afraid—horribly afraid."

The trembling again seized him, and he put his hands over his eyes as if to shut out some terrible sight.

"Don't repeat a word of what I have told you to Allen or any one else," he said suddenly. "It is possible that some day I may ask you to help me; and remember, Bell, I trust you."

He held out his hand, which I took. In another moment the butler entered with the lamps, and I took advantage of the interruption to make my way to the drawing-room.

The next day the Curzons arrived, and a hasty glance showed me that Phyllis was a charming girl. She was tall, slightly built, with a figure both upright and graceful, and a handsome, somewhat proud face. When in perfect repose her expression was somewhat haughty; but the moment she spoke her face became vivacious, kindly, charming to an extraordinary degree; she had a gay laugh, a sweet smile, a sympathetic manner. I was certain she had the kindest of hearts, and was sure that Allen had made an admirable choice.

A few days went by, and at last the evening before the day when I was to return to London arrived. Phyllis's mother had gone to bed a short time before, as she had complained of headache, and Allen suddenly proposed, as the night was a perfect one, that we should go out and enjoy a moonlight stroll.

Phyllis laughed with glee at the suggestion, and ran at once into the hall to take a wrap from one of the pegs.

"Allen," she said to her lover, who was following her, "you and I will go first."

"No, young lady, on this occasion you and I will have that privilege," said Sir Henry. He had also come into the hall, and, to our astonishment, announced his intention of accompanying us in our walk.

Phyllis bestowed upon him a startled glance, then she laid her hand lightly on his arm, nodded back at Allen with a smile, and walked on in front somewhat rapidly. Allen and I followed in the rear.

"Now, what does my father mean by this?" said Allen to me. "He never goes out at night; but he has not been well lately. I sometimes think he grows queerer every day."

"He is very far from well, I am certain," I answered.

We stayed out for about half an hour and returned home by a path which led into the house through a side entrance. Phyllis was waiting for us in the hall.

"Where is my father?" asked Allen, going up to her.

"He is tired and has gone to bed," she answered. "Goodnight, Allen."

"Won't you come into the drawing-room?" he asked in some astonishment.

"No, I am tired."

She nodded to him without touching his hand; her eyes, I could not help noticing, had a queer expression. She ran upstairs.

I saw that Allen was startled by her manner; but as he did not say anything, neither did I.

The next day at breakfast I was told that the Curzons had already left the Abbey. Allen was full of astonishment and, I could see, a good deal annoyed. He and I breakfasted alone in the old library. His father was too ill to come downstairs.

An hour later I was on my way back to London. Many things there engaged my immediate attention, and Allen, his engagement, Sir Henry, and the old family curse, sank more or less into the background of my mind.

Three months afterwards, on the 7th of January, I saw to my sorrow in the *Times* the announcement of Sir Henry Clinton's death.

From time to time in the interim I had heard from the son, saying that his father was failing fast. He further mentioned that his own wedding was fixed for the twenty-first of the present month. Now, of course, it must be postponed. I felt truly sorry for Allen, and wrote immediately a long letter of condolence.

On the following day I received a wire from him, imploring me to go down to the Abbey as soon as possible, saying that he was in great difficulty.

I packed a few things hastily, and arrived at Clinton Abbey at six in the evening. The house was silent and subdued—the funeral was to take place the next day. Clinton came into the hall and gripped me warmly by the hand. I noticed at once how worn and worried he looked.

"This is good of you, Bell," he said. "I cannot tell you how grateful I am to you for coming. You are the one man who can help me, for I know you have had much experience in matters of this sort. Come into the library and I will tell you everything. We shall dine alone this evening, as my mother and the girls are keeping to their own apartments for tonight."

As soon as we were seated, he plunged at once into his story.

"I must give you a sort of prelude to what has just occurred," he began. "You remember, when you were last here, how abruptly Phyllis and her mother left the Abbey?"

I nodded. I remembered well.

"On the morning after you had left us I had a long letter from Phyllis," continued Allen. "In it she told me of an extraordinary request my father had made to her during that moonlight walk—nothing more nor less than an earnest wish that she would herself terminate our engagement. She spoke quite frankly, as she always does, assuring me of her unalterable love and devotion, but saying that under the circumstances it was absolutely necessary to have an explanation. Frantic with almost ungovernable rage, I sought my father in his study. I laid Phyllis's letter before him and asked him what it meant. He looked at me with the most unutterable expression of weariness and pathos.

"'Yes, my boy, I did it,' he said. 'Phyllis is quite right. I did ask of her, as earnestly as a very old man could plead, that she would bring the engagement to an end.'

"'But why?' I asked. 'Why?'

"'That I am unable to tell you,' he replied.

"I lost my temper and said some words to him which I now regret. He made no sort of reply. When I had done speaking he said slowly,—

"'I make all allowance for your emotion, Allen; your feelings are no more than natural.'

"'You have done me a very sore injury,' I retorted. 'What can Phyllis think of this? She will never be the same again. I am going to see her today.'

"He did not utter another word, and I left him. I was absent from home for about a week. It took me nearly that time to induce Phyllis to overlook my father's extraordinary request, and to let matters go on exactly as they had done before.

"After fixing our engagement, if possible, more firmly than ever, and also arranging the date of our wedding, I returned home. When I did so I told my father what I had done.

"'As you will,' he replied, and then he sank into great gloom. From that moment, although I watched him day and night, and did everything that love and tenderness could suggest, he never seemed to rally. He scarcely spoke, and remained, whenever we were together, bowed in deep and painful reverie. A week ago he took to his bed."

Here Allen paused.

"I now come to events up to date," he said. "Of course, as you may suppose, I was with my father to the last. A few hours before he passed away he called me to his bedside, and to my astonishment began once more talking about my engagement. He implored me with the utmost earnestness even now at the eleventh hour to break it off. It was not too late, he said, and added further that nothing would give him ease in dying but the knowledge that I would promise him to remain single. Of course I tried to humour him. He took my hand, looked me in the eyes with an expression which I shall never forget, and said,—

"'Allen, make me a solemn promise that you will never marry.'

"This I naturally had to refuse, and then he told me that, expecting my obstinacy, he had written me a letter which I should find in his safe, but I was not to open it till after his death. I found it this morning. Bell, it is the most extraordinary communication, and either it is entirely a figment of his imagination, for his brain powers were failing very much at the last, or else it is the most awful thing I ever heard of. Here is the letter; read it for yourself."

I took the paper from his hand and read the following matter in shaky, almost illegible writing:—

My dear Boy,

When you read this I shall have passed away. For the last six months my life has been a living death. The horror began in the following way. You know what a deep interest I have always taken in the family history of our house. I have spent the latter years of my life in verifying each detail, and my intention was, had health been given me, to publish a great deal of it in a suitable volume.

On the special night to which I am about to allude, I sat up late in my study reading the book which I saw you show to Bell a short time ago. In particular, I was much attracted by the terrible curse which the old abbot in the fourteenth century had bestowed upon the family. I read the awful words again and again. I knew that all the other details in the volume had been verified, but that the vault with the coffin had never yet been found. Presently I grew drowsy, and I suppose I must have fallen asleep. In my sleep I had a dream; I thought that some one came into the room, touched me on the shoulder, and said "Come." I looked up; a tall figure beckoned to me. The voice and the figure belonged to my late father. In my dream I rose immediately, although I did not know why I went nor where I was going. The figure went on in front, it entered the hall. I took one of the candles from the table and the key of the chapel, unbolted the door and went out. Still the voice kept saying "Come, come," and the figure of my father walked in front of me. I went across the quadrangle, unlocked the chapel door, and entered.

A death-like silence was around me. I crossed the nave to the north aisle; the figure still went in front of me; it entered the great pew which is said to be haunted, and walked straight up to the effigy of the old abbot who had pronounced the curse. This, as you know, is built into the opposite wall. Bending forward, the figure pressed the eyes of the old monk, and immediately a stone started out of its place, revealing a staircase behind. I was about to hurry forward, when I must have knocked against something. I felt a sensation of pain, and suddenly awoke. What was my amazement to find that I had acted on my dream, had crossed the quadrangle, and was in the chapel; in fact, was standing in the old pew! Of course there was no figure of any sort visible, but the moonlight shed a cold radiance over all the place. I felt very much startled and impressed, but was just about to return to the house in some wonder at the curious vision which I had experienced, when, raising my startled eyes, I saw that part of it at least was real. The old monk seemed to grin at me from his marble effigy, and beside him was a *blank open space.* I hurried to it and saw a narrow flight of stairs. I cannot explain what my emotions were, but my keenest feeling at that moment was a strong and horrible curiosity. Holding the candle in my hand, I went down the steps. They terminated at the beginning of a long passage. This I quickly traversed, and at last found myself beside an iron door. It was not locked, but hasped, and was very hard to open; in fact, it required nearly all my strength; at last I pulled it open towards me, and there in a small cell lay the coffin, as the words of the curse said. I gazed at it in horror. I did not dare to enter. It was a wedged-shaped coffin studded with great nails. But as I looked my blood froze within me, for slowly, very slowly, as if pushed by some unseen hand, the great heavy door began to close, quicker and quicker, until with a crash that echoed and re-echoed through the empty vault, it shut.

Terror-stricken, I rushed from the vault and reached my room once more.

Now I know that this great curse is true; that my father's spirit is there to guard the door and close it, for I saw it with my own eyes, and while you read this know that I am there. I charge you, therefore, not to marry—bring no child into the world to perpetuate this terrible curse. Let the family die out if you have the courage. It is much, I know, to ask; but whether you do or not, come to me there, and if by sign or word I can communicate with you I will do so, but hold the secret safe. Meet me there before my body is laid to rest, when body and soul are still not far from each other. Farewell.

—Your loving father,

Henry Clinton.

I read this strange letter over carefully twice, and laid it down. For a moment I hardly knew what to say. It was certainly the most uncanny thing I had ever come across.

"What do you think of it?" asked Allen at last.

"Well, of course there are only two possible solutions," I answered. "One is that your father not only dreamt the beginning of this story—which, remember, he allows himself—but the whole of it."

"And the other?" asked Allen, seeing that I paused.

"The other," I continued, "I hardly know what to say yet. Of course we will investigate the whole thing, that is our only chance of arriving at a solution. It is absurd to let matters rest as they are. We had better try tonight."

Clinton winced and hesitated.

"Something must be done, of course," he answered; "but the worst of it is Phyllis and her mother are coming here early tomorrow in time for the funeral, and I cannot meet her—no, I cannot, poor girl!—while I feel as I do."

"We will go to the vault tonight," I said.

Clinton rose from his chair and looked at me.

"I don't like this thing at all, Bell," he continued. "I am not by nature in any sense of the word a superstitious man, but I tell you frankly nothing would induce me to go alone into that chapel tonight; if you come with me, that, of course, alters matters. I know the pew my father refers to well; it is beneath the window of St. Sebastian."

Soon afterwards I went to my room and dressed; and Allen and I dined *tête-à-tête* in the great dining-room. The old butler waited on us with funereal solemnity, and I did all I could to lure Clinton's thoughts into a more cheerful and healthier channel.

I cannot say that I was very successful. I further noticed that he scarcely ate anything, and seemed altogether to be in a state of nervous tension painful to witness.

After dinner we went into the smoking-room, and at eleven o'clock I proposed that we should make a start.

Clinton braced himself together and we went out. He got the chapel keys, and then going to the stables we borrowed a lantern, and a moment afterwards found ourselves in the sacred edifice. The moon was at her full, and by the pale light which was diffused through the south windows the architecture of the interior could be faintly seen. The Gothic arches that flanked the centre aisle with their quaint pillars, each with a carved figure of one of the saints, were quite visible, and further in the darkness of the chancel the dim outlines of the choir and altar-table with its white marble reredos could be just discerned.

We closed the door softly and, Clinton leading the way with the lantern, we walked up the centre aisle paved with the brasses of his dead ancestors. We trod gently on tiptoe as one instinctively does at night. Turning beneath the little pulpit we reached the north transept, and here Clinton stopped and turned round. He was very white, but his voice was quiet.

"This is the pew," he whispered. "It has always been called the haunted pew of Sir Hugh Clinton."

I took the lantern from him and we entered. I crossed the pew immediately and went up to the effigy of the old abbot.

"Let us examine him closely," I said. I held up the lantern, getting it to shine on each part of the face, the vestments, and the figure. The eyes, although vacant, as in all statuary, seemed to me at that moment to be uncanny and peculiar. Giving Allen the lantern to hold, I placed a finger firmly on each. The next moment I could not refrain from an exclamation; a stone at the side immediately rolled back, revealing the steps which were spoken of by the old man in his narrative.

"It is true! It is true!" cried Clinton excitedly.

"It certainly looks like it," I remarked: "but never mind, we have the chance now of investigating this matter thoroughly."

"Are you going down?" asked Clinton.

"Certainly I am," I replied. "Let us go together."

Immediately afterwards we crept through the opening and began to descend. There was only just room to do so in single file, and I went first with the lantern. In another moment we were in the long passage, and soon we were confronted by a door in an arched stone framework. Up till now Clinton had shown little sign of alarm, but here, at the trysting-place to which his father's soul had summoned him, he seemed suddenly to lose his nerve. He leant against the wall and for a moment I thought he would have fallen. I held up the lantern and examined the door and walls carefully. Then approaching I lifted the iron latch of the heavy door. It was very hard to move, but at last by seizing the edge I dragged it open to its full against the wall of the passage. Having done so I peered inside, holding the lantern above my head. As I did so I heard Clinton cry out,—

"Look, look," he said, and turning I saw that the great door had swung back against me, almost shutting me within the cell.

Telling Clinton to hold it back by force, I stepped inside and saw at my feet the ghastly coffin. The legend then so far was true. I bent down and examined the queer, misshapen thing with great care. Its shape was that of an enormous wedge, and it was apparently made of some dark old wood, and was bound with iron at the corners. Having looked at it all round, I went out and, flinging back the door which Clinton had been holding open, stood aside to watch. Slowly, very slowly, as we both stood in the passage—slowly, as if pushed by some invisible hand, the door commenced to swing round, and, increasing in velocity, shut with a noisy clang.

Seizing it once again, I dragged it open and, while Clinton held it in that position, made a careful examination. Up to the present I saw nothing to be much alarmed about. There were fifty ways in which a door might shut of its own accord. There might be a hidden spring or tilted hinges; draught, of course, was out of the question. I looked at the hinges, they were of iron and set in the solid masonry. Nor could I discover any spring or hidden contrivance, as when the door was wide open there was an interval of several inches between it and the wall. We tried it again and again with the same result, and at last, as it was closing, I seized it to prevent it.

I now experienced a very odd sensation; I certainly felt as if I were resisting an unseen person who was pressing hard against the door at the other side. Directly it was released it continued its course. I allow I was quite unable to understand the mystery. Suddenly an idea struck me.

"What does the legend say?" I asked, turning to Clinton. "'That the soul is to guard the door, to close it upon the coffin?'"

"Those are the words," answered Allen, speaking with some difficulty.

"Now if that is true," I continued, "and we take the coffin out, the spirit won't shut the door; if it does shut it, it disproves the whole thing at once, and shows it to be merely a clever mechanical contrivance. Come, Clinton, help me to get the coffin out."

"I dare not, Bell," he whispered hoarsely. "I daren't go inside."

"Nonsense, man," I said, feeling now a little annoyed at the whole thing. "Here, put the lantern down and hold the door back." I stepped in and, getting behind the coffin, put out all my strength and shoved it into the passage.

"Now, then," I cried, "I'll bet you fifty pounds to five the door will shut just the same." I dragged the coffin clear of the door and told him to let go. Clinton had scarcely done so before, stepping back, he clutched my arm.

"Look," he whispered; "do you see that it will not shut now? My father is waiting for the coffin to be put back. This is awful!"

I gazed at the door in horror; it was perfectly true, it remained wide open, and quite still. I sprang forward, seized it, and now endeavoured to close it. It was as if some one was trying to hold it open; it required considerable force to stir it, and it was only with difficulty I could move it at all. At last I managed to shut it, but the moment I let go it swung back open of its own accord and struck against the wall, where it remained just as before. In the dead silence that followed I could hear Clinton breathing quickly behind me, and I knew he was holding himself for all he was worth.

At that moment there suddenly came over me a sensation which I had once experienced before, and which I was twice destined to experience again. It is impossible to describe it, but it seized me, laying siege to my brain till I felt like a child in its power. It was as if I were slowly drowning in the great ocean of silence that enveloped us. Time itself seemed to have disappeared. At my feet lay the mis-shapen thing, and the lantern behind it cast a fantastic shadow of its distorted outline on the cell wall before me.

"Speak; say something," I cried to Clinton. The sharp sound of my voice broke the spell. I felt myself again, and smiled at the trick my nerves had played on me. I bent down and once more laid my hands on the coffin, but before I had time to push it back into its place Clinton had gone up the passage like a man who is flying to escape a hurled javelin.

Exerting all my force to prevent the door from swinging back by keeping my leg against it, I had just got the coffin into the cell and was going out, when I heard a shrill cry, and Clinton came tearing back down the passage.

"I can't get out! The stone has sunk into its place! We are locked in!" he screamed, and, wild with fear, he plunged headlong into the cell, upsetting me in his career before I could check him. I sprang back to the door as it was closing. I was too late. Before I could reach it, it had shut with a loud clang in obedience to the infernal witchcraft.

"You have done it now," I cried angrily. "Do you see? Why, man, we are buried alive in this ghastly hole!"

The lantern I had placed just inside the door, and by its dim light, as I looked at him, I saw the terror of a madman creep into Clinton's eyes.

"Buried alive!" he shouted, with a peal of hysterical laughter. "Yes, and, Bell, it's your doing; you are a devil in human shape!" With a wild paroxysm of fury he flung himself upon me. There was the ferocity of a wild beast in his spring. He upset the lantern and left us in total darkness.

The struggle was short. We might be buried alive, but I was not going to die by his hand, and seizing him by the throat I pinned him against the wall.

"Keep quiet," I shouted. "It is your thundering stupidity that has caused all this. Stay where you are until I strike a match."

I luckily had some vestas in the little silver box which I always carry on my watch-chain, and striking one I relit the lantern. Clinton's paroxysm was over, and sinking to the floor he lay there shivering and cowering.

It was a terrible situation, and I knew that our only hope was for me to keep my presence of mind. With a great effort I forced myself to think calmly over what could be done. To shout for help would have been but a useless waste of breath.

Suddenly an idea struck me. "Have you got your father's letter?" I cried eagerly.

"I have," he answered; "it is in my pocket."

My last ray of hope vanished. Our only chance was that if he had left it at the house some one might discover the letter and come to our rescue by its instructions. It had been a faint hope, and it disappeared almost as quickly as it had come to me. Without it no one would ever find the way to the vault that had remained a secret for ages. I was determined, however, not to die without a struggle for freedom. Taking the lantern, I examined every nook and cranny of the cell for some other exit. It was a fruitless search. No sign of any way out could I find, and we had absolutely no means to unfasten the door from the inner side. Taking a few short steps, I flung myself again and again at the heavy door. It never budged an inch, and, bruised and sweating at every pore, I sat down on the coffin and tried to collect all my faculties.

Clinton was silent, and seemed utterly stunned. He sat still, gazing with a vacant stare at the door.

The time dragged heavily, and there was nothing to do but to wait for a horrible death from starvation. It was more than likely, too, that Clinton would go mad; already his nerves were strained to the utmost. Altogether I had never found myself in a worse plight.

It seemed like an eternity that we sat there, neither of us speaking a word. Over and over again I repeated to myself the words of the terrible curse: "And whoso entereth into the cell shall be the prisoner of the soul that guardeth the door till it shall let him go." When would the shapeless form that was inside the coffin let us go? Doubtless when our bones were dry.

I looked at my watch. It was half-past eleven o'clock. Surely we had been more than ten minutes in this awful place! We had left the house at eleven, and I knew that must have been many hours ago. I glanced at the second hand. *The watch had stopped.*

"What is the time, Clinton?" I asked. "My watch has stopped."

"What does it matter?" he murmured. "What is time to us now? The sooner we die the better."

He pulled out his watch as he spoke, and held it to the lantern.

"Twenty-five minutes past eleven," he murmured dreamily.

"Good heavens!" I cried, starting up. "Has your watch stopped, too?"

Then, like the leap of a lightning flash, an idea struck me.

"I have got it; I have got it! My God! I believe I have got it!" I cried, seizing him by the arm.

"Got what?" he replied, staring wildly at me.

"Why, the secret—the curse—the door. Don't you see?"

I pulled out the large knife I always carry by a chain and swivel in my trouser pocket, and telling Clinton to hold the lantern, opened the little blade-saw and attacked the coffin with it.

"I believe the secret of our deliverance lies in this," I panted, working away furiously.

In ten minutes I had sawn half through the wooden edge, then, handing my tool to Clinton, I told him to continue the work while I rested. After a few minutes I took the knife again, and at last, after nearly half an hour had gone by, succeeded in making a small hole in the lid. Inserting my two fingers, I felt some rough, uneven masses. I was now fearfully excited. Tearing at the opening like a madman, I enlarged it and extracted what looked like a large piece of coal. I knew in an instant what it was. It was magnetic iron-ore. Holding it down to my knife, the blade flew to it.

"Here is the mystery of the soul," I cried; "now we can use it to open the door."

I had known a great conjurer once, who had deceived and puzzled his audience with a box trick on similar lines: the man opening the box from the inside by drawing down the lock with a magnet. Would this do the same? I felt that our lives hung on the next moment. Taking the mass, I pressed it against the door just opposite the hasp, and slid it up against the wood. My heart leapt as I heard the hasp fly up outside, and with a push the door opened.

"We are saved," I shouted. "We are saved by a miracle!"

"Bell, you are a genius," gasped poor Clinton; "but now, how about the stone at the end of the passage?"

"We will soon see about that," I cried, taking the lantern. "Half the danger is over, at any rate; and the worst half, too."

We rushed along the passage and up the stair until we reached the top.

"Why, Clinton," I cried, holding up the lantern, "the place was not shut at all."

Nor was it. In his terror he had imagined it.

"I could not see in the dark, and I was nearly dead with fright," he said. "Oh, Bell, let us get out of this as quickly as we can!"

We crushed through the aperture and once more stood in the chapel. I then pushed the stone back into its place.

Dawn was just breaking when we escaped from the chapel. We hastened across to the house. In the hall the clock pointed to five.

"Well, we have had an awful time," I said, as we stood in the hall together; "but at least, Clinton, the end was worth the ghastly terror. I have knocked the bottom out of your family legend for ever."

"I don't even now quite understand," he said.

"Don't you?—but it is so easy. That coffin never contained a body at all, but was filled, as you perceive, with fragments of magnetic iron-ore. For what diabolical purposes the cell was intended, it is, of course, impossible to say; but that it must have been meant as a human trap there is little doubt. The inventor certainly exercised no small ingenuity when he devised his diabolical plot, for it was obvious that the door, which was made of iron, would swing towards the coffin wherever it happened to be placed. Thus the door would shut if the coffin were *inside the cell*, and would remain open if the coffin were *brought out*. A cleverer method for simulating a spiritual agency it would be hard to find. Of course, the monk must have known well that magnetic iron-ore never loses its quality and would ensure the deception remaining potent for ages."

"But how did you discover by means of our watches?" asked Clinton.

"Any one who understands magnetism can reply to that," I said. "It is a well-known fact that a strong magnet plays havoc with watches. The fact of both our watches going wrong first gave me a clue to the mystery."

Later in the day the whole of this strange affair was explained to Miss Curzon, and not long afterwards the passage and entrance to the chapel were bricked up.

It is needless to add that six months later the pair were married, and, I believe, are as happy as they deserve.

THE ORDINARY HAIRPINS

E. C. Bentley

Even if it is fair to say that Edmund Clerihew Bentley (1875–1956), a journalist and humorist who invented the Clerihew verse form, only dabbled in detective fiction, it must be added that he did so to astonishingly significant effect. His debut novel *Trent's Last Case* (1913) was a landmark title in the genre's history, a well-written and cleverly plotted country house mystery that influenced writers of the Golden Age of detective fiction such as Agatha Christie and Dorothy L. Sayers. It scarcely mattered that Bentley's original intention was to satirise the notion of the supposedly omniscient Great Detective. The book was filmed three times and remains a good read. And it earned Bentley election to the prestigious Detection Club, presided over by his old school friend G. K. Chesterton. When Chesterton died, Bentley succeeded him as President of the Club.

Although he had not originally intended Philip Trent to become a series character (hence the title of the novel), Bentley achieved such success with the book that he came under pressure to write short stories about Trent and, in 1936, to publish *Trent's Own Case*, co-written with his friend H. Warner Allen. The second novel was a minor effort compared to its predecessor, but the short stories are generally of high calibre and they were eventually collected in *Trent Intervenes* (1938); the first appearance of this story, however, was in the *Strand Magazine* in October 1916.

A SMALL COMMITTEE OF FRIENDS HAD PERSUADED LORD Aviemore to sit for a presentation portrait, and the painter to whom they gave the commission was Philip Trent. It was a task that fascinated him, for he had often seen and admired, in public places, the high half-bald skull, vulture nose, and grim mouth of the peer who was said to be deeper in theology than any other layman, and all but a few of the clergy; whose devotion to charitable work had made him nationally honoured. It was not until the third sitting that Lord Aviemore's sombre taciturnity was laid aside.

"I believe, Mr. Trent," he said abruptly, "you used to have a portrait of my late sister-in-law here. I was told that it hung in the studio."

Trent continued his work quietly. "It was just a rough drawing I made after seeing her in *Carmen*—before her marriage. It has been hung in here ever since. Before your first visit I removed it."

The sitter nodded slowly. "Very thoughtful of you. Nevertheless, I should like very much to see it, if I may."

"Of course." Trent drew the framed sketch from behind a curtain. Lord Aviemore gazed long in silence at Trent's very spirited likeness of the famous singer, while the artist worked busily to capture the first expression of feeling that he had so far seen on that impassive face. Lighted and softened by melancholy, it looked for the first time noble.

At last the sitter turned to him. "I would give a good deal," he said simply, "to possess this drawing."

Trent shook his head. "I don't want to part with it." He laid a few strokes carefully on the canvas. "If you care to know why, I'll tell you. It is my personal memory of a woman whom I found more admirable than any other I ever saw. Lillemor Wergeland's beauty and physical perfection were unforgettable. Her voice was a marvel; her spirit matched them; her fearlessness, her kindness, her vigour of mind and character, her feeling for beauty, were what I heard talked about even by people not given to enthusiasm. She had weaknesses, I dare say—I never spoke to her. I heard her sing very many times, but I knew no more about her than many other strangers. A number of my friends knew her, though, and all I ever gathered about her made me inclined to place her on a pedestal. I was ten years younger then; it did me good."

Lord Aviemore said nothing for a few minutes, then he spoke slowly. "I am not of your temperament or your circle, Mr. Trent. I do not worship anything of this world. But I do not think you were far wrong about Lady Aviemore. Once I thought differently. When I heard that my eldest brother was about to marry a prima donna, a woman whose portrait was sold all over the world, who was famous for extravagance in dress and what seemed to me self-advertising conduct, I was appalled when I heard from him of this engagement. I will not deny that I was shocked, too, at the idea of a marriage with the daughter of Norwegian peasants."

"She was country-bred, then," Trent observed. "One never heard much about her childhood."

"Yes. She was an orphan of ten years old when Colonel Stamer and his wife went to lodge at her brother's farm for the fishing. They fell in love with the child, and having none of their own, they adopted her. All this my brother told me. He knew, he said, just what I would think; he only asked me to meet her, and then to judge if he had done well or ill. Of course I asked him to introduce me at the first opportunity."

Lord Aviemore paused and stared thoughtfully at the portrait. "She charmed every one who came near her," he went on presently.

"I resisted the spell; but before they had been long married she had conquered all my prejudice. It was like a child, I saw, that she delighted in the popularity and the great income her gifts had brought her. But she was not really childish. It was not that she was what is called intellectual; but she had a singular spaciousness of mind in which nothing little or mean could live—it had, I used to fancy, some kinship with her Norwegian landscapes of mountain and sea. She was, as you say, extremely beautiful, with the vigorous purity of the fair-haired northern race. Her marriage with my brother was the happiest I have ever known."

He paused again while Trent worked on in silence, and soon the low meditative voice resumed. "It was about this time six years ago— the middle of March—that I had the terrible news from Taormina, the day after my return from Canada. I went out to her at once. When I saw her I was aghast. She showed no emotion; but there was in her calmness the most unearthly sense of desolation that I have ever received. From time to time she would say, as if she spoke to herself, 'It was all my fault.'"

At Trent's exclamation of surprise Lord Aviemore looked up. "Few people," he said, "know the whole of the tragedy. You have heard that a slight shock of earthquake caused the collapse of the villa, and that my brother and his child were found dead in the ruins; you have heard, I suppose, that Lady Aviemore was not in the house at the time. You have heard that she drowned herself afterwards. But you have evidently not heard that my brother had a presentiment that this visit to Sicily would end in death, and wished to abandon it at the last moment; that his wife laughed away his forebodings with her strong common sense. But we belong to the Highlands, Mr. Trent; we are of that blood and tradition, and such interior warnings as my brother had are no trifles to us. However, she charmed his fears away; he had, she told me, entirely lost all sense of uneasiness. On the tenth day of their stay her husband and only child were killed. She did not think, as you may think, that there was coincidence here. The shock had changed her whole mental being; she believed then, as I believed, that my brother inwardly foreknew that death awaited him if went to that place." He relapsed into silence.

"I know slightly," Trent remarked, "a man called Selby, a solicitor, who was with Lady Aviemore just after her husband's death."

Lord Aviemore said that he remembered Mr. Selby. He said it with such a total absence of expression of any kind that the subject of Selby was killed instantly; and he did not resume that of the tragedy of the woman whom the world remembered still as Lillemor Wergeland.

It was a few months later, when the portrait of Lord Aviemore was to be seen at the show of the N.S.P.P., that Trent received a friendly letter from Arthur Selby. After praising the picture, Selby went on to ask if Trent would do him the favour of calling at his office by appointment for a private talk. "I should like," he wrote, "to put a certain story before you, a story with a problem in it. I gave it up as a bad job long ago myself, but seeing your portrait of A. reminded me of your reputation as an unraveller."

Thus it happened that, a few days later, Trent found himself alone with Selby in the offices of the firm in which that very capable, somewhat dandified lawyer was a partner. They spoke of the portrait, and Trent told of the strange exaltation with which his sitter had spoken of the dead lady. Selby listened rather grimly.

"The story I referred to," he said, "is the Aviemore story. I acted for the countess when she was alive. I was with her at the time of her suicide. I am an executor of her will. In the strictest confidence, I should like to tell you that story as I know it, and hear what you think about it."

Trent was all attention; he was deeply interested, and said so. Selby, with gloomy eyes, folded his arms on the broad writing-table between them, and began.

"You know all about the accident," he said. "I will start with the 15th of March, when Lord Aviemore and his son were buried in the cemetery at Taormina. That was before I came on the scene. Lady Aviemore had already discharged all the servants except her own maid, with whom she was living at the Hotel Cavour. There, as I gathered afterwards, she seldom left her rooms. She was undoubtedly overwhelmed by what had happened, though she seems never to have lost her grip on herself. Her brother-in-law, the present Lord Aviemore, had come out to join her. He had only just returned from Canada"—Selby raised a finger and repeated slowly—"from Canada, you will remember. He had gone out to get ideas about the emigration prospect, I understood. He remained at the hotel, meaning to accompany Lady Aviemore home when she should feel equal to the journey.

"It was not until the 18th that we received a long telegram from her, asking us to send some one representing the firm to her at Taormina. She stated that she wished to discuss business matters without delay, but did not yet feel able to travel. At the cost of some inconvenience, I went out myself, as I happen to speak Italian pretty well. You understand that Lady Aviemore, who already possessed considerable means of her own, came into a large income under her husband's will."

"She was a client who could afford to indulge her whims," Trent observed. "If you were already her adviser, she probably expected you to come."

"Just so. Well, I went out to Taormina, as I say. On my arrival Lady Aviemore saw me, and told me quite calmly that she was acquainted with the provisions of her late husband's will, and that she now wished to make her own. I took her instructions, and prepared the will at once. The next day the British Consul and I witnessed her signature. You may remember, Trent, that when the contents of her will became public after her death they attracted a good deal of attention."

"I don't think I heard of it," Trent said. "If I was giving myself a holiday at the time, I wouldn't know much about what was going on."

"Well, there were some bequests of jewellery and things to intimate friends. She left £2,000 to her brother Knut Wergeland, of Myklebostad in Norway, and £100 to her maid, Maria Krogh, also a Norwegian, who had been with her a long time. The whole of the rest of her property she left to her brother-in-law, the new Lord Aviemore, unconditionally. That surprised me, because I had been told that he had disapproved bitterly of the marriage, and hadn't concealed his opinion from her or any one else. But she never bore malice, I knew; and what she said to me at Taormina was that she could think of nobody who would do so much good with the money as her brother-in-law. From that point of view she was justified. He is said to spend three-fourths of his income on charities of all sorts, and I shouldn't wonder if it was true. Anyhow, she made him her heir."

"And what did he say to it?"

Selby coughed. "There is no evidence that he knew anything about it before her death. No evidence," he repeated slowly. "And when told of it afterwards he showed precious little feeling of any kind. Of course, that's his way. But now let me get on with the story. Lady Aviemore asked me to remain to transact business for her until she should leave Taormina. She did so on the 27th of March, accompanied by Lord Aviemore, myself, and her maid. To shorten the railway journey, as she told us, she had planned to go by boat first to Brindisi, then to Venice, and so home by rail. The boats from Brindisi to Venice all go in the daytime, except once a week, when a boat from Corfu arrives in the evening and goes on about eleven. She decided to get to Brindisi in time to catch that boat. So that was what we did; had a few hours in Brindisi, dined there, and went on board about ten o'clock. Lady Aviemore complained of a bad headache. She went at once to her cabin, which was a deck-cabin, asking me to send some one to collect her ticket at once, as she wanted to sleep as soon as possible and not be awakened again. That was soon done. Shortly before the boat left, the maid came to me on her way to her own quarters and told me her mistress had retired. Soon after we were out of the harbour I turned in myself. At that time Lord Aviemore was leaning over the rail on the deck on to which Lady Aviemore's cabin opened, and some distance from the cabin. There was nobody else about that I could see. It was just beginning to blow, but it didn't trouble me, and I slept very well.

"It was a quarter to eight next morning when Lord Aviemore came into my cabin. He was fearfully pale and agitated. He told me that the Countess could not be found; that the maid had gone to her cabin to call her at 7.30 and found it empty.

"I got up in a hurry, and went with him to the cabin. The dressing-case she had taken with her was there, and her fur coat and her hat and her jewellery-case and her handbag lay on the berth, which had not been slept in. The only other thing was a note, unaddressed, lying open on the table. Lord Aviemore and I read it together. After the inquiry at Venice I kept the note. Here it is."

Selby unfolded and handed over a sheet of thin ruled paper, torn from a block. Trent read the following words, written in a large, firm, rounded hand:

"Such an ending to such a marriage is far worse than death. It was all my fault. This is not sorrow; it is complete destruction. I have been kept up till now only by the resolution I took on the day when

I lost them, by the thought of what I am going to do now. I take my leave of a world I cannot bear any more."

There followed the initials "L.A." Trent read and reread the pitiful message, so full of the awful egotism of grief, then he looked up in silence at Selby.

"The Italian authorities found that she had met her death by drowning. They could not suppose anything else—nor could I. But now listen, Trent. Soon after her death I got an idea into my head, and I have puzzled over the affair a lot without much result. I did find out a fact or two, though; and it struck me the other day that if I could discover something, you could probably do much better."

Trent, still studying the paper, ignored this tribute. "Well," he said, "what is your idea, Selby?"

Selby, evading the direct question, said, "I'll tell you the facts I referred to. That sheet, you see, is torn from an ordinary ruled writing-pad. Now I have shown it to a friend of mine who is in the paper business. He has told me that it is a make of paper never sold in Europe, but sold very largely in Canada. Next, Lady Aviemore never was in Canada. And there was no writing-pad in her dressing-case or anywhere in the cabin. Neither was there any pen or ink, or any fountain pen. The ink, you see, is a pale sort of grey ink."

Trent nodded. "Continental hotel ink, in fact. This was written in a hotel, then—probably the one where you had dinner in Brindisi. You could identify her writing, of course."

"Except that it seems to have been written with a bad pen—a hotel pen, no doubt—it is her usual handwriting."

"Any other exhibits?" Trent asked after a brief silence.

"Only this." Selby took from a drawer a woman's handbag of elaborate bead-work. "Later on, when I saw Lord Aviemore about the disposal of her valuables and personal effects, I mentioned that there was this bag, with a few trifles in it. 'Give it away,' he said. 'Do what you like with it.' Well," Selby went on, smoothing the back of his head with an air of slight embarrassment, "I kept it. As a sort of memento—what? The things in it don't mean anything to me, but you have a look at them." He turned the bag out upon the writing-table. "Here you are—handkerchief, notes and change, nail-file, keys, powder-thing, lipstick, comb, hairpins—"

"Four hairpins." Trent took them in his hand. "Quite new ones, I should say. Have they anything to tell us, Selby?"

"I don't see how. They're just ordinary black hairpins—as you say, they look too fresh and bright to have been used."

Trent looked at the small heap of objects on the table. "And what's that last thing—the little box?"

"That's a box of Ixtil, the anti-sea-sick stuff. Two doses are gone. It's quite good, I believe."

Trent opened the box and stared at the pink capsules. "So you can buy it abroad?"

"I was with her when she bought it in Brindisi, just before we went on board."

Again Trent was silent a few moments. "Then all you discovered that was odd was this about the Canadian paper, and the note having obviously been prepared in advance. Queer enough, certainly. But going back before that last day or two—all through the time you were with Lady Aviemore, did nothing come under your notice that seemed strange?"

Selby fingered his chin. "If you put it like that, I do remember a thing that I thought curious at the time, though I never dreamed of its having anything to do—"

"Yes, I know, but you asked me here to go over the thing properly, didn't you? That question of mine is one of the routine inquiries."

"Well, it was simply this. A day or two before we left Sicily I was standing in the hotel lobby when the mail arrived. As I was waiting to see if there was anything for me, the porter put down on the counter a rather smart-looking package that had just come—done up the way they do it at a really first-class shop, if you know what I mean. It looked like a biggish book, or box of chocolates, or something; and it had French stamps on it, but the postmark I didn't notice. And this was addressed to Mlle. Maria Krogh—you remember, the Countess's maid. Well, she was there waiting, and presently the man handed it to her. Maria went off with it, and just then her mistress came down the big stairs. She saw the parcel, and just held out her hand for it, and Maria passed it over as if it was a matter of course, and Lady Aviemore went upstairs with it. I thought it was quaint if she was ordering goods in her maid's name; but I thought no more of it, because Lady Aviemore decided that evening about leaving the place, and I had plenty to attend to. And if you want to know," Selby went on as Trent opened his lips to speak, "where Maria Krogh is, all I can tell you is that I took her ticket in London for Christiansand, where she lives, and where I sent her legacy to her, which she acknowledged. Now then!"

Trent laughed at the solicitor's tone, and Selby laughed too. His friend walked to the fireplace and pensively adjusted his tie. "Well, I must be off," he announced. "How about dining with me on Friday at the Cactus? If by that time I've anything to suggest about all this, I'll tell you. You will? All right, make it eight o'clock." And he hastened away.

But on the Friday he seemed to have nothing to suggest. He was so reluctant to approach the subject that Selby supposed him to be chagrined at his failure to achieve anything, and did not press the matter.

★

It was six months later, on a sunny afternoon in September, that Trent walked up the valley road at Myklebostad, looking farewell at the mountain far ahead, the white-capped mother of the torrent that roared down a twenty-foot fall beside him. He had been a week in this remote backwater of Europe, seven hours by motor-boat from the nearest place that ranked as a town. The savage beauty of that watery landscape, where sun and rain worked together daily to achieve an unearthly purity in the scene, had justified far better than he had hoped his story that he had come there in search of matter for his brush. He had worked and he had explored, and had learned as much as he could of his neighbours. It was little enough, for the postmaster, in whose house he had a room, spoke only a trifle of German, and no one else, as far as he could discover, had anything but Norwegian, of which Trent knew no more than what could be got from a traveller's phrase-book. But he had seen every dweller in the valley, and he had paid close attention to the household of Knut Wergeland, the rich man of the valley, who had the largest farm. He and his wife, elderly and grim-faced peasants, lived with one serv-ant in an old turf-roofed steading not far from the post office. Not another person, Trent was sure, inhabited the house.

He had decided at last that his voyage of curiosity to Myklebostad had been ill-inspired. Knut and his wife were no more than a thrifty peasant pair. They had given him a meal one day when he was sketching near the place, and they had refused with gentle firmness to take any payment. Both had made on him an impression of com-plete trustworthiness and competency in the life they led so utterly out of the world.

That day, as Trent gazed up to the mountain, his eye was caught by a flash of sunlight against the dense growth of birches running from top to bottom of the steep cliff that walled the valley to his left. It was a bright blink, about half a mile from where he stood; it remained steady, and at several points above and below he saw the same bright appearance. He perceived that there must be a wire, and a well-used wire, led up the precipitous hill face among the trees. Trent went on towards the spot on the road whence the wire seemed to be taken upwards. He had never been so far in this direction until now. In a few minutes he came to the opening among the trees of a rough track leading upwards among rocks and roots, at such an angle that only a vigorous climber could attempt it. Close by, in the edge of the thicket, stood a tall post, from the top of which a wire stretched upward through the branches in the same direction as the path.

Trent slapped the post with a resounding blow. "Heavens and earth!" he exclaimed. "I had forgotten the *saeter*!"

And at once he began to climb.

A thick carpet of rich pasture began where the deep birch-belt ended at the top of the height. It stretched away for miles over a gently sloping upland. As Trent came into the open, panting after a strenuous forty-minute climb, the heads of a score of browsing cattle were sleepily turned towards him. Beyond them wandered many more, and two hundred yards away stood a tiny hut, turf-roofed.

This plateau was the *saeter*; the high grassland attached to some valley farm. Trent had heard long ago, and never thought since, of this feature of Norway's rural life. At the appointed time, the cattle would be driven up by an easier detour to the mountain pastures for their summer holiday, to be attended there by some peasant—usually a young girl—who lived solitary with the herd. Such wires as that he had seen were kept bright by the daily descent of milk churns, let down by a line from above, received by a farm-hand at the road below.

And there, at the side of the hut, a woman stood. Trent, as he approached, noted her short rough skirt and coarse sack-like upper garment, her thick grey stockings and clumsy clogs. About her bare head her pale-gold hair was fastened in tight plaits. As she looked up on hearing Trent's footfall, two heavy silver earrings dangled about the tanned and careworn face of this very type of the middle-aged peasant women of the region.

She ceased her task of scraping a large cake of chocolate into a bowl and straightened her tall body. Smiling, with lean hands on her hips, she spoke in Norwegian, greeting him.

Trent made the proper reply. "And that," he added in his own tongue, "is a large part of all the Norwegian I know. Perhaps, madam, you speak English." Her light blue eyes looked puzzlement, and she spoke again, pointing down to the valley. He nodded; and she began to talk pleasantly in her unknown speech. From within the hut she brought two thick mugs; she pointed rapidly to the chocolate in the bowl, to himself and herself.

"I should like it of all things," he said. "You are most kind and hospitable, like all your people. What a pity it is we have no language in common!" She brought him a stool and gave him the chocolate-cake and a knife, making signs that he should continue the scraping, then within the hut she kindled a fire of twigs and began to boil water in a black pot. Plainly this was her dwelling, the roughest Trent had ever seen. He could discern that on two small shelves were ranged a few pieces of chipped earthenware. A wooden bed-place, with straw and two neatly folded blankets, filled a third of the space in the hut. All the carpentry was of the rudest. From a small chest in a corner she drew a biscuit tin, half full of flat cakes of stale rye bread. There seemed to be nothing else in the tiny place but a heap of twigs for fuel.

She made chocolate in the two mugs, and then, at Trent's insistence in dumb show, she sat on the only stool at a rude table outside the hut, while her guest made a seat of an upturned milking pail.

She continued to talk amiably and unintelligibly, while he finished with difficulty the half of a bread-cake.

"I believe, madam," he said at last, setting down his empty mug, "you are talking simply to hear the sound of your own voice. In your case, that is excusable. You don't understand English, so I will tell you to your face that it is a most wonderful voice. I should say," he went on thoughtfully, "that you ought to have been one of the greatest sopranos that ever lived."

She heard him calmly, and shook her head as not understanding.

"Well, don't say I didn't break it gently," Trent protested. He rose to his feet. "Madam, I know that you are Lady Aviemore. I have broken in on your solitude, and I ask pardon for that; but I could not be sure unless I saw you. I give you my word that no one else knows or ever shall know from me, what I have discovered." He made as if to return by the way he had come.

But the woman held up a hand. A singular change had come over her brown face. A lively spirit now looked out of her desolate blue eyes; she smiled another and a much more intelligent smile. After a few moments she spoke in English, fluent but with a slight accent of her country.

"Sir," she said, "you have behaved very nicely up till now. It has been an amusement for me; there is not much comedy on the *saeter*. Now, will you have the goodness to explain?"

He told her in a few words that he had suspected she was still alive, that he had thought over such facts as had come to his knowledge, and had been led to think she was probably in that place. "I thought you might guess I had recognised you," he added, "so it seemed best to assure you that your secret was safe. Was it wrong to speak?"

She shook her head, gazing at him with her chin on a hand. Presently she said, "I think you are not against me. I can feel that, though I do not understand why you wanted to search out my secret, and why you kept it when you had dragged it into the light."

"I dragged it because I am curious," he answered. "I have kept it and will keep it because—oh well, because it is your own, and because to me Lillemor Wergeland is a sort of divinity."

She laughed suddenly. "Incense! And I in these rags, in this hovel, with what unpleasantness I can see in this little spotty piece of cheap mirror!... Ah well! You have come a long way, curious man, and it would be cruel not to gratify your curiosity a little more. Shall I tell you? After all, it was simple.

"It was very soon after the disaster that the resolve came to me. I never hesitated. It was my fault that we had gone to Sicily—you have heard that? Yes, I see it in your face. I felt I must leave the world I knew, and that knew me. I never really thought of suicide. As for a convent, unhappily there is none for people with minds like mine. I meant simply to disappear, and the only way to succeed was to get the reputation of being dead. I thought it out for some days and nights. Then I wrote, in the name of my maid, to an establishment in Paris where I used to buy things for the stage."

"Ha!" Trent exclaimed. "I heard of that, and I guessed."

"I sent money," she went on, "and I ordered a dark-brown trans-formation—that is a lady's word for wig—some stuff for darkening the skin, various pigments, pencils, *et tout le bazar*. My maid did not know what I had sent for; she only handed the parcel to me when it came. She would have thrown herself in the fire for me, I think, my maid Maria. When the things arrived, I announced that I would return to England by the route you have heard of, perhaps."

He nodded. "The route that gave you a night passage to Venice. And you disguised yourself in your cabin at Brindisi, and slipped off in the dark before the boat started."

"Indeed, I was not such a fool!" she returned. "What if my absence had been discovered somehow before the boat left Brindisi? That could easily happen, and then goodbye to the fiction of my suicide. No; when we reached Brindisi, we had, as I knew, some hours there. We left our things at an hotel, where we were to dine, and then I put on a thick veil and went out alone. At the office near the harbour I took a second-class passage to Venice for myself, in the name of Miss Julia Simmons, in the same boat I had planned to take. It would be at the quay, they told me, in an hour. Then I went into the poorer streets of the town and bought some clothes, very ugly ones, some shoes, toilet things—"

"Some black hairpins," Trent murmured.

"Naturally, black," she assented. "My own gilt pins would have looked queer in a dark-brown wig, and I had to have pins to fasten it properly. I bought also a little cheap portmanteau-thing, and put my purchases in it. Then I took a cab to the quay, found the boat had arrived, and gave one of the stewards a tip to show me the berth named on my ticket, and to carry my baggage there. After that I went shopping again on shore. I bought a long mackintosh coat and a funny little cap—the very things for Miss Simmons—took them to the hotel, and pushed them under the things my maid had already packed in my big case.

"On the steamer, when Maria had left me and I had locked the cabin door, I arranged a dark, rather catty sort of face for myself, and fitted on Miss Simmons's hair. I put on her mackintosh coat and cap. When the boat began to move away from the quay, I opened my door an inch and peeped out. As I expected, every one was looking over the rail, and so—the sooner the better—I just slipped out, shut the cabin door, and walked straight to Miss Simmons's berth at the other end of the ship... There is not much more to say. At Venice I did not look for the others, and never saw them. I went on to Paris, and wrote to my brother Knut that I was alive, telling him what I meant to do if he would help me. Such things do not seem so mad to a true child of Norway."

"What things?" Trent asked.

"Things of deep sorrow, malady of the soul, escape from the world... He and his wife have been true and good to me. I am supposed to be her cousin, Hilda Bjoernstad. In my will I left them money, more than enough to pay for me, but they did not know that when they welcomed me here."

She ceased and smiled vaguely at Trent, who was considering her story with eyes that gazed fixedly at the skyline.

"Yes, of course," he remarked presently in an abstracted manner. "That was it. As you say, so simple. And now let me tell you," he went on with a change of tone, "one or two little details you have forgotten.

"At Brindisi you bought, just before going on board with the others, a box of the stuff called Ixtil, because it looked as if there might be bad weather. You took a dose at once, and another a little later, as the directions told you. You might have needed more of it before reaching Venice, but as Mr. Selby was with you when you bought it, you thought it wiser to leave it behind when you vanished. Also, you left behind you four new black hairpins, which had somehow, I suppose, got loose inside your handbag, and were found there by Selby. You see, Lady Aviemore, it was Selby who brought me into this. He told me all the facts he knew, and he showed me your bag and its contents. But he didn't attach any importance to the two things I have just mentioned."

She raised her eyebrows just perceptibly. "I cannot see why he should. And I cannot see why he should bring in you or anybody."

"Because he had some vague notion of your brother-in-law having either caused your death, or at least having known of your intention to commit suicide. He never told me so outright, but it was plain that that was in his mind. Selby wanted me to clear that up if I could. You see, your brother-in-law stood to benefit enormously by your death, and then there was the matter of the note announcing your suicide."

"It announced," she remarked, "the truth; that I was leaving a world I could not bear any longer. The words might mean one thing or another. But what about the note?"

"The perfectly truthful note was written with pen and ink, of which there was none in your cabin. It was written on paper which had been torn from a writing-pad, and no pad was found. Also that make of paper is sold in Canada, never in Europe. You had never been in Canada. Your brother-in-law had just come back from Canada. You see?"

"But did not Selby perceive that Charles is a saint?" inquired the lady with a touch of impatience. "Surely that was plain! More Dominic than Francis, no doubt; but an evident saint."

"In my slight knowledge of him," Trent admitted, "he did strike me in that way. But Selby is a lawyer, you see, and lawyers don't understand saints. Besides, your brother-in-law had taken a dislike to him, I think, and so perhaps he felt critical about your brother-in-law."

"It is true," she said, "he did not care about Mr. Selby, because he disliked all men who were foppish and worldly. But now I will tell you. That evening in the hotel at Brindisi I wanted to write that note, and I asked Charles for a sheet from the block he had in his hand and was just going to write on. That is all. I wrote it in the hotel writing-room, and took it afterwards in my bag to the cabin."

"We supposed you had written it beforehand," Trent said, "and that was one of the things that led me to feel morally certain you were still alive. I'll explain. If, as we thought, you had written the note in the hotel, your suicide was a premeditated act. Yet it was afterwards that Selby saw you buying that Ixtil stuff, and it was plain that you had taken two doses. And it struck me, though it didn't seem to have struck Selby, that it was unlikely any one already resolved to drown herself at sea would begin treating herself against sea-sickness.

"Then there were those new black hairpins. The sight of them was a revelation to me. For I knew, of course, that with that hair of yours you had probably never used a black hairpin in your life."

The Countess felt at her pale-gold plaits and gravely held out to him a black hairpin. "In the valley we use nothing else."

"It is very different in the valley, I know," he said gently. "I was speaking of my world—the world that you have left. I was led by those hairpins to think of your having changed your appearance, and I even guessed at what was in the parcel that came for your maid, which Selby had told me about."

She regarded her guest with something of respect. "It still remains," she said, "to explain how you knew it was in Norway, and here, as a poor farm servant, that I should hide myself. It seemed to me the last thing in the world—your world—that a woman who had lived my life would be expected to do."

"All the same, I thought it was a strong possibility," he answered. "Your problem, you see, was just what you say—to hide yourself. And you had another—you had to make a living somehow. Everything you possessed—except some small amount in cash, I suppose—you left behind when you disappeared. And a woman can't go on acting and disguising herself for ever. A man can grow hair on his face, or shave it off; for a woman, disguise must be a perpetual anxiety. If she has to get employment, and especially if she has no references, it's something very like an impossibility."

She nodded gravely. "That was how I saw it."

"So," he pursued, "it came to this: that the world-famous Lillemor Wergeland had to come to the surface again somewhere, and in no long time—Lillemor Wergeland, whose type of beauty and general appearance were so marked and unmistakable, whose photographs were known everywhere. The fact is that for some time I couldn't see for the life of me how it could possibly have been done. There were only a few countries, I supposed, of which you knew enough of the language to attempt to live in any of them; and if you did, you would always be conspicuous by your physical type and your accent. If you attracted attention, discovery might follow at any moment. The more I thought of it, the more marvellous it seemed that you had not been recognised—assuming you were still alive—during the six years or so that had passed before I heard the full story and guessed at the truth.

"And then an idea came. There was one country in which your looks and speech would not betray you as a foreigner—your own country. And if there were any corners of the world where you could go with a fair certainty of being unrecognised, the remoter villages of Norway would be among them. And at Myklebostad, on the Langfjord, which the map told me was one of the remotest, you had a brother who was two thousand pounds richer by your supposed death. You see how it was, then, that I came to this place on a sketching holiday."

Trent stood up and gazed across the valley to the sunlit white peaks beyond. "I have visited Norway before, but never had such an interesting time. And now, before I return to the haunts of men, let me say again that I shall forget at once all that has happened today. Don't think it was merely a vulgar curiosity that brought me here. There was once a supreme artist whose gifts made me her debtor and servant. Anything that happened to her touched me; I had a sort of right to go seeking what it really was that had happened."

She stood before him in her coarse and stained clothes, her hands clasped behind her, with a face and attitude of perfect dignity. "Very well; you stand on your right and I on mine—to arrange my own life, since I am alone in it. I will spend it here, where it began. My soul was born here before it went out to have adventures, and it has crept home again for comfort. Believe me, it is not only that as you say, I am safe from discovery here. That counts for very much; but also I felt I must go and live out my life in my own place, this faraway lonely valley, where everything is humble and unspoilt, and the hills and the fjords are as God made them before there were any men. It is all my own, own land!

"And now," she ended suddenly, "we understand one another, and we can part friends." She extended her hand, saying, "I do not know your name."

"Why should you?" he asked. He bent over the hand, then went quickly from her. At the beginning of the descent he glanced back once; she waved to him.

Halfway down the rugged track he stopped. Far above a wonderful voice was singing to the glory of the Norse land.

> "Ja, herligt er mit Fodeland
> Der ewig trodser Tidens Tand,"

sang the voice.

Trent looked out upon the wild landscape. "Her fatherland!" he soliloquised. "Well, well! They say the strictest parents have the most devoted children."

THE VANISHING HOUSE

Will Scott

Will Scott was the writing name of William Matthew Scott (1893–1964), who was born in Leeds, where he began to establish a reputation as a caricaturist prior to moving to London with his wife Lily. After the First World War, the couple relocated to Herne Bay in Kent, which remained his hometown for the rest of his life. In the early part of his career, Scott was a prolific writer of detective fiction, including novels, plays, and short stories, although from the 1950s he wrote fourteen books for children, *The Cherrys* series, which enjoyed a good deal of popularity and have drawn comparisons to the work of Enid Blyton. *Disher—Detective* (1925) is a novel featuring an apparently impossible disappearance as well as the eponymous private investigator; Scott adapted his book for the stage and the play enjoyed success in the West End before being filmed.

This story comes from the highly-regarded book *Giglamps* (1924), about a tramp who sometimes solves mysteries and sometimes sails on the windy side of the law himself.

ON A DAMP EVENING IN LATE SUMMER, IN AN ESSEX LANE, A gentleman turned into a broken barn and took off his boots. It is appropriate that you should meet him first thus, by the feet. The action, like some subtle inversion of the handshake of custom, is fitting for an introduction. Other men might remove a glove. But he takes off his boots.

Strange? Not so very, when you know. For he was a gentleman whose feet were out of his boots much oftener than his hands were out of his pockets. His hands did never a thing for him; but his feet took him here, there and everywhere, and showed him as much of the world as one can reasonably expect to see in one lifetime, going at five miles a day, three days a week. His feet were very nearly his fortune.

Paying the piper, they called the tune. They led, he followed. And knowing what was best for them, they led him now into the broken barn, where they could be dried with derelict straw, and where what remained of the boots could be propped up toe to toe and left to dry. The English climate being what it is—whatever it is—it follows obviously that he was very often taking off his boots. It was not good for the kind of boots, but what could a fellow do?

"I wonder how much I could get from the firm that made 'em not to wear 'em?" he mused, as he made his back comfortable against a pile of abandoned sacking and located flints with his bare heel, moving them aside.

He yawned and fixed his glasses.

Now, if you like, that was strange. Balanced on his nose—their presence here no doubt incapacitating their lawful owner in the search for them—were a pair of *pince-nez*. The man was something between a somebody of the nobodies and a nobody of the some-bodies, and the gulf was bridged by eyeglasses. But, conceivable that he had seen better days, it was inconceivable that he had seen them through these. Stolen thread secured their frame, unclean stamp-edging gripped frantically one glass, and a cable of grocer's string held the lot to a moth-hole in a wrecked lapel. Eyeglasses. But only just. Nothing to boast of. And yet not all the farce of them, nor all the ivy of indolence, could destroy the last crumbling hint of archi-tecture that clung to the ruin because of them. The gentlemen of the highway, the other Sons of Dust, called him Giglamps. And other things. But very nearly they might have called him sir.

The rest of this artist in ease, after the glasses and the feet, though equally picturesque, was of minor importance. He was sockless, tieless, collarless and shaveless. His attire was a pair of inadequate trousers, a cutaway coat that had once belonged to somebody else—and probably did still—and a straw hat that could not imaginably ever have belonged to anybody. Twenty in heart, sixty in experience, he was somewhere between the two in years. By inclination he was always disinclined. By profession he did not practise any.

He folded his arms and closed his eyes and fell asleep.

He was an expert sleeper. To none of his achievements did he give such care as to his sleep. There was an art in it, a quiet power that was the master's touch. If genius be the art of taking pains car-ried to ridiculous limits, then here was the genius of slumber; the sustained effort of which only the great are capable. For Giglamps slept not only well, but long; so that when at length he opened his eyes and tried to peep about, the sun was down and the night was up, and not the moon nor a star nor a light at all interrupted the blackness. He could see nothing, and there was no sound to be

heard, save—perhaps, doubtfully—a church chime far away. Eight.
Or twelve. It might have been two.

Sitting up from the forsaken sacking, he shook himself and
rubbed his feet together. Dry, but cold. Wherefore he buttoned his
coat where a button remained and put out a hand for his boots. But
he did not get his boots. With a little gasp of surprise he quickly drew
back his hand and began fumbling excitedly in his pockets.

"Fairy godmothers!" he exclaimed.

He had a matchbox and the luxury of two matches, which did not
permit of much recklessness. But here, surely, was occasion for the
use of a match; and so, banking one against the future, he rubbed
the other on the sandpaper striker and held it aloft.

"Thanks for yours," he called to the ill-lit emptiness. "What's it
all about?" And after a lengthy wait: "Anybody there?"

Nobody there. The broken barn was as empty as when he had
entered it, nor was there any response from the darkness outside.
He took a swift glance at the floor, at the wildly fantastic change that
had come over things whilst he had slept. The boots. The wonderful
boots. But—not his boots!

His own were gone, vanished apparently beyond recall, but from
out the nothingness that had claimed them another pair had come,
and this other pair were now reposing side by side on the very spot
where his own had been. And they *were* boots, these new ones. Good
boots. Great boots. Boots worthy of being sung; fit to pass into the
epics and the legends of highway and casual ward.

The match expired. Then Giglamps put out his hand again and
drew the boots towards him.

"Perhaps it ain't fairy godmothers, though," he murmured.
"Lunatics, more like. Another o' them Little Corporals."

He put on the boots, laced them as best he could in the darkness,
and shuffled to the door.

"H'm," he said, after listening for some moments and hearing nothing. "If this ain't the limit! Any use leavin' my trousers here for five minutes, I wonder?" He bent his feet to right and left, easing the new boots and making them acquainted with his peculiarities, both of foot and conduct. "Bit big," was his verdict, after experimental creakings and slurs; "but better big than little, anyway. Never look a gift-egg in the birth certificate. They *are* boots; an' it's the dotty 'll get the squeeze, not me. There'll be corns in St. Helena tomorrow."

He gave another call, but when this too remained unanswered he turned away. The rain had stopped and a few stars were out, reflected grotesquely in the pools along the lane, as if great holes had been torn out of the world and one could see through to the other skies beyond. But soon they were blotted out again and the darkness became a chaos. The road led over a wide and rolling heath and lost itself and the lonely traveller it had lured from the comforts of the broken barn. Falling into ditches and falling out of them, clutched at by hidden bushes, struck by unseen trees, and suddenly pitched forward into an unwilling run by unsuspected hills, for three hours or more Giglamps stumbled on, hungry and hopeless of any refuge but dawn, cursing himself for leaving the barn on the slim fear that the unknown lunatic might return and claim the better boots. He was, indeed, beginning to wonder if he had taken an unfortunate leap out of the frying-pan. And then, quite suddenly, far across the lonely heath he saw the little square gleam of a lighted window.

"Aha!" he cried in high glee. "A sail!" And he made off towards it, trying to hurry.

But the light was a mile or more away, and the heath was roughest hereabouts. The little square window shone larger, but very slowly, and half an hour had tumbled by before he came up to the place. "A woman could have put her hat on in the time," he grumbled.

There was neither gate nor fence, the rough heathland flowing to the very steps before the door. He judged it to be a woodman's cottage or perhaps a keeper's hut—not a land likely to be flowing with milk and honey; nevertheless, pretty sure to hold prospect of food of some kind. The only trouble might be the keeper himself—if he happened to be at home.

Beside the lighted window a thin line shone through a chink where the door was not properly closed. For this Giglamps was thankful. He planned to spy out the land before declaring his presence.

But as he came near, about a dozen yards off, the silence was suddenly broken by the drunken warbling of a long-dead music-hall song, strangely incongruous and unexpected in this remote corner.

> "Down east, New York, in Chinatown,
> There lives a coloured gal named Brown,
> Keeps a little laundry sto-er…"

Before Giglamps, stopped with surprise, could continue forward, a sudden and violent voice interrupted the singer behind the door, threatening many things if the song did not immediately cease and commanding that a certain bottle, unseen, be at once set down. The door was gently closed and a blind drawn across the window. But then the song flowed on again more drunkenly than before, laughter now hiccuping in it:

> "Carolina Brown,
> Bell'er Chinatown—
> Mekkin's 'eaps o' dolluz,
> I'nin' cuffz an' colluz…"

"Kelly!" the violent voice cried sharply. "Do you want the whole bloomin' county round? Gimme that bottle, do yer 'ear? You never was safe near booze."

"Until," laughed the drunk—"until you says wot you is goin' to do, I sits 'ere an' I keeps on boozin' an' I keeps on singin' an'—"

"Do?" In the sudden added violence of the other voice its earlier violence faded away to geniality. "Do? Nothing! That's what I'm goin' to do!"

A fierce argument ensued, both voices locked in a pandemonium of noise. There appeared to be something of which the owner of the violent voice desired keenly to be rid, and Giglamps, listening outside, heard enough to understand that the something was the other man, Kelly. A reference of Kelly's to a thirty-year-old friendship provoked sarcastic laughter. "Yes, but not all the time, eh? What-o! What you say—friend? Then you prove it, cocky, by packin' up an' 'oppin' it. You know very well how it is. I wouldn't mind doin' it for yer, but it ain't safe."

To which Kelly retorted: "I goes when I gets what I come for. Until then I sits and boozes and sings…"

The voices mingled in a fresh crash of abuse, and then, in the following silence of exhaustion, clink of glass and bottle came once more.

"Kelly! For the Lord's sake! D'yer 'ear me? Get off that blighted booze! You was never safe within a mile of a bottle. An' you'll want to keep a clear 'ead for the mornin'—"

"Until I gets what I came for!" said the Kelly voice, and the phrase trailed away in drunken laughter. "Luckiest thing on earth, ol' man, me findin' you 'ere. Gawd knows wot I sh'd done if I *ain't* found you 'ere. But I did. See? I did. An' I ain't mug enough—" He broke off, and a tingling silence followed. "Listen!" he went on quietly. "Was that somebody outside? Open the door an' take a peep—an' if yer catch anythin' listenin', shoot it. I'll just be 'avin' another drop—"

Giglamps drew well away and dropped flat in the heather. The door opened and the figure of a heavy man showed black in the sudden light. He waited a moment, peering into the gloom, and then returned and closed the door, leaving the blackness blacker. Then the tramp clambered to his feet and turned away as the song burst out afresh, or was continued:

> "Busy as a bee,
> You will alw'ys see
> Carolinerbrowner Chi... na... town."

"No place for me," Giglamps decided.

Wearily he plodded on, keeping a sharp eye for other and more friendly cottages, even strangely hopeful for a village, puzzling over the affair of the two voices, the Kelly voice and the other, and wondering why the resurrection of a decade-interred song should occur on this lonely heath of all places, and on this night of all times.

"P'raps," he thought, "the person ain't heard nothin' newer. There's places where a thing can be soakin' in for years, an' then they're hardly damp. Mebbe this village, when I come to it, if there is one, will have the banners out for the Battle of Hastings, not havin' heard yet that we had it slipped across us."

His thoughts switched back to the quarrel. Why was the violent one so eager to be rid of Kelly? Kelly was an uninvited and unwelcome guest; a guest demanding something and being firmly assured that he wouldn't get it. What was it Kelly wanted?"

The ground began to rise, suggesting wonderful retreats beyond. Over the hill there might be many things—a village, at least a farm, turnips to make off with, larders to rob, *something* to eat...

He groped his way forward; but before he could top the rise in the rough ground an unexpected thing happened. From far away behind a cry trailed across the loneliness.

"Help!"

He swung round. The door was open again, and silhouetted in the little square of light was the figure of a man. For the briefest second it stood there, sharp and clear; then it was gone. The door closed, the light was shut off, and the empty silence was as it had been before.

With a sigh of resignation Giglamps turned back.

In ten minutes he was again before the closed door, and, treading carefully, his hand outstretched before him, at last he came upon the crumpled figure of a man lying motionless at the foot of the steps. Kneeling beside it he said in a whisper:

"Anythin' I can do? What's up?"

He shook the still form, but there was no response. From behind the closed door came the sounds of feverish pacing and muttered curses. Giglamps fumbled at the man's coat and laid a hand on the heart. Then, shaking his head, he felt in his pocket for the last treasure of a match, shielded this with his body that no stray beam could escape to watching eyes behind, struck it and looked.

He saw a rough-looking man, half dressed, his face cut open and wet with blood. But the most startling thing of all was the unfamiliar marking on the strange grey cloth of the lifeless man's attire. Convict's uniform! One hand was pressed close to the throat, the other was tightly clutching a bunch of thick heath grass, on a strip of which the body lay.

The light went out. Giglamps rose from his knees and tossed the spent match aside.

"Here's a go!" he thought. "An escaped convict! That's what he wanted—the other feller's togs. Nearly got 'em too, before he was outed. I'll bet it was a daisy of a scrap!" He glanced uncertainly in the direction of the door, closed and invisible now in the utter darkness. "Question now is," he muttered, "what? Was there anyone else besides that feller an' this feller? How many have I got to slosh if it comes to a scrap? An' if they tries to hop it, what chance have I of followin' on a night like this? Now, if there was a village over the hill there, I could get some help, mebbe."

He considered it a moment, and then walked softly towards the rise. When he was at a safe distance from the scene of the crime he began to hum, slowly, to lull his racing thoughts to rest, the old-time song that he had so strangely come upon this night:

> "Busy as a bee,
> You will alw'ys see
> Carolinerbrowner Chi… na… town."

"So that's why he was singin' a song with moths in it," he reflected. "Must have been the last song he heard before he was put away. Must have been put away for a fair old stretch."

This time he topped the rise, but he saw only darkness beyond. Of other house or village there was not the faintest sign. And yet, there must be something, somewhere out there. If far away, a community must lie ahead. He would have to seek and find. Behind—back there—what help could he give alone?

He went on.

II

Many miles from anywhere the village of Sunset slept, a futile, untidy place of many beginnings and no climax. When Giglamps came to it at dawn he found it calm and at peace, and represented solely by its constable, who stood perplexed before the Sunset Inn, thumbs stuck in belt and chin thrust out. He turned pompously as the tramp stopped before him.

"And what have you done?" he demanded.

"Made the mistake of thinkin' p'raps you was a policeman," Giglamps retorted, resenting the other's tone.

"Do you want me?"

"Don't exactly *want* you; but just at the moment p'raps you ain't quite so unnecessary as usual. There's been a murder. An' mebbe there'll be another, if you keep on forgettin' your company manners like this."

"What's this?" snapped the constable.

"An escaped convict, by name of Kelly. There's a feller lives in a little cottage back across the heath there, an' Kelly called on him an' tried to get some new clothes or somethin'. They had a Number One row about it, an' the other feller he done Kelly in."

"When was this?" the policeman asked.

"I couldn't tell you the time exactly," said Giglamps. "You see, the Duke of Westminster begged my watch as a keepsake an' I don't have one now. But it was some time in the night. I wasted hours tryin' to find a village and a copper. I'm too tired to go on any further now. You'll have to do."

The constable grunted.

"There was a convict, name of Kelly, got out of Essex County Gaol yesterday," he said. "He's been leadin' us a fine old chase all night, when we ought to have been in bed. It's because of him I'm awake now."

"Are you really?" said Giglamps. "It must be pretty depressin' to see you when you're asleep, then."

"We'll have less of that, if you don't mind," said the policeman. "An' I shall want you to come back with me right away to the cottage. If you was the only witness I shall want you on the spot."

"Like a shot, Freddy," Giglamps smiled. "Just wait till I catch a sandwich."

"You'll find no sandwiches here at this time o' day," said the constable. "You can sandwich when we get back. Come on."

"Just a bite!"

"Not even a bite. Come on!"

Giglamps sighed.

"Yours faithfully," he said softly, dropping into line.

If the constable knew nothing else, at least he knew the country around his native village of Sunset. Turning from the village street he made straight for a sandy road that led across the heath to the distant rise in the land. "There's only one 'ouse, only one building of any kind, for seven miles," he explained surlily. "So we don't have far to look. A feller called Hermit Percy lives there. Bit silly…"

"Hope he's silly enough to have left the larder door open."

As they plodded up the long hill Giglamps' well-exercised tongue got the better of his hunger and he began to gossip about the crime and reconstruct the fatal happening.

"You can see what it was. Old Kelly blows in an' wants a new set o' fittin's off of the Hermit Percy, and most likely Perkin only had one set o' fittin's, an' he got annoyed. So would I. So would you. You can hardly blame the Perkin, can you? Case o' manslaughter, eh?"

The constable gave no sign of having heard.

"Don't you think?" Giglamps prompted.

The constable did not speak.

"Preservin' an official silence, or what?" Giglamps asked, with a curl of the lip.

"I'm not in the 'abit of discussin' my cases with tramps," said the policeman.

It was some moments before Giglamps responded to this. He breathed heavily on his glasses and polished them carefully on his sleeve, keeping his eyes on the officer all the time.

"If manners was a race, Freddy," he said at length, "you'd finish scratch. You would—bang on the startin' post. You can't tell a gentleman by the crease in his trousers, you know—any more 'n you can judge a copper by the intelligent light in his buttons. Ever tried bein' civil?"

No reply from the constable. After a moment's silence Giglamps went on:

"You know, Freddy, filthy lucre's a thing I ain't ever had to take baths for. We never seemed to have much in common. But don't I just wish I had a million or two at this moment." And as the other was still silent, he concluded: "So's I could leave you out o' my will!"

After a lonely mile or two the crest of the hill was reached and the solitary cottage of the hermit was espied below across a little plain. Smoke was rising from the chimney, but nobody was in sight. The great wide heath was empty. The two men walked down in silence, and as they turned the corner by the little window and came to the door with the three uneven steps before it, Giglamps began to look around curiously.

"Somebody's moved the body," he whispered.

"We shall soon see," said the constable, tapping on the door.

Hermit Percy proved to be a tall and elderly man with tremendous whiskers, and a skull cap thrown without art or aim on one side of his head. He seemed rather bored with existence.

"Morning, Jodd," he said casually.

"Mornin', Percy," said the constable. "I 'ear you 'ad a bit o' trouble last night, Perce."

"Me?" said Percy.

Constable Jodd turned to Giglamps.

"Yes," said the tramp. "The feller Kelly. Kelly—who was done in on your doorstep here. The convict."

"Here?" said Percy. "Oh, yes?"

The others were watching him closely. With one hand he covered a yawn; with the other he fumbled for the door-knob.

"Well, Perce," said Jodd, "anything to say?"

"No," said Percy, finding the knob at last. "Good morning."

"Just a minute." The constable slipped his foot over the step. "Tell me what happened here last night."

"Nothing," said Percy.

"We'll have a look."

They all went in, and Jodd began a tour of inspection, first in the little rooms and then in the tiny sheds at the back of the house. The tramp stood before the table and stared meaningly at half a pie. Without a word Percy pushed it towards him.

"Thanks for yours to hand," Giglamps smiled. "Contents noted."

Hermit Percy, plainly one not to be put out by anything under the sun, calmly went about the business of breakfast-making that had been interrupted by the others' arrival. A time-worn teapot was on the table. Taking this to the door, he emptied the tea-leaves in a damp pile beside the steps. A few seconds later he stopped before Giglamps and said nonchalantly, nodding across the room:

"There's another pie in the cupboard."

"Not now!" Giglamps grinned, pointing to the crumbs on his coat.

"Oh well, of course…" said Percy resignedly.

Constable Jodd returned from the sheds with a lined brow and a puzzled stare in his eyes.

"Funny!" he murmured. "You—you're sure about this?"

Giglamps nodded.

"And you heard nothing, you say, Perce?"

"Asleep since eight o'clock," replied Percy.

"You didn't hear the cry this man mentions?"

"Asleep," said Percy.

"H'm!" Jodd looked at the tramp. "Tryin' somethin' on?"

"Freddy," said Giglamps, "if you was a man an' not somethin' which has dropped off a procession, you'd know very well I haven't come all this way for the walk. I can't help what old Perkin says. What I said is right. Kelly was done in at this door here last night. I heard the row. I saw the body. I dunno if old Perkin slept through it. Only I know it happened."

"H'm!" said Jodd. "Well, I think you'd better both come back with me until a search has been made on the heath. You'll not 'ave to wait long, if it's a straight tale. But I don't see how you can both be right. I shall send for the inspector from Cherry Hill. He'll be here by evening."

"Why both of us?" Percy demanded.

"Because I say so!" snapped Jodd.

"But—"

"Leave him alone," said Giglamps. "It's only his way. He'll plonk all the village into the police station, and then let out the innocent ones, one by one, an' hang what's left. It'll be a bit crowded, but he has sent for the inspector, remember. The inspector ain't comin' to see us. He's comin' to open a new wing."

"Come on," said Jodd; and they went out, Percy locking the cottage door and Jodd taking the key.

Giglamps jumped from the steps on to the pile of damp tea-leaves, crushing it flat; and as he moved aside Jodd gave a cry and pointed.

"Ho!"

They all looked at the impression the tramp's foot had made, and saw in its centre another and deeper impression—that of a broad arrow.

"Ho!" cried Jodd.

"Oh, that," said Giglamps. "Yes, I'd forgotten that. Of course. Yes, I had my boots changed last evenin' while I was asleep in an old barn over the heath. Somebody took mine and left me these. I wondered what the game was. Must have been our old friend Kelly, before he came across his pal. Plain as daylight, now, eh?"

"I ought to tell you," Jodd warned him, "that it'll be better for you if you don't say anything."

"Me?" said Giglamps. "I couldn't help talking."

Jodd turned to Percy.

"You might as well see it through, Perce," he said; "but p'raps I shan't have to detain you, after all."

They made across the low stretch on which the hermit's cottage stood towards the rise, and were perhaps half a mile upon their way when Jodd, who was leading, suddenly pulled up and stopped, staring at something lying in the heather. It was the half-dressed body of a man.

"Aha!" he cried.

Giglamps and Hermit Percy too looked and saw. And having seen, Giglamps drew himself up and glanced sideways at the policeman.

"Now," he said, "who's right now? Didn't I say the body'd been moved? What about it now?"

A new sternness towards Percy crept into Jodd's manner.

"P'raps I shall have to detain you, after all, Perce," he said. "D'you still say you heard nothin' last night?"

"Nothing," said Percy.

"All right—we'll see. Come along, both of you. Don't touch the body there!"

Giglamps had been kneeling beside the corpse, peering intently at it. Now he knelt up and stared at the policeman and the hermit with a strange look in his eyes.

"Lumme!" he gasped.

"What?" said Jodd.

Giglamps stood and stared at the cottage across the heath, then back at the body, and then for a second time at the cottage. He ran his fingers through his hair and gave a long, low whistle.

"What is it?" Jodd testily demanded.

"That body," Giglamps said slowly, "that body, I'm pretty sure—*it ain't been moved!*"

"Please yerself!" snapped Jodd. "First you say he was killed at the door and moved here; then you say he's killed here an' ain't been moved. Please yerself, of course. Only there's a good half a mile between 'em now. P'raps you mean the cottage has been moved away from the body?"

"Look here," said Giglamps. "You see his hand clutchin' the grass there? A dead man don't clutch at grass like that once he's dead; an' if they move him it tears away. You see this match what I told you about, just where I threw it? This corpse, what I saw killed at the door there, half a mile away, ain't been moved from where it is now! What's that mean? Hanged if I know. But it means something—there's a clue there, somewhere."

"It strikes me," said Jodd, "that I better send for the doctor as well as the inspector. Cottages can't walk, my lad—not in these parts. Come on!"

They walked away, turned up the rise and over towards Sunset.

"You know," said Giglamps, a little later, "if there's one thing 'd make me believe a cottage *could* walk, it's a country cop's statement that it *couldn't*. What'll you do now, Freddy? Take no notice of what I just told you?"

Jodd did not reply.

"Because, you know," Giglamps went on, "it's true. The body both has been moved and hasn't been moved; or else the house has—or hasn't. Mad, ain't it? It's goin' to take a bit o' thinkin' out. But it's true, Freddy."

Jodd threw out his chest, but answered not.

"There's some things the police'll never believe unless you prove it to 'em," Giglamps proceeded; "and this affair's one o' the things. The police are such simple-minded little angels. A yarn like this is too complicated for 'em. They'll either say that the feller was done in at the cottage door an' ain't there now, and so of course he has been moved; or else that he ain't been moved because he was done in where we found him and not at the cottage door. Very difficult to get the little sweets to believe both sides of the matter, I know. But I got an idea the police is goin' to be wrong both ways this time—wrong twice, if you understand me. Sounds mad, I admit. But—I dunno…"

"By the way, Freddy," he said a little later, hurrying on to be at the policeman's side. "*Re* this murderer merchant. All the time we're gallopin' on here and missin' the scenery we're forgettin' about him. You'll try to get him, won't you?"

Jodd, silent, flicked the dust from a shining button.

"Awaitin' the favour of your kind reply," said Giglamps. "Ain't you listenin', Freddy?"

Jodd did not appear to be. His eyes were on distant Sunset. Giglamps shrugged his shoulders and fell back a pace.

"Burstin' with news, ain't he?" he said, addressing Percy. "Simply packed with information! No home complete without him. Mebbe they're bringin' him out in fortnightly parts, an' there's another thirteen days to go before the next one?"

III

"Perkin," said Giglamps late that afternoon, across the little cell of Sunset; the little cell that once had housed coal where now it

harboured criminals, in the days before the cottage of Giles Grey
had become the "police station" of Constable Jodd: "Perkin, we're
trapped. Right on the cheese!"

Hermit Percy said nothing to this, contenting himself with trying
to squeeze comfort out of a hard board.

"These country cops are deadly," Giglamps proceeded. "Deadly.
So long's you haven't anything you ain't safe near 'em. They'll get
you! Now, if it'd been Scotland Yard I wouldn't have worried. They
never get anybody. All they're good for is anecdotes in the penny
papers. 'Twenty-five Wasted Years at the Yard, or Criminals Who've
Dodged Me'—you know. But these rustics!"

"No need to burst into tears," said Percy. "We're not arrested
yet. Only detained."

"Sure," Giglamps agreed; "but why? 'Cos you've got the house,
and I've got the boots. That's the reasonin' power, an' it ain't safe,
Perkin, my bright lad. Believe me, if only Freddy can find a bunch
o' leeks out there on the heath he'll have Lloyd George in here with
us before mornin'. He'd be great on point duty in a desert, but he
ain't safe here."

"Suspicions are nothing," Percy yawned.

"Perkin," said Giglamps patiently, "in the hands of a country cop
a mere suspicion is to a conviction what Carlisle is to Scotland. Y'
understand me? Too near to be nice. Can't you see the hole we're
in? If they don't believe me, my number's up. I've admitted I was
present at the doin's. I've got the johnny's boots. If the feller he quarrelled with ain't produced, what do they say? That I'm the feller he
quarrelled with. On the other hand, if they do believe me, or some
of me—you can't expect 'em to believe it all—*your* number's up.
Don't you see? Now, Perkin, we only got one hope. We got to find
the feller who's done this. We just simply got to find him, Perkin.
If you'll help me, I'll help you. You may be a sound sleeper or a liar

or a fool, but I'm pretty sure you ain't a murderer. You've an open, unmurderous face, same as mine. So we got to help each other, Perkin. The cops is too interested in us to look for the right johnny. We got to do it ourselves."

"Easy!" said Percy.

"I know it ain't! For one thing, I shouldn't know the murderer if I saw him—there isn't a thing I could spot him by. For another thing, here we are both locked up. *But*, Perkin—every minute we're here he's gettin' farther and farther away from it all, an' that's not healthy for either of us. One of us has *got* to get out and spot him, whether we can reckernize him or not. I *know* it's not easy."

"No clue," said Percy. But Giglamps shook his head.

"You're wrong there. There's that rummy clue about the body and the door. I dunno what it's all about, but it's there. You'll find the whole thing rests on it. One of us'll thank his stars I had a match left to see that dead hand clutchin' the grass. The body and the house, together at the time of the doin's, is half a mile apart now—but neither of 'em's moved! Ain't it mad? Same time, there it is, an' it's up to us. You can't expect a cop to believe it."

"House can't move," said Percy, with another yawn.

"And the body hasn't."

"And here we are."

"And here we are, as you remark. First thing is to be not here."

Jodd's shuffling footsteps were heard at the top of the cellar steps. Giglamps stood over Percy with a smile.

"Goin' to help me, Perkin?" he said.

"In what way can I help you?"

"I dunno. P'raps this way."

With a sudden jab his fist shot out and Percy toppled to the floor. Before he could rise knees were on his chest and the tramp's two fists were pounding his face. He gave a savage yell that brought Jodd hurrying down the steps and the clink of keys to the door, and then he attempted futile retaliation. The door crashed open, Percy swore, Jodd bellowed and made a dash, and the next moment Giglamps was erect like a released spring, and a well-directed kick had sent Jodd spinning into the corner of the cell. It had all occurred in a short minute, and at the end of it Giglamps was halfway up the cellar steps.

"Worry him, Perkin!" he shouted. "Sorry, an' all that, but it had to be done. Had to take him by surprise. Your sake as much as mine."

Leaving Jodd and Percy to their surprise, he sped across the cottage and through the door.

But the tumult had stirred Sunset in its sleep. Men and boys were running down the street and cottage doors were spilling rustics. One, only a yard away, Giglamps sent crashing and bleeding across the pavement.

"Sorry!" he cried.

To right and left the way was blocked. Only over the street did a doubtful sanctuary offer. Racing across, he kicked open a cottage door and jumped inside. Just in time he got the door closed and the bolt shot. Outside, a hundred feet were pattering on the road.

Breathing heavily from the rare exertion, he rested against the door and looked around. It was a humble cottage-room with blue-washed walls and tired furniture. A kettle sang merrily on the hob. A cat slept. An old woman sat in a rocking chair, tirelessly endeavouring to insert a length of cotton in a needle's eye. She had been near to success when the interruption occurred and "jumped" the cotton away again. She lowered the needle and looked up with a sigh.

"You might have knocked," she said wearily.

He smiled.

"I'm sorry. I jus' came in to borrow your kettle an' a bedroom. I'm after a murderer."

"I hope there will be no unpleasantness," said the old woman.

He plucked the kettle from the fire and hurried upstairs. She raised the needle and peered at it again.

"My eyes ain't what they used to be," she sighed.

Above in the bedroom Giglamps pushed open the window and leaned out over the gathered crowd wildly waving the kettle of boiling water.

"Get out of it an' let me talk!" he cried. "The first bright spark what comes near that door gets extinguished. Back!"

They looked up. And jumped back.

Jodd was with them, very battered, but of Percy there was nothing to be seen. Two villagers, guarding the "police station" door, told his story in his absence.

"Are you goin' ter come down?" Jodd shouted, shaking his fist.

Giglamps smiled upon him sweetly.

"Dear sir," he said. "Thanks for kind inquiries. In reply to yours— yes, I'm coming down. Trustin' this meets with your requirements. Yours truly."

A countryman sat in a trap in the middle of the street, watching the fun with a straw in his mouth. Giglamps hailed him.

"Hey—you! See this?" He waved the kettle aloft. "It's boilin' worse 'n old Freddy here, an' I've got a aim like a false clue goin' to meet a policeman. Bring your trap under this window."

The man's jaw dropped and he hesitated, looking at Jodd.

"Shan't ask yer twice."

Jodd and the villagers made terrible threats. The driver swore and asked vain questions of the clouds. Giglamps waited a moment and then swung the kettle.

"All right! Hopin' this finds you as it leaves me—"

"Kimmip!" shouted the driver in panic, tugging at the reins.

He brought the trap beneath the window and Giglamps climbed through and dropped to the seat. Sunset yelled; and one youth more daring than the rest, sprang forward, to spring back the next moment with a scalded finger thrust into his mouth.

"Off we go!" Giglamps shouted to the driver. "An' stop before I tell you an' you'll never be repaired. Get on with it!"

The trap shot forward, turned a bend and was gone. Then Sunset shook itself and thought of pursuit.

IV

The sun had been down an hour and the last light of day was fading as Giglamps, running with difficulty, turned over the heath hill and began the descent to the village of Cobb's Corner. Jodd and a score of Sunsetters were close behind, gaining every moment. The race was near the end, and Giglamps knew it.

Before the cooling of the kettle had driven him to part with trap and driver a useful lead had been gained; but almost all of it had been lost in a futile search of Percy's house and the place where the body had been found. Nor had he discovered anything new, seen anything that might give sanity to his mad and only clue. Not a thing. His story was as senseless now as when he had first told it.

"If I can't understand what I'm talkin' about, there ain't a dog's chance the cops 'll even try to," he gasped.

He glanced behind. Superior physique and general fitness were telling; not two hundred yards now separated him from Jodd's party; and soon their cries must rouse Cobb's Corner and trap him ahead. Hopeless mess... He thought of surrender...

And then, suddenly, turning a bend on the road, he pulled up, all the breath going from him in a long whistle of amazement.

"Pee-ee-eew! Lor' lumme!"

Insanity gone suddenly sane! Thoughts fell over each other in his brain. Never in all his restful life had he been called upon to think so swiftly or so eagerly. Turning to his pursuers, he wildly waved a hand, beckoning them to hurry; then he turned off the road, plunged into the woods on his right and ran down into Cobb's Corner by back ways.

At the end of a dark alley near the High Street the others overtook him at last and Jodd grasped him savagely by the shoulder.

"You're arrested!"

"Only for the moment," Giglamps smiled.

"Eh!"

"Be a good boy now, an' keep quiet an' watch. Did you see a johnny comin' down the hill into the village there, just below where I cut off into the trees? He'll be along here in a minute or two. A hundred quid to a farthing he's your man."

Jodd's grip did not relax, but he gave a queer glance at the other villagers. Then, to his captive:

"Reckernize him, I s'pose?"

"That's the trouble," Giglamps admitted. "I can't. But I been thinkin' hard comin' down that hill, an' I got one lonely little chance to make him put his foot right in it. Tickle his conscience an' make him confess. See? Now all be mammy's little darlings—keep quiet an' listen."

Through the fast-gathering shadows of the village street a heavy man slouched towards them, glass-frame and tinker's outfit strapped to his back. At the lighted window of a little shop five yards from the alley he stopped.

"Now!" Giglamps whispered to his companions. And then, keeping well back in the shade brewed by the alley walls, in a low voice little above a whisper he began to sing:

> "Carolina Brown,
> Bell'er Chinatown—
> Mekkin' 'eaps o' dolluz…"

With a loud and awful cry, half roar of rage, half scream of terror, the big man spun round, raising his arm as if to ward off a blow.

"Don't! What—"

He balanced a moment on his toes, and then, as Jodd flashed officialdom before his eyes, he turned and fled cursing along the street.

"Quick!" Giglamps shouted. "Get him!"

They got him.

"All the same," Jodd grumbled, as the little crowd turned up the hill on its way back to Sunset, "all the same, I'd like to know how you *knew*."

Giglamps laughed.

"Yes? Oh, well—easy enough, but not so easy, so to speak. Through not havin' a country cop's intellect. Through bein' mad enough, when the evidence pointed that way, to keep a open mind about a cottage bein' able to walk. You see, the minute I set eyes on that body I knew it hadn't been moved; and, of course, as you said, the cottage hadn't been moved either. But Kelly was killed at the door of somebody's happy little home, 'cos I was on the spot and seen it done, and so, although you swore that old Perkins's happy little home was the only happy little home on all the heath, I began to see I'd just got to look around for some other happy little home, see? One that had 'opped it. I know it sounded mad. I admit I didn't see daylight a ha'porth, an' I didn't know what I was goin' to do— until I saw *this*. Then I reckoned I was near enough to somethin' to take a chance."

He raised his hand and pointed. They were now come to the brow of the hill where he had stopped and turned aside on his run down to Cobb's Corner.

"*This!*" he repeated. "Yes, I reckon it's lucky for me a house *can* walk, now an' again."

They peered through the gloom and saw, half hidden beneath the trees, with light shining brightly through a chink in the door and dimly where a blind was drawn across the window, a caravan.

"A caravan!" Jodd gasped. And a dozen Sunsetters together echoed: "A caravan!"

Giglamps laughed softly. By the side of the road where they stood, outside a little cottage was a battered dustbin.

"Only one place for a country cop, when it comes to business," he said.

"What yer mean?" Jodd snarled.

Giglamps tapped the dustbin with his foot.

"Yours—very truly!" he said with a grin.

THE BORDER-LINE CASE

Margery Allingham

Margery Allingham (1904–66) was one of the acknowledged "Queens of Crime" who rose to prominence during the Golden Age of detective fiction. Indeed, her work was discussed by the journalist and politician John Strachey in his influential article "the Golden Age of English Detection" which appeared in the *Saturday Review* in 1939. Strachey went so far as to describe Allingham not only as a "young master" (whom he bracketed with Michael Innes and Nicholas Blake) but also as "a more sophisticated Dorothy Sayers", a judgment with which Sayers' fans would no doubt quarrel. He heaped praise on Allingham's novel *Flowers for the Judge* (1936) and argued that she, like Sayers in *Murder Must Advertise* (1933), was at her best when describing a setting with which she was closely familiar. However, one admirable quality that both women shared as authors was a willingness to experiment within the genre and to keep trying something different rather than simply to persist with the same-old, same-old because there is always a market for it.

In more recent times, Allingham's admirers have included John le Carré and J. K. Rowling and she has been the subject of a well-researched biography by Julia Jones, while the Margery Allingham Society, founded in 1988, is still going strong. This story first appeared in the *Evening Standard* on 25 August 1936.

I T WAS SO HOT IN LONDON THAT NIGHT THAT WE SLEPT WITH the wide skylight in our city studio open and let the soot-blacks fall in on us willingly, so long as they brought with them a single stirring breath to move the stifling air. Heat hung on the dark horizons and beneath our particular bowl of sky the city fidgeted, breathless and uncomfortable.

The early editions of the evening papers carried the story of the murder. I read it when they came along about three o'clock on the following afternoon. My mind took in the details lazily, for my eyelids were sticky and the printed words seemed remote and unrelated to reality.

It was a straightforward little incident, or so I thought it, and when I had read the guarded half-column I threw the paper over to Albert Campion, who had drifted in to lunch and stayed to sit quietly in a corner, blinking behind his spectacles, existing merely, in the sweltering day.

The newspapers called the murder the "Coal Court Shooting Case", and the facts were simple.

At one o'clock in the morning, when Vacation Street, N.E., had been a deserted lane of odoriferous heat, a policeman on the beat had seen a man stumble and fall to the pavement. The intense discomfort of the night being uppermost in his mind, he had not unnaturally diagnosed a case of ordinary collapse and, after loosening the stranger's collar, had summoned the ambulance.

When the authorities arrived, however, the man was pronounced to be dead and the body was taken to the mortuary, where it was discovered that death had been due to a bullet wound neatly placed between the shoulder-blades. The bullet had made a small blue hole and, after perforating the left lung, had furrowed the heart itself, finally coming to rest in the body structure of the chest.

Since this was so, and the fact that the police constable had heard no untoward sound, it had been reasonable to believe that the shot had been fired at some little distance from a gun with a silencer.

Mr. Campion was only politely interested. The afternoon certainly was hot and the story, as it then appeared, was hardly original or exciting. He sat on the floor reading it patiently, his long thin legs stretched out in front of him.

"Someone died at any rate," he remarked at last and added after a pause: "Poor chap! Out of the frying-pan... Dear me, I suppose it's the locality which predisposes one to think of that. Ever seen Vacation Street, Margery?"

I did not answer him. I was thinking how odd it was that a general irritant like the heat should make the dozens of situations arising all round one in the great city seem suddenly almost personal. I found I was desperately sorry for the man who had been shot, whoever he was.

It was Stanislaus Oates who told us the real story behind the half-column in the evening paper. He came in just after four, looking for Campion. He was a Detective-Inspector in those days and had just begun to develop the habit of chatting over his problems with the pale young man in the horn-rimmed spectacles. Theirs was an odd relationship. It was certainly not a case of the clever amateur and the humble policeman: rather the irritable and pugnacious policeman taking it out on the inoffensive, friendly representative of the general public.

On this occasion Oates was rattled.

"It's a case right down your street," he said briefly to Campion as he sat down. "Seems to be impossible, for one thing."

He explained after a while, having salved his conscience by pointing out that he had no business to discuss the case and excusing himself most illogically on grounds of the heat.

"It's 'low-class' crime," he went on briskly. "Practically gang-shooting. And probably quite uninteresting to all of you who like romance in your crimes. However, it's got me right down on two counts: the first because the man who shot the fellow who died couldn't possibly have done so, and second because I was wrong about the girl. They're so true to type, these girls, that you can't even rely on the proverbial exception."

He sighed as if the discovery had really grieved him.

We heard the story of Josephine as we sat round in the paralysingly hot studio and, although I never saw the girl then or afterwards, I shall not forget the scene; the three of us listening, breathing rather heavily, while the Inspector talked.

She had been Donovan's girl, so Oates said, and he painted a picture of her for us: slender and flat-chested, with black hair and eyes like a Russian madonna's in a transparent face. She wore blouses, he said, with lace on them and gold ornaments, little chains and crosses and frail brooches whose security was reinforced by gilt safety-pins. She was only twenty, Oates said, and added enigmatically that he would have betted on her, but that it served him right and showed him there was no fool like an old one.

He went on to talk about Donovan, who, it seemed, was thirty-five and had spent ten years of his life in gaol. The Inspector did not seem to think any the less of him for that. The fact seemed to put the man in a definite category in his mind and that was all.

"Robbery with violence and the R.O. boys," he said with a wave of his hand and smiled contentedly as though he had made everything clear. "She was sixteen when he found her and he's given her hell ever since."

While he still held our interest he mentioned Johnny Gilchick. Johnny Gilchick was the man who was dead.

Oates, who was never more sentimental than was strictly reasonable in the circumstances, let himself go about Josephine and Johnny Gilchick. It was love, he said—love, sudden, painful and ludicrous; and he admitted that he liked to see it.

"I had an aunt once who used to talk about the Real Thing," he explained, "and embarrassingly silly the old lady sounded, but after seeing those two youngsters meet and flame and go on until they were a single fiery entity—youngsters who were pretty ordinary tawdry material without it—I find myself sympathising with her if not condoning the phrase."

He hesitated and his smooth grey face cracked into a depreciating smile.

"Well, we were both wrong, anyway," he murmured, "my aunt and I. Josephine let her Johnny down just as you'd expect her to and after he had got what was coming to him and was lying in the mortuary he was born to lie in she upped and perjured her immortal soul to swear his murderer an alibi. Not that her testimony is of much value as evidence. That's beside the point. The fact remains that she's certainly done her best. You may think me sentimental, but it depresses me. I thought that girl was genuine and my judgement was out."

Mr. Campion stirred.

"Could we have the details?" he asked politely. "We've only seen the evening paper. It wasn't very helpful."

Oates glared at him balefully.

"Frankly, the facts are exasperating," he said. "There's a little catch in them somewhere. It must be something so simple that I missed it altogether. That's really why I've come to look for you. I thought you might care to come along and take a glance at the place. What about it?"

There was no general movement. It was too hot to stir. Finally the Inspector took up a piece of chalk and sketched a rough diagram on the bare boards of the model's throne.

"This is Vacation Street," he said, edging the chalk along a crack. "It's the best part of a mile long. Up this end, here by the chair, it's nearly all wholesale houses. This sandbin I'm sketching in now marks the boundary of two police divisions. Well, here, ten yards to the left, is the entrance to Coal Court, which is a cul-de-sac composed of two blank backs of warehouse buildings and a café at the far end. The café is open all night. It serves the printers from the two big presses farther down the road. That's its legitimate trade. But it is also a sort of unofficial headquarters for Donovan's mob. Josephine sits at the desk downstairs and keeps an eye on the door. God knows what hours she keeps. She always seems to be there."

He paused and there came into my mind a recollection of the breathless night through which we had all passed, and I could imagine the girl sitting there in the stuffy shop with her thin chest and her great black eyes.

The Inspector was still speaking.

"Now," he said, "there's an upstairs room in the café. It's on the second floor. That's where our friend Donovan spent most of his evening. I expect he had a good few friends with him and we shall locate them all in time."

He bent over the diagram.

"Johnny Gilchick died here," he said, drawing a circle about a foot beyond the square which indicated the sandbin. "Although the bobby was right down the road, he saw him pause under the lamp post, stagger and fall. He called the Constable from the other division and they got the ambulance. All that is plain sailing. There's just one difficulty. Where was Donovan when he fired the shot? There were two policemen in the street at the time, remember. At

the moment of the actual shooting one of them, the Never Street
man, was making a round of a warehouse yard, but the other, the
Phyllis Court chap, was there on the spot, not forty yards away, and
it was he who actually saw Johnny Gilchick fall, although he heard no
shot. Now I tell you, Campion, there's not an ounce of cover in the
whole of that street. How did Donovan get out of the café, where
did he stand to shoot Johnny neatly through the back, and how did
he get back again without being seen? The side walls of the cul-de-
sac are solid concrete backs of warehouses, there is no way round
from the back of the café, nor could he possibly have gone over the
roofs. The warehouses tower over the café like liners over a tug. Had
he come out down the road one or other of the bobbies must have
been certain to have seen him. How did he do it?"

"Perhaps Donovan didn't do it," I ventured and received a pitying
glance for my temerity.

"That's the one fact," said the Inspector heavily. "That's the one
thing I do know. I know Donovan. He's one of the few English mob
boys who carry guns. He served five years with the gangs in New
York and has the misfortune to take his liquor in bouts. After each
bout he has a period of black depression, during which he may do
anything. Johnny Gilchick used to be one of Donovan's mob and
when Johnny fell for the girl he turned in the gang, which was adding
insult to injury where Donovan was concerned."

He paused and smiled.

"Donovan was bound to get Johnny in the end," he said. "It was
never anything but a question of time. The whole mob expected it.
The neighbourhood was waiting for it. Donovan had said openly
that the next time Johnny dropped into the café would be his final
appearance there. Johnny called last night, was ordered out of the
place by the terrified girl, and finally walked out of the cul-de-sac. He
turned the corner and strolled down the road. Then he was shot by

Donovan. There's no way round it, Campion. The doctors say that death was as near instantaneous as may be. Johnny Gilchick could not have walked three paces with the bullet in his back. As for the gun, that was pretty obviously Donovan's too. We haven't actually picked it up yet, but we know he had one of the type we are after. It's a clear case, a straightforward case, if only we knew where Donovan stood when he fired the shot."

Mr. Campion looked up. His eyes were thoughtful behind his spectacles.

"The girl gave Donovan an alibi?" he inquired.

Oates shrugged his shoulders. "Rather," he said. "She was passionate about it. He was there the whole time, every minute of the time, never left the upper room once in the whole evening. I could kill her and she would not alter her story; she'd take her dying oath on it and so on. It didn't mean anything either way. Still, I was sorry to see her doing it, with her boy friend barely cold. She was sucking up to the mob, of course; probably had excellent reasons for doing so. Yet, as I say, I was sorry to hear her volunteering the alibi before she was asked."

"Ah! She volunteered it, did she?" Campion was interested.

Oates nodded and his small eyes widened expressively.

"Forced it on us. Came roaring round to the police station with it. Threw it off her chest as if she were doing something fine. I'm not usually squeamish about that sort of thing, but it gave me a distinct sense of distaste, I don't mind telling you. Frankly, I gave her a piece of my mind. Told her to go and look at the body, for one thing."

"Not kind of you," observed Mr. Campion mildly. "And what did she do?"

"Oh, blubbered herself sick, like the rest of 'em." Oates was still disgruntled. "Still, that's not of interest. What girls like

Josephine do or don't do doesn't really matter. She was saving her own skin. If she hadn't been so enthusiastic about it I'd have forgiven her. It's Donovan who is important. Where was Donovan when he fired?"

The shrill chatter of the telephone answered him and he glanced at me apologetically.

"I'm afraid that's mine," he said. "You don't mind, do you? I left the number with the Sergeant."

He took off the receiver and as he bent his head to listen his face changed. We watched him with an interest it was far too hot to dissemble.

"Oh," he said flatly after a long pause. "Really? Well, it doesn't matter either way, does it?... Still, what did she do it for?... What?... I suppose so... Yes?... Really?"

He seemed suddenly astounded as his informant at the other end of the wire evidently came out with a second piece of information more important than the first.

"You can't be certain... you are?... What?"

The faraway voice explained busily. We could hear its steady drone. Inspector Oates's exasperation grew.

"Oh, all right, all right," he said at last. "I'm crackers... we're all crackers... have it your own damned way."

With which vulgar outburst he rang off.

"Alibi sustained?" inquired Mr. Campion.

"Yes." The Inspector grunted out the word. "A couple of printers who were in the downstairs room swear he did not go through the shop all the evening. They're sound fellows. Make good witnesses. Yet Donovan shot Johnny. I'm certain of it. He shot him clean through the concrete angle of a piano warehouse as far as I can see." He turned to Campion almost angrily. "Explain that, can you?"

Mr. Campion coughed. He seemed a little embarrassed.

"I say, you know," he ventured, "there are just two things that occur to me."

"Then out with them, son." The Inspector lit a cigarette and wiped his face. "Out with them. I'm not proud."

Mr. Campion coughed again. "Well, the—er—heat, for one thing, don't you know," he said with profound uneasiness. "The heat, and one of your concrete walls."

The Inspector swore a little and apologised.

"If anyone could forget this heat he's welcome," he said. "What's the matter with the wall, too?"

Mr. Campion bent over the diagram on the boards of the throne. He was very apologetic.

"Here is the angle of the warehouse," he said, "and here is the sandbin. Here to the left is the lamp post where Johnny Gilchick was found. Farther on to the left is the P.C. from Never Street examining a courtyard and temporarily off the scene, while to the right, on the other side of the entrance to Coal Court, is another constable, P.C. someone-or-other, of Phyllis Court. One is apt to—er—think of the problem as though it were contained in four solid walls, two concrete walls, two policemen."

He hesitated and glanced timidly at the Inspector.

"When is a policeman not a concrete wall, Oates? In—er—well, in just such heat… do you think, or don't you?"

Oates was staring at him, his eyes narrowed.

"Damn it!" he said explosively. "Damn it, Campion, I believe you're right. I knew it was something so simple that it was staring me in the face."

They stood together looking down at the diagram. Oates stooped to put a chalk cross at the entrance to the cul-de-sac.

"It was *that* lamp post," he said. "Give me that telephone. Wait till I get hold of that fellow."

While he was carrying on an excited conversation we demanded an explanation from Mr. Campion and he gave it to us at last, mild and apologetic as usual.

"Well, you see," he said, "there's the sandbin. The sandbin marks the boundary of two police divisions. Policeman A, very hot and tired, sees a man collapse from the heat under a lamp post on his territory. The man is a little fellow and it occurs to Policeman A that it would be a simple matter to move him to the next lamp post on the other side of the sandbin, where he would automatically become the responsibility of Policeman B, who is even now approaching. Policeman A achieves the change and is bending over the prostrate figure when his colleague comes up. Since he knows nothing of the bullet wound, the entrance to the cul-de-sac, with its clear view to the café, second-floor room, has no significance in his mind. Today, when its full importance must have dawned upon him, he evidently thinks it best to hold his tongue."

Oates came back from the phone triumphant.

"The first bobby went on leave this morning," he said. "He was an old hand. He must have spotted the chap was dead, took it for granted it was the heat, and didn't want to be held up here by the inquest. Funny I didn't see that in the beginning."

We were all silent for some moments.

"Then—the girl?" I began at last.

The Inspector frowned and made a little grimace of regret.

"A pity about the girl," he said. "Of course it was probably an accident. Our man who saw it happen said he couldn't be sure."

I stared at him and he explained, albeit a little hurriedly.

"Didn't I tell you? When my sergeant phoned about the alibi he told me. As Josephine crossed the road after visiting the mortuary this morning she stepped under a bus... Oh yes, instantly."

He shook his head. He seemed uncomfortable.

"She thought she was making a gesture when she came down to the station, don't you see? The mob must have told her to swear that no one had been in the upstairs room; that must have been their first story until they saw how the luck lay. So when she came beetling down to us she must have thought she was risking her life to give her Johnny's murderer away, while instead of that she was simply giving the fellow an alibi... Funny the way things happen, isn't it?"

He glanced at Campion affectionately.

"It's because you don't get your mind cluttered up with the human element that you see these things so quickly," he said. "You see everything in terms of A and B. It makes all the difference."

Mr. Campion, the most gentle of men, made no comment at all.

THE SHOT THAT WAITED

Vincent Cornier

"For over sixty years the work of Vincent Cornier has been something of a secret treasure within the vaults of mystery fiction." So said Mike Ashley in his introduction to *The Duel of Shadows: the Extraordinary Cases of Barnabas Hildreth* (2011), which presented what Ellery Queen had, not long after the Second World War, called "one of the great series of modern detective stories". Hildreth was a secret agent also known as "The Black Monk" and he was adept at making sense of seemingly impossible crimes; his first case was "The Catastrophe in Clay", which presented the puzzle of how a trickster was turned overnight into a block of stone. Cornier, whose real name was William Vincent Corner (1898–1976), was by birth a Yorkshireman, although much of his success in the field of detective fiction resulted from the enthusiasm of Fred Dannay at *Ellery Queen's Mystery Magazine* for his ingenious way of telling a story. Mike Ashley argues that "even after all these years there is nothing like them in the annals of mystery fiction".

Cornier's best stories are highly entertaining, but changes in literary fashion seem to have caused his career as an author to peter out in the 1960s. By that time, he had left his wife and family and run off abroad with his secretary. He returned to England in 1970 and, as Mike Ashley says: "was injured in a riot in London. He settled in Hastings, unbeknown to his family, who happened to discover his whereabouts by chance" prior to his death from a heart attack. This story, originally entitled "The Duel of Shadows", was first published in *Pearson's Magazine* in April 1934.

I N THE CALCULATION AN ALLOWANCE HAS TO BE MADE FOR THE *Gregorian Correction* of the calendar in 1752. Then it becomes apparent that the time elapsed between the firing of that bullet and its plunge into Westmacott's body was exactly two hundred and twenty-two years, two months, one week, five days, twelve hours and forty-seven minutes...

The duelling pistol from which it was shot was fired by Ensign the Honourable Nigel Koffard. He was a young officer in one of Marlborough's crack squadrons and had but recently homed to England after the decisive bloodiness of Malplaquet. The man whom his shot wounded two hundred odd years after was Mr. Henry Leonard Westmacott, a branch-cashier of the London and Southern Counties Bank.

Nigel Koffard pressed the trigger of that pistol, in the park of Ravenshaw Hall, Derbyshire, at precisely eight o'clock on the radiant morning of August the second, 1710.

Henry Westmacott was sitting by his own hearthside in the drawing-room of The Nook, Bettington Avenue, Thornton Heath, Surrey, when Koffard's bullet struck him and shattered his right shoulder. He had just settled down—on the dismal and rainy night of October the twenty-third, last year—intending to listen to a concert broadcast from the Queen's Hall. The ball hit him as the B.B.C. announcer was concluding an apology for the programme being late by saying: "It is now eight forty-seven, and we are taking you straight over—"

Thus was the second time most accurately determined.

*

All the day long, young Mrs. Westmacott had been anxious about their little boy, Brian. He was running a slight temperature.

Hence she no sooner had dinner ended when she needs must go up to the nursery. In the swift way of tummy-troubled baby boys, Brian had contrived to lose his pains. He was sleeping serenely.

Pamela Westmacott smiled ruefully as she rearranged his cot clothes...

The shot, the groan, and the stumbling fall among the fire-irons all sounded on that instant. With mechanical acumen Mrs. Westmacott also noted that some china crashed to ruin in the kitchen, and that the opening chords of the Symphony Orchestra's performance were lost to a thud and a sudden silence.

She rushed down the stairs to collide with her maidservant, who had burst with almost equal speed from her domain.

"Oh, ma'am! Wh-what in the name o'glory's happened?"

"Hush, Biddy, and stay there! I—I'll see what's the matter."

Westmacott had raised himself to his knees and was delicately pawing at his right shoulder.

"Henry! Henry—darling!" Pamela Westmacott was down beside him. "What's gone wrong?" Then she saw the sodden red horror of his shoulder. "Oh, my poor old boy!... *Biddy*—'phone Doctor Smithers and the police. Tell them to hurry. Say Mr. Westmacott has been shot!"

When doctor and police arrived Westmacott had been got to bed. He was fully conscious and calm, despite his excruciating pain. His wife had managed him in a way that won Doctor Smithers' admiration.

Smithers turned to her with a smile as he unscrewed the nozzle of the syringe with which he had administered an opiate.

"Sensible woman, Mrs. Westmacott! You made everything very easy... What's that?... *Dangerous?* Oh, no, not at all! Direct compound fracture of the *scapula* socket and a flake chipped off the head of the *humerus.* Painful, but that's all."

Old Smithers patted her hands and definitely pressed her to the door. "Now run along and leave hubby to me. Go down and satisfy the curiosity of those exceedingly impatient policemen. Above all, don't—worry."

The police were certainly impatient. Their cross-examination had foundered poor Biddy. After their dismissal of her she had gone back to the kitchen to blubber among the neglected crockery.

In Mrs. Westmacott was discovered harder and less hysterical material. She told them all she knew. Essentially because it tallied so exactly with Biddy's account, the officers became more and more confounded...

"But are you absolutely *sure*, Mrs. Westmacott, no one came out of this room as you rushed down the stairs? Or slipped out by the front door."

"Oh, dear, how many more times must I tell you? No!" Wearily she smoothed her forehead. "Who could have done so?"

"Whoever fired that shot," grunted Inspector Ormesby. "There's no weapon to be found. The windows are all properly secured. There isn't any glass broken. Your husband wasn't potted at by someone lurking in the garden—that's self-evident. And he couldn't possibly have shot himself." The Inspector nodded toward the radio cabinet which the bullet had struck. "The position of his wound and the subsequent flight of the missile settles *that*... Somebody shot him! Then who was it?"

A plainclothes officer turned from his inspection of the damaged cabinet. He had been pencilling notes referring to the tarnished ball of lead which showed itself, half-embedded, in the seven-ply veneered woodwork. It had struck a spot directly in front of a radio tube, and the impact had been sufficient to shatter filaments, so stopping reception.

This man's talking was far less truculent than that of Inspector Ormesby. But it was deadlier.

"You've told us that the front door was locked for the night. Have I got that right?"

"Yes, you have."

"I noticed that a little brass bolt is on the inner side of the door. Then there's the main lock and a Yale latch. All of 'em secured?"

"No. The key of the big lock wasn't turned, but the bolt was pushed home. Naturally the latch held as well."

"Had you to open those to let us in?"

"I had."

The plainclothes man watched her through half-closed eyes.

"Now, you remember, you also told us that you came helter-skeltering down the stairs at such a rate that you bumped into this Bridget O'Hara woman at the bottom. And she'd just flown out of the kitchen?"

"Perfectly correct. When the shot was fired, Biddy dropped a plate or something. Then she rushed here. We—we converged on the room."

"No one went out of the door." It seemed that the plainclothes man was musing aloud. "No one, so you say, went up the stairs past you. No one could have doubled out by way of the kitchen, and no one could have doubled out of here back into the dining-room or into the cupboard under the stairs, without you or your servant seeing 'em... *Um-m-m!*" He paused, and ignored Mrs. Westmacott completely, to smile past her at Inspector Ormesby. *"And no weapon found,"* he slowly murmured. "You carry on here, Inspector. Strikes me I'll have to have another heart-to-heart talk with our faithful Bridget."

Pamela Westmacott flinched as though a viper had reared itself before her eyes as she watched the inimical C.I.D. man saunter from the room. Mad as it seemed, fantastic and unreal as it was, nevertheless she realised she was the suspect here.

Now let interpolation be made of the somewhat astounding experience of an official police photographer, called Coghill.

A genial little fellow, Egbert Coghill; a craftsman of infinite patience and capability. He was the man who went to The Nook the next day and acting on police instructions, set about securing photographs of the drawing-room and, more especially, the bullet-splintered radio set.

Cheerily, with an incessant whispering whistle, he moved about and made himself quite at home. He dumped his big camera on a table. The black leather case, which contained his plates in their mahogany slides, he placed in front of the radio cabinet. Still softly whistling, he pottered around, making his notes and selecting his objects and angles.

Thereafter he erected his camera and made various long exposures. He took photographs of the door, the windows, the bloodstained rug, the untidy hearth, and the armchair in which Westmacott was sitting when he was wounded. After these, Coghill concentrated on his most important work. He removed his plate carrier from its place in front of the radio set and focused on the half-embedded bullet and the starry matrix wherein it lay. He expended his remaining four plates on this.

When he came to the development of his material, Coghill was astonished and alarmed. Without exception, each dripping negative held—superimposed on its actual detail—a wee portrait of something that appeared to be an astronomical portrait view of the planet Saturn. These were ring-impounded orbs which had a quality of eerie brilliancy that had struck the plates with something amounting almost to halation. Yet they were mottled by shadows of an intensity and a delicacy Mr. Egbert Coghill had never previously developed out of any sensitive emulsion.

More than this phenomena, the four exposures of the radio cabinet were useless. These, which should have been Coghill's acme, not only bore the eerie imprint of the tiny incandescent "planet," but a great maelstrom of fog about the place where the bullet should have been. The cabinet was clear enough. Only that area which should have been occupied by a representation of the leaden slug was at fault.

Mr. Coghill equipped himself with another camera and a new assortment of plates. Back he went to the drawing-room of The Nook. He duplicated his previous exposures and again developed them.

None of this second group of negatives showed the Saturn-like globe. Equally, none of the seven plates he had, secondarily, exposed on the cabinet front was in any better state than the former four. Except for the non-appearance of the queer orb, there were the identical coils of fogginess about the splintered woodwork—*and no sign of the bullet.*

Mr. Egbert Coghill made a number of prints from all these negatives. Together with his notes and the plates themselves, he gave into police keeping. This done, he fared forth and drank deeply.

Without much loss of time those photographs went, by way of Scotland Yard, to a Home Office department in Whitehall: to Barnabas Hildreth. He studied them and puzzled over them, as he afterwards told me, until he was sick to death of the very sight of them. Bewildered, Barnabas then interviewed the Westmacotts.

The unfortunate Henry had nothing of much value to relate. He had been reading, he said, and had just put aside his evening paper to listen to the broadcast. As he leaned back in his chair, he heard a curiously violent hissing as of air escaping from a pin-punctured tire. Then there was a detonation and a fiery enormous blow at his shoulder.

He scouted the idea that anyone could have been in the room with him without his knowledge. And on the subject of the police theory—that his wife had shot him and, in collusion with Bridget O'Hara, had thereafter established incontestable *alibi*—he was sardonically and sulphurously vehement. When he discovered Hildreth so far agreed with him under that head as to veto further official brow-beating, Westmacott became a different man. He was so relieved, so pathetically relieved, that Hildreth was touched—actually was humanised sufficiently to accept an invitation to stay for tea!

So it came about that the grim Intelligence Service officer and Master Brian Westmacott became friends. Hildreth chuckled over this.

"There was no resisting the little beggar, Ingram. He's a sturdy kid and as sensible as the deuce. No sooner had I finished examining the drawing-room than he lugged me off to build what he called a 'weal twue king's palace'—from bits of wood; wood such as I've never seen a child playing with before. He had a big box full of sawn-up chair legs and rails; 'pillars' for his palace. And he'd scores of miniature arches and so forth—all shaped out of carved walnut and mahogany and oak and elm—little blocks, battens, and angle-pieces that had originally been parts of furniture. One glance at 'em showed they were scores of years old and had come from the workshops of masters like Hepplewhite and Chippendale."

I sensed something of extraordinary import here.

"*Oh,* and where'd he got 'em from?"

"Out of the family woodshed. Or, at least, his father had." Hildreth grinned. "I looked it over—lots of the same stuff there. Y'see, Westmacott has a brother in the antique furniture trade: does restorations and repairs and so forth. Westmacott gets all the waste from his brother's workshops. The likely bits he cuts up to add to Brian's collection of blocks and pillars. The remainder is burned.

"While I was in the drawing-room, old man"—he deliberately went off at a tangent—"I poked that bullet out of the radio set and took a pair of callipers to it. It's a pistol ball right enough. But where in the name of glory did it come from? And, who cast it—and *when*?"

"'Who cast it?'" I echoed. "What, isn't it an ordinary revolver slug?"

"Mass-produced?" Barnabas rubbed his hands together in glee. "Not on your life! It's as big as a marble and perfectly spherical. And it has marks on it that only the closure of a beautifully accurate bullet-mould could have made. More than that. It's of an unusual calibre—one so unusual that it opens up a tremendous field of conjecture, yet, at the same time, defines the narrowest of tracks. A track, indeed, that a fool could follow.

"Calibres of firearms," he softly stated, "are not little matters left to individual discretion, Ingram. They're registered and pedigreed better than bloodstock—at least, in this country. Ever since 1683 any armourer or gunsmith drilling a new size of bore has had to deposit a specimen barrel and exact measurements with the Tower authorities before he could fit it to a stock or sell or exploit it in any way.

"Remembering that, I asked for records to be searched. The answer is, that ball was cast to be shot out of only two particular types of weapons. It's of a size that's quite obsolete today. Either it could have been shot from a long gun, registered in London by Adolph Levoisier, of Strasbourg, in 1826, or out of a duelling pistol fashioned by Gregory Gannion, a gunsmith who had an establishment in Pall Mall between 1702 and 1754.

"The exact date of Gannion's application for a license to put on the market a weapon of a new type and calibre which he called '*an excellently powerful small-arm, for the practise of the duel, or in other uses, for delicacy and swiftness of discharge in defence or offence'*... was February the ninth, 1709. And according to all accounts, the blood-thirsty young bucks of that day went daffy about it. Y'see, it was the first hair-trigger' pistol on the market: ugly but useful.

"I'm working up from that. I've a shrewd idea that good English lead wouldn't come out of a Continental long-gun. *No,* a Gannion duelling pistol seems indicated."

I am getting ever more used to Barnabas Hildreth's tortuous tricks. The queerly precise ordination of those words, "good English lead," made me curious.

"How does one determine the nationality of—er—lead?" I asked.

"All as easily as one differentiates between a Chinese man and a Zulu," he sourly grinned. "By looking at it and studying it.

"According to the assay-notes, furnished me this morning, the lead from which that ball was cast came from one particular area of Derbyshire—*and nowhere else!* What's more, it's almost pure native stuff"—his face shone with some inner ecstatic light—"and so absolutely unique... that it's worth its weight, and more, in gold. In fact, if the fervours and excitements of the metallurgical chemists are anything to go by—and they're simply frazzling over it—it's the clue to a pretty fat fortune for someone!"

He got up then, and calmly stalked across to my tantalus and mixed whisky and sodas. Then he challenged me across the brim of his glass.

"Well, old man, all the best! And here's to the speedy solution of one of the neatest mysteries I've struck for months."

So far as I recollect, it was two days later that Hildreth descended on me. He wanted me to go to Thornton Heath with him, and I went. We visited the premises occupied by Westmacott's brother

Ralph—Westmacott and Company, Ltd.: "Antique Furniture Restored, Renovated, Repaired, and Reproduced."

Admittedly, Ralph Westmacott had certain specimen pieces in his workshops. These were the magnificent possessions of connoisseurs, to whom the factor of financial worth hardly counted. They were all undergoing tiny but incredibly painstaking forms of restoration, and guarded jealously for the treasures they were.

However, as Hildreth said, these were not our meat. Westmacott took us to the larger, general workshop. Here we saw really valuable, but ordinary, examples of olden furniture in the processes of repair and "faking."

"We pride ourselves," Westmacott told us, "on our ability to replace a faulty participle with a sound one, so meticulously reproduced and fitted—grafted on, one might say—that no one outside first-flight experts can detect the addition."

"That, of course, necessitates," smoothly came Hildreth's question, "your carrying an amazing stock of old cabinet-making woods, I presume?"

Westmacott looked curiously at my friend.

"*Aye*, amazing is the word," he laughed. "Come and have a look!"

He preceded us to a vast loft that was filled by racks and shelving—and all of them packed with broken parts of old-fashioned furniture.

"Here you are," he exulted, "from Tudor to Early Victorian; from linen-fold panelling to pollard-oak sideboard doors... gathered together from the auction rooms of half the globe. We couldn't carry on a day without 'em. Unless similar old stuff is used on replacement jobs—"

"Stuff like this, for instance," Hildreth interrupted to point at a great stack of dirty wood, looking to me like huge half-cylinders of amber-flecked bog oak: split tree trunks.

"This lot seems to be pretty ancient."

Ralph Westmacott moved delicately to Hildreth's side.

"*Aye,*" he concurred, "it's old enough! That wood's been buried in the earth for a century and more."

Brightly, blandly, almost with the alert cockiness of a schoolboy, Barnabas Hildreth replied:

"I don't doubt that for a moment, Mr. Westmacott! They're elm-wood water conduits, aren't they? And judging from their boggish appearance, they've come out of country where there's plenty of peat about."

Ralph Westmacott scratched his grizzled hair.

"Yes, they *are* conduits, and they certainly came out of peaty loam—from Derbyshire, as a matter of fact. We've men on the job up there now. They came from Ravensham Park, near a place called Battersby Brow... we bought the whole line of wooden water-pipes that used to serve the hall and the village."

Grimly enough Hildreth chuckled.

"What a game it is!" he drily stated. "Now, 'Battersby Brow,' in Derbyshire"—he was jotting down these particulars in a notebook—"and 'Ravensham Park,' you say?"

"Yes, that's all correct." Westmacott seemed puzzled.

"And this hall you mentioned?"

"Ravensham Hall, the residence of General Sir Arthur Koffard."

Hildreth put away his book and began to fumble among the blackened elm-wood.

"Might I have a chunk to take away with me?" he inquired. "I want it for certain experiments that have to be made." Westmacott nodded. "And will you ratify this? Certain lumps of this wood that you knew would be useless for your work you gave to your brother Henry, didn't you?"

"I—I did! What's the—"

"That's right! I thought I recognised the stuff again. I saw some in his wood shed." Hildreth smiled. *"Thanks!"*

With that we went back to London.

From the "Black Bull," at Battersby Brow in Derbyshire, a letter came to me on October 29th:

"MY DEAR INGRAM,

If you can leave your mouldy rag to look after itself for the weekend, come over here and be interested. Of all the intricate bits of work I've ever struck, this is the trickiest! Don't let me down, old chap. I promise you a really noble *dénouement* for the mystery of the Westmacott bullet: an ending that, I suppose, you'll stick on one of your scandalous chronicles of my cases and complacently claim as your own.

Sincerely,

B. H."

So I set out for Battersby Brow and the "Black Bull" as soon as I put my paper to bed in the early hours of Friday, the thirty-first. At nine o'clock the next morning I was in a beautiful and brilliant country of whistling airs and mighty hills.

Over breakfast, Barnabas crowed mightily.

"Done a lot of work since I saw you, old man! Only one tiny coping-stone to be put on, and the job's complete.

"It *was* a Gannion duelling pistol that fired that ball. I've seen it. There's a pair of 'em, and they've been laid away in a case since 1710… One was discharged. The other was loaded, but I got permission to draw the charge. I drew it right enough!" He chuckled. "D'you know, it was a curious experience. There I had in hand another ball, similar to the one that wounded Westmacott. And there were tiny, tattered fragments of a newspaper that had been used for a wad between bullet and powder—an issue of the *Northern Intelligencer* for August the first, 1710.

"The Koffards of Ravensham Hall have been awfully decent about everything. At first they were inclined to be stand-offish, but when I told old General Koffard the story you know, he tucked into things like a good 'un."

"Sorry to butt in, Barnabas—but, tell me, what story *do* I know? It occurs to me that I've only a few strikingly dissimilar and baffling incidents in mind, all hazily mixed up with lead that's 'worth its weight in gold' and old elm logs which you proved had come from this district."

Hildreth lit a cigarette.

"Listen, old man, and follow me carefully... Go back in thought to the night of the twenty-third. You have Westmacott sitting in his chair. A bullet, apparently fired out of the void, strikes his shoulder and is deflected into the radio set. Point the first to be made: direction of bullet's flight proved it was shot from somewhere in the region of Westmacott's feet. Got that?" I surveyed the scene in mind... I had to agree. "Now for point the second. Had a ball of that size possessed a high velocity, it'd have made the dickens of a mess of the *humerus*. It'd have caused a comminuted fracture and, without much doubt, it would have glanced across and gone through his throat.

"But no, it was a missile of low velocity—only a direct compound fracture of the *scapula* socket and a lazy glide off, to smack the front of the radio set.

"No one can say where the ball came from. The ineffable Egbert Coghill goes to photograph it... He puts his plate-carrier dead in front of the set, incidentally in front of the bullet. For fully a quarter of an hour he footles about; then, when he comes to take his photographs, he carries on each plate he afterwards exposes a portrait of the ball, transmitted by its own power through the leather case, through the whole clutter of his mahogany slides and, in fact, through everything within eighteen inches of the radio cabinet!"

I jumped at that.

"D'you mean those Saturn-like globes were—"

"Photographs of that ball! *Precisely!* It emitted a short, hard ray of far more intensity than the usual X-ray apparatus employs!"

"But how could that come about?"

"*Pitchblende,*" said Barnabas Hildreth, "that's why! Apart from certain areas in Cornwall, only the Peak district of Derbyshire and some isolated caverns round about Ingleborough in Yorkshire have pitchblende deposits. Usually, it's in association with lead that has a high silver content… The assay of that ball not only showed lead and silver, but definite traces of pitchblended striations, all melted together.

"To clinch that part of the business, however"—Hildreth glanced at the time—"remember that the second batch of Coghill's prints did *not* show the eerie little 'planet.' That was because he did not bung his plate-carrier in front of the radio set on his second venture. The active emissions were powerless outside a small range.

"But neither set of plates would betray anything except a fogginess where the bullet should have been. What could you reasonably expect?" Hildreth shrugged. "A long exposure, with powerful lens concentrating radium rays on a speedy photographic emulsion— nothing but fog *could* result!"

In the end I realised that Hildreth was right. Radio-active properties in that leaden slug would explain everything. Incidentally I caught the drift of what he meant when he spoke about the value of the bullet and its potentiality as the clue to a fortune.

"Do you mind"—Hildreth was on his feet and again looking at his watch—"if we hustle? We've a walk of a few miles if we're to get that coping-stone set, y'know. And I want it done today."

*

That long tramp across the sage-green acres of the Derbyshire countryside terminated in the park of Ravensham Hall. A group of navvies, excavating a snakish trench, paused in their work and watched us curiously. And from out of a nearby hut a podgy and bespectacled man clad in a white coat, and an old iron-haired fellow with a face of claret, came to greet us. One was a chemist called Sowerby and the elder man was Major-General Sir Arthur Koffard.

"Well, Sowerby," Hildreth briskly questioned when introductions were completed, "had any luck?"

Sowerby smiled unctuously and beckoned us back to the hut. In there he pointed to a fire-clay retort that glowed above a fierce petrol-air lamp. Around the squat nozzle of the retort a big plume of intensely blue and brilliant flame was glowing.

"Yes, Mr. Hildreth, your surmise! was right enough. It's *methyl hydride* without a doubt." He pointed to the halcyon fire. "Almost pure, to burn like that."

"Most 'strordinary—most 'strordinary thing," this was the crisp clacking of Koffard, "'tha' one can live a lifetime, 'mong things like these, an never know—never know. 'Course, this land's been full o' will-o-th'-wisp lights for years, but one never stops to, give 'em much thought."

Barnabas abstractedly nodded and walked out. We followed him to the side of the trench. For a long while he studied the enormous hollow trunks that the navvies had dug out of the black and oozy earth.

"Magnificent trees," he muttered. "Veritable giants! Took some labours I should say, to gouge their innards out!" Then he turned to Koffard and asked him something about a map.

"Aye, I've got it here." The rattle-voiced old officer produced a tin cylinder and drew out of it a scroll inscribed by rusted lines of ink.

"The avenue stood across there. Nigel Koffard fought his duel"—he pointed to a level sward forty yards away—"just on that patch. At the beginning of the avenue, exactly."

When we went to this place we could plainly see a series of little hummocks stretching, in parallel, for almost half a mile. It was explained to me that here had been a hundred and more elms making a great avenue that was felled in 1803—under each knoll was a mighty stump. The trunks, hollowed out, had gone into the formation of that pipe-line (for conveying drinking water from a hillside spring) the navvies were excavating.

Hildreth stopped exactly on the spot on which one Nigel Koffard had taken his stance to fight a duel on the morning of August the second, 1710.

"Now Sir Arthur," Hildreth murmured, "let's work things out. Your ancestor challenged his cousin to a duel, primarily over the intentions of that cousin toward your ancestor's sister. When the affair came to its head, Nigel Koffard was fully determined to put a ball through his cousin. But that doughty lad, conscious of honour and innocence, did not so much as lift his own pistol. Refused, point-blank, to defend himself."

"Tha's right; quite right!" Koffard applauded. "He must ha' had guts, y'know—simply stood there. Completely broke Nigel's nerve."

"And the said Nigel," Hildreth grinned, "thereupon did a bit of quick thinking. It dawned on him that he had misjudged his man. So, to show his regret and to extend an olive branch, he turned and fired his bullet straight into the nearest elm. Whereupon the youngsters shook hands. The cousin got permission to marry Nigel's fair sister, and the Gannion duelling pistols—one discharged and the other loaded—were put back in their case and guarded thereafter, for the sake of the episode, as family heirlooms."

"Precisely, sir!" said General Koffard. "Admirably put, sir!"

"Then, if that's so"—Hildreth was already on the move—"we'll trouble that invaluable plan of yours once again. Now we want to see this place called Skelter's Pot, where lead was mined in those days."

… We tramped a full mile up a mountainous slope and were eventually rewarded by the view of a bite into a pinkish face of spar, which the old map told us was "Skelter's Pot."

"Out of here," Sir Arthur Koffard told us, "came all the lead used hereabouts. The hall is roofed by it. That pistol-ball was certainly cast from it."

Hildreth took a geologist's hammer from his pocket and knocked away at a piece of semi-translucent quartz in which dull grey patches showed and on which strangely green filaments were netted.

"I would like," he softly returned as he put this specimen away, "to own your roof! At a modest estimate it'll be worth more than the hall and this estate put together."

"Now, you see, old chap"—Hildreth tapped the rough pencil sketch he had made—"this was the way of it." I leaned across the table, and under the steady oil-lamp light of the old Black Bull, I looked at the drawing. "Here we've all we need."

"When Nigel Koffard shot that ball, at closest range, into the living elm-tree it made a deep cavity, a tunnel, in which it stopped. In a few more years a 'rind-gall' was formed. The elm closed over the wound in its structure by a growth of annular rings. The cylindrical little tunnel remained and the ball remained.

"Then our elm showed signs of what is called 'doatiness'—incipient decay. It, together with all the others in the avenue, was felled, hollowed out, and used for an aqueduct. Y'see, old man, elm is the *one* wood which never changes if kept constantly wet.

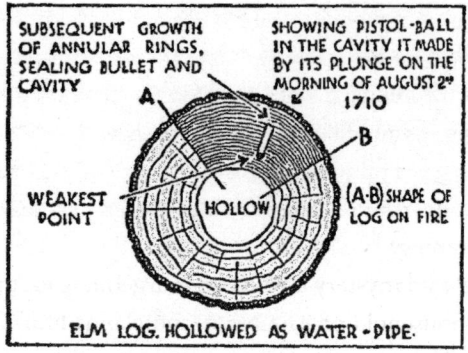

DIAGRAM OF THE ELM LOG BURNT IN THE CASHIER'S FIRE.

"This is a queer countryside, Ingram. And the elm's a queer tree. Get those facts in mind.

"That chamber which held the bullet also held the gases of the elm's former disruption, and to these were added those similar gases which lurk in peaty land. 'Similar,' did I say: *Identical* would be a better word... You heard old Koffard talk about marsh-gas; natural gas, that is... Well, that's what we're considering. You saw that chemist fellow, Sowerby, with a retort full of elm-wood burning such gas at the mouth of the apparatus.

"*Methyl-hydride; methane; carburetted-hydrogen*—call it what you will, and still you're right—is marsh-gas. Also it's the dreaded and terribly explosive thing which miners call *fin-damp*... when mixed with air.

"You see it burning away in every fireside in the land. It's the illuminating property of coal. And it *always* results when bodies of a peaty, woody, or coaly constituent are subjected to great heat."

I began to have an inkling of what Hildreth was getting at.

"However, to the mechanics of the situation." He laughed and drank some beer. "Ralph Westmacott, the furniture man, buys some old weathered elm-wood from Derbyshire in order to fake his manu-factures. What he has to spare—useless—he gives, as usual, to his brother, Henry Leonard. Our good Henry Leonard diligently saws it up into chunks and fills the family woodshed.

"Now comes a rainy and dismal October night. Henry puts a log on the open-hearth fire, extends his slippered feet, and prepares to enjoy the evening.

"But the wild mystery of the ever-burgeoning earth comes into the simple household of The Nook and claims him... He hears a violent hiss. That was air rushing into the vascular tissue of that hot elm-log, combining with the incredible chemistry of Nature with the terrible potential of that hydrocarbon, *methane, in the hollow where the bullet lay concealed.*

"Nigel Koffard's powder had not half the fulminating property, in the steel barrel of his pistol, that *fire-damp* had in the smooth wound of the elm log... Pressure increased, since the hollow was filling every second with more and more gas, and air was in combination with it. At last, the hungry fire, eating away the inner face of the log, reached the terribly explosive mixture. Then *bang*, up and outwards shot the ball into Henry's shoulder.

"So we're back at our beginning—the very first point I made: that the ball was fired from somewhere about Westmacott's feet. I recalled flying fragments of coal and co-related things... allowing, always, for the unusual.

"But, instead of coal and cinders, the well of the grate was filled with half-burned fragments of wood—like fragments of furniture, surmounted by a big tricorne hunk of charred elm-wood. I won-dered, vastly, about those fragments. Then, when I saw the little boy, Brian, playing with his homemade building blocks, I was definitely set on the second line which led me to solution."

He picked up his tankard and smiled.

"That green network you saw on the surface of that spar *was* pitchblende! I'm told it's more than usually rich in radium and uranium salts.

"The land on which Skelter's Pot is situated belongs to the Commissioners. It's an open common land. Anyone procuring the necessary faculty, and entering into serious negotiations, can mine it... So, with the joyous approval of Mr. Henry Leonard Westmacott, I have entered my innocent ally Master Brian's name on our list—"

"'Our list'?" I was puzzled by his most deliberate pause. "What list?"

"Oh, the little company I'm forming: myself, yourself, Koffard, Westmacott and young Brian, to exploit the pitchblende deposits of our property in Skelter's Pot, Derbyshire." He laughed and stretched his long arms. "It ought to provide for us in our old age, if nothing else!"

... Judging by my latest returns from that adroitly-contrived concern, I am inclined, stoutly, to agree.

THE GOLD OF TSO-FU

Anthony Wynne

Anthony Wynne was the crime writing alias of Robert McNair Wilson (1882–1963), a Glaswegian who came from Maryhill, later immortalised on television as the setting for the long-running TV series *Taggart*. A doctor by profession, Wilson was also a journalist, writer of detective fiction and non-fiction, and politician. Under his real name he published such books as *Napoleon the Man* and *The History of Medicine*, as well as several titles dealing with economics such as *The Defeat of Debt*. He was also medical correspondent for *The Times* for more than a quarter of a century. In 1924 his first detective novel was serialised, and it appeared in book form the following year as *The Mystery of the Evil Eye*.

Few British crime writers have shown such devotion to the "impossible crime" story as Anthony Wynne. As Robert Adey said in *Locked Room Murders*, which lists twenty-one of his novels as well as two short stories, he was a master of one particular branch of the locked room sub-genre, i.e. "death by invisible agent. Time after time he confronted his… detective with situations in which the victim was killed, quite on his own, in plain view of witnesses who were unable to explain how a close-quarters blow could have been struck." This story, which first appeared in *Flynn's Magazine* on 13 February1926 and features his Great Detective Dr. Eustace Hailey, concerns a death by shooting in a room under observation.

A CLERK CAME INTO THE WAITING-ROOM OF EVANS' CHINA BANK in Kingsway. He held Doctor Hailey's card between his thumb and forefinger.

"You have an appointment with Sir Thomas Evans?" he asked.

"I imagine so. He sent me a telegram this morning asking me to meet him here at this hour."

"Very well. I will see if he is in his room."

The man retired. Doctor Hailey glanced round the astonishing apartment in which he found himself. No wonder Evans had the reputation of being a super-man! Who but himself would have dared to furnish a business office after the manner of King Louis XIV in the most prodigal moments of his palace-building? His eye travelled from colossal mirrors with wrought iron frames which seemed to have been fashioned by Vulcan himself, so bold and stark were the mountings of them, to delicate gildings full of the old sweetness of Venice and filigree work of wrought silver full of the cold ecstasy of winter moonlight. It was all grotesque, strange, a wild mingling of the harsh and the gentle, of beauty and sweetness, of iron and gold, and yet it expressed something clear and distinct—something magnificent beyond the splendours with which merely rich men often surround themselves. This man—

The door of the room was flung open. The clerk who had taken the doctor's card staggered in with pallid cheeks and eyes which seemed to bulge from their sockets.

"For God's sake, doctor, come quickly!" he cried in hoarse tones, "something—something awful has happened."

Doctor Hailey followed him across the immense entrance hall of the building, where tremendous groups of statuary threatened or glowed upon the astonished visitor, to a room of the same size as that which he had just quitted. The man shrank back and allowed him to enter the room alone.

The sight which met his eyes caused him to gasp, so strange and terrible was it. Facing him, its round, sinister face illuminated by a shaft of sunlight, was a huge effigy in freshly gilded wood, of some oriental deity seated on his throne. Just below the throne, lying with outstretched hands and pallid features, was the body of a young man.

Doctor Hailey crossed the room and came to the body. He stooped down to examine it.

The man had been stabbed through the heart.

He opened his waistcoat and shirt. The wound was a small one. He decided that the dagger with which it had been inflicted must have been wielded with the greatest precision and vigour. He turned to the trembling clerk who remained at the doorway.

"Do you know him?" he asked sharply.

"Oh, yes. It is Mr. Harrier, of this office." The clerk's voice shook as he spoke.

The doctor bent again and completed his examination. The dead man had evidently been struck down close to the spot where he lay, because he had clutched at the god in his fall. There were small flakes of the gold-beater's skin, used to gild the effigy, on his finger-tips. Doctor Hailey stood up and surveyed the magnificent room with eyes which quailed. The thought came to him that the mind that had planned these decorations was a mind that horror, no matter how stark, would not intimidate, a mind as ruthless as the sea.

"Did Mr. Harrier often come to this room?"

"Not very often, sir. But he is one of the directors of the Bank."

Doctor Hailey continued his inspection. In addition to the gilded god there was a beautiful replica in marble of Michael Angelo's statue of the young David, which, by comparison with that dull effigy, seemed strangely instinct with vision and power. The floor was a marble chequerboard in black and white. Here and there glowing carpets had been laid on it. The huge fireplace was carved in lines as swift as the flames which leaped on its hearth. In the centre of the apartment was a desk fashioned, as it seemed, out of a single block of ebony and crusted with dull brass along its margin. Great lamps hung from the fretted roof; they were of coloured glass like the tall windows on the wall. Above the head of the god was an exquisite cabinet of Japanese lacquer—the kind of lacquer work which is seen as a rule only in museums and palaces.

"Sir Thomas has not come in today?"

The clerk shook his head. He had been joined by a uniformed attendant who volunteered the information that he had watched the door of the room from the time when the murdered man entered it until the time when the crime was discovered.

"I 'appened to be standing in the entrance 'all and I can swear that no one went in or came out during the 'ole time."

Doctor Hailey contracted his brow.

"These windows," he remarked, "do not seem to open. Am I right?"

"They don't open, sir. They're built in."

A quick step sounded in the hall without. The men at the door stood to attention. A thick-set individual with a round face came bustling into the room.

Doctor Hailey had an immediate impression of vigour both of mind and body. But that impression was less definite than the sense of aversion he felt. He stiffened instinctively as he turned to greet the newcomer.

"Good God, what's this…?"

The man stood still and gazed at the spectacle disclosed to him. The doctor thought that he grew paler for an instant, but it was difficult to be sure about that, because he was naturally pale.

"Harrier!"

He glanced round the room, his small eyes gleaming excitedly. Then he seemed to pull himself together. He turned abruptly and held out his hand.

"Doctor Hailey?" he asked, fixing his eyes on the doctor in the fashion often adopted by men of this kind.

"That is my name."

Doctor Hailey's tones were not cordial.

"My name is Evans. I wanted to talk to you on a personal matter. But that must wait now."

He demanded to be told about the tragedy. Yet he scarcely seemed to listen when the facts were stated.

"We must send for the police," he cried. "We must ring up Scotland Yard at once. This is a terrible business—terrible. There is not a moment to be lost. The murderer"—he turned suddenly to the doctor—"I am right in thinking that poor Harrier was murdered, am I not?" he asked in a sharp parenthesis.

"I do not see that there can be any doubt on that score. Had he committed suicide, the weapon must have been in his hand or, at least, near his body."

"Of course. Quite so, I agree with you entirely." Sir Thomas's voice jerked. He told his clerk to summon the police. Then he went to the door of the room and shut it. He turned the key in the door and came back towards the place where Doctor Hailey was standing. He stood a moment gazing down at the dead face. Then he raised his eyes and fixed them on those of his companion.

"I asked you to come here this morning," he declared, "in order to tell you that I murdered this man. You will do me the credit of confessing that the appointment was well timed."

The doctor started in spite of himself. His huge shoulders seemed to square as though he made ready to cope with sudden danger. His lack-lustre eyes narrowed.

"So!" he remarked.

"You do not believe me. Of course not. I had expected that." Sir Thomas Evans laughed harshly and there was a horrible, crackling sound in his laughter. "Nevertheless it is the truth. There are ways of entering and leaving this room which are not apparent to a casual visitor."

He strode to the fireplace and stood in front of the fire with his sinister face thrust forward. A smirk played on his lips.

"So now," he continued, "I have set you a puzzle to solve. As an amateur detective you will have full scope for all your talents, you and the policemen who will soon be here. Meanwhile I propose to go out and have a bite of lunch."

Doctor Hailey took his snuff-box from his pocket. He opened it with great deliberation and took a somewhat prolonged pinch. His eyes continued to observe the little banker closely.

"Harrier was one of your directors, I understand," he remarked in casual tones.

"He was. And a damned interfering fellow into the bargain. For which reason I killed him." Sir Thomas emitted a chuckle which reminded the doctor of the sound made by broody hens. He took a big gold cigar-case from his pocket and proceeded to light up.

"My business," he remarked, "is one which requires a very high degree of courage as well as of imagination."

He picked up his hat, which he had laid on the ebony desk and put it on his head.

"If the police want me," he declared, "I can be found at the Automobile Club."

He moved to the door. The doctor saw his fat hand reach out to the key. He awaited the click of the lock.

Instead of that sound, however, he heard another of the man's formidable chuckles.

Next moment he was looking down the barrel of a pistol.

Sir Thomas chuckled again.

"I have changed my mind," he said. Then his voice rose to a shout as he cried: "Put up your hands, you damned scoundrel!"

His pallor had given place to redness. His eyes were glowing. Doctor Hailey took a step back.

"Up! and be quick about it."

The little man advanced across the floor holding his gun out stiffly in front of him. He began to count, "One, two, three, four," in a peculiarly menacing tone of voice. The doctor glanced about him and then, apparently as an afterthought, raised his eyeglass and screwed it into position.

"Have the goodness to put that thing away," he ordered in a quiet voice.

His words appeared to startle the banker, for he stopped counting and stood still. Nevertheless he repeated his order that the doctor should put up his hands.

"For what reason, may I ask?"

"Because I tell you."

Doctor Hailey took more snuff.

"Is it not enough," he inquired in conciliatory tones, "to have killed one man?"

Sir Thomas chuckled once more. His chuckle became a laugh. With a sudden, swift gesture he flung his pistol to a corner of the room.

"Good! Damned good," he cried. "Let me congratulate you, my dear Doctor Hailey, on the possession of a very pretty wit—a very pretty wit."

He advanced with outstretched hand. He shook the doctor's hand warmly.

There was a loud knocking at the door.

"Ha! The police!"

Sir Thomas drew himself up. He went to the door and threw it open. An inspector and two constables were standing behind it.

"Permit me, gentlemen," he said, "to give myself up as the murderer of that young man—that most foolish and interfering young man."

He indicated the dead body with a sweep of his arm.

The inspector was nonplussed for a moment. He inquired if Sir Thomas was serious and was informed that he had never been more serious in his life. At a signal from him the policemen moved closer to the banker.

Late that evening Inspector Biles of Scotland Yard was shown into Doctor Hailey's smoking-room at twenty-two Harley Street. He found his old friend deeply immersed in a volume of lectures by Sigismund Freud and had difficulty in avoiding being dragged there and then into a discussion of the Psycho Analytic Theory as applied to the criminal world. He declared:

"I have just seen Sir Thomas Evans. It is absolutely certain that he did not murder Harrier. He was in Hampstead at the time the murder was committed."

The doctor closed his book and stood up. He was in evening clothes and looked, Biles thought, bigger than usual.

"And yet," he remarked in slow tones, "I do not think that the worthy banker is nearly as mad as he pretends."

Biles nodded.

"My dear doctor, that is the conclusion I have reached myself. The fellow is shamming. What I don't understand is why he should wish to accuse himself of such a crime."

"Have you looked into his affairs at all? It is just possible, isn't it, that he may be attempting to cover one crime by assuming responsibility for another?"

"His affairs are in perfect order. The credit of the China Bank was never higher than it is today."

Doctor Hailey shook his head.

"In that case," he said, "I must confess myself entirely at a loss."

"I took him home," Biles continued, "and told his wife to summon a doctor. I explained to her that you had seen him shortly after the discovery of the murder and that he had threatened you. In the circumstances it seems best that he should be placed under medical control."

The doctor nodded. He asked whether or not any light had been obtained on the murder itself and was told that the police were entirely without a clue.

"Both the doorkeeper and one of the clerks are ready to swear that nobody entered or left the room during the whole period of Harrier's occupancy of it. It is just possible that they are lying, but somehow I don't think so."

Biles went away. Doctor Hailey sat down again and gave himself to the contemplation of the puzzle. But no flash of illumination came to lighten his darkness. He was about to go to bed when he heard his front door bell ring sharply. He glanced at the clock on the mantelpiece beside him. It was close on midnight.

He went to the door and opened it himself. A young girl in evening dress was standing on the step.

"Doctor Hailey?" she asked in breathless tones.

"Yes."

The doctor stood back to allow her to enter. She came in quickly and he shut the door behind her.

"My name is Evans," she told him, "Lady Evans. I believe you saw my husband at his office this morning."

Doctor Hailey invited her to enter his smoking-room. He closed the door of the room carefully and then indicated a chair. Lady Evans, he observed with interest, was very young and very beautiful—a pale blonde of the type so greatly admired by second-rate artists. Yet she did not look second-rate.

She sat down and raised her big blue eyes to his face.

"I have come to you," she said in low tones, "because I am in fear of my life. You will help me, won't you?"

"If that is possible."

The doctor raised his eyeglass and put it carefully in position in his eye.

"I think it is possible." Her accents were quite matter of fact. "You are a mind doctor and if you pronounce that my husband is mad no one will dare to dispute that opinion." She added after a moment, "My own doctor has refused to certify him, but he is not a specialist, of course."

"I do not think that he is mad."

He saw her start. The natural pallor of her cheeks was intensified.

"Oh, surely, after what happened at the Bank today! The detective from Scotland Yard told me." She shook her head in a queer, bewildered fashion which was attractive as the ingenuousness of a child is attractive. Doctor Hailey took a pinch of snuff.

"Will you answer one question—a personal question?" he asked in crisp tones.

She nodded, almost as though she knew already what was coming.

"Was the murdered man a friend of yours as well as of your husband's?"

"Yes."

"An intimate friend?"

"Yes"

"So that Sir Thomas may possibly have been jealous of him?"

Lady Evans studied the carpet for a few minutes with, apparently, most minute care. Suddenly she raised her eyes:

"My husband had sworn to kill Jack—Mr. Harrier," she said simply.

"And yet he did not kill him?"

The girl drew a sharp breath.

"Didn't he?"

Her voice broke and a look of deadly anxiety came into her eyes. "He has sworn to kill me also," she said in a whisper.

She jumped up suddenly and seized the doctor by the arm.

"Oh, do this for me!" she cried. "Please, because I am so terribly frightened."

Doctor Hailey persuaded her to sit down again. After a moment she raised her eyes to his face.

"I can trust you?" she asked in whispered tones.

"I hope so."

"I have been very foolish anyway," she confessed. "A year ago I allowed Jack, Mr. Harrier, to make love to me. We exchanged letters, terribly indiscreet letters. My husband has found some of them."

She broke off and raised her hands in a gesture of helplessness.

"Last night, without any warning, the storm broke."

Her eyes quailed. She drew a deep sigh which seemed to stifle her breath.

"He had invited Jack to dinner. Afterwards in the drawing-room he told us that he knew our secret and that he had decided to divorce me. The way he said it was so terrible that I begged Jack to protect me against him. Then Jack lost his head."

She paused. She closed her eyes as if that memory was still too harrowing to be borne. "They fought with one another."

She added in low tones: "Jack was trying to find those letters when he was killed!"

Doctor Hailey bit his lip. "How do you know that?" he asked sharply.

The girl seemed to recoil from him. Her cheeks became deathly pale. She rose and leaned against the mantelpiece.

"I know," she faltered.

She stood, swaying a little on her feet. He thought for a moment that she was about to fall. Then she sat down again and covered her face with her hands.

"You have not told me all the truth about those letters," the doctor said in very quiet tones. He added: "I think it would be well if you made your confidence a complete one."

"I cannot tell you all the truth."

Doctor Hailey opened his snuff-box and took a careful pinch.

"The recovery of a bunch of foolish love letters which your husband had already read," he remarked, "would not have availed either Harrier or yourself much, since Sir Thomas was, no doubt, in possession of evidence against you of a more substantial kind."

He looked at the shrinking girl as he spoke. He saw her lips assent to his proposition.

"On the other hand if the letters contained a suggestion… of a criminal nature—"

Lady Evans uttered a low cry. The fear in her expression was cruelly intensified. She raised her hand in a gesture which seemed to ward off some imminent peril.

"Jack was mad, crazy," she whispered. "We were both mad."

"I see." The doctor's tone had a grim quality.

"He didn't mean it. Oh, I know that he didn't mean it."

She began to weep. The profound silence of Harley Street late at night filled the chamber. Doctor Hailey put his eyeglass in his eye.

"It is very likely that he didn't mean it," he said. "But, all the same, when a man discovers that another man, his business partner, has been suggesting to his wife that it would be a good thing to get rid of him... well, he has some excuse for taking an exaggerated view of the danger threatening him."

He paused. The girl did not raise her head.

"Your husband may have believed quite honestly that you and Harrier meant to murder him."

Still she did not reply. Doctor Hailey stood watching her with a look of pity in his eyes. It was the old, bitter story of a woman's misplaced love: the story, he reflected, which is the beginning and the end of human tragedy.

"When did Sir Thomas find these letters?" he asked after a moment.

"I don't know. I thought at first that he had only just found them. But it is possible that he may have known of them for some months before he went to China. I remember that he scarcely troubled to say goodbye to me when he left for that journey."

She sighed again. At that time, Doctor Hailey realised, she must have been too greatly thankful to obtain even a temporary release from her husband to care how he took leave of her. Nor with her lover at her side was she likely to trouble much about his letters. The thought of the banker faring forth, alone, with the knowledge of his wife's betrayal of him hidden in his heart was not a pleasant one.

"Harrier apparently did not find the letters," he told the girl. "His pockets were searched in my presence."

"I know that. I managed to get that information from the inspector who brought my husband home." She broke off and then added:

"I was so terribly afraid because if the police had found them they would certainly have been read at the inquest tomorrow."

With an impulsive gesture she drew a bunch of keys from the pocket of her coat and held them out to Doctor Hailey.

"I managed to get these tonight," she declared, "after the doctor had ordered my husband to bed. They were in his pocket. As soon as I found them, I rang up the caretaker at the Bank and said I was coming down. I'm going there now because my husband may tell the police about the letters at any moment. I am quite sure they are in his room at the office for I've searched everywhere at home."

Her cheeks were flushed and her eyes had become bright. It was difficult to realise that this was the woman who, a few moments before, had seemed to be the victim of a deadly and paralysing fear, the woman who had just lost her lover at the hands, as she believed, of her husband. The doctor regarded her with a thoughtful expression which betrayed the process of his mind. He had encountered her like before, often enough, but seldom so extreme an example of the type. She was, he thought, selfishness incarnate, selfishness without a single backward glance or a single hesitation. Husband and lover were no more than dream figures in this restless mind, figures easily replaced and therefore scarcely to be regretted. Only her fears and anxieties for herself were real. If she could secure the letters and persuade some doctor to certify the little banker as a lunatic she would turn without a qualm to fresh excitements.

The telephone bell began to ring. He strode across to the instrument and lifted it. A moment later he turned to the girl with new anxiety in his face.

"This is Scotland Yard speaking," he declared. "Your husband has just returned there. They want me to go down at once."

Lady Evans' lips parted in an exclamation of delighted surprise. She succeeded in suppressing it.

"I was quite sure that he had lost his reason," she declared. She took a step towards Doctor Hailey. "You will certify him now for certain, won't you?"

He did not reply. He promised to come to the Yard and then set the telephone down. He turned to the girl.

"It is sheer craziness," he said, "this idea of yours about going to the Bank. I will take you home, on my way to Westminster."

She shook her head. "No. I can't risk that. Tomorrow it may be too late."

The look of fear had crept back again to her eyes.

Doctor Hailey adjusted his eyeglass.

"Has it not occurred to you," he asked, "that such an action, at such an hour of the night, must arouse suspicion?"

She shrugged her shoulders.

"What can they suspect me of? My husband hasn't been murdered."

"Exactly. And so tomorrow he will learn what you have done."

"Tomorrow it will not matter. Tomorrow he will be locked in an asylum. Besides, I am going away to the country to stay with my sister until this trouble has blown over. Once the letters have been burned I shall be safe."

She moved to the door. He opened it for her. In the hall, as he was about to open the front door, he caught sight of her beautiful face reflected in one of his mirrors. She wore the expression of a child; a mingling of wistfulness and innocence. He caught his breath in the realisation that there was no artfulness in that expression. Lady Evans was entirely sincere. He called a cab and handed her into it. A few minutes later he was on his way to Scotland Yard.

Biles met him and conducted him up the famous staircase to his own room.

"This business," the detective declared, "is the most mysterious I have ever handled. The man will take no denial that he murdered

Harrier and yet it's absolutely certain that his story is a tissue of nonsense."

He indicated a chair and Doctor Hailey sat down.

"At the same time, my dear Biles," he said, "there remains the fact that Harrier was murdered and that nobody either entered or left the room in which the crime took place. It would seem to follow that only an individual with special secret knowledge of the building can be guilty. After all, if one is sure of one's alibi, self-accusation is not a bad way of disarming suspicion."

He took a pinch of snuff as he spoke. The detective shook his head.

"We have absolute proof that Evans was nowhere near his office yesterday morning until after the crime was committed."

He rang a bell on the table and when his summons was answered directed that Sir Thomas Evans should be brought to the room.

"I am most anxious," he declared to the doctor, "that his mental state should be fully reported on by a competent observer. So far as I am concerned he seems to be absolutely sane."

Sir Thomas came striding into the room with brisk steps. He recognised Doctor Hailey at once and greeted him in his eager manner. He repeated nearly everything he had said in his office using almost the identical form of words.

"The mystery remains," he concluded, "because it appears to be easier to suppose that I am crazy than to verify the precise statements which I have made."

"Such as?" Doctor Hailey's tones were crisp.

"That there exists a trap-door leading from the room to the cellar."

Biles interrupted sharply: "We have spent a whole day attempting to verify your statements. They cannot be verified because they are untrue."

The little banker raised his hands in a gesture of resignation. His face, for all the smirk which adorned it, had a sinister look entirely out of harmony with the character to which he seemed to be pretending. But Doctor Hailey did not observe that expression. He had stiffened in his seat and was gazing now, with horrified eyes, at the man's left shoulder. Biles, who was watching him, followed his gaze. But he saw nothing to justify it. His eyes travelled to the banker's face. He restrained an exclamation. Evans who was also watching the doctor, had become livid.

"My God!"

Doctor Hailey sprang up suddenly and snatched his hat.

"Arrest him!" he shouted to the startled detective. "Arrest him as Harrier's murderer."

Before the words were spoken he had flung open the door of the room and was already in the corridor. He dashed down the stairway with such violent haste that one of the policemen on duty came running to obstruct his passage.

"A cab. For God's sake," the doctor ordered him.

The man, who had seen him enter with Biles, hesitated a moment. Doctor Hailey pushed past him and they came to the yard together. The policeman blew a whistle shrilly.

"I didn't realise, sir," he apologised.

A cab appeared. The doctor jumped in.

"Evans' China Bank in Kingsway," he cried, "and drive like hell."

He flung himself back on the cushions. He could feel his heart thumping against his ribs. It was just the barest chance that he might be in time. He seized the speaking tube.

"Quick! Quicker for God's sake!"

The vehicle swung into Aldwich, narrowly escaping a collision with a big market wagon on its way to Covent Garden. It raced up Kingsway and stopped: the great wrought iron gates of the China

Bank stood like grim sentinels in the empty street. Doctor Hailey sprang across the pavement and seized the bell-handle. He tugged at it. He shouted.

"What do you want?"

"Is Lady Evans here? Oh, for God's sake open quickly. It's life or death… death probably."

The gates fell part. He was back again among the dim statues in the entrance hall. For a moment, in the darkness, he lost his bearings so that he scarcely knew how to advance. Then his eye caught a gleam of light. He staggered towards it; he seized the handle of the door beneath which the light was shining. The handle rattled in his grasp.

"Locked!"

He cried out, and his voice echoed in the wide spaces above him. The caretaker snatched up one of the big roof-lamps. Doctor Hailey was bending with his ear to the door. He remained thus for a second. Then he called:

"Lady Evans! Lady Evans!"

There was no reply from the room. He turned to the man beside him.

"Your keys."

"It is no use, sir. The key is turned in the lock."

The caretaker's face was white. The story of the murder had evidently shaken his nerves. He pointed with a finger which trembled to the end of the key protruding from the hole in the door.

"Have you an axe—a bar?"

The man ran across the hall to his lodge. Doctor Hailey listened again. He thought he heard the sound of a light footfall on the marble floor. Then another sound reached his ears, a faint creaking as of an old wooden stair. He sprang erect and beat on the panels of the door with his hands.

"For Heaven's sake," he shouted, "keep away from the god... from the steps."

He stepped back into the hall and then flung his whole weight against the door. But its stout panels resisted him. Biles' voice beside him made him turn sharply. The detective held an iron bar which he had evidently just taken from the caretaker. He thrust one end of it into the jamb of the door with the deft skill of a professional burglar. He threw his weight on the other end.

The door burst open with a loud cracking and splintering of wood.

The three men started back in speechless horror. Before them, standing on the topmost step of the throne on which the gilded god was seated, was Lady Evans. Her hands were clutched to her breast tearing at it convulsively; her eyes stared and her face was white as the white marble of the floor. She swayed a moment, backwards and forwards.

Doctor Hailey leaped towards her. But he was too late. Before he reached the god, she had fallen.

He knelt beside her and put his finger on her pulse. Then he tore open, her dress. As he did so Biles, who was bending beside him, cried out:

"The same wound, in the same place!"

Doctor Hailey set the girl's hand down. He rose and leaned for a moment against the table. His kindly face was furrowed by pity.

"What does it mean?" the detective asked in hoarse tones. He added: "This time, at any rate, it cannot be Evans because, before I followed you, I saw him securely locked up."

Doctor Hailey seemed to pull himself together. Very slowly he adjusted his eyeglass. He came to the back of the golden effigy and pointed to a tiny button protruding from among the richly carved robes of the deity.

"Observe," he remarked, "that if I wish to reach the button I must bend over the god."

He put out his hand as he spoke and demonstrated the truth of what he had said. Then he stood erect again and pointed to his left shoulder. Biles saw a number of small flakes of gold adhering to the black cloth.

"The effigy has been gilded recently, my dear Biles. It so happened that I noticed a number of similar flakes of gold on Evans' shoulder at the Yard. And then I remembered the Chinese cult of Tso-fu, 'the god who executes judgement,' and the fact that the banker has recently returned from a journey to the Far East."

He turned to the caretaker as he spoke:

"When was this figure placed here?" he asked.

"About a month ago, sir. Sir Thomas fetched it back with 'im from China."

Doctor Hailey went to the door and picked up the bar of iron which Biles had left there. He approached the god and set one end of the bar on the upper step of the throne, retaining the other end in his hands. He invited the caretaker to lean his weight on the bar.

The man bent forward. Suddenly, from the breast of the god, like a tongue of some horrid snake, a blade leaped forth, flashed in the lamplight and, while yet the cry of new amazement, with which he had greeted its appearance, was on Biles' lips, vanished again behind the heavy gilding.

The doctor set the iron bar down and pointed to the lacquer cabinet above the head of the effigy.

"Before he went to China," he declared in calm tones, "Evans found some letters written by Harrier to his wife in which that unhappy fellow went the length of hinting at murder as a possible means of obtaining the woman he loved. Last night the banker told the guilty pair about his discovery and threatened an immediate divorce. At the same time he seems to have let it be known that the letters were hidden somewhere in this room. In the circumstances it is scarcely surprising, I think, that Harrier should have ransacked every likely receptacle this morning, including that most inviting cabinet."

Doctor Hailey paused a moment and took a pinch of snuff.

"A second murder performed in the same way as the first and soon after it," he added, "is necessarily an immensely risky business for the murderer. That, I imagine, was why Evans sent me a telegram asking me to meet him here at midday today and behaved as he did. It was a part of his plan that we should be convinced that he had lost his reason, because such a conviction, or so he believed, apparently, would ensure his custody by my profession—supposing that the police rejected his self-accusation of murder, refrained from arresting him—while the second crime which he foresaw with certainty—was being committed. An alibi of that kind might be counted on to disarm even the blackest suspicion."

"But the button?" Biles asked. "I do not see how you connect that with the tragedy."

Doctor Hailey took a second pinch.

"My dear Biles," he said, "the priests of Tso-fu are wont to exercise a strict control over the judgments of their deity. When the button is turned in one direction the spring which releases the knife is held back and the steps of the throne are quite safe. When, on the contrary, it is turned in the opposite way—"

He broke off and raised his huge shoulders.

"Our friend Evans," he added, "naturally kept his infernal machine at 'safe' till the day of vengeance arrived. His only mistake seems to have been that he forgot, or did not know, that fresh gilding is a little apt to rub off when one leans heavily against it."

THE TWO FLAWS

Hal Pink

Hal Pink was the principal writing name of Harry Leigh Pink (1906–73), who is today so little remembered that this little story somehow escaped the eagle eye of Bob Adey and has never been mentioned in any edition of *Locked Room Murders*, although his novel *The Rodeo Mystery* (1941; the problem concerns a death by shooting of someone astride a wildly bucking bronco) is included. I became aware of his work through Jamie Sturgeon, who tracked down a copy of this story, while the main online source of information about his life is the Bear Alley blog.

Pink was born in the "model village" of Port Sunlight in Wirral and the family later moved to Nottingham. He began to write western stories in the 1920s and travelled regularly to the United States and also to Canada, marrying a woman from Toronto. His pseudonyms included Barrington Beverley, H. Carson Marksman, and Charles van Horn. He wrote five detective novels featuring Inspector Docker, but moved to Canada, gave up writing, and became a church minister. Having relocated once again to California, he served as rector of Long Beach Episcopal Church and remained in the state for the rest of his life. "The Two Flaws" dates from 1934 and seems to have been syndicated to a number of newspapers.

"**I**T'S WHAT I CALL AN 'OPEN-AND-SHUT' CASE," SAID CHIEF-Inspector Wenshall.

Superintendent Carson, Wenshall's superior, ignored the remark, and continued to peer intently at the polished surface of the office table.

"Marriott is the killer," went on Wenshall, who liked to hear the sound of his own voice. "See how everything fits in? The constable on patrol in the street outside sees the electric light burning in this office after the usual closing time. He investigates, finds the door locked, peeps through the letter-slot, and sees the dead body of Burgess. The key of the room is on the table. Only one other man except the landlord—and he is in Germany—has a key to the office, and that is Marriott, the dead man's partner. An 'all-stations' call goes out for Marriott. He is arrested at Dover in the act of boarding a ship for France. The tailor in the shop on the ground floor below this office testifies to having heard the two men quarrelling earlier in the day. Marriott admits having quarrelled with Burgess. On a writing pad near the dead man's hand are scrawled the letters 'M-A-R': obviously he was trying to write 'Marriott.' What more do you want?"

He rubbed his hands together. "Open and shut, that's what—"

"If you'd open your eyes and shut your mouth," said Carson, who could be very offensive when irritated, "you might be more use to me. Look here."

He pointed a finger at the surface of the table, where, until a moment ago, the office key had lain. The object of interest was a very tiny fragment of steel embedded in the wood. Carson extricated the sliver of steel from the table, and, wrapping it in paper, stowed it away in a matchbox.

Wenshall sniffed. "I don't know why you are wasting time here. There is still the statement of the tailor to be taken."

"There are a lot of things that you don't know," snapped Carson. They locked the office door behind them and proceeded down the stairs.

The firm of "Burgess and Marriott," the two partners of which earned a meagre living as "Business Transfer Agents," occupied a small office on the fourth floor of a building in Cheapside.

At first glance the murder of Clive Burgess—he had been found sprawled in his chair by the table, a stiletto in his heart—had seemed to be what Chief Inspector Wenshall described as an "open-and-shut" case. Naturally, Marriott protested his innocence. Questioned as to the cause of the quarrel, he stated that Burgess had been idling instead of working, that he was too fond of women's company, and spent little time in assisting his partner, and that on the day of the murder he had dissolved the partnership after heated words on both sides. Pressed as to why he left London, en route for France, after having drawn the bulk of his savings from the bank, he answered that he had friends in Paris, and thought that there might be better business opportunities across the Channel.

Maxwell, the tailor, a thin little man with myopic, bespectacled eyes, and bald head, turned nervously as the detectives entered the shop. He gave his statement quickly. The wash-basins for the use of tenants were on the top floor in a recess opposite the door of the Burgess-Marriott office. He had gone upstairs, after locking the door of his shop, to wash his hands, and it was then that he overheard the quarrel. He returned to his shop, and sometime later saw Marriott emerge by the side door.

"What time did this occur?" interrupted Carson.

"About 4 p.m., I think," was the reply. "It was nearly dusk."

"Did you know the dead man?"

"Intimately," said the little tailor. "He was a customer of mine, poor fellow."

"As you say you knew him intimately, perhaps you can tell me the names of one or two of his lady friends. I want to find out a lot of things about this man's private life," went on Carson.

"Well, to tell you the truth, I never met any of them," said Maxwell. "When I say I knew him intimately, I mean that he was such a good customer to me that I invited him home to dinner once or twice. Personally, I always found him a very charming and companionable man, and I know that Mary—my wife—did so, too."

"Have you reason to believe that Marriott and Burgess quarrelled over anything else besides business?" asked Carson. "A woman, for instance—"

Maxwell shook his head. "I really do not know," he said slowly. "Poor Burgess! A pity Marriott lost his temper and did this dreadful act—"

"You seem very sure of his guilt," said Carson, drily.

"Why, aren't you?" stammered Maxwell, taken aback.

"Maybe—and maybe not," was the non-committal reply, as Carson turned to leave—"I'd like to hear a woman talk about Burgess first."

Three hours later Maxwell paid a visit to Scotland Yard, in response to a polite request from Carson. He was ushered into the superintendent's office. The accused man, haggard and defiant, sat in a corner under guard.

"Ah, come in, Mr. Maxwell," said Carson, genially. "Sorry I had to take you away from business, but there are several points on which you can help us. In your statement this morning you said that the time when you overheard the quarrel would be about four o'clock in the afternoon, nearly dusk."

"That is correct."

"It's a lie—" burst out the angry Marriott. "I admit we had a few words, but it was nearer three o'clock than four."

The little tailor shook his head. "You are mistaken. I know, because it was so dark that I had to put on my shop lights as soon as I returned."

The door opened, and a detective entered.

Carson looked across at him. "You found it?" he said.

The newcomer nodded. "In the box," he said, and handed to him a small plain envelope. Carson slipped it into his pocket.

"You may remember me saying this morning that I would like a woman's opinion on Burgess, Mr. Maxwell," he said casually.

Maxwell nodded.

"I got it," said Carson crisply—"from your wife!"

"My—my wife?" gasped Maxwell.

"I wanted an opinion, and your wife was the only woman who had met him, so far as I knew, so I went to your house and saw her," was the calm reply. "When I told her Burgess had been murdered she fainted."

Maxwell drew in his breath sharply. "Fainted? Do you mean—you don't infer that there was—was anything between my wife and Burgess?"

"I don't infer it. I know there was. She confessed it to me. You did wrong to introduce a handsome young fellow like that into your home, Mr. Maxwell."

"I know," moaned the other, mopping his brow with a handkerchief. "Good God! This is terrible—I never even suspected. But why drag this in? It does not alter the fact Marriott is the one man who could have killed Burgess."

"On the contrary, Marriott did not kill Burgess."

"Then—then who did?"

"You did!" flashed Carson. "And I'll tell you why! You discovered that Burgess had betrayed your trust, had been visiting your home in your absence. You seized the opportunity yesterday, when the quarrel occurred and Marriott left, to accuse Burgess—"

"You can't prove it!" cried Maxwell, white to the lips. "How could I get into a locked room when the only key was on the table?"

"We'll come to that in a moment," said Carson. "There are two flaws in this case against Marriott. One is the conflicting times at which it is stated the quarrel took place. You say 4 p.m., nearly dusk. Marriott says 3 p.m. Marriott is right, because his bank state that he came to them to withdraw his money shortly before closing time— and that is 3:30 p.m. in London. When you went to talk to Burgess his office light was switched on, and you forgot to turn it off before leaving! That is why you wanted to establish the fact that the light could have been on when Marriott was in the office."

The little tailor swayed unsteadily. Carson pushed a chair towards him with his feet, and the other collapsed into it.

"Then we come to the mystery of the locked room and the key on the table. And here we come to the second flaw—the flaw in the needle which you had on your person. Even the best needle manufacturing works turn out a flawed product occasionally, and yours happened to be one of them. Your problem was to prove that you could not possibly have gained access to the room. Your method was highly ingenious, and but for the flaw you might have got away with it."

He produced the envelope and his matchbox from his pocket. From the envelope he drew out a long length of strong black thread, from the end of which dangled a needle broken off short at the point.

"You took the key from the key-ring in the dead man's pocket. You stuck your needle upright in the wood of the table-top, you carried the thread over to the door and through the letter-slot in the door. You cleaned the handle of the stiletto to leave no fingerprints, and came out of the office, bringing the door-key with you. You locked the door, slipped the ring on to the thread, slid it through the letter-slot and down the sloping thread, so that it fell on to the table, with the needle sticking up through the hole in the key-handle. Then you jerked on the thread to release the needle, and it broke at the point, leaving this tiny bit still embedded in the wood. You put the needle into your needle-box in your shop, where a C.I.D. man found it soon after you left to come here."

When they had led the stricken man away Marriott came over to shake Carson's hand.

"One thing puzzles me," he said. "They told me that Burgess left some writing on a pad, and that it spelt 'M-A-R', the first letters of my name. Do you think that he was trying to write my name?"

Carson shook his head. "When a man is dying, and knows it—especially a man like Burgess—if he tries to write at all, it is usually to a woman. Maxwell's wife is named Mary."

MURDER GAME

Christianna Brand

Christianna Brand (1907–88), born Mary Christianna Milne, was a writer who emerged as the Golden Age of detective fiction was coming to an end, but who excelled at writing the sort of ingenious puzzles—often offering multiple possible solutions to the mystery posed—that had been fashionable in the years between the two world wars. Her debut novel, *Death in High Heels* (1941), gave a clear indication of her potential as a crime writer, and she fulfilled her early promise quickly. *Green for Danger* (1944) is a superb whodunit, blending a vivid setting—in a hospital—with sound characterisation and a clever plot. The book was successfully filmed a couple of years after its publication, with Alastair Sim playing Brand's most popular detective, Inspector Cockrill.

Several of Brand's novels have been reprinted in recent years as British Library Crime Classics, and readers' enthusiasm for them underlines the enduring merit of her crime writing. After 1955, however, she did not publish another detective story for more than twenty years, although her three children's books about Nurse Matilda proved popular. In her later years, she returned to the genre with only modest commercial success, although this was partly due to the fact that ingenious mysteries of the kind in which she specialised had fallen out of critical favour. Her short stories are often at least as impressive as her novels. This story first appeared—as "The Gemminy Crickets Case"—in *Ellery Queen's Mystery Magazine* in August 1968 and as "Murder Game" in her collection *What Dread Hand?* in the same year.

T HE OLD MAN WAS SIMPLY DELIGHTED TO MAKE HIS ACQUAINT-
ance. "You're most welcome, my dear boy; not often I see a
fresh face, these days, not one that I like, anyway—and you remind
me a bit of myself when *I* was a lad. You're staying, I hope?" All
about them stretched wide lawns, velvety green in the bright spring
sunshine; over the shining flower-beds, men were working with spud
and hoe. "What brings you here?"

"The Gemminy case," said Giles.

"Yes, well you know, I'm pretty hot on a murder puzzle; I've heard
a lot of confessions in my time." He thought about it. "Gemminy.
The solicitor? The name's familiar but my memory's all to pieces,
these days. A good chap, I seem to recall?" His old mind searched back
over recent months. "I do remember something in the papers, that
brought the name back. Sealed Room Mystery, didn't they call it?"

"He was in his office, bolts drawn inside the door, window
broken—glass still vibrating: but four storeys up. He'd been strangled
and then tied to his chair and then stabbed. The wound so fresh that it
was still bleeding when the police broke in. But nobody in the room."

"Well, my goodness!" He hooked his heavy, veined old hand
into the young man's arm. "Give us a haul up this slope and we'll sit
on a bench under the mulberry tree—not many gardens nowadays
can boast a mulberry, can they?—and you can tell me all about it.
I've forgotten, I forget everything nowadays, so you can start from
scratch." And his bright eyes shone. "Test me!" We'll play a sort of
game of Hunt the Thimble—Hunt the Murderer, if you like. Tell
me the outlines, tell it to me as the police will have got it, clues, bits

of evidence—not necessarily the truth, you know, but as it came to them. Let me work it out and see if I can beat them to it…"

Now that it had come, a sort of horror grew in Giles' mind, a sort of sickness at the thought of going over it all yet again, of dragging Helen's name again through the blood and the terror and the doubt. But they had said to talk about it as much as he could, to get it out of his system, to try to forget. Try to forget me, Helen had said, try to forget… And so…

And so they came to the bench; Giles Carberry sat with the old man there and told him the story of the Gemminy case.

Old Gemminy's office: a bare, square room, not very large. Strong, heavy door. Opposite the door, the single window—one large pane of glass, the glass broken to form a jagged hole, perhaps two feet in diameter. A little broken glass on the floor beneath the sill; much more in the deserted warehouse yard below. As Giles had said, the window four storeys up.

And at the desk, between window and door, Thomas Gemminy, solicitor dealing largely in criminal matters; seventy years old. Tied to the chair with a length of cord torn from the blind, tipped sideways, half asprawl across the paper-strewn desk, staring with empurpled face towards the door; his own silk handkerchief twisted about his neck and, for good measure, a knife thrust between the shoulder-blades; only a little blood, but the wound still oozing. The paper knife, which had always lain on his desk, not there.

And at the door, as the police came pounding up the stairs, Rupert Chester hammering, double-fisted, shouting out that there was smoke coming from under the door, that Uncle Gem wouldn't answer…

"Rupert Chester?"

"Rupert was one of his wards. We were all his wards—he constituted himself guardian to all sorts of children he came across with—well, with unhappy backgrounds. You must remember that? Anyway, I'll tell you later. But Rupert was one of them."

"All right, well…" The old man considered it, forming the picture in his mind's eye. "The general scene? The buildings opposite?"

Giles Carberry drew angles on the gravelled path. "This is the office block; big old house, actually—we took up the whole top floor of it. Stairs, no lift. No one else working there of course on a Saturday afternoon—and the day of the World Cup Final, what's more. Street here. These are Rupert's rooms and mine, looking across the street to the police station opposite. Uncle Gem's the end room, the corner room; only one window and that overlooked the warehouse yard, at right angles to the street."

"Narrow yard?"

"Yes, but don't start on rope bridges and pulleys and things from the opposite roof; or ledges or painters' cradles and the rest of the gimmicks. They've all been considered and counted out."

"Don't tell me, don't tell me," said the old man like a child playing a game.

"Well, but these are facts, not evidence which might or might not be true. And the fact is that no one could have got out of the jagged hole in that window, fifty feet up."

"All right. Well?" He twiddled his gnarled old thumbs. "This Rupert Chester? Another of old Gemminy's wards, you say?"

"Wards, adopted children, whatever you like to call us. His 'Crickets'. Rupert and me and Helen; and lots more of us, of course…"

A *good* chap, the old man had said; and so indeed he had been, Thomas Gemminy—good, kind and compassionate. Thrown by his work a great deal among criminals, his heart had bled for innocent families, left to the mercy of an undiscriminating world. Financial help, help in finding new jobs, new homes, often even new lives far

away from England where the past would not catch up on you...
"We used to think that the ones he encouraged to emigrate were the
ones with really dangerous pasts," said Giles. "But of course we never
knew; none of us ever knew about the others, he said it would not
have been fair." While his wife had lived, his own home, even, had
been open to pitiful children, often too young to know, themselves,
what their parentage had been. The Gemminy Crickets, he called
them: one of his foolish, gentle jokes. There was a Gemminy Crickets
Trust, to which all those who had passed through his hands might
turn for help in time of need; his will left everything to the trust.
("So no clues there; you can leave money out of it.") He had been
to great lengths to cover their tracks, even from themselves; (not
with Giles, however—Giles had been old enough to remember that
night, the night his mother and father had been hacked to death by
the madman with an axe—it was not only the children of criminals,
Thomas Gemminy befriended: there had been the victims too.)

Of them all, in his old age three had been most close to him—
Giles, Rupert, Helen: Giles and Rupert because they had qualified
and gone into partnership with him, and Helen, his pet, his darling,
last to be adopted in his own home before his wife had died: Helen
with her great eyes looking out so bravely from beneath the cloud
of her soft, dark hair...

"His Talking Orchid he used to call her," said Giles. "But she's
very tough, really. Spent all her life with us boys doing everything
we did, and most things better..." The smile died out of his eyes.
"All that emerged at the trial."

"Don't tell me, don't tell me," said the old man again. "Let me
guess." He eyed the young man shrewdly. "You were in love with her?"

There came upon him the sickness, the stab of sickness and pain
that came whenever he thought too closely about Helen; but he said,
keeping his tone light: "What do you think?"

"And Rupert?"

"Rupert too."

"Which did she favour?"

Rupert, gay, sweet-tempered Rupert with his smiling blue eyes and his heavy, curling auburn hair, so ruthlessly brushed flat only to come curling up again... Himself, dark, slender, serious, who could yet be so full of jokes and laughter... "One day it was one of us, one day the other; she just made hay with us. And then when this third party came along—"

"Oh, there was a third party then? Not just between you three?—the murder I mean, of course. Suspects one, two, three and four: you and Rupert and Helen and—A.N. Other?" The old man rose, hoisting himself forward with a jerk of his heavy arms and shoulders. "Let's walk a little; it's chilly sitting still. And wasn't there something about a policeman murdered too? Old Gemminy rang up the police station with some message?—and later a policeman also rang up?"

Thomas Gemminy in his "sealed room", dying—ringing up the police station across the street with that wild, mad, urgent summons—something about something or somebody "vanishing into thin air", something about the window, and then on a note of sheer, squealing terror, something about "the long arms..." And an hour later Police Constable Cross, supposed to be pounding his unsensational beat a couple of miles away, ringing up also, with crazy gabblings, "Got me by the throat..." and something about the window and something about vanishing into thin air and something, on a suddenly rising note of terror about "the long arms..." A 'phone box had been traced at last with a pane of glass broken; and a hundred yards away, submerged in a tank of water in a half-demolished old factory, his body—bound and strangled; and stabbed in the back with the missing paper-knife from Mr. Gemminy's office...

"He came from the same police station?"

The only police station in that small country town—just across
the street from the office, where they had all been known so well:
Thomas Gemminy and his two young men, in and out every other
day pleading, arguing, deliberating, fighting, on behalf of their dubi-
ous clientèle. There had been half a dozen of the lads getting their tea
when the first message had come through—down in the basement
canteen, from whose windows they could actually see the windows
of Gemminy's offices, five storeys above. They'd all dropped everything the minute the name of Gemminy was mentioned and, hardly
waiting for permission let alone orders, caught up their helmets and
gone dashing across the street. "So it couldn't have been two minutes
from the time he rang—"

"What exactly did he say?"

"I've told you. That he was dying. That someone or something,
the operator couldn't make sense out of it, had strangled him; that
the desk was on fire, he must have help quick. And then this thing
about 'through the window' and then about 'vanishing into thin air'.
The operator kept trying to interrupt him, trying to get the name
and address and at last he choked out the name Gemminy and then
there was this dreadful scream about 'the long arms'. As I say, within
a couple of minutes a sergeant and at least five of the boys were
trying to break down the door."

But Rupert had been already there, beating at it with a closed
fist, barging at it with a bruising shoulder, yelling "Uncle Gem!
Uncle Gem!" The sergeant had told off a man to stand at the head
of the stairs and watch for anyone escaping and then with the rest
had launched himself against the door. Rupert had yelled at last:
"It must be bolted. There's bolts top and bottom." And a panel was
stove in and an arm thrust through and up and a panel kicked in and
an arm thrust through and down; and as they stood back for one
more concerted effort against the stout lock still holding—into the

momentary silence there came from within the room, thin and clear and eerily tinkling, the sound of breaking glass.

And the door gave at last and burst inwards and suddenly the smoke-filled room was a flurry of blue-uniformed arms and legs; and there was nobody there, not a living soul.

Not a living soul. A dead man, only: strangled, staring at them across the burning desk, the wound in his back still oozing blood, and the jagged edges of the broken window pane behind him still vibrant, as though someone had that moment gone diving through.

But the hole was two feet in diameter and the window fifty feet up.

Rupert Chester and a couple of the men rushed over to the body, the sergeant with another made a dash for the window. Nothing moving, not a sign of life in the yard below—a warehouse yard, used for deliveries, swept clean, a shell, an empty space enclosed by blank walls and a high barricaded gate. "Watch," said the sergeant to the man, "don't take your eyes off it." But he knew there would be nothing to see and already a sort of dread was forming in him, a dread and a confusion. In the centre of the room all was pandemonium as, coughing and choking in the smoke belched out from the burning desk, men beat at the flaming papers; and out of the confusion, Rupert Chester's voice cried, sharp and high: "For God's sake!—look at this! It's Helen—she's in danger. I must go."

And he was gone. "Shall I go after him?" yelled one of the men, but, "No, no," the sergeant yelled back, "leave him, get on with the job." There was too much to do, no one could be spared; and after all, Rupert Chester was known to them, it wasn't like a suspect disappearing, unidentifiable. And besides—there he'd been outside the locked and bolted door, trying to get *in*. And the smoke was getting thicker, a man was calling out that the body was beginning to scorch, a voice cried, "For God's sake, aren't there any extinguishers?", a voice cried,

"I'll go for the fire brigade…" What was one to do?—move the body with all its tell-tale clues or risk the whole lot being consumed by the fire? He fought his way over to the flaming desk, looked briefly at the old man's body, trying to take in the whole scene and impress it on his memory; ordered, "Yes, move him, chair and all, carry him outside." No time to worry about Rupert Chester now; and if there really were some danger to Helen Crane, at least someone was coping with it. And anyway, thank God!—here was the fire brigade.

"Was the room badly burnt?"

"Most of the woodwork," said Giles. "The furniture and the door itself and so on; and papers, of course, there was masses of paper in the room. Not much left in the way of clues, once the hoses had soused it all. And of course no sign of the note."

"What note?"

"The note that had made Rupert shoot off to look for Helen. He said it was on a scribbling pad; huge letters, scrawled—HELEN—DANGER—some such thing."

"Did anyone else see it?"

"He said he'd shown it to one of the men; but they all deny having seen it."

"That was predictable," said the old man dryly.

Giles did a double take. "You mean you're *there*?"

"What's 'there'? I'm in a dozen places. If you mean do I see how it could have been done—"

"You haven't heard yet about the dead policeman."

"I don't see how he complicates things. We now have all our suspects—all of them," said the old man with a significant wink, "outside the locked room and free to be running around murdering policemen or doing anything else. Still, tell me about him."

"He was killed about five o'clock. Uncle Gem's call came through to the station at near enough three minutes to four; at five the policeman rang up. And saying almost the same words, that's what made it so uncanny—about the long arms and something vanishing into thin air. First he said 'George?'—that was the chap on the switchboard—'this is Dinkum.' Dinkum was his nickname at the station—and he gave his number and was just saying where he was calling from when he seemed to be disturbed and there came this frightful shouting, again about somebody strangling him, just like Uncle Gem, and the word 'window' and 'vanished into thin air'—and then a sort of gurgling scream and the operator could just make out the words 'the long arms...' And as I told you, they finally found a call box with a broken window pane and they searched around there and the body was in a half-demolished factory, a hundred yards away."

They came to the end of the gravelled path and turned back. "The murderer seems to have been very fortunate in the privacy of his arrangements."

"Well, but they *were* arrangements, weren't they? And what arrangements! Saturday afternoon and the final of the World Cup: every soul in the place glued to the telly—and for good measure a wet, blustery day: gorgeous weather over most of the country, but with us a wet, blustery day."

They came to the bench and sat down again; the old man tired easily. From below came the whirr of a motor-mower, the lawn was striped in paler and darker green as the grass bent beneath the cropping blades. But the old man's mind was in a sealed room, locked and bolted, where glass broke, a dying man was stabbed—and yet where no living man could have been; in a 'phone box where a country-town policeman choked and yammered and presumably within a few moments, also died. "Any actual tie between the two deaths?"

"The same words spoken—'into thin air' and this terrifying thing about 'the long arms'. And it was the knife from Uncle Gem's office; and traces of his blood group were mingled with the man's own.

It was all a good bit diluted with the water—he'd been heaved into this sort of half-destroyed tipped-up water tank. Tied up with some wire rope which had been lying about there."

"I see. All right. Well, those are the facts," said the old man, rubbing his hands. "So then, let's have the alibis."

"Rupert's and Helen's and mine—?"

"And A.N. Other's. We mustn't forget Helen's third suitor. I am assuming," said the old man, "that if money was out of it, the motive was something to do with Helen?"

And they were back to Helen. But he had to go through with it now. "That was the conclusion the police came to at this stage," said Giles.

"Yes, well we want to play it from the police angle. But first— what authority had Mr. Gemminy over Helen? With regard to her marrying, I mean. Could he prevent it?"

"Not legally, probably, if that's what you mean. But he could advise; and his advice was based upon knowledge of the past. He could prevent it by—well, warnings; to her, to us, to other people. He knew our life histories, our heredities…"

"Sufficient motive certainly, for silencing him. More potent, in fact, than actual authority."

"Somebody thought so," said Giles, grimly assenting.

"Very well. Let's move on now to what actually happened, the order of events." Like a child, excited and eager, he wriggled himself heavily into a more comfortable sitting position on the bench. "True or false—as the police got them. Leave me to do the sorting out. *They* had to."

In a way, the ball had started with P.C. Cross: finishing his dinner in the canteen, pedalling off to his beat, not remarked again until the telephone call at five o'clock; his body found an hour or so later in the disused factory.

"The next exact time we know is when I went to the office to see Uncle Gemminy…"

Mr. Gemminy had stayed on there because he wanted to talk to them—to Giles and Rupert: but separately. "I was to go at half past two, Rupert at four. He didn't want to talk at home because Helen might be there—she still lived with him. Rupert and I shared a flat in a block about fifteen minutes' drive from the office. Anyway, the thing was that this third party had turned up and the old man didn't like it. Who the chap was we didn't then know but I think *he* knew, or he'd guessed, and he wasn't too pleased. He thought she'd had her head turned, he thought she didn't know her own mind; and anyway he would secretly have liked it to be Rupert or me, he wanted to keep it in the family. Anyway, his idea was to sort it out first with us two and find out how each felt about her before he did any more. But nothing terrific you know—just a family discussion."

"All right. So at half past two you went along?"

"M'm. Leaving Rupert at the flat. We had a very affable chat, the old man and I, I told him my side of the thing—"

"He didn't tell you the identity of A.N. Other?"

"No, he didn't," said Giles.

"Well, never mind; that we can easily enough deduce. And so—?"

"And so at half past three I came away and he was safe and sound then. And don't say he wasn't," said Giles, "because he was. He rang up Rupert after I'd left—and it wasn't till four o'clock that he rang the police."

"Yes. Well?"

"Well, I drove home. I parked the car and just as I came round the corner to the front door of the flats, I saw Rupert come running down the steps, hatless and carrying his mac. in spite of the rain, as though he'd just snatched it up all anyhow—and he scrambled into his car and went shooting off."

"Why in such a hurry? His appointment wasn't till four?"

"Because, so he says, Uncle Gem had just rung him up—"

"The exact words, please."

"Well, he said first, 'Haven't you started?' and Rupert said 'I was just leaving; isn't Giles still with you?' and Uncle Gem said, 'No, he went at half past,' and he was just saying something about 'a very good talk' or something like that when he suddenly broke off and said, 'There it is again. I don't like it, Rupert. There seems to be something funny happening outside the window.'"

"Fifty feet up?"

"Well, that's what he said; and then he said, 'Do come quickly, Rupert, there's something wrong.' So naturally Rupert whizzed off not even taking time to put on his mac."

"Or to ring the police station first?—just across the road from your uncle."

"Well, I don't think one would, do you?" said Giles. "He says it just never entered his head."

The old man thought it over. He said dryly: "All very convenient for *you*, dear boy? Because if you were seeing Rupert outside your flats, you weren't back at the office, fifteen minutes' drive away, murdering your uncle—were you?"

"*If* I was seeing Rupert," said Giles. "The police thought of that one, too—don't worry! They thought I might have noted earlier where his car was parked, deduced that he'd have run out—he always does everything at the double. Faked up the alibi, in fact. But there was the macintosh."

"You could hardly have guessed that on such a day he wouldn't be wearing it. I think it does let you out."

"And Rupert. Because if I saw him outside the flats, he couldn't have been back at the office a couple of miles away, murdering Uncle Gem, either."

"Your uncle didn't die until after Rupert could have had time to arrive there."

"Yes, but things had already started. He said so to Rupert."

"We have only Rupert's word for that," said the old man. He changed his tack. "And meanwhile—Helen?"

"Helen was out of it," said Giles quickly. "She was up on the heath, walking—and the heath's fifteen miles away."

"What, the whole afternoon? On a wet, blustery day?"

"She does it to keep fit. She does film work—stunt stuff, really, in a mild sort of way: the stand-ins, riding and diving and skiing and shooting, all that lot. I told you we boys brought her up tough."

"Lots of people saw her on the heath, I dare say?"

"You said it yourself—who else would be up there on such a day?"

"Then who says she was there?"

"I say so. I'd arranged to meet her there."

"And did you?"

"No," said Giles. "But that was my fault. I mucked up the arrangements. The heath's a huge place. I said to go on and I'd meet her—well, after I'd left Uncle Gem, but I couldn't tell her that, she didn't know I was seeing him. I just said about half past four by the Bell, which is a pub. But she thought I said at the Dell, which is a place where we sometimes picnic. They do sound the same if you mumble."

"And did you mumble?"

"Yes, because I didn't want Rupert to hear. The fact is, I thought I'd get in first, after seeing Uncle Gem. All's fair?" said Giles with a faintly self-deprecatory air.

"All right. A quarter to four. Helen's up on the heath, without an alibi; you and Rupert alibi one another outside your flats. What's your story next?"

"My story, as you so flatteringly call it, is that I went in, made myself a cup of char—as I hadn't said I'd meet her till half past; and

I'd left Uncle Gem a bit early—and then drove up to the Bell. And Rupert's story is that he couldn't get into Uncle Gem's office and was hammering at the door when the police arrived and broke it open. He went in with them and then he saw this note on the desk and he was so shaken by the murder and this on top of it that he never stopped to think but just rushed off to look for Helen. She wasn't at home, he rang round frantically to a few friends, nothing doing there; so he got into the car again and drove about just stupidly searching in places where he thought she might be—"

"Did the places where he thought she might be happen to take him near the scene of the policeman's murder?"

"It's all within a smallish area," said Giles, briefly. "A couple of miles or so. Except of course for the heath and that's where she was, half an hour's drive away from any of it. Rupert went out there eventually, knowing she often walked there at the weekend. But as I say it's a huge place and in the end we all missed one another."

"So at the time of the policeman's killing—about five you said?— Helen and Rupert have in fact no alibis? And you?"

"I'm afraid you will find this very convenient too," said Giles. "But yes, I have one for this time also. I waited for Helen for about twenty minutes and then I thought she might have decided not to come, it being such a filthy day; so I rang up the house to ask. The housekeeper will tell you so."

"You could have done that from anywhere."

"Well, I'm sorry to disappoint you, but I did it from the call box outside the Bell. And I can prove it because I could see the people inside all crowded round the television—the pub was closed, but we know the people, we often go there; and I knocked on the window and made signs asking the score and they signalled back that extra time was being played, so I knew it was all square; and we all made praying signals through the glass…"

"Well, I must say that sounds pretty conclusive."

"The police thought so too," said Giles; dry in his turn.

"So that leaves Rupert and Helen."

"And your dear friend A.N. Other. And perhaps you'll explain to me," said Giles, "not so much which of them killed Uncle Gemminy as how any of them *could* have. The door locked—the key was in the debris of the burnt-out desk, by the way—and bolted from the inside. The window was fifty feet up and a child couldn't have got through the hole in the glass. Yet it had just that moment been broken and Uncle Gem had that minute been stabbed. So before we have accusations—I think there should be explanations."

The old man shrugged huge shoulders up to the thick lobes of his ears. "Oh, well, as to that there are probably half a dozen. I can think of three, straight off—one for each of them: One for Rupert, one for Helen, one for my dear friend, as you call him, A.N. Other..."

Giles reacted immediately. "Why should Helen do such a thing? You agree that this crime was committed *because* of her."

"If it was," said the old man, "who more interested than herself?" He brushed aside interruptions. "Thomas Gemminy was discussing the marriage of this precious ewe lamb of his. He knew all the past histories, the heredities—he could tell what might for ever put an end to any idea of marriage between Helen and—somebody. So—somebody silenced him. Somebody set fire to the desk where dangerous documents might be kept; and silenced him."

"All right—so you say. But I say—how?"

The old man was silent, sitting deep in thought, the sunshine beating down through the leafless branches of the mulberry tree, dappling his big bald head with light and shadow. Giles prompted at last, trailing a red herring across that other name: "Take Rupert—"

He seemed to come awake. "All right, very well: take Rupert! Rupert pretends a telephone call to give him an excuse to hurry off and get there early; or perhaps even actually gets one, telling him simply that you've left and he may as well come along now—but either way is sure that you are out of the way. He strangles the old man, ties him to the chair, conceals the knife about himself somewhere and comes out, locking the door behind him. When the police arrive, he's pounding on it. He suggests that it's bolted on the inside and when the panel's broken, is the first to thrust through his arm and pretend to draw back the bolts: which in fact, of course, never were shot at all. The lock gives way, they all tumble in and he goes with them. Chucks the key into the fire raging round the desk; and that's all there is to it." He asked as a child asks, playing Hunt the Thimble: "Am I getting warm?"

"Not frightfully," said Giles. "What about the stabbing, for example?"

"The oldest trick in the crime thrillers, boy. Bends over the body pretending to be frantic with anxiety, jabs in the knife. So recently dead, there'd still be a little ooze of blood."

"All this in front of half a dozen policemen?"

"In a crowded room filled with smoke; everyone excited and milling about…"

Giles clutched at a straw. "But the window! They heard the glass being shattered just as they were actually breaking in."

"They heard glass being shattered," said the old man. "Which is rather a different thing."

"The broken pane was still quivering."

He shrugged again. "Something thrown while Rupert's hand was through the panel—a piece of the panel itself, perhaps; it would be burnt up afterwards in the fire. Or the window broken in advance and a piece of the glass kept back for just this purpose—there was a little inside the window-sill, wasn't there? Threw it while his hand was through the broken panel, out of sight; and a lucky shot hit the broken pane and started it vibrating again. But all that was needed was the sound."

"Good God!" said Giles. He could not help a grudging admiration. "You certainly have it all worked out."

"You said it couldn't be done. I'm only telling you one of half a dozen ways in which it could. This is the way it could have been done by Rupert."

"Well, all right then—Rupert. What about the note?"

"No note, of course. An excuse to get himself out of the room."

"Why?" said Giles.

"Ah, why? To deal with the policeman? The policeman, on his beat, had seen something, perhaps?"

Giles' scepticism began to revive a little. "Seen what? There was nothing to be seen. Rupert got there a bit early—so what? He makes no secret of it, he's accounted for it anyway by saying that Uncle Gem 'phoned him. He had no reason to kill the policeman."

"I agree," said the old man, calmly. "And if he didn't then no doubt he also didn't kill Mr. Gemminy."

"You don't believe this about Rupert at all?"

"I told you—this is one way it could have been done—by Rupert."

"But then if he's out—well, there really was a note saying that Helen was in danger."

"I dare say there was," said the old man.

"But Helen wasn't in danger."

"I dare say she wasn't," said the old man.

"Then—who put the note there about Helen?"

"Helen put it there," said the old man.

A tough girl. A girl trained to ride and climb, to shoot straight, to throw straight—a girl beating boys at their own games. A girl in love, whose guardian disapproved of her romance and had the power to end it for ever—he who knew the secrets of so many pasts. A girl

with half an hour to work in, between one interview and the next…
"Am I getting warm?"

That cold shudder again, that sickness at the heart, when Helen's
name was dragged forward into the ugly light. "Of course not,"
said Giles. "It's all nonsense. How could she have done it? She was
nowhere near when the door was broken down. And in that case the
bolts really were drawn, inside."

"Oh, well—bits of string passed under the door, you know—all
that lark. The door was destroyed by fire and the bits of string with
it. One good reason why the fire was ever started at all."

"But the knife wound! The broken glass!"

"The glass was broken in advance, of course—a hole two feet in
diameter. And the victim, dying or dead, tied to his chair—with his back
to that hole in the glass. For the rest—a warehouse roof opposite: a
narrow yard. She could throw straight, couldn't she?—a knife no doubt,
as well as anything else. As to the breaking glass—why assume that the
glass was broken, at the time they heard it breaking, from the inside?
After all, there was some as we've just seen, inside the sill. She'd be
pretty handy with a catapult, I dare say? You boys will have seen to that."

"Why should she have done it? Why should she do such a thing?
Why all this—mystification?"

"To mystify. To make it all happen when she was supposed to
be nowhere near." He looked into the young man's white face curiously. "It's only a game," he said. "We're only playing a game. But
you don't like even to hear it said."

"I've heard it said several times already," said Giles, "when it was
not a game. The police are not fools, you know, either. Only—not
being fools—they asked themselves two further questions. Why
leave the note—?"

"To make Rupert do just what he did. Run out and leave himself
without an alibi for the time the policeman was killed."

"—and so that brings us again to: why kill the policeman, anyway?"

"The policeman came from the station just across the road from the office. As he pedalled off to his beat—may he not have glanced up and seen—a boy on the roof of the warehouse with a catapult...? But when the news of the murder broke—then he'd have put two and two together, wouldn't he? So she had to shut his mouth. She'd recognise him? Like the rest of you, she'd know all the chaps at the station, at any rate by sight?"

"Yes, we all knew him. And by the same token," said Giles, "a strapping great chap he was. So how—?"

"You told me she was a tough girl," said the old man.

"Tough enough to drag him, dead or dying, to that place a hundred yards away from the call box, heave him into that tank...?"

"That has to be accounted for," acknowledged the old man with an odd glance.

"And the knife—if she'd thrown the knife, it would still have been in the wound when the police broke in. She wasn't in the room, to take it away. You'll hardly suggest, I suppose," said Giles, heavily sarcastic, "that she yanked it back with a piece of string? Or some sort of boomerang knife, perhaps...?" He relaxed against the hard back of the bench with an absurd relief. "You old devil!—you never really believed she killed Uncle Gem."

Bright eyes, alight with mockery: not very kindly mockery. "No. Not that."

"And so—we come to A.N. Other?"

"And the boomerang?"

"Boomerang—what boomerang? What I said just now—a boomerang knife? I was only joking."

"Not a boomerang knife, no. Just any old boomerang." He left it at that; sat for a long time, thinking. "We have at this stage, I take

it, all the information the police had to work on. True or false. So…
So I put myself in the position of the police; and I think what I do
is to ask myself what are the most important questions. And I think
I reply to myself as follows: First—why was the policeman killed?
And secondly—why was he killed in the way he was?—why were
both men killed in such a way?—strangled, tied up and then, dying
or already dead, stabbed in the back. And thirdly, why did both ring
up with this strange phrase about something vanishing into thin
air?—and what was meant by the horrible screaming about the long
arms? And fourthly—why, when Rupert says that he showed the note
to somebody, does everybody deny having seen it? And fifthly and
sixthly and seventhly and for ever ad infinitum, the most important
question of all: in that room that afternoon—dead man locked in,
wound still bleeding, window just broken, desk in flames and all the
rest of it—why did someone call out that he was going for the fire
brigade?" And he asked again, like a child playing a drawing-room
game: "Am I getting warm?"

"Very warm now," said Giles. "Very warm."

"The call to the police station said that the room was on fire.
Surely to goodness, while the men rushed across the street to the
rescue, they could leave it to the remaining staff to follow the obvious routine and send for the fire brigade?"

"Fire or no fire," said Giles, "if you get any hotter you'll burn
yourself."

"And P.C. Cross had not been seen since he'd left after his midday
dinner and gone off to his beat?"

"Scorching," said Giles.

"Which brings us back to the boomerang, you see."

"I don't know what you mean by this boomerang."

"Only that it's an Australian word; and when you used it a
moment ago, it made me think. Because 'dinkum' is an Australian

word too, isn't it? And that was the policeman's nickname, wasn't it? Dinkum Cross."

We used to think that the ones he encouraged to emigrate were the ones with really dangerous pasts.

A child with a bad background, sent away for his own safety and peace of mind. Returning in manhood, under the wing of the kindly old guardian, joining the police force with his help and encouragement—a Gemminy Cricket like the rest of them, unacknowledged as such only lest the past should catch up on him still. Through his work coming in contact with his brother Crickets; getting to know Helen, his sister Cricket: falling in love. His heredity such that their guardian would never permit a marriage between them.

"Helen, of course, would have told him all about the arrangements for that afternoon; she could hardly have been so incurious as you men all seemed so innocently to suppose, when it was her business you were going to discuss. From the corner of the warehouse yard, he watched you come and saw you leave. Mr. Gemminy observed him there, rang up Rupert and told him to hurry, there'd been something rather odd going on under the window—"

"He could have rung across to the police."

"But he had this young man's secrets still to respect."

"Yes," agreed Giles. "That would have been in character. So?"

"So he rang Rupert. And in the middle of the conversation the murderer came into the office." He broke off. "Still hot?"

"Very hot; but also very cold," said Giles.

"Still, let's go on through with it. He must work fast—our murderer—because he hasn't as much time as he'd hoped, Rupert's been warned, he's on his way. He strangles the old man, stabs him for good measure, sets the desk alight, smashes the hole in the window to create a draught and fan the flames. And it's done: his secrets are burnt to ashes, the only one in the world who was aware that they even existed is dead. No one knows who he is, not even Helen will connect him with Thomas Gemminy, let alone with his murder. He closes the door and is starting to hurry off down the stairs when he hears—?"

"He hears Rupert arriving, I suppose," said Giles. "It's too late to escape that way; and there's no other."

"What would he do?" said the old man. He thought that one over too. unhurriedly. "I think he would dodge into the nearest room—would that be your office? Oh, Rupert's, well it makes no difference—he'd dodge in there, meaning to wait until Rupert was inside the smoke-filled room trying to cope with what he found there—and then slip out and away down the stairs before he called the police. But—"

"But?"

"But he'd locked the door. An automatic gesture, a symbolical gesture, closing the door upon the terrible past and the terrible thing he'd done to conceal it. He'd locked the door of the murder room, simply not thinking: and Rupert couldn't get in."

"And he was a few feet away in Rupert's room—and couldn't get out?"

"Until—?"

"Until a whole lot of men in blue uniform just like himself came pounding up the stairs and started banging at the locked door. Who was to notice in that confined space on the landing, with smoke already belching out from under the door, that they had been joined by another of themselves, all barging, heads down, one, two, three, all together now! against the door. And someone says something about bolts and he thinks very quickly; and stoves in the panel and thrusts in his arm and pretends to draw them back. But surely," said Giles, "he wouldn't really have gone unrecognised?"

"The room was on fire, filling with dense smoke; doubtless no one would notice if you kept a handkerchief up to your face—probably they all were doing it. Voices were choking and unrecognisable— voices saying something about fire extinguishers, something about going for the fire brigade…"

"So as to get out of the room?"

"There you have it, boy. And how clever after all! Not a suspect escaping, you see, but just one of themselves, shouting to the man at the top of the stairs that he'd been sent—and something about the fire brigade. He'd tried a better way; while he waited in the other room, he'd scrawled the note about Helen, hoping to be allowed to go after Rupert when Rupert, predictably, dashed off. But that one didn't wash so he had to fall back on the fire brigade. For improvisation, it wasn't too bad." He humphed and smiled. "Hot?"

"In parts," said Giles. "One small point, however, strikes a little chill. What about Uncle Gem's 'phone call to the police? What about these strange remarks—vanishing into thin air, the long arms…"

"Your Uncle Gemminy's—? But my dear fellow, good heavens! you haven't got the point at all. You don't suppose…?" He broke off rubbing his thick hands together with a self-satisfied chuckle. "Just put yourself into the picture, boy! Rupert beating on the door. Murderer crouching in a room a few feet away: in Rupert's own room. And very soon indeed, what is Rupert going to do? He's going to stop panicking, dear boy, he's going to use his loaf—he's going to come to his own room and telephone to the station just across the way. Only one thing will prevent him—and that is the arrival of the police, before he calls them. So… From the window, the murderer can see down into the canteen—half a dozen chaps there who will, as he knows from his own experience, leap up and come dashing to the scene of an emergency call—if it's urgent enough. So—the gasping and the choking—to disguise the voice—the mystification of a lot of nonsense about long arms and thin air. And duly—over they come; and in due course also, as we've seen—off he goes!"

"To a telephone booth where he binds and gags himself, rings up the police with a message almost identical with the earlier one and then moves on to a convenient hiding place and there quietly murders himself?"

"Murder?" said the old man. "Would you call it murder?" And he turned his big frame so that he stared directly into the tense, white face. "I thought you would be more likely to regard it as—an execution."

Giles sat up very straight. "Are you suggesting that I—?"

"You were up on the heath, dear boy; you have your alibi and there's no breaking that, if people actually confirm having seen you there."

"Rupert then—?"

"But could Rupert have known who had murdered your guardian?"

"Nobody could have known at that stage," said Giles. "No one even knew that Uncle Gem had been killed, except for the police—and of course the murderer. How could somebody kill the murderer, by way of revenge, when nobody else knew there had even been a murder?"

"Perhaps the murderer himself told somebody?"

"Told who? He'd hardly have come to Rupert or me—"

"No," said the old man. "So who *would* he have gone to?"

"Dear God!—you mean he told Helen?"

"Need he actually have told her? But... You see, may he not well have had an assignation with Helen for that afternoon—that important afternoon when their joint future was being discussed. She has a date with you, but she'll ditch that, pretend she confused the meeting place. And... Well, she is waiting for him somewhere near that telephone booth. Something shows in his face perhaps; or in his manner; and we know there was blood on his uniform—traces were found despite his having been in the water."

"The blood was from the knife. Why should he have brought away the knife?"

"To defend himself, perhaps? Maybe Rupert had a lucky escape not actually meeting him on the stairs. Or maybe he was frightened of leaving fingerprints—we know he was hurried, he had less time than he'd bargained for—Mr. Gemminy would have warned him, very likely, that Rupert was on his way. The old man wouldn't die quick enough, perhaps, so he snatched up the knife—that would explain why two methods were used. But then—had he been careful enough about prints? if they're found on the knife, that's the end of him. So he plucks it out of the wound, wraps it round with something, conceals it under his uniform jacket..."

"And Helen?"

"Helen goes close up to him to embrace him—feels the hard ridge of the knife against his chest... Or he drops it, perhaps—he'll have been pretty nervous, no doubt. At any rate she deduces what has happened—gets it away from him and in her rage and agony about her uncle, strikes out at him—"

"The man was strangled," said Giles, white-lipped.

"Are they sure which happened first?—after the immersion in the tank, I dare say it wasn't easy to be certain. Anyone can stab a man in the back; and once he was weakened by the knife wound, it wouldn't be too hard for a strong young woman to finish him off. And that might explain how she got him to the final hiding place—dragged him along, still alive but stupefied by pain and weakness, tied him up when she got him there and once he was totally helpless—"

"Dear God!" said Giles. He fought against it, the very thought was revolting. "The telephone call—"

"At the knife point? Perhaps he'd told her how he'd tricked the police with the faked call from Gemminy's office, perhaps he'd confessed it all—freely or at the knife point, as I say. So she forced him to do the thing again, use the same phrases, carry on the mystery, the strangeness, the hint of some horrible magic that he'd already begun when he'd impersonated Mr. Gemminy." He looked suddenly, keenly, into the white sick face. "My dear boy—it's still only a game, isn't it? Or if it's the truth, you surely can't go on caring for such a girl? Yet you can't even bear to have her name mentioned in such a connection."

"You could hardly expect it," said Giles. "I've been in love with her all my life. To ask me to accept…" His mind was sick, swooning with the horror of the thought of it. "That even for revenge, even in a red hot rage she could do such a thing—"

"Better, all the same than doing it dispassionately; not in grief or anger but deliberately, in cold blood?" And he asked: "What, after all, did you know about this girl? What if it was really a case, not of what Mr. Gemminy could tell Helen about her lover, but what he could tell the lover about *her*?"

The sun was going down, it was growing a little chilly. "Let's walk up and down just one more turn and then we'll go in and have tea." And he got up, seized Giles by the arm and walked with him again along the sanded path. "This young policeman—his past can't after all have been so very bad? He'd been brought back to this country, encouraged by your uncle to join the police force; or only permitted, but at any rate your uncle knew all about it. Would the old man have been so rigidly, so positively against the marriage, if there hadn't been something on the other side also? Or perhaps it was *only* on Helen's side that the bad heredity lay? Perhaps he knew that she should not marry at all?"

"She's as good as gold," said Giles. "As good as gold."

"But we're speaking not of *her* sins but of the sins of her fore-fathers." Giles jerked away his arm but the old man caught at it again, and held him fast. "Supposing Helen was not in love with the policeman at all? Supposing it was one of you two, yourself or Rupert?—she was just teasing you, making you both jealous, play-ing hard to get. But Mr. Gemminy doesn't know that. He sees the young man below the window, watching, wondering what's being said up there about him—and Helen. He calls him up—and tells him for his own sake as well as for Helen's, that two such heredities shouldn't mix. So the young man—predisposed, you see, by his own bad heredity—kills him. And coming to her with the blood of her belovèd guardian still fresh on his hands, reveals that he now knows secrets of her own past—and if she will not 'consent unto him' as the Bible says, may he not well reveal these secrets to prevent her marrying anyone else? Would you have married her under these circumstances? Would Rupert? Would you not always have been looking over your shoulders, asking yourselves what your children would become...?" He was silent again. "I think," he said, "that this perhaps was not an execution, though that may have been the excuse that the killer gave, even to herself. I think it was like the setting fire to the desk—a safety measure." And his bright old eye swivelled again to the set face. "Am I not getting very hot?"

"You are getting as cold as ice," said Giles; very cold himself. "You were burning your fingers but now you have taken your hand away from the truth, and you're cold again." And he pointed out: "The whole object of the exercise was that Uncle Gem wanted to 'keep it in the family'—he *wanted* her to marry either Rupert or me. And he'd hardly have done that if her heredity had been so bad that she would commit murder to keep it a secret."

They had come to the end of the path; turned now and started back towards the great spread of the mulberry tree and the bench beneath. From afar off a gong sounded; and below them as they started down the incline of the little hill, gardeners were straightening up, hands to loins, stretching, looking about them, gathering up their tools. "So," said the old man, "we are to leave Helen out of it, are we?"

"Of course," said Giles. "As if Helen…" And the hot white mist that invaded his mind always at the thought of Helen accused, welled up now like a miasma and sickened and stupefied him. When he emerged from it, the old man had embarked again upon his five questions. "Only they have perhaps changed a little bit now in order of importance. We asked ourselves why none of the police admitted having been shown the note about Helen, and we asked ourselves why someone should have gone for the fire brigade which would have been already on its way: and we found the answer to both questions—the murderer failed to get himself out of the room by the one means and resorted to the other. And we asked ourselves the meaning of those strange phrases about 'vanishing into thin air' and 'the long arms'—and we know now that they were only dragged in to confuse the issue. And we asked ourselves why your uncle was killed in the way he was—tied up, strangled, stabbed—and we know that this also was to cause confusion: that all the details of the recent stabbing and the newly broken window and the undrawn bolts, were all to cause confusion, to suggest that he had at that moment been killed by someone inside a locked room which in fact proved empty. But we asked ourselves one question which has not yet been answered and this now becomes the crucial question—why was the policeman killed? Because when we outlined an otherwise watertight case against Rupert, this was the point that exonerated him. Rupert had no reason to kill the policeman."

Giles walked beside him, slowly, supporting the shuffling steps down the gentle slope. "You are very hot now. Burning. Because, yes, that is the crucial question. Why was the policeman killed?"

"To avenge the murder of your Uncle Gemminy," said the old man. "What other reason could there possibly be? And that means—one of you three: you or Helen or Rupert. But you're out of it, that we do know; and I accept that Helen also is out of it—all that was only a tarradiddle because you challenged me, you said she couldn't have done it. So we have to come back to Rupert."

"And come back to the question you asked before. Why should Rupert have killed the policeman? Revenge, you say. But how could he have known that the policeman was the murderer?"

"Because in searching for Helen," said the old man, "he simply did the obvious thing. He stopped every policeman he saw and asked if they'd seen any sign of her. And recognised the man he'd shown the note to—back there in the murder room."

And he dropped Giles' arm and turned and faced him, the big, lined face alight with triumph. "*Now* am I hot?" he said.

And the white mist was back, brilliant and stupefying, pierced through with pain. And out of the mist, Giles heard himself answering: "Yes. White hot."

Rupert—whom also she loved, though surely one might believe, surely one might even yet hang on to the knowledge: not as she had loved himself. Rupert whom their guardian had chosen to be the favoured one. In Giles' mind now, the white light blazed: the white mist that came ever more frequently nowadays, to flood his mind with its terrible brilliance, its terrible pain. "Am I hot?" asked the old man, still playing the game, the game of Hunt the Killer which suddenly was only ugly and frightening, to be covered over and, please God, forgotten—the game which, unless something were said now, firmly and finally to bring it to an end, would never be covered over, never forgotten—never forgotten by this heavy old man with his cruel, sadistic mind, playing over old agonies like a cat with a mouse. And so: "Am I hot?" he said; and "White hot," Giles answered conceding victory. "The end of the game."

"Yes," said the old man. "The end of the game. And the beginning of reality." And he hooked a veined old hand into the trembling arm and started the long stroll in towards a nice hot cup of tea. "I told you I'd heard many murder confessions," he said. "Now tell me yours."

No answer: only the terrible trembling, the terrible, uncontrollable shaking of the arm he held, of the whole suddenly sick and shambling body. He prompted: "The policeman first—for perhaps the oddest reason ever known for killing a policeman: that you wanted to borrow his uniform. Knowing in advance what your Uncle Gemminy was going to say—"

Knowing in advance what Uncle Gemminy was going to say: because you remembered that night, you knew all about that long ago night—that you had within you the seed passed down through the generations, the terrible seed. The hot white light which, off and on, had visited him since that hideous night of his childhood, had taken possession of Giles' whole mind now: brilliant, dazzling—confusing yet clarifying, muffling all emotion, intensifying thought... One thought paramount: that Helen would be lost to him, that as always Rupert would win, that she would turn from him, back to Rupert whom also she had always loved...

The plan emerging: long thought-out, elaborate, nursed to perfection, a wish, a dream, a game, growing insensibly into a reality of purpose, springing into action because it must be now, today, this moment, if ever it was to be set going at all. Kill a policeman—no, don't kill him immediately, he must not seem to have died until after his uniform has been used and returned to him. Tie him up then—choose a man who knows you well (that young chap that's been making sheep's eyes at Helen recently—he'll do; and serve him right!)—and, knowing you, will trustingly come with you into the derelict building if you tell him some story of strange goings-on there: who'll trustingly turn his back. Wearing his uniform, get to the office—World Cup day, not a soul about; and anyway, who notices a uniformed copper going about his every-day duties? Kill Uncle Gemminy, silence him for ever—he who alone knows the seed of madness you carry within you, he who alone knows that you should never marry, never bring tainted children into the world... Tie him to his chair: for good reasons you must tie up the policeman and also stab him—an "uncanny" resemblance between the two murders will confuse the issue; and you can throw in a few strange references when you make your necessary telephone calls, cast over it all an air of netherworld horror.

Ring Rupert, ask him to come quickly; you well know Uncle Gem's mannerisms and for the rest, pretended alarm will disguise your voice. Ten minutes now, before he—hurrying—will arrive. Break the window, keep back a piece of the glass. Set fire to the desk. A moment before Rupert is due, ring over to the police station with wild talk of a mysterious attack, so urgent as to bring them all tearing across: you know their habits, you have watched them from your window, often enough, snatching up their helmets, tumbling over one another to answer a hurry-call; and there must be several of them, that is the essence of your plot. Now the desk is well alight, the room filling with smoke, the doors bolted. As Rupert's fist begins to pound, inflict the stab wound, observe the satisfactory trickle of blood, showing how recently the wound was made. Take out the knife, wrap it in the plastic sheet you have brought for the purpose and button the whole tight inside your uniform jacket. If Uncle Gemminy's blood is on the uniform, the fact that this same knife was used to kill the policeman will account for it; no one must catch the smallest glimpse of the fact that that uniform was in the office at the time Uncle Gem was killed.

Move back to the door, stand to one side and wait. They break in the panels at last, stand back a moment for the final onslaught—and in that moment you fling the piece of glass you have preserved from the broken pane. You are lucky in actually hitting the remaining glass and setting it vibrating; but all that you really needed was the sound, the sound of someone smashing that hole in the window and diving out "into thin air".

And the door gives, opening back against you as you stand flattened against the wall; and as the men surge forward, you surge forward with them. In that smoke-filled room, filled with blue uniforms—who will observe that one blue uniform came, not through the door but from behind it...

Rupert is there with them, of course, and now you have a little extra bit of luck to add to that alibi about having seen him leave the flat. You have noted where his car was parked, of course, and for the rest you could deduce that he'd rush out in a hurry—you've arranged for that by the telephone call and you know your Rupert; (his being early made no difference either way, of course—all you wanted was to be able to pretend this alibi for yourself, to describe Rupert rushing out, to know pretty exactly at what time that would happen; and it had the added advantage of your knowing just how long it would be before he arrived.) And now you observe that he can't even have stopped to put on his macintosh. As you stand with your handkerchief up to your face, against the smoke and the heat, he comes up close to you, he shows you the note about Helen, and you are able to see that the shoulders of his light jacket are soaked through. (You must look round the flat and just see that he did take the mac. even if he didn't wait to put it on.) Meanwhile, he's reacting to the note as you knew he would—rushing off to look for Helen without stopping for a moment's thought. The sergeant won't let you follow him, as you'd rather hoped; so you shout out something not too specific about the fire brigade and, not waiting for consent or refusal, dash off, flinging a word to the man on duty at the top of the stairs. And from then on—a uniformed bobby, hurrying about some professional duty—slowing down as you get clear of the building, just a man strolling his beat. Back to the derelict factory, get the constable back into his uniform—easier when he's alive than if he were, literally, a dead weight. Finish him off, heave him into the water tank: the longer they take to find him, the harder to deduce the time of death, and immersion in the water of course will further confuse it. The old man's blood on the knife will account, as you've planned, for any on the uniform.

Twenty minutes later, you are coming up to the heath, scorching hell for leather along the empty roads. You had intended to knock up the pub people, ask them for change for the public telephone outside; but through the window you can see them all crowded round the television set watching the World Cup final; and what more natural than to tap on the pane—you know them quite well—and make questioning faces, sketch a query mark on the pane: clasp hands in mock prayer as they signal back, "All square; extra time," and turn back to huddle over the set again.

Helen safely out of the way, of course; you told her to meet you at the Dell. So you can go to the call box, make the legitimate call to the house to ask if she's there; and then…

Five o'clock; and the policeman has been dead for half an hour and more—yet here is his voice asking for "George"—you know well enough that George is on the switchboard today—giving his nickname, all the little authenticities… Breaking off with vague alarms, coming back to scream out in gibbering fear that he's being attacked... P.C. Cross: alive and speaking on the telephone at five o'clock when you are known to be fifteen miles away from the scene of his death.

He had reckoned on suspicion fastening, possibly, upon Rupert; but Helen—that had been horrible... The white light had grown more and more frightening then, blazing day and night inside his mind with a dazzling confusion as when one looks into the eye of the sun and sees only blackness. But this had been a whiteness, infinitely more terrible—a pain-filled, terror-filled radiance that blotted out all but the pain and the terror of the ensuing days. They had been very kind; considering what had happened, they had all been kind. They'd told him that he should not die nor even go to prison, but to a place where he might hide himself from the light inside his head. He'd been afraid of that, afraid of the truths that would face him when he was no longer blinded by the light. But they'd said that he hadn't been—what they called "responsible"; because of that heredity, because of that very thing that Uncle Gemminy had been going to speak about—because of that long ago day when he had fled, a small boy, shrieking with mortal fear, away from Grandad, standing suddenly in the doorway carrying the great hatchet and stained down his front and all over his hands, with blood...

The gardeners had left the flower-beds and now at a discreet distance followed them; keeping a wary eye also—no point in humiliating and antagonising them, the trick psychs, said nowadays—upon other couples, other little groups all strolling in towards the big, barred buildings ahead; jingling the heavy keys, herding in their charges, sheep-like, to the grazing grounds. The old man stood aside, courteously, to usher the newcomer through the huge door with its wire-netted, splinter-proof glass. "Well, thank you, I enjoyed that. Someday I'll tell you about *my* murder. Killed off my whole family one night, you know, with an axe. Not my fault; my father was mad before me, as mad as a hatter. And it's years ago now; my goodness, yes!—when that happened, you'll have been no more than a child."

TOO MANY MOTIVES

James Ronald

James Ronald (1905–72), who was born in Glasgow and later lived in the United States for a number of years, was a prolific crime writer whose work slipped into obscurity for half a century until the efforts of Chris Verner (whose father Gerald was himself a crime writer) led to his rediscovery and republication. Those long years of neglect make it sobering to realise how successful he was in his day. *Murder in the Family* (1938), for instance, was made into a film, and the poet and detective fiction addict W. H. Auden wrote in the *Daily Telegraph* that the book might be "confidently recommended." *This Way Out* (1939) was compared by its American publishers to two classic novels of psychological suspense, *The Lodger* by Marie Belloc Lowndes and *Before the Fact* by Francis Iles. This was a bold claim, but more than mere publicity hype; the novel was adapted for the stage and then filmed in 1944 as *The Suspect* with Charles Laughton excelling as the protagonist Philip Marshall.

There was, perhaps, a pulpy element to some of Ronald's writing (reflected in the titles of novels such as *They Can't Hang Me* and *Six Were to Die*) which may have contributed to his work falling out of fashion, but he had a knack of creating tense situations and the revival of interest in his work is welcome. This story first appeared in the *20-Story Magazine* in April 1930.

M OST PEOPLE GIVE DINNER PARTIES TO THEIR FRIENDS. MARK
Savile displayed his grim sense of humour by giving a dinner
party to four men who hated him. It would have been impossible
for him to find four friends to be his guests; indeed, it is doubtful
whether he had made one single true friendship in his entire fifty-
four years of life. That did not trouble him. It would almost seem
that it pleased him to be hated.

The book of Savile's life held a lengthy reckoning of the misery
to which he had brought others in his meteoric rise to a position of
power in the world of finance.

When Eldoradian Concessions Limited failed, there were those
who said that the investigations of the receiver would result in prison
for Savile. They said that he had gone just a little too far. And had
overstepped the shadowy division between robbery legal and illegal.
These were false profits. Thousands of small investors lost their savings in the crash of his bubble company, but Savile went his way the
richer by one hundred thousand pounds.

At the age of fifty-four he was reputed to be enormously wealthy;
he was despised even by fellow-financiers, which is degradation
indeed; and he had not a single friend—excepting the women who
flocked to him like flies to a jam pot.

He celebrated his fifty-fourth birthday by a dinner-party to four
men of the many who hated him.

Why Savile's invitation was accepted each of the four would
have found difficulty in explaining. Perhaps his audacity piqued
them.

Of the four, Borrow was the only one whom Savile had never directly injured. Financially, John Borrow was too sound an opponent for Savile to cross swords with. But Borrow's best friend had shot himself, driven out of his mind by the ruin that Savile had brought upon him, and that was a score John Borrow intended to settle one day.

Harold Denholm came to Savile's dinner-party because he was afraid to stay away. Savile had a powerful hold over him, and in the invitation to dine Denholm read a fugitive hope that the financier intended to make things easier for him.

Lord Clavering accepted the invitation to dine because of his uneasiness over Fortuna Copper of which he was a director, and because Savile was the only person who knew the real condition of the company's affairs.

Dennis Barclay was drunk when Savile's invitation came. For a week he had scarcely drawn a sober breath. When he read the letter and realised from whom it came, he tore it into shreds.

All four came to dinner at Savile's flat.

As each of the guests arrived, he was shown into the tastefully furnished library of the flat. When all four were present, dry Martinis were served, and it was not until they had finished their cocktails that their host made his appearance. He did not offer to shake hands with them, but bowed slightly to each in turn with just a hint of mockery in his eyes.

Borrow nodded gravely in return. Denholm muttered something in a low voice. Lord Clavering shrugged his shoulders philosophically. Dennis Barclay flushed and took a single step forward, but was just sufficiently sober to hold his peace.

Savile smiled suavely.

"I am informed that dinner is ready to serve," he said. "You will excuse the informality? I have only a single manservant."

They followed him in silence to the dining-room. The table, which had a plate-glass top, was tastefully laid. A single alabaster electric light bowl directly above the centre effectively illuminated the table but left the remainder of the room in darkness.

A soft-footed manservant left the room by another door as they entered.

"My man Simpson, is both cooking and serving tonight," said Savile in his rich, silky voice. "It has been necessary therefore to arrange a simple menu. I hope that you will enjoy it."

The meal, while not an elaborate one, was deliciously cooked. Each of the four courses of which it consisted had been chosen with the discrimination of a connoisseur.

Savile's dark, sinister eyes were all that showed his grim enjoyment of the jest he had perpetrated. He knew that they hated him and it pleased his grotesque sense of humour to dine and wine them as though they were the finest of good friends. Otherwise, he was a perfect host.

Savile's manservant came into the room and walked to his master's chair. Savile nodded.

"You may go now, John," he said. To his guests he remarked:

"It is one of my peculiarities that I prefer my servant to sleep out. I value privacy."

In a smooth, even tone, he continued his discourse upon vintage wines.

It is impossible to talk of wines without talking of countries and to a man like Savile countries meant capitals. The conversation drifted to Berlin, Vienna, to Budapest and Madrid. Gradually, Savile's guests took part in the conversation and it became almost animated, for they had all travelled.

Lord Clavering mentioned Venice as the city which appealed to him most of all the cities in the world. He had spent a year there; the happiest year of his life.

They had come now to coffee, brandy, and cigars. Savile pierced the end of his cigar with precious care and lit it without permitting the flame actually to touch the cigar.

"Venice is a city of beautiful dreams," he remarked, exhaling a cloud of fragrant blue smoke, "but there are two things that must be remembered about Venice. If one goes alone, it is a city of ghosts. One must be accompanied by a beautiful woman—and one must not go twice with the same woman."

There was an awkward little silence.

Dennis Barclay flushed angrily.

"You have ugly ideas—about women, Savile," he said harshly.

Savile shrugged his shoulders.

"Ugly? Perhaps—to you, who regard a woman as a goddess, to be placed upon a pedestal. I have my own ideas of everything. They do not often please others but they frequently amuse me." His eyes travelled to the face of each of his guests in turn. It amused him to see contempt written plainly on each. The artificial atmosphere which he had created was gone, and open hostility had replaced it.

"This dinner is one of my ideas," Savile continued in a calm, even voice. "It is even more amusing than I had anticipated. I wonder what would be said if it was known—publicly—that we five men dined together. I think there are many who would share the exquisite humour of my jest with me."

No one answered him. Dennis Barclay was white with fury, but he restrained himself.

Savile smiled, and continued slowly.

"It would probably be said that if the object of the dinner was to discuss finance, Barclay would not be here, and that if the finance was—shall we say 'shady'?—Borrow would not be with us."

Denholm leapt to his feet, his eyes blazing.

"Look here, Savile," he cried, "you've gone too far. What rotten suggestion are you making against Clavering and me?"

Savile met his eyes squarely.

"Does it matter?" he parried with a sardonic smile. "Do you particularly mind what I say? I think not."

Denholm's face was set and grim, but he sat down in silence.

"It would seem that I am quite alone in the enjoyment of my joke," went on Savile smoothly. "Perhaps you have all too much on your minds to see the humour of this situation. Clavering is wondering how he will answer the questions the police will put to him when—"

Lord Clavering blanched and his hands clutched the arms of his chair so tightly that his knuckles showed white.

"My God, Savile," he gasped. "Then the rumours about Fortunas Copper are true?"

Savile spread his hands in a deprecatory gesture.

"How should I know? I am not even on the board."

"You took damn good care of that!" Clavering whispered hoarsely. "But if there's anything wrong with the company, you're responsible."

Savile laughed harshly.

"My dear fellow, I'm only a shareholder," he replied, "and I'll have to bear my loss philosophically. The directors must do the explaining. But don't worry about the police, Clavering. They're notoriously easy to hoodwink. All they are fit for is laying traps for speeding motorists. The—er—higher branches of crime are beyond them. Think of the murders that go undetected my dear chap! And murder is the kingpin of crimes."

There was silence for a moment, save for the stertorous breathing of Lord Clavering, whose face was as colourless as putty. There was something diabolical about the way Mark Savile had piled on the agony that astounded the others, even with their knowledge of

Savile's vileness. John Borrow was the first to speak, and his voice, sharp and harsh, cut the silence like a knife.

"There are times when murder is commendable, Savile," he said.

Savile's expression was bland, even a shade amused.

"And those times?" he asked.

John Borrow took a deep breath.

"To kill a man who has ruined a friend who trusted him," he replied slowly, "would be no more reprehensible than to decapitate a snake."

"You think so, do you?" replied Savile. "I too have ideas about murder. It is a fascinating subject. Not as a vehicle for revenge—but as an art. It can be an art you know, when a man of intelligence turns to it. But when the police investigated your hypothetical murder, it would be too easy to trace the motive, my dear Borrow. The undetected murder must be motiveless—there must be no traceable strings to lead to the murderer. Kill your wife, or your aunt or your enemy, and you are instantly suspected. Kill, for instance, someone you do not know—stab a stranger in an Underground crowd, or push a passer-by under a bus—and there are no traceable motives to lead to you. What do you think, Denholm, or do you shrink from the topic? You are looking very white."

Denholm leaned across the table and stared as one fascinated into his host's saturnine eyes.

"I will tell you what I think," he retorted in a voice filled with emotion. "When a damned Shylock gets hold of a man and makes him repay a debt half a dozen times, and still holds it like a whip over him, and makes his life a living hell till he can't call his soul his own, I think that death is too merciful a punishment."

Savile's eyes were filled with ironic amusement at the other's vehemence.

"But the motive is damning," was his only comment. "What do you say Clavering?"

Lord Clavering looked up. His ashy face wore a tortured expression.

"I have nothing to say," he replied slowly, rising from his chair as he spoke. "Excuse me please—I cannot stay any longer."

He stumbled towards the door, a broken, beaten, man. Savile's voice held him back.

"But won't you add your opinion to this very enthralling discussion? I am sure that it would be interesting."

Lord Clavering did not turn to face his tormentor. His voice, when he replied, was toneless.

"If Fortuna Copper is a swindle, and you have shifted the blame to men whose only crime is—stupidity, you will discover my conception of a guiltless murder," he said.

Dennis Barclay, whose suppressed fury had come to fever pitch, sprang to his feet, upsetting his chair. His fists were clenched and his eyes menaced Savile.

"You swine! You unmentionable cad!" he raved. "I don't know why you invited us here, unless it was to gloat over us in your filthy mind. I don't know why I came. The thought of eating your food makes me sick. Savile, you rat, you defiler of women, I'll kill you if I hang for it!"

He sprang at Savile, and his first wild swing struck the financier on the temple, dazing him. Barclay's hands were at Savile's throat, squeezing the life out of him, when Borrow and Denholm interfered and dragged the infuriated young man back.

Savile lay unconscious in his chair. His breath was coming in short gasps.

"Leave me alone!" cried Barclay, struggling desperately. "Let me get at the swine and finish him off!"

John Borrow's grasp on Barclay's arm did not relax.

"We had better go," he said quietly. "He's not worth it, Barclay."

Somehow, they got Barclay out of the flat. By the time they were in the street he was calmer and he went off alone, leaving the others to go their several ways.

It was fully five minutes before Mark Savile opened his eyes with a groan. He looked about him wildly, until his glance fell upon the debris of the dinner and he remembered what had happened.

His neck was raw and sore and his head was throbbing viciously. He put up a hand and rubbed his neck ruefully. He eased himself out of his chair and staggered rather than walked to the sideboard, where he mixed himself a stiff brandy and soda. Remembering the grim humour which had prompted him to hold his amazing dinner-party, he smiled a twisted, bitter smile.

He went to the library and turned on all the lights. The brilliant illumination gave him courage, for he was a coward at heart. Now, although he had enjoyed his joke, he shivered with fear.

He sat down at his desk and produced writing-paper and an envelope. In a shaky hand he wrote an inscription on the envelope. It ran:

"Should anything happen to me, this envelope must be handed to the proper authorities."

Then he drew the paper towards him and commenced to write.

Just then the doorbell rang, and he rose and went to answer it.

Dennis Barclay did not arrive at his home in St. James's Street that night until half-past ten, although he had no engagement following the dinner which broke up so abruptly. He fumbled with his latch-key, placing it everywhere but in the lock, until his valet, hearing the scrapings at the door from the kitchen, where he was entertaining a friend, came and let him in.

Consternation was written on the valet's face when he beheld his master. Barclay was dead drunk and swaying on his feet. His clothes were rumpled and muddy and his tie was gone.

The valet had been employed by Dennis Barclay for some years, and he was very fond of his master. He helped him in and got him to bed where Barclay immediately lapsed into a sleep that was akin to stupor.

Herbert, the man servant, returned to the kitchen with a long face. His guest, the butler from next door, looked up at his entrance.

"What's up?" he asked.

Herbert shook his head dolefully.

"It's Mr. Barclay—he hasn't been quite himself lately," he responded.

The butler nodded sympathetically.

"I know. Is he—?"

Herbert nodded.

"You won't let it go further," he said. "If I thought you would, I wouldn't tell you—"

"You know me, Herbert," replied the butler. "'Aven't we been the best of friends for years?"

Herbert smiled.

"The very best, old boy," he agreed. "Have another drink?"

He poured two glasses of his master's rare old port. They sipped the wine gratefully in silence—in their own way they were almost connoisseurs.

"Mr. Barclay's been terribly upset lately," Herbert began at last. "He had a nasty shock some time ago. His young lady jilted him for another man—a man named Savile. Mr. Barclay took it hard. You know how it is when a thing like that happens; he's been drinking a lot, and hardly eating a thing. One night I came across him with *her* picture in his hand, and I could see that the way he's been treated had knocked the stuffing out of him, so to speak. But he's a mild type of man, Mr. Barclay is, though one of the best, and he took it quietly. I never heard him utter a word against the other man—drunk or sober."

The butler nodded sympathetically.

Herbert looked up; his face very grave.

"He's been to dinner tonight with the other fellow—the man who pinched his girl," he said earnestly.

"Go on!" gasped the butler incredulously.

Herbert nodded.

"The swine wouldn't let him alone. He wrote to Mr. Barclay and invited him to dinner. When the guv'nor got the letter, he took on something awful. It was the first time I've ever seen him violent. I was scared he would do something crazy. You can imagine my surprise when at the last moment he decided to go. Go he did, and now he's back as drunk as a lord and with his clothes in a rare mess. Gawd, I hope he hasn't been up to anything—"

The butler put down his glass, and leaning forward, pressed Herbert's arm sympathetically. Herbert nodded gratefully.

"*You* can understand, old pal," he said. "He's always been a gentleman to me."

The following morning two men called at Dennis Barclay's flat and asked to see him. Barclay was in bed, sound asleep, but the callers were so insistent that Herbert grudgingly wakened his master.

When Dennis Barclay entered the small sitting-room where the two men were waiting, one of them rose and said:

"I am Detective Harris, of the Criminal Investigation Department, Mr. Barclay, and I must ask you to accompany me. Mr. Mark Savile has been killed and your presence at his flat is urgently requested by the inspector in charge."

Dennis Barclay looked queer for a moment, then he laughed shakily.

"Dead, is he?" he remarked. "Then the world is a better place. If you will wait for a few minutes, gentlemen, I will be ready to accompany you."

His face was very white, but he mounted the stairs to his room steadily.

Doctor Britling arrived at Mark Savile's flat fully an hour after the police. His delay was due to the fact that he had been consulting works of reference and piles of old clippings for information about the dead man, knowledge of which was none of his concern as a police surgeon. A policeman was on duty at the door of the flat, which stood open. Daniel crossed the hall quickly and entered a room in which there were six men—and the body of Mark Savile. Taking the occupants in with one swift glance, he nodded briskly to the inspector in charge.

"Ha, Evans! Good morning," he added cheerfully. "Glad to see you. *You* won't cramp my style, hey?"

Without waiting for an answer, he crossed the room to the fireplace, and knelt down beside the body, which lay on the hearthrug. His examination did not take long. Mark Savile had been dead for hours, and the cause of death was obvious; he had been shot in the right temple. The shot had been fired at close quarters, for the wound was blackened with powder marks.

"Well, the man's dead alright," remarked Daniel, rising to his feet. "He's been dead from between eight to twelve hours. Death was instantaneous, of course. What is it, Evans, suicide?"

Evans shook his head.

"Quite impossible, doctor," he replied. "There's no trace of a weapon anywhere in the room. It is quite obviously murder."

Daniel nodded gravely.

"Humph! Who are all these people?" he demanded suddenly.

Evans permitted himself a little smile.

"This is Lord Clavering," he said, indicating one of those present. "And this gentleman is Mr. Dennis Barclay. Both of them dined here last night. The man in uniform is the commissionaire of the building who was on duty last night. That chap over there is the dead man's valet, and that completes the list."

The Inspector explained that they were awaiting the arrival of the other two guests of the previous evening's dinner. Daniel nodded briskly.

"You don't mind if I look round a bit on my own?"

"Not at all. I'll be glad of your help, doctor," Evans replied easily. "But the case looks pretty obvious. Look here!" He produced a note in the dead man's handwriting. "I found this under the blotting pad on the desk."

He read it aloud:

"'I have reason to fear that one of the men who dined with me tonight has designs on my life. Should anything happen to me, he is responsible. His name is—' You see, Mr. Britling, he was probably in the middle of writing this when he was interrupted—doubtless by someone at the door. He was alone in the flat, so he answered the summons himself, first slipping the unfinished note under the blotter. His visitor killed him before he had the opportunity of finishing the letter."

Daniel nodded slowly.

"And his visitor was?"

The Inspector smiled.

"One of his guests," he replied, "which one we will know shortly. The commissionaire here was on duty last night and saw all four leave. He was absent from the hallway for a time after that, but returned in time to see one of the four—he didn't know his name—coming downstairs. He had left with the others—but returned later."

"He will recognise the man again?"

"Yes, he's positive of that. It wasn't either Lord Clavering or Mr. Barclay, so it rests between the other two"—he consulted a piece of paper—"Mr. Borrow or Mr. Denholm. I've sent for them, of course. They should be here shortly."

Daniel nodded.

"Who found him?" he asked.

The dead man's valet moved uneasily.

"I did, sir," he said.

"Did you disturb anything?"

The valet shook his head decisively.

"Everything's exactly as I found it, sir," he replied in a tremulous voice. "Gave me a turn, it did, finding him like that. I could see he was dead, and I didn't wait to see anymore. I went in the other room quickly and 'phoned the police."

"What time was that?"

"About eight o'clock, sir. I don't sleep in the flat, and I arrived this morning at my usual time, half-past seven. I didn't come in here, and it wasn't until I had started on Mr. Savile's breakfast and had his bath running that I found out there was anything wrong. I went to call him and found that his bed hadn't been slept in. I came in here—and that's what I found."

He pointed a shaky finger at the body. Daniel nodded, but did not look at the body.

"What sort of master was Mr. Savile?" he asked.

The valet hesitated.

"Well, you know how it is, sir. He wasn't bad—paid me on the nail and all that. Maybe he was a bit mean, but lots of guv'nors are."

"Locked up the cigars and liquor?"

The valet ventured a shaky smile.

"Yes, sir, that sort of thing. He splashed the drink about when he had a party, but he always made sure I didn't get a little nip on the quiet."

Daniel smiled.

"Did he have many friends?"

"Well, no sir, not many. Mostly women. Lots of *them* came here. He didn't have many gents calling."

"Have you noticed anything unusual about him lately?"

The valet reflected for a moment or two, then shook his head.

"No, sir, I can't say I have. I *did* think it queer that he should invite four gentlemen to dinner last night. I didn't think—"

"That he had four gentlemen friends?"

The valet did not answer, but it was obvious that Daniel had read his thoughts.

"That was all?"

"Now I come to think of it, sir," replied the valet seriously, "there was one thing that struck me as being unusual. Last night, when I was replenishing the brandy decanter, Mr. Savile, who was watching me do it—he always watched—says: 'A fresh bottle, John—you can pour what's left in that decanter into an empty bottle.' Then he laughs, sort of queer, and says: 'On second thoughts, John, you can drink it yourself, after you're off duty.' Well, I was quite taken aback, sir, but he really meant it. It was as good a glass of the real stuff as I ever tasted."

The strained atmosphere in that room of death relaxed. There were smiles on the faces of all those present, except the valet, who was very serious, and the commissionaire, who was overawed in the presence of murder.

"That is all John," said Daniel gravely. Then, turning to the others, he added: "An amusing little detail, gentlemen. But those things are often important, eh, Inspector?"

Without waiting for an answer, he started on a painstaking tour of the room. His first objective was the single large window, which investigation proved to be efficiently locked from the inside. Foot by foot he examined the flooring, moving furniture, and opening such drawers as were not locked. His investigation brought him back again at last to the body of Mark Savile.

The body lay very stiff and straight upon the rug before the fire-place. The trunk and legs were stretched out in an orderly fashion as though already arranged for burial. The feet were pointing to the window and the right arm was outstretched towards the fireplace, the fingers curved but not clenched. The left arm was pressed close to the body and the hand was clenched tightly.

"What about the explosion?" Daniel asked, rising to his feet. "Did anyone hear it?"

Inspector Evans smiled ironically.

"There wasn't one—or the whole building would have been roused," he replied. "The occupant of the flat next door says that he heard a 'plop' like the sound of a cork being drawn, at about a quarter to ten. That, of course, is the noise made by an automatic which has a silencer attached."

"Death instantaneous—no time to dispose of a revolver—and no revolver found," said Daniel reflectively.

"Answer, 'murder'," responded Inspector Evans. "And, by the way, 'about a quarter past ten' is the time the commissionaire saw one of the murdered man's guests leave the building—for the second time."

At that moment the door of the flat opened, and four men entered. Two of them were detectives, and the other two were John Borrow and Harold Denholm. As they advanced into the room, the commissionaire clutched the inspector's arm.

"'That's 'im, sir," he said in a hoarse penetrating whisper, pointing to Denholm. "That's the gent as I saw last night."

Inspector Evans nodded briskly. He advanced to meet the new-comers. Their eyes had already fallen on the thing which lay on the hearthrug and they were looking pale.

"Mr. Borrow or Mr. Denholm?" Evans asked, addressing Harold Denholm.

Denholm gave his name in a jerky voice. The sight of the corpse had shaken him. Evans submitted him to a searching scrutiny.

"Well then, Mr. Denholm," he said brusquely, "as you can see for yourself, there's been murder done here. It was done, as near as I can make out, at a quarter past ten last night. At approximately that time you were seen to leave this building, although you had previously left it half-an-hour earlier with the other dinner guests. Why did you return?"

Denholm hesitated, and his eyes travelled round the room. He flinched when the body of Mark Savile came within his line of vision. He half turned so that the sight was hidden from him.

"I—I came—on purely personal business," he said at last, in a slow, husky voice.

"What business?" insisted the Inspector.

"Nothing that can possibly concern this affair."

The Inspector's lips tightened.

"That is for me to judge, sir," he snapped.

Denholm shook his head wearily.

"I am afraid that I must refuse the information," he replied shakily.

Inspector Evans gave him a hard look.

"In that case," he said grimly, "it is my duty to place you under arrest—and to warn you that anything you say may be taken down and used in evidence against you!"

Harold Denholm's face had been white. Now it turned ash-grey.

"You are going to arrest me?"

Inspector Evans moved impatiently. He pointed a stubby finger at Denholm.

"Can't you understand your position?" he snapped. "You dined here last night with a man whom you dislike, you leave with your fellow guests in an agitated condition, you return afterwards, and at the appropriate time when you are in the building your host is murdered. Can't you see that the circumstantial evidence against you is damning?"

Denholm glowered defiance.

"And what about Barclay," he demanded. "He was in the building, too, after we had all left it. I saw him leave. He tried to strangle Savile last night. Are you going to arrest him as well?"

The Inspector's jaw dropped. His face was a picture of astonishment. He wheeled round and stared at Dennis Barclay.

"Is this true?" he demanded.

Barclay nodded.

"Yes," he said simply.

Inspector Evans stood stock still for a moment. His large red face wore a perplexed expression. The case which he had seen forming against Denholm was crumbling, and a new line had opened up before him.

"Sit down—all of you," he said suddenly. "There's a lot in this affair that wants explaining. Mr. Denholm—you first. Tell me why you returned here last night, and exactly what happened."

They all found chairs, except the valet and the commissioner, who felt it in keeping with their positions to remain standing. Daniel, who seemed engrossed in an inspection of the corpse, and the Inspector, who perched himself upon the desk.

"Well, Mr. Denholm," he demanded.

Denholm licked his lips nervously.

"I came back last night," he began slowly, "to have it out with Savile about—about a loan which I had repaid several times over. I was desperate—worried—and determined to put an end to paying him, no matter what it meant. I rang the bell, but there was no answer. That's the truth—I swear it. I rang several times, but the flat was quite silent. Savile was probably dead already. I saw Barclay leaving the building as I approached it. He didn't see me, because he went the other way."

The Inspector considered this, nodding his head heavily at each point which he turned over in his mind.

"There's something else you should know," Denholm continued, with a sidelong glance at his fellow guests of the previous night. "Barclay was engaged to a girl whom—well, Savile persuaded away from him. Last night, Barclay half-killed Savile and left him unconscious in his chair—if we'd let him, he'd have finished the job there and then."

Inspector Evan's eyes did not waver from Denholm's face.

"You think Barclay killed Savile because of this girl?" he suggested evenly.

Denholm glanced nervously at Barclay, who neither stirred nor spoke.

"I don't suggest that—quite," he said, in a tone that testified to his feelings of shame. "But I didn't do it. I think that Savile was dead before I arrived—and Barclay left the building as I arrived."

There was a silence after he spoke. Those who were present knew perfectly well that he was implicating Dennis Barclay to save his own skin, but it was undeniable that no matter what the motives were that prompted his indirect accusation, there was no lack of justification for it.

All eyes were turned on Dennis Barclay, except those of Daniel Britling, who was gazing with marked interest at Lord Clavering. Behind the tired-looking eyes of the peer, Britling read something more than merely horror of the murder, or even concern for his friend.

John Borrow was the first to break the silence.

"Look here," he said crisply. "In the interests of justice—and common decency—it is only right that you should know, Inspector, that none of us had any great liking for—er—the deceased. In fact, I think we each had a motive for wishing his death."

Inspector Evans wheeled round to face him.

"And those motives were?" he demanded.

Borrow returned his gaze calmly.

"On my part, friendship for a poor young fellow whom Savile ruined, and who shot himself." He was silent for a moment, then continued: "Yes, I think I would have killed Savile for that."

He recounted simply and briefly the conversation of the previous evening, when Savile had given his views on murder, and the others had been provoked into adding their opinion of justifiable murder—and had given their own motives for wishing ill to their host. He spoke without bitterness, as one should speak of the dead, but the impression of Savile which he gave to those who had not known him was not a pleasant one.

"He seems to have been a thoroughly nasty customer," commented Evans. "But that doesn't alter the fact that murder has been done. He was right too, mind you, about his motiveless murders. I should say that the motive is the greatest factor in tracing a murderer. But with four motives! Well, let's hear from you, Mr. Barclay. What happened when you returned here last night?"

Dennis Barclay moistened his lips. He glanced around at the others and was encouraged by a look of sympathy from John Borrow. He smiled gratefully. "To be frank I came back to kill him," he commenced, with a gesture towards the corpse, which Daniel Britling had thoughtfully covered with a rug. "I meant to kill him in cold blood, then give myself up to the police. He deserved death if ever a man did. I rang the bell, and he was alive then, for he answered my ring. He wouldn't open the door, though. He spoke to me from the other side, and told me to go to hell. I rang several times but he didn't answer after the first ring. At last, I came away and—well I fancy I must have got drunk, for I don't remember anything after leaving the building."

Harold Denholm rose to his feet and pointed an eager finger at the Inspector.

"Don't you see," he cried, "Barclay admits that Savile was alive when he arrived. I rang the bell only a few minutes later, and there wasn't an answer. Savile must have been dead when I rang, so—"

Daniel interposed smoothly:

"You overlook the fact that Savile may have assumed that it was still Mr. Barclay who was ringing the bell," he pointed out, "and I must remind you that if Mr. Barclay had murdered Mark Savile he would not have admitted that Savile was alive, and answered his ring. He would have said, as you have said, that Savile did not answer."

Denholm whitened and sat down abruptly. He tried to speak, but the words would not form themselves. As though he had lost all interest in Denholm, Daniel turned to Lord Clavering and gave him a benevolent smile.

"Won't *you* tell us why *you* returned here last night?" he asked politely.

Lord Clavering started as though he had been shot.

"How did you know?" he gasped.

Daniel shrugged his shoulders.

"I didn't—that was chance shot, but it is obvious that you did return. Why?"

"I suppose I should have made a clean breast of it," Lord Clavering replied steadily. "Yes, I returned. I was worried about the condition of a company of which I am director and I intended to force the truth out of Savile. My experience was the same as Denholm's—Savile didn't answer when I rang the bell."

On Inspector Evans' face there was an expression of extreme perplexity. It was almost the expression that a prize fighter wears directly after he has been the recipient of a punch in the solar plexus. His case was running away with itself and opening up so many possibilities that they bewildered him.

He almost glared at John Borrow.

"Well, sir? What about you?" he demanded.

John Borrow smiled apologetically.

"I'm not in this, Inspector," he replied. "I went straight home last night and went to bed."

"You can prove that, of course?"

Borrow reflected for a moment or two.

"Why, no, I'm afraid I can't," he said at last. "I have no servant and I didn't meet anyone who knew me. I'm afraid—"

Evans cut him off short with a wave of his hand.

"Alright," he said bitterly, "we'll count you in."

He turned to Daniel.

"What on earth do you make of this?" he demanded.

The doctor shrugged his shoulders philosophically.

"We must use the things we know as a basis for learning the things we should like to know," he replied.

"Well, what *do* we know?" the Inspector snapped. "We know that murder has been done. That is proved by the complete absence of a weapon which might have been used for suicide. A man who dies immediately has no time to dispose of an automatic, and there is not one in the room."

The doctor nodded gravely.

"We know that three of the dead man's guests returned to this building after leaving it last night, that the fourth cannot prove his alibi, and that all four had strong motives for murdering Mark Savile," the Inspector went on.

Daniel crossed to the body and kneeling down pulled the covering rug back and made a careful examination. He prised open the clenched hand, which was empty, and examined the curved fingers of the other hand which trailed across the fender of the fireplace.

The cuffs of the dead man's shirt seemed to interest him intensely; also, the type of his cuff links. His examination was thorough, extending as it did even to the soles of his shoes.

"Did you ever play 'Red Indians' as a child, Inspector?" he asked casually, speaking over his shoulder.

Inspector Evans' jaw dropped. For a moment he wondered whether the little surgeon had lost his senses.

The doctor smiled.

"It was a long time since *I* was a child," he remarked, "but I can remember how artistically I used to 'die' when pierced by an imaginary arrow of the enemy. I would spin round, fall on my back, and lie stretched out very stiff, and very neat—just as the body of Mark Savile is lying now. But when a man is really shot and has dropped in his tracks, his attitude is more ungainly. His arms and legs are sprawled out. Now why did the murderer leave his victim's body so tidy? Why take time to adjust the limbs? And why spoil the job by leaving one arm sprawled out to call attention to the preciseness of the rest of the body?"

He rose to his feet, and turned to the dead man's valet.

"Among your duties, you assist your master in dressing?"

The valet nodded.

"And you put the studs and cuff links in his shirts?"

"Yes, sir, always."

Daniel's next remark was addressed more to himself than to the valet.

"Then why, I wonder, did Mark Savile change his dress shirt last night?" he mused. "If you will look at the cuffs, Inspector," he continued, "you will see that they are quite soiled with fingerprints. No capable servant would do that. Therefore, Mr. Savile must have changed his shirt after dinner—or perhaps rolled up his sleeve and had trouble readjusting his cuff links." To the valet he added: "Suppose you see whether you can find a soiled shirt."

As the valet left the room, Daniel picked up the dead man's last epistle, and read it aloud:

"I have reason to fear that one of the men who dined with me tonight has designs upon my life. Should anything happen to me, he is responsible. His name is—"

"Having written so far," remarked Daniel, "why not continue?"

Inspector Evans made a deprecatory gesture.

"The doorbell rang, he went to answer it, and was killed before he could finish the letter," he urged.

The little doctor gave him a mildly reproving glance.

"One word, Inspector, was all that he need write. One word— 'Borrow' or 'Barclay' or 'Denholm' or 'Clavering.' Wouldn't you have written that one little word before answering the doorbell?"

Evans did not answer.

"With his pen in his hand," Daniel continued, "it would have been natural for Savile to add the name that gave value to his letter—but he didn't. Why?"

He paced up and down the room slowly. There was a suggestion of a schoolmaster lecturing his class as he talked.

"Mr. Borrow said that Mr. Savile was a man of grim humour," he remarked. "Perhaps his humour was the humour of lunacy. He must have been a wicked man, at least—as wicked as the blackest imp of hell. Giving a dinner to four enemies was only the beginning of his joke. Working his four guests into a fever against him was only a preparation.

"To unravel the mystery of his death we must use guesswork to connect our links. One guess I shall make is that Mark Savile's affairs had reached a crisis. Perhaps, Lord Clavering, your fears about

Fortuna Copper were well founded, and perhaps Savile had been unwily enough to implicate himself for once. At any rate the time had come when Mark Savile must commit his greatest crime. He chose to add others to it.

"Had he wanted to live, he would not have dined four enemies and inspired them with the desire to kill him. That would have been suicide—or shall I say that *was* suicide?

"At all events, he trapped his guests into their several threats and half-threats, and when they had gone he wrote his letter, which would implicate whichever one was rash enough to come back. Probably he had considered the possibility of more than one coming back—that would add spice to the jest. His murder could not be proved against one of them—but it would be suspected against them all.

"Four men with admitted motives, Inspector—and you could never get a strong case against any one of them to bring him to court. But the public would try them. They would be marked men wherever they went. The newspapers would display their photographs. The sensation-loving public would gloat over every particular about the private lives of these four men who were suspected of murder. Private lives!—they would have no privacy. The pointing fingers would follow them everywhere. Worst of all, these four men would suspect each other. Convict a murderer and hang him and his punishment is over, but cast a doubt which cannot be proved or disproved against a man and his trial goes on forever.

"Mark Savile knew the hell to which he was condemning his four enemies. Death came to him on the wings of his last hellish joke.

"He lay down on the hearthrug, as he is lying now. His legs were straight and pressed together, but he had forgotten that a man who is shot and falls to the ground and does not lie neatly. His left hand was clenched tightly to give him courage. He pulled the trigger of his automatic pistol and, almost as the shot that killed him was fired, the weapon vanished!"

He halted in his stride, and beamed benevolently at Inspector Evans.

"The weapon vanished!" he repeated softly.

The valet, who had previously returned to the room but who had hesitated to interrupt the little surgeon's discourse, now advanced and handed him a dress shirt which he identified as the one his master had worn at dinner on the previous evening.

"But the weapon?" said Inspector Evans in a tone of bewilderment. "Where is it?"

Daniel exposed the sleeve of the shirt. Almost to the shoulder it was soiled and grimy.

"In a well-kept room there is only one place where such dirt is allowed to gather," he remarked.

"But we've already looked in the fireplace!" expostulated Evans.

"Not *in* the fireplace," responded Daniel quietly. "*Up* the chimney."

In a moment Evans was on his knees and was turning the rays of a flashlight into the gloom of the chimney. Then he thrust an arm up and, after considerable tugging and pulling, brought down a stout piece of wood which had been wedged in the chimney.

To it was attached a length of strong elastic and attached to the elastic was an automatic pistol with a Maxim silencer.

Evans stared at the apparatus in silence.

"When the shot was fired the weapon vanished," murmured the little surgeon softly. "Tugged out of the dead man's unresisting hand and whisked up the chimney by the elastic. A simple device beloved by conjurors."

He picked up his pearl-grey hat and placed it on his head at a jaunty angle.

"I think that's all for the present, Inspector," he said pleasantly, drawing on his gloves. "I'll see you at the yard later. Good morning gentlemen."

THE CASE OF THE MAN WHO
WAS TOO CLEVER

Ernest Dudley

Vivian Ernest Coltman-Allen (1908–2006) was a man of many parts. Among other things he was an actor, playwright, and crime writer better known as Ernest Dudley, the surname inspired by the town of his birth. Marcelle Bernstein, who wrote his obituary for the *Guardian,* said: "He grew up in Cookham, Berkshire where his father owned a public house and the artist Stanley Spencer, lived next door and paid for his meals by washing up. Spencer's friends included writers and actors such as Ivor Novello and Jack Buchanan and the latter steered the boy toward acting—Ernest later wrote a stage show for him." After some years of acting, Dudley concentrated on writing professionally, and he worked for the BBC at the same time as John Dickson Carr.

Dudley's breakthrough came in 1942 with the creation of Dr. Morelle, of whom Bernstein said: "Conceived in a Bristol cellar during an air raid, he was based on film actor and director Erich von Stroheim, whom Ernest had met briefly in Paris in the 1930s. With his secretary Miss Frayle... Dr. Morelle featured in novels, short stories, a film—*The Case of the Missing Heiress* (1949) –, a play and three radio serials." This story is taken from *Meet Dr. Morelle* (1943).

ONE EVENING DOCTOR MORELLE HAD BEEN VISITING A SCIEN-tist acquaintance who resided in a block of flats which the Doctor has sardonically described as "reminiscent of native cliff-dwellings". Miss Frayle had accompanied him on his visit, and they had said "Goodnight" to their host and were descending the staircase from the second floor on their way out. As the distance down was so short they did not bother to call the lift. Suddenly Miss Frayle was shocked and horrified to hear the sound of what appeared to be a woman screaming.

The screams came from a flat on the first floor, and the creature sounded as if she were in great agony.

Miss Frayle turned a white face to the Doctor and grasped his arm.

"Doctor, listen! That awful screaming—! It's some woman—!"

"I was not under the impression it was the squeaking of a mouse!" he replied, pausing, and glancing along the passage leading to the flats.

"It's coming from that flat along there!" gasped Miss Frayle, stepping forward as if to hurry in the direction she was indicating. "It must be someone in terrible pain—"

The Doctor's eyes narrowed speculatively. He walked quickly past her, speaking to her over his shoulder.

"I think perhaps it would be advisable to ascertain the reason for such distress."

She caught up with him and was saying breathlessly: "Perhaps we can do something—" when there came the humming of the lift ascending. The lift-gates opened with a slam and the hall-porter shot out, his eyes popping, and rushed after them.

"Here's the porter," Miss Frayle told the Doctor unnecessarily, for he had already observed the man's approach. "We'll go in with him."

"Blimey! Who's kicking up the song-and-dance?" he gulped as he joined them.

"It's from the flat along here," she said.

The screams continued, and they hurried in the direction from whence they came.

"Fancy practising scales this time o' night!" exclaimed the porter with an attempt at heavy-handed humour.

Doctor Morelle turned his head and eyed him with extreme disfavour. "I feel fewer abortive attempts at misplaced humour and more imperative action is indicated!" he snapped.

"Something awful's happening, I'm sure—" cried Miss Frayle as she ran alongside in order to keep up with the Doctor's raking strides, the porter was breathing stertorously as he laboured after them.

Suddenly the screaming subsided, dying away into moans. Then silence.

"She's chucked it now, anyway!" grunted the porter. "Flat nineteen it sounded from. That's Mr. and Mrs. Collins—"

They reached the door that bore the number nineteen, and the porter produced his passkey. There came no sound from within the flat as he turned the key in the lock.

Doctor Morelle and Miss Frayle found themselves in a small hall with a glimpse of the lounge beyond. Chromium, glass and light oak predominated. There was a faint smell of perfume pervading the atmosphere. As the porter stood uncertainly in the entrance to the lounge there came a rapid movement and a youngish man appeared, wearing a blue silk dressing gown. His face was ghastly.

"Mr. Collins!" exclaimed the porter.

"Thank heavens—! Thank heaven, you've come!" the man cried.

"What's happened?" Miss Frayle said. "We heard—"

"My wife—!" was the agitated response. "Locked herself in the bathroom! She—she's—" he broke off incoherently, and they followed him as he rushed back the way they had come. The bathroom was at the end of a short passage on either side of which two bedrooms faced each other.

"Blimey! We'd better bust the door in!" said the porter as Collins rattled vainly at the lock.

"Diana! Diana!" he called, and turned to them frantically. "We must get in!" he gasped. "Something's happened to my wife! Something's happened to her!"

"Let's shove together. Come on, sir," addressing the Doctor, "and you, Mr. Collins." Doctor Morelle murmured: "No doubt our combined efforts will prove efficacious!"

"Yes—! Yes—!" babbled Collins.

Miss Frayle stood aside as they rushed at the bathroom door together. The door was not built to withstand such vigorous treatment, and when the three of them charged at it the second time there was a sound of splintering wood.

"Once more!" shouted Collins, and after the third attempt the door crashed open.

"Kindly remain in the bedroom, Miss Frayle!" Doctor Morelle said over his shoulder, as he caught sight of the crumpled figure of a woman on the bathroom floor.

"Better get a doctor!" grunted the hall-porter.

"Fortuitously," murmured Doctor Morelle, "I happen to be one—I am Doctor Morelle."

The man shot him a surprised look. "Oh? Lucky you was passing! Even though it's a bit too late by the look o' things!"

Collins cried; "The key's on the floor. Diana must have locked the door before she—she—!" He broke off and knelt down beside the woman. "She's—she's dead!" he muttered brokenly.

She was dead, the Doctor saw at a glance. Thoughtfully he stooped to pick up the fragments of a broken tumbler, which had apparently fallen from the dead woman's grasp. He sniffed at the pieces, then carried them into the lounge.

"Miss Frayle, perhaps you will kindly occupy yourself by finding something in which to wrap these fragments?" As she took them he added: "Possibly you may have noticed the aroma of poppy about them?"

"I was wondering what it was," she said sniffing.

"The poison which the unfortunate woman drank from the tumbler is undoubtedly laudanum—opium prepared in spirits of wine. Hence the aroma of poppy."

"Was it suicide—?" Miss Frayle began to ask, and then gave a sudden exclamation of pain. "Oh! I've cut my finger on one of these bits of glass."

"Tck! Tck! How careless of you! Let me observe the extent of the damage." He examined the cut.

"It's nothing much."

"Quite a superficial injury. Nevertheless it would be wiser to bandage the wound. I can use my handkerchief as a temporary measure."

"Oh Doctor, it seems a shame to spoil it." But in spite of her protest, he produced his handkerchief from his breast pocket and proceeded to bandage the cut finger.

"How neatly you've done it!" Miss Frayle smiled up at him admiringly, as he finally tied the knot. "And so quick."

"Quite comfortable?"

"Beautiful! Thank you so much, Doctor. Er—may I have it back please?"

"Um—?" He seemed to be deep in thoughtful contemplation of her hand.

"My hand—you're holding on to it!"

He appeared to snap out of his musing.

"Ah yes! I was momentarily somewhat preoccupied. I was considering one or two questions I wish to put to Mr. Collins. Perhaps you would be good enough to acquaint him of my identity—if the porter has not already advised him—and ask him to come here. Just call him out of the bathroom, no need for you to venture inside."

Miss Frayle shuddered in agreement and went out of the lounge to find Collins.

In a moment he came in and sat dejectedly in an armchair, his head between his hands. Miss Frayle observed him with pity and glanced at the Doctor who was contemplating him with a look of calculation. Poor man, she thought, it must have been an awful shock to him. Surely the Doctor could leave the business of questioning him till later?

The porter appeared and poured a glass of whisky for Collins, but the latter, however, decided he didn't need it. The porter continued to hold the glass and took an occasional sip himself.

Doctor Morelle leaned negligently against a radiogram. He lit a cigarette thoughtfully.

"What—what could have happened—?" Collins turned to him with a haggard face. "Why should she do such a thing?"

The Doctor shook his head. "The circumstances point to the fact that your wife died from the effects of laudanum poisoning, Mr. Collins," he said quietly.

"Poor lady, what a shocking business!" muttered the porter, and Miss Frayle noticed that he consoled himself with another sip of whisky.

Collins suddenly stood up in a distracted manner and began to pace the room.

"I never dreamt she'd—she'd take her own life!" he cried. "You see, we'd quarrelled—Diana was temperamental—she was an actress on the films and radio—imagined and exaggerated all sorts of things—and when she slammed out of the bedroom, I didn't take what she said about committing suicide seriously."

"She threatened to commit *felo-de-se*?" put in Doctor Morelle softly.

"Yes. But as I say, I thought she was just being melodramatic. I called out to her something to that effect, as a matter of fact, then went to bed. As you see I'm in my dressing gown."

"I had already observed that fact."

Miss Frayle gave the Doctor a quick look and saw that his face wore an enigmatic expression.

Collins went on, speaking jerkily:

"And then suddenly I heard her screaming in terrible pain. I got out of bed, rushed to the bathroom, but the door was locked—"

At that moment the telephone rang in the hall. Collins broke off with a frown. He made as if to answer it himself, then turned to the porter. "Will you see who it is?"

When the man had gone, Doctor Morelle murmured:

"Please continue, Mr. Collins. You were describing how you hurried to the bathroom and found the door secured on the inside."

"Well, there's not much more to tell. I tried to force the door but couldn't, and—and—well, the rest you know."

The porter returned. He said to him:

"A lady to speak to you, sir. Wouldn't give no name," the other's frown deepened. He hesitated and then moved towards the hall. "Perhaps I'd better answer it," he apologised, and went out. He carefully pulled the door after him, but Doctor Morelle made no attempt to overhear the conversation on the telephone; on the contrary, he stood with his head slightly on one side, his eyes narrowed thoughtfully.

"What is it, Doctor?" began Miss Frayle in a hushed whisper.

He waved her into silence. She and the porter stood staring at him wonderingly. Suddenly he gave an exclamation of satisfaction.

"Ah! The almost imperceptible sound of some mechanical device in motion," he said.

"Eh?" grunted the porter.

"Whatever do you mean?" asked Miss Frayle.

Doctor Morelle, who had moved from the radiogram to the centre of the lounge, waved his hand casually.

"I should imagine it emanates from that radiogram."

He crossed to it with a swift movement and raised the light oak lid.

"H'm... As I had imagined, the turntable is still in motion."

"So it is," exclaimed the porter. "It hasn't been switched off—!"

At that moment Collins returned and saw them by the machine. He paused in the doorway, then came forward eyeing them somewhat suspiciously. The Doctor turned to him with a bland expression.

"I was admiring your radiogram," he said suavely.

The other nodded. "Yes... It was a present to my poor wife. She was very fond of the radio, naturally."

"The—ah—deceased also possessed a comprehensive selection of gramophone records," continued the Doctor, indicating a number which had been placed on a chair by the cabinet. He was turning them over as he spoke.

"You goin' to play us a tune, Doctor?" muttered the porter in a somewhat censorious tone. "I must say it don't seem quite the moment—"

Collins cut in, his voice high-pitched: "What's this all about? What's the radiogram got to do with my wife's suicide?"

Imperturbably the Doctor observed:

"This seems to be a somewhat unusual record." He had picked up a disc that bore a plain white label. He glanced at the inscription cursorily. An expectant silence had fallen. Miss Frayle, who had given Collins a quick look, heard Doctor Morelle murmur as if speaking to himself: "It might be interesting to hear this played…"

"This is fantastic!" Collins protested, stepping forward. "Horrible!"

The Doctor seemed not to hear him. He was about to place the record on the revolving turntable when there came a shout.

"Leave that record alone! Put it down—!"

The next moment the disc was almost knocked from his hand as Collins made a sudden lunge. Miss Frayle gasped with sudden apprehension as she saw the look on the man's face. The porter, too, gave an exclamation of surprise, but reacted quickly and grappled with him. There was a fierce struggle, but the porter's weight soon told. Collins was forced back and subsided, breathing heavily, into an armchair, with the porter standing over him, dour and menacing. As if nothing had happened to mar the equanimity of the proceedings, Doctor Morelle placed the record on the turntable and adjusted the volume control.

It proved to be an excerpt from what was apparently a highly dramatic playlet. But what caused the porter's jaw to drop and Miss Frayle to goggle from behind her spectacles was the part where a series of piercing screams issued from the radiogram.

"Blimey!" said the porter hoarsely. "Why, that's Mrs. Collins, and them's the screams wot we heard outside!"

"Exactly the same voice—!" gulped Miss Frayle.

"A voice raised from the grave, is it not, Mr. Collins?" said Doctor Morelle. "And accusing you!"

"Yes…" Doctor Morelle mused through a cloud of cigarette smoke. "It was patently a clear-cut case!" He gave a thin smile of self-satisfaction, and went on:

"Mrs. Collins had undoubtedly succumbed as a result of laudanum poisoning, but the drug had been administered by her husband. How exactly the police will ascertain as a result of their examination of the culprit."

He was sitting before his desk in the study of the house in Harley Street. It was some time later; Collins had been removed by the police summoned to the flat, and he, accompanied by Miss Frayle, had returned home.

Miss Frayle asked:

"But how did the poor woman come to be found locked in the bathroom?"

He regarded her with what he imagined was an expression of extreme tolerance.

"For the simple reason," he explained carefully, "that the husband had dragged her there. He had thereupon locked the door on the inside and made his exit through the window to the fire escape, closing the window after him. It was a simple manoeuvre to return to the flat through the front door. In point of fact, he aroused my suspicions somewhat in the first instance by his manner of drawing attention to the key on the floor. A shade too obviously performed, it occurred to me. Whereupon I took the precaution of ascertaining if there was easy egress from the window. That was merely a minor indicative that all might not be what it purported to be, however."

Miss Frayle duly obliged by looking at him questioningly, and he went on:

"The major clue which attracted my attention was one very obvious fact which would have been apparent to any student with the most elementary knowledge of first-aid!"

She wriggled uncomfortably under the reproach implied in his tone.

"Well, I once took a course of first-aid, Doctor," she said, making a somewhat feeble attempt not to appear intimidated.

"Then I can only presume, my dear Miss Frayle, that even your superior intelligence had failed to absorb the fundamental fact that laudanum is a narcotic which induces a condition of painless stupor!"

She blushed, fiddled with her spectacles, and stammered:

"Why yes—Yes, of course! I remember now—"

"It followed, therefore, the wife would never have screamed out as she was supposed to have done."

He flicked the ash from his cigarette.

"Why did he deliberately attract attention by playing a record of Mrs. Collins screaming like that?" Miss Frayle asked.

"His purpose was to establish a somewhat subtle alibi. He calculated that on hearing the screams the hall-porter would rush to the scene and find him attempting to force the bathroom door—"

"You mean the way we did?"

"Precisely. Thus adding colour and credence to the story he had prepared. It would appear Mr. Collins transferred his affections elsewhere. As his wife, however, was in possession of considerable wealth which would become his upon her demise, he decided to precipitate her death in order to be in a position to embark upon a second marriage." His nostrils quivered with repugnance. "A sordid sequence of events, culminating inevitably in tragedy and disaster."

"Was it the—the other woman who 'phoned?"

He nodded. "I understand it was his inamorata."

Doctor Morelle puffed at his Le Sphinx.

"Umm…" he mused, "were I proposing to include this in a collection of tales of—ah—ratiocination, I should be inclined to entitle it 'The Man who was too Clever'." He gave a thin smile of self-satisfaction. "Yes…a singularly appropriate title."

Miss Frayle frowned. "Oh, but surely, Doctor," she corrected him after a moment's thought, "he wasn't clever enough?"

He closed his eyes with a painfully elaborate sigh.

"That will be the subtle implication conveyed—to the discerning reader!"

"Well," she persisted obstinately, "I don't see how anyone can be too clever and not clever enough all at the same time."

He replied, his voice grating with growing irritation: "The operative word in my last observation happened to be the word, 'discerning'!"

The implication sank in and she challenged him with:

"Meaning, I suppose, that I'm not?" It was her turn to sigh, only there was nothing forced about it. Her sigh came from the heart. Then she shrugged her shoulders. "However," she said, "no doubt I should be grateful to you for thinking I can read at all!"

"I confess I often suspect it is largely a matter of guesswork on your part!"

But she was determined not to be defeated this time. With what for her must have seemed to have been an inspired riposte, she flashed back at him: "Rather in the same way that you guess at these clues you talk about... eh, Doctor Morelle?"

His eyebrows shot up. This was unlike Miss Frayle. For one fraction of a moment his face almost registered surprise. Then, with eyes narrowed but in a voice smooth as silk, he murmured:

"Except that *I* always happen to guess correctly, my dear Miss Frayle!"

Miss Frayle subsided.

THE BROADCAST BODY

Grenville Robbins

Information about Grenville Robbins is hard to come by, and if any readers of this anthology can supplement my meagre stock of knowledge about him, I'd be glad to hear from them. He was a journalist who worked for *The Times* and wrote song lyrics and short stories; I included his "The Broadcast Murder" in *Miraculous Mysteries* and the fact that this story also involves broadcasting suggests that he may have had some involvement with the BBC.

My understanding is that he was born in 1893 and that his father was Sir Alfred Robbins, a prominent journalist, political writer, and Freemason. His brother Clifton Robbins published nine Golden Age detective novels between 1931 and 1940, boasting titles such as *Methylated Murder* (1935), but his work has fallen into obscurity, just like Grenville's. This story first appeared in *The 20-Story Magazine* in June 1936.

"You may think I'm mad, my boy; but let me assure you that I'm not. Tomorrow, at noon precisely, I'm going to broadcast my bodily self from my laboratory here at Hampstead to my brother's—your uncle George's—laboratory at Dulwich. And, what is more, you shall be present to watch the experiment.

"At noon I shall be at Hampstead. At 12.1 p.m., or even earlier, I shall, by means of wireless, have projected myself to Dulwich. I don't care a pin if you *do* think I'm mad now. You won't at 12.1 p.m. tomorrow."

I certainly did think my uncle John—in other words, the celebrated Professor Manfred—was mad, as he lay back in his armchair and looked at me in triumph.

And yet I had to admit that, in most particulars, his behaviour seemed to be sane enough.

His eyes were glittering with excitement now, but they were certainly not the eyes of a madman; his fingers were twitching with eagerness, but they were not the twitchings of a lunatic.

In everything he seemed sane enough—except in this one important particular.

Of course, he couldn't project himself through the ether like a sound or even like a picture. The thing was obviously impossible.

And, yet, I had to admit that wireless itself would have seemed impossible only a few years ago and that ordinary telegraphy would have seemed incredible before that.

There was no doubt whatever that the professor was a brilliantly clever man. He knew more about electricity, especially in its relation to wireless and broadcasting, than any man in the world.

He *might* just conceivably have struck some epoch-making discovery by which he could actually broadcast solid bodies through the ether. And yet it *must* be impossible!

I gave it up.

He had been looking at the play of these various ideas, as the different expressions flitted across my face, and now when the final expression showed that I had given it up, he laughed outright.

Out of his chair he sprang with the agility of a trained athlete, for he was only about forty-five years old and as unlike the common conception of a "professor" as it was possible to imagine.

Well over six feet in height and without any superfluous flesh, he was still a perfect picture of health.

He walked quickly across the room to a sideboard and came back with a bottle of champagne and a couple of glasses. He filled them and passed one over to me.

"Well, my young journalistic nephew Henry," he said gaily, "you may not believe a word I say and you may think me mad; but you can't refuse to toast the possible success of my new invention. Here's to it!"

The champagne was Bollinger 1917. I could not refuse to drink that, even if he was mad, and so I drank deeply to the health of the thing I had already irreverently decided to describe as "The Body Broadcaster."

"Now that's better," said the other. "As you've wished the thing well, I'll tell you something about it. That's so long as you promise not to publish anything in your third rate rag until after tomorrow's demonstration."

I promised.

"Apart from my excellent assistant Angus Macdonald, whom you know, you will be the only person allowed to witness the most amazing invention that has ever been made. Henry, you are being honoured above all men, and don't you forget it!"

I murmured something non-committal.

"Ah, I see. You are still unconvinced. Well, just listen to me for a minute."

He held me with his glittering eye, something after the manner of the Ancient Mariner, and so, perforce, I had to listen.

"You see," he began, "a thing that must have seemed mad a thousand, a hundred, or even ten years ago need not necessarily seem—or be—mad today. The telegraph seemed incredible until it came into being; then came the telephone, which was even more surprising.

"Then, from the communication of words by wire we came—and only comparatively recently, too—to the communication of words without wires—that is, to wireless in its original form."

I nodded.

"But see how quickly even wireless has developed during the few years of its existence! First there was wireless telegraphy; then wireless telephony with its illegitimate offspring 'Broadcasting,' as we know it today; and then came the broadcasting of images.

"Phototelegraphy was followed by television, and, with the new scheme of television which I patented only last year—a scheme, mind you, which shows the image in its original colours—we have brought wireless as far as it will go—until noon tomorrow."

I smiled slightly, but luckily for my peace of mind he didn't notice it.

"Just consider my system of television for a minute," he went on. "That is an established fact, and it reproduces in any desired place a perfect two-dimensional representation of whatever is going at the other end, and reproduces it in colour.

"I stand at one end and, practically simultaneously, I am at the other in two dimensions. With the aid of the older inventions my voice can be there, too."

"But," I objected, "your image and your voice—"

"A moment," he interrupted. "I am about to make myself clear. Just consider now how far we have advanced and how rapidly. A few years ago nothing; and now I can project my own voice and my own appearance through the ether at will to any selected spot. Even *you* will admit that this is a remarkable step forward in so short a time."

I had to admit that it was.

"About a year ago, it began to occur to me that there was only one thing more needed to make it possible to project through the ether not merely a two-dimensional image of oneself, but oneself in very fact. Add a third dimension to the two we have already managed to broadcast successfully and the thing is done!"

My brain began to reel, but I tried to look as intelligent as I could.

"And, moreover," he went on, with a bellow of triumph, "if this thing could be achieved it would obviously make the process absolutely different from anything that had preceded it.

"It would no longer be a question of transporting images through the air; it would be a matter of transporting actual things.

"At present, in the two-dimensional form of broadcasting, known as television, there is always the presence of the third dimension at the transmitting end to keep the thing imperfect.

"The thing transmitted can send out images, but its third dimension keeps it firmly pegged down at its own end of the apparatus. Release this third dimension and everything is different.

"Now, you release the whole body and are able to transport through the air to wherever you wish, not only an image of any particular thing, but the thing itself. Do you get me now?"

I answered in the affirmative. It certainly sounded reasonable enough, as he said it, and I had no time to examine it for any flaws in the logic before he plunged rapidly into his argument once more.

"So far as that had gone, the problem was an easy one. I had my starting point—two-dimensional broadcasting—and I knew where I wanted to get to. It was a big step I had to cover, but it was only one step, and that was something.

"I devoted all my energies to that single thing. The solution had narrowed itself down to one single point."

"Oh?" I said blankly.

"How do sounds travel over the ether?"

"Waves," I answered, hoping for the best.

"Right first time. And two-dimensional images in colour travel in the same way, with the help of my own discovery, which is still called only HLC2VO. This mixture, in other words, modifies the images, so that they can span the ether.

"What I had to do, therefore, was to find some new material which would do to the body what this substance did to the image. Now do you get my point?"

I did.

"Good! Now the whole thing had narrowed itself down amazingly. To broadcast, say, the human body, as I am going to do mine tomorrow"—here he broke off and looked at the clock, which said five minutes after midnight—"no, today, I must first reduce the body to a state where its components can be in a condition to be changed into their appropriate wireless waves at the transmitting end.

"They will then travel through the ether to a receiving instrument at the other end, which must have the proper corrective to turn the waves into components and the components into the human body again.

"I had to behave rather like Dr. Jekyll; but, instead of merely separating the good from the evil, I had to separate everything, until the body was reduced to its simplest possible components.

"All the atoms into which it was then turned would create their own appropriate waves, if treated in the right way, and would speed through space, to be reunited at the other end as a human body once more."

"But—" I ventured.

"No buts," he snapped back, "until another twelve hours are over. Then you can follow the example of a famous Lord Chancellor and 'say whatever seems fitting in another place'!

"After all, my boy, my triumph is only a few hours old. Don't spoil my joy in it already.

"For I have indeed found the stuff that renders the body fit for broadcasting—and, what is more, I have also just found the antidote.

"I am not going to tell even you what these two bodies are made of. I won't even tell you if they're vegetable, animal, mineral, or none of them. Let it suffice that the discovery has been made.

"At noon I am going to prove it. I step into the transmitting chamber here. I use my new discovery and am dissolved, until I become a series of waves, which travel with inconceivable rapidity to George's house at Dulwich.

"There, the antidote is ready to receive the waves on arrival and reconvert them into my body once more. The thing cannot fail and shall not fail!

"At noon, I stand by you. A portion of a second later I shall have projected myself by wireless over a distance of a dozen miles.

"You shall be there to see it, my boy; and to you will fall the honour of first writing of my triumph. It is the most profound discovery of two thousand years!"

After this long dissertation, he lay back and ruminated; but he was too excited to keep quiet for more than a few seconds at a time.

"Just think of it!" he said, breaking out again. "A man can be anywhere he wishes in a second. In Hampstead, in America, in China.

Press a lever and his journey's over. No, taxis, no trains, no boats; but straight from door to door.

"The thing's epoch-making! Travelling, as we know, it now, will cease—for who will ride when he can be broadcast? Railways will be useless—for goods can be broadcast as easily as men and women.

"Wars must stop, for they would be over before they had almost begun. The possibilities are limitless. And at noon I shall finally prove them all."

I looked at him again as he lay back, and pondered. He was certainly not mad. Could there conceivably be anything in this extraordinary idea after all? It seemed absolutely impossible, and yet—

Oh, I didn't know!

He was not worrying about me any more. He just lay back with a rapt expression and hardly noticed me until I rose to go.

"Be here at 11.30," was all he said, and dismissed me.

I walked home through the lovely summer night, and as I walked I thought deeply—very deeply, indeed.

As a matter of fact, I wasn't really taken altogether by surprise. The whole thing had been going on for months now, and being the professor's favourite nephew—for the simple reason that I was his only nephew—I had got a pretty fair inkling, weeks before, of the precise kind of bee that had taken up permanent residence in his bonnet.

It was only on this particular evening that I discovered out of his own mouth that it was a bee of such virility and such prodigious size.

Of course, some idea of what was going on had been bound to slip out in one way or another, and vague suggestions had even got into the papers—but not into mine, the *Daily Comet*.

The reason for this was not so much that I was the soul of honour as that I should have got the sack for, in the vernacular, trying to sell them what they would be bound to consider a pup.

One or two of the other papers had not been quite so scrupulous. The *Morning News* had a long article, on what they chose to describe as "The Literary Page," dealing with the idea of broadcasting solid objects and suggesting that it might become a feasible proposition.

This article, I well remember, was sandwiched between an article on "Religion: Does it Help the Housewife?" and the daily ration of "Snappy Jests for Subtle Readers." It was written by a boxer who had recently made a name by winning a fight after having been hit by his opponent in the first round.

A light article on the same subject had also appeared in the *Daily Almanack*, in the course of which the writer waxed desperately witty over the possibilities of using such an invention for the confounding of errant married folk.

That, however, had been about all, and the great public was not in the least stirred. Very sensibly, it preferred to lie low and say nothing.

At the same time, I could not help realising that, whatever happened, the coming experiment was going to be a definitely first-class newspaper story. And I was to be the only outsider present!

Supposing that by any amazing stroke of fortune my uncle actually had stumbled on a miracle—what a story that would make! And the more I pondered on his rational demeanour and his altogether abnormal brain power, the more I began to feel that there was just one chance in two million that the thing might come off according to plan.

When I awoke in the morning I was not quite so sanguine. I hurried to the house at Hampstead and the assistant Macdonald opened the door to me on the stroke of half-past eleven.

I followed him up the stairs to the top storey of the solidly built four-floored house, and was taken straight into the room where the actual experiment was obviously going to take place.

Professor Manfred was already there. He was wearing a dressing-gown. It was clear that he intended to make his unprecedented journey in the garb of Adam.

The room was lighted by electric light and there was no window to be seen. In the middle of the wall opposite the door was a kind of metal cabinet, something like a telephone box, which reached from the floor right up to the ceiling. That was obviously where the transmission was going to take place.

My uncle shook me warmly by the hand. He still seemed perfectly normal. A little excited, that was all.

"Here's the box of tricks," he said, leading me over to the cabinet and flinging open the door. The room was instantly flooded with daylight. The back wall of the box was the wall of the room itself, and in the middle of this was the window. It had no glass in it but was heavily and closely barred.

"There, you see," he said, shaking the bars of the window as though he would tear the side of the house out, "there's absolutely no deception. I'm not going to slip through these and run all the way to Dulwich without any clothes on. A fly couldn't get through there.

"All the same, that window looks towards Dulwich and faces the direction I've got to take. That's why it's there. Straight across, your uncle George is waiting for me. I shall be at his house, twelve miles away, in ten minutes' time."

I nodded,

"Here," he went on, pointing to a great mass of apparatus at the side of the box, "is an adaptation of the regular television transmitter. And here," pointing to another collection of gadgets underneath the window on the floor, "is the new machine that is going to do the business."

I moved towards it.

"Don't touch it," he snapped. "It's only thrown together at present and is terribly fragile. But, even with this delicate machinery, all I have to do is to turn that little handle, which sets all the apparatus in motion, and science does the rest. Hey presto! I'm gone."

He looked at his watch again.

"Five minutes," he muttered. "Here, Angus, be a good fellow and ring up my brother, to make sure that everything's all right that end."

The telephone was on the wall, just by the cabinet, and the call was through in a minute. Everything was apparently ready.

At one minute to noon the professor slipped off his dressing-gown and stood naked in front of us, while he gave us a parting admonition.

"I turn on the handle directly I have shut the door behind me," he said. "Give me a whole minute, whatever happens, and then come in. If it takes longer than that, the thing's a failure and I'm a fool."

So saying, he slipped into the cabinet and slammed the door behind him. It fitted exactly and we were left with only the subdued glow of the electric light again.

Neither of us said a word. We were both too excited for that. I had my watch in my hand, and at last the second hand crawled round to noon. I could just hear a neighbouring church clock striking the hour, and then I bent over my watch again.

The professor should have his sixty seconds and not a second more. Ten seconds had passed when there was a slight sound from within. That was all until, just as the minute was up, there was a tremendous explosion from inside. It sounded as though all the glass in the world had been smashed at the same time.

Angus and I sprang at the door simultaneously. It was stiff and so a couple of seconds elapsed before we could open it.

There was an acrid smell inside and a good deal of smoke, but the sunlight was now streaming through and every corner of the little cabinet could be seen.

Every component of the apparatus was smashed into bits. The floor was absolutely covered with metal and glasswork.

But otherwise the cabinet was empty!

Automatically, I tugged at the bars of the window. They were as solid as a rock. Nothing could have got through them.

I was too surprised to speak, but Angus echoed my thoughts when he suddenly gave a yell.

"Good Lord!" he shouted. "He's done it!"

I stood there stupefied. It certainly did seem as though the professor had indeed "done it." It seemed clear that he really had managed to broadcast his body through the ether, over twelve miles of London roofs, from Hampstead as far as Dulwich.

Angus dashed to the telephone; but after an impatient wait was reluctantly convinced that the line had gone out of order. "It's those confounded electrical disturbances, I suppose!" he cried excitedly.

"Look here, be a sport. The professor's car is outside. Hop into it and drive like blazes to Dulwich and see what's happened. Hurry up."

I hurried, and my uncle's chauffeur was soon making his way to Dulwich with a celerity that at any other time would have frightened me clean out of my wits.

My uncle George at Dulwich was a very different kind of person from my uncle John at Hampstead. Ten years younger and without a tithe of the other's brains, he had spent most of his life and earned most of his money by acting as a pallid reflection of his brilliant brother.

He dabbled in science a bit; he, in fact, dabbled in most things a bit, and was able to help the other in some of the easier parts of his experiments.

No doubt he received a regular remuneration for these slight services, and during the last great series of experiments, which had just had such a momentous culmination, they had been working together practically the whole time.

I had never had very much to do with Uncle George; but, if he had never done me any good, he had certainly never done me any harm. As long as he was left alone he did not worry much.

So I was distinctly surprised when, after a mad drive, we drew up outside his house at Dulwich, to find him dancing on his own doorstep. When he saw me, he stopped.

"Whatever's happened?" he cried.

"That's just what I came here to find out," I answered, in surprise.

He looked at me blankly, and almost dragged me into the house after him.

"I don't understand," he said. "There was a loud explosion here and that was all. And when I tried to ring you up, the line was out of order. Has anything happened to John? Was he hurt when the experiment started?"

"What do you mean?" I asked stupidly. "Isn't he *here?*"

"Isn't he *there?*" retorted the other.

"No," I said. "There was an explosion at Hampstead, too, and when we opened the door of the cabinet he'd vanished."

"Good gracious!" said poor Uncle George, brandishing his arms in the air. "Whatever *can* have happened?"

I quietened him down a bit, and eventually we both simply had to come to the same conclusion.

The first part of the experiment had been a success and the second hadn't. In other words, the professor had been able to transform his body into its elements and to project himself from his starting point at Hampstead. That much seemed obvious.

But then something must have gone wrong, and he had not been able to transform those elements back into a body again, and so to reappear at Dulwich.

He had, in short, simply vanished into the ether—where, so far as present human knowledge was concerned, he was likely to remain in his present disembodied state for ever, since he alone knew the secret, and his precious apparatus was all smashed to atoms.

"You see," said my uncle George, who must know more about the professor's plans than anyone, "he knew that the first part of his invention was perfect.

"He knew for certain that he could project himself from his laboratory at Hampstead, and he was *practically* sure that he could reconstitute himself at this end.

"*Practically* sure, but not quite; and he admitted to me that he had to take a chance to test the apparatus at this end. Poor John! He was a martyr to science, if there ever was one."

He paused for a second.

"But I saw him," he went on with an hysterical shout, "after anyone else. Even after you."

I looked at him incredulously.

"Yes," he went on. "Just as the clock struck twelve I was looking into the shut cabinet here—it has a glass door this end—and for a portion of a second I saw him in the mirror of the televisor inside, as clearly as I can see you now.

"That was the very start of the process, and then came the explosion which smashed all the wonderful apparatus to smithereens."

By this time we had reached the laboratory. It was almost a replica of the other. So was the cabinet, with the sun streaming through a barred window and the floor ankle deep in broken apparatus.

It was clear that, whatever part of the ether the disembodied professor was tenanting now, his secret was lost for ever.

There was obviously nothing else to be done at Dulwich. So, leaving the place in the care of its housekeeper, an aged and deaf old lady who was the only other inhabitant, I bustled my stupefied relation into the car and we returned post haste to Hampstead.

My companion talked volubly all the way. His nerves seemed to be quite unstrung, and it was really not very surprising. Apparently, he had been as confident of the success of the experiment as the professor.

I did my best to cheer him up, but it was not much good. My uncle George had never been a very strong character, and now he seemed to have gone to bits altogether. His excessive grief rather surprised me.

When we arrived back at the laboratory at Hampstead, everything was as it had been left. Macdonald was at the telephone when we went in, and as he saw us he slammed it down impatiently.

"Thank goodness, you've come!" he cried. "I've been trying to get through ever since you left. Is it all right? Where's the professor?"

We told him the other end of the story, and then all three of us just stood and gaped at each other. The thing seemed inexplicable, unless we agreed that the professor had started his mysterious journey—and never ended it.

In the most literal sense, in fact, he had vanished into thin air.

"What are we going to do?" bleated Uncle George.

That was an easy question to ask, but a pretty difficult one to answer. What *did* one do next?

Of course, we should have to tell the police, who would undoubtedly want to have us all put into a lunatic asylum.

But what exactly could one do about a body that was not in existence? It was no good going to the Hampstead coroner and asking him to hold an inquest on nothing.

And, yet, there seemed to be no doubt that, if not dead, the professor had at least shuffled off his mortal coil. If he wasn't a corpse within the meaning of the Act, he certainly wasn't alive within the meaning of the Act.

It was all very difficult.

Anyhow, we had to tell the police, and the lot fell on me. They obviously thought I was mad, but they condescended to make a thorough search of rooms and there the matter rested for several weeks.

It made a first-class sensation, but eventually the great British public, through their newspapers, were simply compelled to believe that the unlucky professor was wandering in a disembodied state in some curious fourth dimension which he alone inhabited.

As the circumstances were distinctly unusual it was something more than a nine days' wonder, but gradually it began to be forgotten—another actress had some pearls stolen—and Uncle George having at his own wish gone to the Riviera to pull himself together, I had almost stopped thinking about it, too.

Then I had a visit from our family solicitor.

He had been going through the professor's papers, preparatory to inviting the law to presume his death, and the chaotic state of his affairs had given the methodical legal gentleman something of a shock.

The professor seemed to be pretty heavily in debt all round. I hadn't expected that—although it was no real surprise, for he was notoriously careless about practical details of this kind. He lived in his scientific world and seemed to let the rest take care of itself.

What was surprising, however, was that, although he had been very heavily insured in several companies some years before, he had left no will.

All that could be found was a draft of an unfinished, unsigned and unwitnessed document which left all his possessions, on his death, to his "beloved assistant, Angus Macdonald."

There was not even a date to the draft which, of course, would not hold water any way. Try as they would, they could find no other will, so automatically any money would pass to Uncle George.

Although the draft will was valueless from a legal point of view, it had occurred to the solicitor, and it now occurred to me, that it might be very valuable as a pointer. We started to argue the matter out, there and then, and our cogitations were somewhat like this:

Either the professor had done the apparently impossible and projected himself into the ether, or—as seemed more likely—his incredible experiment had failed, and some human being had taken the opportunity of getting rid of him in as unsuspicious a way as possible.

Supposing someone *had* wanted to get rid of my uncle, and supposing that that someone was a person who knew him well, what better time to choose than the moment when, as he had announced many hours before, he was in fact definitely going to disappear?

Granting, then, that my uncle had not vanished into thin air but that he had been murdered, who was the most likely person to have committed the deed?

The thing was clear. It was Angus Macdonald, his "beloved assistant"! He was, moreover, more than likely to have known that the professor intended to leave his money to him, and to have assumed that he had done so.

Once, then, the professor were out of the way, Angus would come into all the insurance money—which, even after the debts were paid, would amount to some £15,000.

What could be better than to arrange to come into it at the convenient time when the professor had announced that he was going to disappear anyhow?

The facts fitted together like a jig-saw puzzle.

★

On the other hand, what had happened to the body? That was a bit of a poser. I certainly thought that there was nothing in the cabinet—I could have sworn it—but I was allowed only a short glimpse, and when there was the smoke of the explosion still inside. Then I had been bundled off to Dulwich.

What a fool I had been! I saw it all now. He had got rid of me while he completed his plans.

But what of the two explosions? It seemed obvious now. As my uncle's assistant, he would have had ample opportunity to tamper with the machine; and, if he could smash the Hampstead end, it was quite conceivable that the other would follow, for that the two were *en rapport* was obvious from Uncle George's glimpse of his brother in the televisor.

Everything seemed to fit in, and I was confident that the mystery was solved. My uncle had not vanished into thin air. He had been murdered and his assistant was the murderer! The body must be in that Hampstead house somewhere.

I told the police, who seemed more interested now, and next morning had a telegram from the Riviera.

Uncle George was dead. He had succumbed to a heart attack. Banishing every other thought, I left London post haste. Two days later I entered the private suite he had been occupying at his Riviera hotel. Someone was sitting in an armchair. He turned round as I came in.

It was the professor!

He smiled bitterly as he saw me.

"Sorry, my boy," he said. "The game's up. I've behaved like a cad and a swine, and now I've got to take what's coming to me."

I could do nothing but stare at him.

He looked at me defiantly enough, but suddenly he pillowed his face in his hands.

"Poor George," he murmured. "He never liked it, and then, when everything was plain sailing, he died. Yes. Every detail had been worked out to the nth, and then Death stepped in and took a hand in the game. Well, I'd better tell you everything."

He led the way to a balcony overlooking the sea and, sitting there in the glorious sunshine, I heard all the details of this tangled business.

"You see," began the professor, "to put things in a nutshell, I've become nothing more or less than a professional crook. I never was any good at business, as you know, and, during the last four or five years my affairs had got into a terrible tangle. I was wrapped up in my scientific work. It was all I lived for then."

He sighed heavily.

"A year or so ago I took stock of my position. Things were coming to a climax, and the matter had got to be faced. I owed nearly £10,000, and I had probably less than a thousand in the bank. The thing was hopeless.

"Then I thought of that insurance money. When I started some dangerous work some years ago, I was advised to go in for it and, as a matter of fact, it never cost me a penny. All the premiums were paid by people interested in the experiments.

"Altogether I reckoned that, at my death, my insurances would bring in about £25,000. That meant £25,000 less £10,000 dead; and minus £10,000 alive.

"The result was that, there and then, I schemed that my next experiment would not be so scientific as everyone would be led to believe. It was to be planned with the definite idea of producing that insurance money, and of producing it while I was still able to enjoy it—while I was still alive. Do you begin to see things now?"

I did.

"That was the only reason that started me on my alleged new invention. The whole thing was a plant."

"Do you mean to say," I said, "that that night you were talking to me you were only acting?"

"I am afraid so," he replied. "I'm sorry now. All those months I was only providing local colour. It was a pretty safe assumption that, if I announced that I was going to disappear during a scientific experiment, and then did disappear, people would have eventually to admit that the disappearance was natural."

"They certainly did," I admitted reluctantly. "But how on earth did you get Angus Macdonald to help you?"

"Macdonald?" he asked in astonishment. "He knew nothing about it whatever. He must be as surprised as you were."

"But they found a draft will—"

"A draft will? Good heavens! That's two years old. I had a quarrel with George and was doing it to spite him. I soon decided not to be such a fool. I thought I'd torn it up. No; it wasn't Angus who was in it. It was poor George, of course."

"Was Uncle George in it?"

"I'm afraid so. You see, when I was eventually presumed dead the money would go to George, whether I made a will or not, and it seemed better not to attract attention by making one.

"He had to be in the plot so as to pass the money on to me. In the meantime, I had enough ready cash to carry on with.

"No; the scheme was worked out to the very last detail. It was perfect, until poor George fell down dead. That, of course, ruined everything. You see, you're the next-of-kin now. Anything else you want to know before I go?"

"Before you go?"

"Yes, before I go."

"What were the explosions?"

"Easy. We'd arranged them at each end, so as to leave no incriminating apparatus behind. George touched his off, and I touched mine. Then, in a second, I was through the window and along the ledge outside to the window of the room next door, where I had left a suit of clothes."

"Through the window? The bars were as firm as rock."

"I know they were. That was an ingenious idea of mine. The *bars* didn't move, but the whole window did. It opened inwards like a shutter and was fixed to with an ordinary spring catch. No one could spot it who didn't know, and once it was shut it was as firm as the wall of a prison."

He shivered.

"I was in the next room in a second and down the stairs and out of the house while you were still peering into the cabinet. I'd arranged for that telephone to go dead. I knew that would keep you a bit."

"Well, you certainly had everything well planned," I said bitterly.

"Yes," he said musingly, "I thought I'd covered every eventuality until George died. And I've got a way of getting over that."

The professor paused for a second and suddenly I saw his meaning. I sprang forward, but it was too late. He slipped something into his mouth and fell with a crash at my feet.

He was stone dead.

Perhaps it was the best way.

I still think that he was a little unlucky. If Uncle George hadn't had a bad heart, they would probably both be living very comfortably abroad to this day.

And somehow one can't worry too much about the feelings of insurance companies.

THE COULMAN HANDICAP

Michael Gilbert

For more than half a century, Michael Gilbert (1912–2006) entertained his readers with a rich variety of stories ranging from classic detection, through police procedurals, legal mysteries, and adventure stories and thrillers, to high-calibre tales of espionage. Perhaps, therefore, it should come as no surprise that this versatile writer began as a published novelist with a story about a seemingly impossible crime, *Close Quarters* (1947). The central mystery, as Bob Adey summarised it, concerns "murder in a guarded area where those present are generally alibied". It was an auspicious start to a distinguished literary career and five years later Gilbert wrote one of his finest books, *Death in Captivity*. Set in an Italian prisoner of war camp and filmed by Don Chaffey as *Danger Within*, the book also earns a mention in Adey's *Locked Room Murders*.

Gilbert was one of the few British crime writers to receive the highest awards in the genre from both the UK's Crime Writers' Association and the Mystery Writers of America. However, he only wrote one other "impossible crime" story, which appeared in *Argosy* in April 1958. This is it.

T HE DOOR OF NO. 35 BOND ROAD OPENED AND A THICK-SET, middle-aged woman came out. She wore a long grey coat with a collar of alpaca wool buttoned to the neck, a light grey hat well forward on her head, and mid-grey gloves on her hands. Her sensible shoes, her stockings, and the large, fabric-covered suitcase, which she carried in her right hand, were brown.

She paused for a moment on the step. Women of her age are often near-sighted, but there was nothing in her attitude to suggest this. She had bold, brown, somewhat protuberant eyes, set far apart in her strong face. They were not unlike the eyes of an intelligent horse.

She looked carefully to left and to right. Bond Road was never a bustling thoroughfare. At twelve o'clock on that bright morning of early April it was almost empty. A roadman, sweeping the gutter; a grocer's delivery boy, pushing his bicycle, nose down in a comic; the postman, on his mid-morning round. All of them were well known to her. She waited to see if the postman had brought her anything, and then set off up the pavement.

In the front parlour of No. 34, a lace curtain parted one inch and closed again. The man sitting on a chair in the bow window reached for the telephone which stood by his hand and dialled.

He heard a click as the receiver was lifted at the other end and said, "She's off. Going west." Then he replaced the receiver and lit himself a cigarette. The stubs in the tray beside the telephone suggested that he had been waiting for some time.

At that moment no fewer than twenty-four people, in one way

or another, were concentrating their attention on Bond Road and on Mrs. Coulman, who lived at No. 35.

"It's a carrier service," said Superintendent Palance of No. 1 District, who was in charge of the joint operation, "and it's got to be stopped." Jimmy Palance was known throughout the Metropolitan Police Force as a fine organiser, a teetotaller, a man entirely lacking in any sense of humour, who worked with a Pawnbrokers' List and the Holy Bible side by side on his tidy desk.

"The first problem of a thief who steals valuable and identifiable jewellery is to get rid of it. What does he do with it?"

"Flogs it?" suggested Chief Inspector Haxtell of Y Division.

"No fence'll touch it," said Chief Inspector Farmer of X Division. "Not while the heat's on."

"Then he hides it," said Haxtell. "In a safe deposit, or a bank. Crooks do have bank accounts, you know."

"Or a cloakroom, or a left-luggage office."

"Or with a friend, or at an accommodation address."

"Or sealed up in a tin, under the third tree from the corner."

"No doubt," said Superintendent Palance, raising his heavy black eyebrows, "there are a great number of possible hiding-places. I myself have listed twenty-seven distinct types. There may be more. The difficulty is that by the time the thief wishes to recover his loot, he is as often as not himself under observation."

Neither Haxtell nor Farmer questioned this statement. They knew well enough that it was true. A complicated system of informers almost always gave them the name of the perpetrator of any big and successful burglary. "All we then have to arrange is to watch the thief. If he goes near the stuff we will be able to lay hands on the man himself, and his cache, and his receiver."

"True," said Haxtell. "So what does he do?"

"He gets in touch with Mrs. Coulman. And informs her where

he has placed the stuff. Gives her the key, or cloakroom ticket, and leaves the rest to her. It is not even necessary to give her the name of the receiver. She knows them all, and gets the best prices. She gets paid in cash, keeps a third, and hands over two-thirds to the author of the crime."

"Just like a literary agent," said Farmer, who had once written a short story.

"Sounds quite a woman," said Haxtell.

"She has curious antecedents," said Palance. "She is German. And I believe, although I've not been able to check it, that she and her brothers were in the German Resistance."

"The fact that she's alive proves she was clever," agreed Haxtell. "Now, I gather you want quite a few men for this. Tell us how you plan to tackle it."

"It's going to be a complicated job," said Palance. "But here is the outline…"

At the end of the street, after turning into the main road, Mrs. Coulman had a choice of transport. She could take a bus going south, or could cross the street and take a bus going north. Or she could walk two hundred yards down the hill to one Underground Station, or an equal distance up it to another. Or she could take a taxi. She was a thick-set woman of ample Teutonic build; and experience, gained in the last month of observation, had suggested that she would not walk very far, and would be more likely to walk downhill than up.

Near each bus stop a man and girl were talking. Opposite the Underground a pair of workmen sat, drinking endless cups of tea. In a side street two taxis waited, a driving glove over the meter indicating that they were not for hire. A small tradesman's van, parked in a cul-de-sac, acted as mobile headquarters to this part of the operation.

It was backed halfway into a private garage, chosen because it was on the telephone.

Mrs. Coulman proceeded placidly to the far end of Bond Road, waited for a gap in the traffic, crossed the main road, and turned up a side road beyond it.

An outburst of intense activity followed.

"Still going west," said the controller in the van. "Making for Highside Park. Details one to eight, switch in that direction. Number one car straight up Loudon Road and stop. Number two car parallel. Details nine and ten, cover Highside Tube Station and the bus stops at the top of the hill."

Mrs. Coulman emerged, panting slightly, from the side road which gave on to the top of Highside Hill, paused, and caused consternation in the ranks of her pursuers by turning round and walking back the way she had come.

Control had just worked out the necessary orders to jerk the machine into reverse when it was seen that Mrs. Coulman had retraced her steps to admire a flowering shrub in a front garden she had passed. Looking carefully about her to see that no one was watching, she nipped off a small spray and put it in her buttonhole. Then she turned back towards Highside Hill and made, without further check, for the Tube Station.

Details number nine and ten were Detective Sergeants Petrella and Wynne. They were waiting inside the station, at the head of the emergency stairs, and were already equipped with all-day tickets. When Mrs. Coulman reached the station entrance, therefore, she found it deserted. She bought a ticket for Euston and took the lift. A young man in corduroys and a raincoat, and an older one in flannel trousers, a windcheater and a club scarf, were already on the platform, waiting for the train. They got into the coaches on either side of her.

Above their heads the machine jerked abruptly into top gear. A word was exchanged with the booking-office clerk and two taxis sped towards Euston.

Mrs. Coulman, however, had disconcertingly changed her mind. Euston, Warren Street, Goodge Street, Tottenham Court Road—station after station came and went and still she sat on. Her seat had been chosen to command the exits of her own and the two neighbouring carriages. She seemed to take a close interest in the people who got on and off. But if she noticed that the men who had come from Highside were still with her, she gave no sign.

It was nearly half an hour later when she quitted the train at Clapham Common Station and made for the moving staircase, looking neither to right nor to left.

Petrella had time for a quick word with Wynne. "It's my belief the old bitch has rumbled us," he said. "Get on the blower and bring the rest of the gang down here, as quickly as possible. Meanwhile, I'll do my best to keep on her tail."

This proved easy. Mrs. Coulman walked down the street without so much as a backward glance, and disappeared into the saloon bar of The Admiral Keppel public house. Petrella made a detour of the place to ensure that it had no back entrance, and settled down to watch. It could hardly have been better situated for his purpose. The doors of its saloon and public bar opened side by side on to the same strip of pavement. Opposite them stood a sandwich bar, with a telephone.

"I don't think we ought to crowd the old girl," said Petrella into the telephone. "It's my impression she's got eyes in the back of her head. If you could send someone—not Wynne, she's seen too much of him already this morning—and put a man at either end of the street, so that *we* don't have to follow her immediately as she goes—"

The voice at the other end approved these arrangements. Time passed. Petrella saw Detective Constable Mote ambling down the pavement, and he flagged him in.

"She's been there a long time," he said. "It must be nearly closing time."

"Sure she hasn't come out?" said Mote.

Petrella looked at his little book. "Two business men," he said. "One youth with a girlfriend, aged about seventeen and skinny. One sailor with a kitbag. That's the score to date."

The door of the public bar opened and three men came out and stood talking to the landlord, who seemed to know them. The men went off down the road together, the landlord disappeared inside, and they heard the sound of bolts being shut.

"Hey," said Petrella. "What's all this?"

"It's all right. There's still someone in the saloon bar," said Mote. "I can see the shadow on the glass. Seems to be knocking her drink back."

"Slip across and have a look," said Petrella.

Mote crossed the road lower down and strolled up past the ground-glass window of the saloon bar.

"It's a woman," he reported. "Sitting in the corner, drinking. I think the landlord's trying to turn her out."

As he spoke the door was flung open and the last of the customers appeared. She was the same shape as Mrs. Coulman, but she seemed to have changed her hat and coat, and to have done something to her face, which was now a mottled red.

She stood on the pavement for a moment, while the landlord bolted the door behind her. Then she ploughed off, straight and strong up the street, dipping very slightly as she progressed.

A thin woman coming out of a shop with a basket full of groceries was nearly run down. She saved herself by a quick sidestep, and said, in reproof, "Carnchew look where you're goin'?"

The massive woman halted, wheeled, and hit the thin woman in the eye. It was a beautiful, co-ordinated, unconscious movement, as full of grace and power as a backhand passing-shot by a tennis champion at the top of her form.

The thin woman went down, but was up again in a flash. She was no quitter. She kicked her opponent hard on the ankle. A uniformed policeman appeared, closely followed by Sergeant Gwilliam, who had been waiting round the corner and felt that it was time to intervene. The massive woman, thus beset, back-heeled at her first assailant, aimed a swinging blow with a carrier-bag full of bottles at the constable, missed him, and hit Sergeant Gwilliam.

Some hours later Superintendent Palance said coldly, to Chief Inspector Haxtell, "I take it that Sergeant Petrella is a reliable officer."

"I have always found him so," said Haxtell, equally coldly.

"This woman, to whom he seems, at some point, to have transferred his attention, is certainly not Mrs. Coulman."

"Apparently not," said Haxtell. "In fact she is a well-known local character called Big Bertha. She is also believed to hold the woman's drinking records for both draught and bottled beer south of the Thames."

"Indeed?" Superintendent Palance considered the information carefully. "There is no possibility, I suppose, that she and Mrs. Coulman are leading a double life?"

"You mean," said Haxtell, "that the same woman is sometimes the respectable Mrs. Coulman of Bond Road, Highside, and sometimes the alcoholic Bertha of Clapham? It's an attractive idea, but I'm afraid it won't wash. Bertha's prison record alone makes it an impossibility. During the month you've been watching Mrs. Coulman, Bertha has, I'm afraid, appeared no less than four times in the Southwark Magistrates Court."

"In that case," said Palance reasonably, "since the lady under observation was Mrs. Coulman when she started, Sergeant Petrella must have slipped up at some point."

"I agree," said Haxtell. "But where?"

"That is for him to explain."

"It's a stark impossibility," said Petrella, later that day. "I *know* it was Mrs. Coulman when she went into the pub. There's no back entrance. I mean that, literally. It's a sort of penthouse, built on to the front of the block. The landlord himself has to come out of one of the bar doors when he leaves. And our local people say he's perfectly reliable. They've got nothing against him at all."

"Could she have done a quick-change act? Is there a ladies' lavatory, or some place like that?"

"Yes. There's a lavatory. And she could have gone into it, and changed into other clothes which she had ready in her suitcase. It's all right as a theory. It's when you try to turn it into fact that it gets difficult. I saw nine people coming out of that pub. The first two were business types from the saloon bar. The landlord didn't know them, but they seemed to know each other. And anyway they just dropped in for a whisky and out again. Then there was a boy and girl in the public bar. They held hands most of the time and didn't weigh much more than nine stone nothing a piece."

"None of them sounds very likely," agreed Haxtell. "And the three workmen were local characters, or so I gather. That leaves the woman and the sailor."

"Right," said Petrella. "And since we know that the woman wasn't Mrs. Coulman, it leaves the sailor. He was broadly the right size and shape and weight, and he was the only one carrying anything. Thinking it over, one can see that's significant. He had a kitbag over his shoulder."

"Just how is a suitcase turned into a kitbag?"

"That part wouldn't be too difficult. The suitcase could easily be a sham. A fabric cover round a collapsible frame, which would fold up to almost nothing and go inside the kitbag with the wig and hat and coat and rest of the stuff."

"Where did the kitbag come from? Oh, I see. She would have had it inside the suitcase. One wave of the wand and a large woman with a large suitcase turns into a medium-sized sailor with a kitbag."

"Right," said Petrella. "And there's only one drawback. The sailor was a man, not a woman at all."

"You're sure?"

"Absolutely and completely sure," said Petrella. "He crossed the road and passed within a few feet of me. He was wearing bell-bottomed trousers and a dark blue sweater. There are certain anatomical differences, you know. And Mrs. Coulman was a very womanly woman."

"A queenly figure," agreed Haxtell. "Yes, I see what you mean."

"It's not only that," said Petrella. "A woman might get away with being dressed as a man on the stage. Or seen from a distance, or from behind. But not in broad daylight, face to face in the street. A man's hair grows in quite a different way, and his ears are bigger, and—"

"All right," said Haxtell. "I'll take your word for it." He paused and added, "Palance thinks you fell asleep on the job, and Mrs. Coulman slipped out when you weren't looking."

"I know," said Petrella. An awkward silence ensued.

Petrella said, "Will they keep up the watch?"

"I should think they'd lay off her a bit," said Haxtell. "It's an expensive job, immobilising a couple of dozen men. And a dinosaur would be suspicious after yesterday's performance. I should think they'd let her run for a bit. There's no reason you shouldn't keep your eyes open, though—unofficially."

Petrella devoted what time he could spare in the next three months to his self-appointed task. His landlady's married sister had a house in Bond Road, so he spent a lot of time in her front parlour and, after dark, prowling around No. 35, the end house on the other side of the road. He also made friends with the booking-clerks at Highside station and Pond End station; and spent an interesting afternoon in the German Section of the Foreign Office.

"One thing's clear enough," he said to Haxtell. "When she's on the job, she starts on the Underground. Taxis and buses are too easy to follow. If you go by Underground, the pursuit has got to come down with you. Or guard the exit of every Underground station in London simultaneously, which is a stark impossibility. Anyway, I know that's what she does. She's been seen three times leaving Highside station, carrying that trick suitcase. She books to any old station. She's only got to pay the difference at the other end. She's a bit more cautious, too, after that last fiasco. She won't get on to the train if there's any other passenger she can't account for on the platform. Sometimes she's let three or four trains go past."

Haxtell reflected on all this, and said, "It seems a pretty watertight system to me. How do you suggest we break in on it?"

"Well, I think we've got to take a chance," said Petrella. "In theory it'd be safer with a lot of people, but actually, I don't think it would work at all. That kind can always spot organised opposition. There's just a chance, if you'd let two or three of us try it, next time we get word that she's likely to be busy—"

"We'll see," said Haxtell.

Three nights after these words were spoken, on a Saturday, the redoubtable twin brothers, Jack and Sidney Ponting, made entry into Messrs. Alfreys' West End establishment by forcing the skylight of an adjacent building, picking three separate locks, cutting their way through an eighteen-inch brick wall, and blowing the lock neatly out of the door of the new Alfrey strong room. When the staff arrived on Monday they found a mess of brickwork and twisted steel. The losses included sixty-four large rough diamonds deposited by a Greek ship-owner. They were to have formed the nuptial head-dress of his South American bride.

"It's a Ponting job," said Superintendent Palance. "It's got their registered trade mark all over it. Get after them quick. They're probably hiding up."

But the Pontings were not hiding. They were at home, and in bed. They raised no objection to a search of their premises.

"It's irregular," said Sidney. "But what have we got to hide?"

"You boys have got your job to do," said Jack. "Get it finished, and we can get on with our breakfast."

Palance came up to see Haxtell.

"They certainly did it. They most certainly did it. Equally certainly they've dumped the diamonds. And none of them has reached a receiver yet, I'm sure of that. And the Pontings use Mrs. Coulman."

"Yes," said Haxtell. "Well, we must hope to do better this time."

"Are you set on trying it on your own?"

Palance was senior to Haxtell. And he was longer in service, and older in experience. Haxtell thought of these things, and paused. He was well aware of the responsibility he was shouldering, and which he could so easily evade. Then he said, "I really think the only way is to try it ourselves, quietly."

"All right," said Palance. He didn't add, "And on your own head be it." He was never a man to waste words.

Four days followed, during which Petrella attended to his other duties as well as he could by day, and prowled round the curtilage of No. 35 Bond Road by night. Four days in which Sergeant Gwilliam,

and Detective Constables Wilmot and Mote were never out of reach
of a telephone; and Haxtell sweated.

On the fifth night Petrella gave the signal: Tomorrow's the day.
And at eleven o'clock next morning, sure enough, the front door
opened and Mrs. Coulman peered forth. She was wearing her travelling coat and hat, and grasped in her muscular right hand was the
fabric-covered suitcase.

She walked ponderously down the road. However acute her
suspicions may have been, there was nothing for them to feed on.
For it is a fact that at that moment no one was watching her at all.

Ten minutes later she was purchasing a ticket at Highside Station.
The entrance to the station was deserted. She waited placidly for
the lift.

The lift and Sergeant Gwilliam arrived simultaneously. He was
dressed as a workman, and he seemed to be in a hurry. He bought
a ticket to the Elephant and Castle and got into the lift beside Mrs.
Coulman. In silence, and avoiding each other's eye, they descended
to platform level. In silence they waited for the train.

When the train arrived, Sergeant Gwilliam hesitated. He seemed
to have an eye on Mrs. Coulman's movements. They approached
the train simultaneously. At the very last moment Mrs. Coulman
stopped. Sergeant Gwilliam went on, the doors closed, and the train
disappeared bearing the Sergeant with it.

Mrs. Coulman returned to her seat on the platform and waited
placidly. By the time the next train arrived, the only other occupants
of the platform were three schoolgirls. Mrs. Coulman got into the
train, followed by the schoolgirls. Two stations later the schoolgirls
got off. Mrs. Coulman, from her customary seat beside the door,
watched them go.

Thereafter, as the train ran south, she observed a succession of
people getting on and off. There were three people she did not see.

Petrella, with Mote and Wilmot, had entered the train at the station before her. Sergeant Gwilliam's planned diversion had given them plenty of time to get there. Petrella was in the first and the other two were in the last carriages of the train.

It was at Balham that Mrs. Coulman finally emerged. Two women with shopping-bags, who had joined her carriage at Leicester Square, went with her. Also a commercial traveller with samples, whom she had watched join the next carriage at the Oval.

Petrella, Mote, and Wilmot all saw her go, but it was no part of their plan to follow her, so they sat tight.

At the next stop, all three of them raced for the moving stairs, hurled themselves into the street, and found a taxi.

"I'm off duty," said the taxi-driver.

"Now you're on again," said Petrella, and showed him his warrant card. "Get us back to Balham Station, as quick as you can."

The taxi-driver blinked, but complied. Petrella had his eye on his watch.

"She's had four minutes' start," he said, as they bundled out. "You know what to do. Take every pub in your sector. And get a move on."

The three men separated. There is no lack of public houses in that part of South London, but Petrella calculated that if they worked outwards from the station, taking a sector each, they could cover most of them quite quickly. It was the riskiest part of the scheme, but he could think of no way to avoid it.

He himself found her.

She was sitting quietly in the corner of the saloon bar of The Gatehouse, a big, newish establishment at the junction of the High Street and Trinity Road.

There was no convenient snack bar this time; there was very little cover at all. The best he could find was a trolleybus shelter. If he stood behind it, it did at least screen him from the door.

The minutes passed, and added up to a quarter of an hour. Then to half an hour. During that time two people had gone in, and three had come out, but none of them had aroused Petrella's interest. He knew, more or less, what he was looking for.

At last the door opened and a man emerged. He was a thick, well-set-up man, dressed in a close-fitting flannel suit which was tight enough across the shoulders and round the chest to exhibit his athletic frame. And he was carrying a canvas bag, of a type that athletes use to hold their sports gear.

He turned left, and swung off down the pavement with an unmistakable, aggressive masculine stride, a mature bull of the human herd, confident of his strength and purpose.

Petrella let him have the length of the street, and then trotted after him. This was where he had to be very careful. What he mostly needed was help. The chase swung back past the Underground and there he spotted Wilmot and signalled him across.

"In the grey flannel suit, carrying a bag," he said. "See him? Then get right after him, and remember, he's got eyes in the back of his head."

Wilmot grinned all over his guttersnipe face. He was imaginatively dressed in a teddy-boy suit and he fitted into the South London streets as easily as a rabbit into a warren.

"Doanchew worry," he said, "I won't lose him."

Petrella fell back until he was a hundred yards behind Wilmot. He kept his eyes open for Mote. The more of them the merrier. There was a long, hard chase ahead.

He noticed Wilmot signalling.

"Gone in there," said Wilmot.

"Where?"

"Small shop. Bit of the way up the side street."

Petrella considered. "Walk past," he said. "Take a note of the name and number on the shop. Go straight on, out of sight, to the other end. If he goes that way, you can pick him up. If he comes back I'll take him."

Ten minutes went by. Petrella thought anxiously about back exits. But you couldn't guard against everything.

Then the man reappeared. He was carrying the same bag, yet it looked different. Less bulky in shape but, by the swing of it, heavier.

He's dumped the hat and coat and the remains of the suitcase at that accommodation address, thought Petrella. Even if we lose him, we know one of the Ponting hide-outs. But we mustn't lose him. That bag's got several thousand pounds' worth of stolen jewellery in it now.

Would it be best to arrest him, and give up any chance of tracing the receiver? The temptation was almost overmastering. Only one thing stopped him. His quarry was moving with much greater freedom, as if convinced that there was no danger. Near the end of the run he would get cautious again. For the moment there was nothing to do but follow.

The man plunged back in the Underground; emerged at Waterloo; joined the queue at the Suburban Booking-Office. Petrella kept well clear for he owned a ticket which enabled him to travel anywhere on the railway.

Waterloo was a station whose layout he knew well. By positioning himself at the central bookstall, he could watch all three exits. His quarry had bought, and was eating, a meat pie. Petrella was quite unconscious of hunger. His eyes were riveted on the little bag, swinging heavily from the man's large fist. Once he put it down, but it was only to get out more money to buy an orange, which he peeled and ate neatly, depositing the remains in one of the refuse bins. Then he picked up the bag again and made for his train.

It was the electric line for Staines and Windsor. He went through the barrier, and walked slowly up the train. There were very few passengers about, and it must have been near enough empty. He walked along the platform, and climbed into a carriage at the far end.

Some instinct restrained Petrella. There were still five minutes before the train left. He waited. Three minutes later the man emerged from the carriage, walked very slowly back down the train, glancing into each carriage as he passed, and got into the carriage nearest to the barrier. The guard blew his whistle.

Two girls who had been sauntering towards the barrier broke into a run—Petrella ran with them. They pushed through the gate. The guard blew his whistle again; they jerked open the door of the nearest carriage and tumbled in together.

"We nearly left that too late," said one of the girls. Her friend agreed with her. Petrella thought that they couldn't have timed it better. But he didn't say so. He was prepared to agree with everything they said. It was the quickest way he knew of getting on with people.

The girls were prepared to enjoy his company too. The dark vivacious one was called Beryl and the quieter mousy one was Doreen. They lived at Staines.

"Where are you getting out?" asked Beryl. "Or is that a secret?"

"I haven't made up my mind yet," said Petrella.

Beryl said he was a case. Doreen agreed.

The train ambled through dim, forgotten places like Feltham and Ashford. No one got out and no one got in. Petrella heard about a dance, and what had gone on afterwards in the car park. He said he was sorry he didn't live at Staines. It sounded quite a place.

"It's all right in summer," said Doreen. "It's a dump in winter. Here we are."

The train drew up.

"Sure you won't change your mind?" said Beryl.

"Perhaps I will, at that," said Petrella. Out of the corner of his eye he saw that his man had got out and was making his way along the platform.

"You'd better hurry up then. They'll take you on to Windsor."

"That'd never do," said Petrella. "I forgot to warn her that I was coming."

"Who?" said Doreen.

"The Queen."

His man was safely past the ticket collector now.

"Come on," said Beryl. They went past the collector together. "Wouldn't you like some tea? There's a good place in the High Street."

"There's nothing I'd like better, but I think I see my uncle waving to me."

The girls stared at him. Petrella manoeuvred himself across the open yard, keeping the girls between him and his quarry. The man had set off up the road without, apparently, so much as a backward glance, but Petrella knew that the most difficult part of the chase was at hand.

"I don't see your uncle," said Beryl.

"There he is. Sitting in that taxi."

"That's just the taxi-driver. I don't believe he's your uncle at all."

"Certainly he is. How are you keeping, uncle?"

"Very fit, thank you," said the taxi-driver, a middle-aged man with a brown bald head.

"There you are," said Petrella. "I'll have to say goodbye now. We've got a lot to talk about. Family business."

The girls hesitated, and then withdrew, baffled.

"You a policeman?" said the taxi-driver. "A detective or something?"

"As a matter of fact, I am."

"Following that man in the light suit? I thought as much. Very pretty, the way you got behind those girls. As good as a book."

His quarry was now halfway up the long, straight, empty road, which leads from Staines Station to the riverside. He had stopped to light a cigarette, and in stopping he half turned.

"Keep behind my cab," said the driver. "That's right, well down. He's getting nervous. I'd say he's not far from wherever it is he's going to. Good as a book, isn't it? Do you read detective stories?"

The man was walking on again now. He was a full three hundred yards away.

"I don't want to lose him," said Petrella. "Not now. I've come a long way with him."

"You leave it to me," said the cab-driver. "I've been driving round here for forty years. There isn't a footpath I don't know blindfold. Just watch which way he turns at the end."

"Turning right," said Petrella.

"All aboard." The taxi shot out of the station yard, and the driver turned round in his seat to say, "Might be making for the High Street, but if he wanted the High Street, why not take a bus from the other platform? Ten to one he's for the ferry?"

"I say, look out for that dog," said Petrella.

The driver slewed back in his seat. Said, "Effie Muggridge's poodle. Asking for trouble," and accelerated. The dog shot to safety with a squeal of rage.

"Got to do this bit carefully," said the driver as they reached the corner. "Keep right down. Don't show so much as the tip of your nose, now."

Petrella obeyed. The taxi rounded the corner, and over it, in a wave, flowed the unmistakable smell of the river on a hot day—weed and water and tar and boat varnish.

"He's in the ferry," said the driver. "Got his back to you. You can come up for air now."

Petrella saw that a ferry punt ran from the steps beside a public house. There were three passengers on her, standing cheek by jowl, and the ferryman was untying and pushing out. He realised how hopeless he would have been on his own.

"What do we do?" he said.

"Over the road bridge, and back down the other side. Plenty of time, if we hurry."

"What were we doing just now?"

The driver chuckled throatily. Petrella held his breath and counted ten, slowly. Then they were crossing Staines Bridge.

"Not much traffic at the moment," said the driver. "You ought to see it at weekends." They did a skid turn to the left, and drew up in the yard of another riverside inn.

"There's two things he could do," said the driver. "Walk up the towpath to the bridge. There's no way off it. Or he could come down the path—you see the stile?—the one that comes out there. I'll watch the stile. You go through that gate and down the garden—I know the man who owns it. He won't mind. You can see the towpath from his summer-house. If you hear my horn, come back quick."

With a feeling that some power stronger than himself had taken charge, Petrella opened a gate and walked down a well-kept garden, full of pinks and roses and stone dwarfs with pointed hats. At the bottom was a summer-house. In the summer-house he found a small girl reading a book.

"Are you coming to tea?" she said.

"I'm not sure," said Petrella. "I might be going to the cinema."

"You'll have to hurry then. The big film starts in five minutes."

Behind him a hooter sounded off.

"I'll run then," said Petrella. He scooted back up the garden. The girl never raised her eyes from her book.

"Just come out," said the taxi-driver. "Going nicely. We'll give him twenty yards. Can't afford too much leeway here. Tricky navigation."

He drove slowly towards the turning, and stopped just short of it.

"Better hop out and look," he said. "But be careful. He's stopped twice already to blow his nose. We're getting pretty warm."

Petrella inched up to the corner, and poked his head round the wall. The man was going away from him, walking along the pavement, but slowly. It was an area of bungalows, some on the road, some on the river bank, with a network of private ways between.

The taxi-driver had got out, and was breathing down the back of his neck.

"Got to take a chance," he said. "If we follow him, he'll spot us for sure. I'll stay here. If he turns right, I'll mark it. If he turns left he's for Riverside Drive. You nip down that path, and you can cut him off."

Petrella took the path. It ran between high hedges of dusty bramble and thorn; hot and sweet-smelling in the sun. It was the dead middle of the afternoon, with hardly a dog stirring. Petrella broke into a jog trot, then slowed for the road ahead.

As he reached the corner, he heard footsteps on the pavement. Their beat was unmistakable. It was his man, and he was walking straight towards him.

Petrella looked round for cover and saw none. He thought for a moment of diving into the shallow ditch, but realised that he would merely be attracting attention. The footsteps had stopped. Petrella held his breath. He heard the click of a latch. Feet on flagstones. The sudden purring of an electric bell.

The chase was over.

★

"I'm not saying," said Palance, "that it wasn't a success. It was a success. Yes."

Haxtell said nothing. He knew just how Palance was feeling and sympathised with him.

"We've got back the Alfrey diamonds, and we've got our hands on that man at Staines. An insurance broker, of all things, and quite unsuspected. Judging from what we found in the false bottom of a punt in his boat-house he's been receiving stolen goods for years. And we've stopped up one of the Ponting middlemen at that tobacconist's in Balham. A little more pressure and we may shop the Pontings, too."

"Quite," said Haxtell sympathetically.

"All the same, it was a mad way to do it. You can't get over that, Haxtell. How long have you known that Coulman was a man?"

"We realised that as soon as we started to think about it," said Haxtell. "It was obviously impossible for a real, middle-aged buxom woman to turn into a convincing man. But, conversely, it was easy enough for a man dressed as a woman, padded and powdered and wigged, to whip it all off and turn back quickly into his own self."

"Then do you mean to say," said Palance, "that the Mrs. Coulman my men were watching for a month—doing her shopping, gossiping, hanging out her washing, having tea with the vicar—was really a man all the time?"

"Certainly not," said Haxtell. Observing symptoms of apoplexy, he said, "That *was* Mrs. Coulman. She had a brother—two, actually. One was killed by the Nazis. The other one got over to England. Whenever she had a big job on hand, her brother would come along at night. The house she lived in was at the end of the row. There was a way in at the side. He could slip in late at night without anyone seeing him. Next day he'd dress up in his sister's coat and hat and go out and do the job. She stayed quietly at home."

"When you realised this," said Palance, "wouldn't it have been better to do the job properly? You could have had a hundred men if necessary."

"It wouldn't have worked. Not a chance. You can't beat a methodical man like Coulman by being more methodical. He'll outdo you every time. The Underground, the change of clothes, the careful train check before he started for Staines, the long straight road, and the ferry. What you want with a man like that is luck—and imagination."

"Yes, but—" said Palance.

"Method, ingenuity, system," said Haxtell. "You'll never beat a German at his own game. Look at the Gestapo. They tried for five years and even they couldn't pull it off. The one thing they lacked was imagination. Perhaps it was a good thing. A little imagination, and they might have caused a lot more bother."

He sounded pleased, and had every reason to be. His own promotion to Superintendent had just come through.

THE LAST MEETING
OF THE BUTLERS CLUB

Geoffrey Bush

Geoffrey Bush (1920–98) is remembered today as a composer and musical scholar. His father was the prolific detective novelist Christopher Bush, but unfortunately his parents split up and Christopher had nothing to do with his son. Geoffrey spent five years as a chorister at Salisbury Cathedral before attending Lancing College and was awarded a Nettleship scholarship in Music by Balliol College. In later years he taught and composed music. He left Oxford during the war and spent some time looking after evacuated children before returning to the city in 1946.

At this point a mutual friend called Margaret Deneke invited him to Glyndebourne for the first performance of Britten's opera *The Rape of Lucretia* and to meet Bruce Montgomery, who shared his love of music, composition, and detective stories. The two men subsequently hired the Wigmore Hall for concerts at which their music was performed, and were members of The Carr Society, a small group of friends who admired the work of John Dickson Carr. Montgomery had by this time established a reputation as a crime writer under the name Edmund Crispin and on one occasion he invited Carr, whom he got to know through the Detection Club, to attend a meeting of the Society named in his honour. Bush, who is name-checked in Crispin's *Frequent Hearses*, offered Crispin an idea for the excellent story that became "Who Killed Baker?" but this is one of his few solo forays into crime writing and appeared in *EQMM* on 10 March 1980.

He pokes fun at the tropes of the Golden Age detective story, with references to great fictional detectives such as Dr. Thorndyke, Lord Peter Wimsey, and Reggie Fortune.

T HE LAST MEETING OF THE BUTLERS CLUB CAN HARDLY BE SAID
to have been a complete success. Meat loaf with ketchup—the
only dish that agreed with both the members' elderly stomachs and
their less elderly teeth—can scarcely be called the *pièce de résistance* of
a gourmet dinner. Nor can the sudden and practically simultaneous
deaths of all those who ate it, some 20 minutes later, be seen—except,
perhaps, from the most judicious perspective—as a fitting climax.

Still, the festivities, while they lasted, were decidedly high-spirited.
At about five o'clock—for the members adhered to the dinner hour
that they had observed during their professional careers—the first
guest arrived at the secluded but unobtrusively elegant section of
London in which the Butlers Club has (or, one must now regretfully
say, had) its permanent headquarters.

Assisted on one side by Morgan, the Club's resident Steward,
and grasping the iron rail on his other side with a gnarled hand, the
first arrival made his way up the front steps, through the hall, and
into the lounge, where he undid the heavy overcoat he had bundled
himself into on that cold Friday evening in January and sank happily
into the most comfortable of the five leather chairs in one corner of
the large oak-panelled room—chairs discreetly redisposed to conceal
the absence of a sixth, which had, alas, been recently removed. (There
was a time, years ago, when the Club's membership numbered in
the dozens, nay, in the scores.)

Soon afterward came the next guest. By five thirty all five members had tottered joyfully in, apart from old Phillips, who made
his entrance in a wheelchair, and old Murgatroyd, whose habitual

expression was one of alert anger. For the next half hour the gurgle of unblended Scotch whisky filled the air—in the matter of the Club's liquid provisions, no expense was spared—together with the crackle of a small fire and the sound of squeaky but animated voices discoursing enthusiastically on their latest ailments.

At exactly six o'clock the figure of Morgan, the thin, deferential, middle-aged Steward—*young* Morgan, he was known as—appeared to announce that dinner was ready.

Nor does he deny that it was *his* dinner. He readily admits that he cooked it in the basement kitchen, he carried it upstairs, and he served it. He was, after all, the only servant on the premises—the Butlers Club's butler.

By a succession of gravity-defying movements old Stanley, the President, levered himself from his chair. Old Murgatroyd followed, looking about him with an angry scowl to see whether anyone was challenging his second, or Vice-Presidential, place. After him old Phillips went into motion, restraining himself out of a sense of decorum, since he was naturally the swiftest, by reason of his wheelchair. And one by one the five surviving members of the Butlers Club trooped and stumbled to their last repast.

"Very tasty," old Phillips remarked, and shovelled in another mouthful.

It was generally agreed that old Phillips, being on wheels, was permitted to eat the main course with a spoon. There had never been an agreement, however, that old Murgatroyd was. He had simply begun to, angrily, three years ago.

"Tangier than last year," old Simpson agreed in a quavering voice. The section of meat loaf he had been conveying to his mouth slipped off his trembling fork and fell with a plop into his ketchup. Poor old Simpson, someone had said earlier in a loud and carrying tone—probably old Phillips, a keen-eyed observer—looked shakier than ever. Undeterred, old Simpson commenced new manoeuvres with his fork.

By this time the slender and retiring hand of young Morgan had filled the wine glasses from a bottle with a label almost as faded and venerable as the diners.

"Gentlemen," the President announced at the head of the table, "a toast."

There was a general clatter of silverware being lowered—or, in the case of poor old Simpson, dropped—and glasses being raised.

"To the old days!"

"To the old days!" repeated a surprisingly strong chorus of reedy voices.

Swallows were swallowed, glasses were set down, lips were smacked.

"Good stuff," old Phillips stated from his wheelchair.

"Very good," old Simpson echoed waveringly, still absorbed in the process of putting down his glass.

"Yours?" inquired old Bates, halfway down the table, looking up at the President. Thanks to an unfortunate malady with a Latin name, old Bates was unable to hold his head more than two or three inches above his plate, from which position, although it was convenient for eating, he had to peer up and sideways at whomever he was addressing.

"Bequeathed to me," the President replied, "by my old master." And for an instant an extra bit of light seemed to dance in his sparkling old eyes.

"To his old master!" old Phillips said, raising his glass.

"To *all* our old masters," old Murgatroyd amended, in a tone that would have been taken as bad-tempered from anyone else.

More swallows. Glasses put down again. And for a moment, for the space of an old heartbeat, an odd sense of something in the air—something like a roar of laughter—about to explode. But kept back, with difficulty, as the five members returned to their dinner. And young Morgan began deftly to refill their glasses.

"Don't suppose," old Bates observed, peering up in his sideways fashion, "they ever thought we'd be enjoying ourselves like this."

"Never *dreamed* it," old Murgatroyd corrected.

"Poor fellows," old Phillips said. And there was another beat of bursting silence, of barely suppressed hilarity, as each pair of ancient eyes looked into another pair, moved on, and gleefully met the next.

Had someone tittered? Old Murgatroyd, the Club crosspatch? Quickly, before anything unseemly could take place at the dinner table, the President looked up and down its shimmering white length. "More meat loaf?" he asked.

Old Bates, his chin down to his chest, struggled to his feet. "Tell young—young what's-his-name"—for it is a curious fact that the members of the Butlers Club were seldom able to remember the name of their own butler, though he had been with them for 20 years—"to bring brandy and cigars to the lounge."

Which was done. And after young Morgan had been casually dismissed, the members found themselves, agreeably full, reinstalled in their leather chairs, except for old Phillips, who retained his private, movable accommodations—though a leather chair was always ready for him, in case he should undergo a miraculous recovery—puffing thick cigars and sipping antique brandy. Plus, for the President and old Murgatroyd, decaffeinated coffee.

"Good meeting," old Simpson declared.

"Excellent," old Phillips agreed.

"So far," old Murgatroyd added, visibly mellowed, with only an undertone of his customary rage.

"Any business?" old Bates asked, his cigar held at a careful distance from his face, which was bobbing close to his lap.

"Not that I know of," the President answered.

"What about the finances?" old Murgatroyd demanded, irascibility boiling nearer to the surface.

"In splendid shape," said old Phillips, who was the Treasurer.

"Investments?"

"Doing well," old Phillips replied. "Sold a block of property in the West End."

"Why?"

"Advised to. By our brokers."

"What did we buy?"

"Saudi Arabia."

"What?"

"Large tract in Saudi Arabia."

"Why did we do that?"

"Said to have oil in it. Seemed like a good idea."

"Hmm," old Murgatroyd said, temporarily appeased.

There was a satisfied pause.

"Remarkable what can be done," old Bates said, looking about the handsome room with a sly, sideways grin, like an ancient Richard III, "with a few modest bequests. A pair of cuff links here. A hundred pounds there. An old family painting. An acre or two of the family land. A few shares of the family business. Put together, by humble fellows like us, and allowed to grow."

"Astonishing," old Phillips said.

"Sobering," the President said, gazing at the end of his cigar.

"And so simple, really," old Bates said.

This time the silence was almost solemn.

"Not many fellows like us left," old Murgatroyd observed.

"Young what's-his-name, I suppose," old Phillips said, waving his cigar toward the door through which young Morgan had departed.

"But not like *us.*"

"Think he should have a raise?" old Bates said.

"Who?" old Murgatroyd said.

"Young Morgan?"

"What for? Hasn't complained, has he?"

"Odd chap," the President remarked. "Never complains about anything."

"What's he got to complain about?" old Murgatroyd asked. "He's the Steward, isn't he?"

Old Simpson lifted a trembling finger. "Cold toilet."

"Eh?" the President said.

"Toilet," old Simpson explained. "Cold."

"Cold?"

"When you sit down on it."

"What are you doing sitting down on young Morgan's toilet?"

"He doesn't mean young Morgan's toilet," old Phillips said. "He means ours."

"Electrically heated," old Simpson said.

"He means," old Phillips said, "he wants an electrically heated toilet seat."

"I'll see what I can do," the President promised.

"Why shouldn't a fellow have an electrically heated toilet seat?" old Bates said. "In his own club? After he's gone through what we've gone through?" And in his single visible eye, peering up and askance was a gleam of triumphant mirth.

"I'll say," old Phillips exclaimed. And blew out an explosive puff of smoke.

"Ha!" old Murgatroyd ejaculated.

It was the President, drawing on his cigar, his lips on either side of it elevated in what those who knew him could tell was Presidential levity—it was he who was the first to give way. "I shall never forget—" he began, and the others understood that the time had come, at last, to indulge themselves in the greatest pleasure of their annual meetings. An hour or two of reminiscences. "I shall never forget the look on my mistress' face, as she stood in the dock in Old Bailey, and the Judge handed down his sentence."

"What was it?" old Phillips asked, settling back in his wheelchair.

"Twenty years, poor lady. Though it was later much reduced, for good behaviour."

"No, no," old Phillips said. "What was the look on her face?"

"Incredulity," the President said, with a faraway look on his own round pink face. "That such a thing should be happening to her."

"But it was," old Phillips said helpfully.

"Yes." The President drew again on his cigar. He tapped the ash from it. "Perhaps you have forgotten the details." No one there had forgotten the details, except old Simpson. They had heard the details annually for more than 30 years, but they were glad to hear the details once more, provided their own turns would come soon. "On the night in question, that resulted in my lady's tragic appearance in the dock six months later, my master was sleeping in the summer-house."

"Why?" old Simpson asked.

"Why what?"

"Why was he sleeping in the summer-house? Wasn't it winter time?"

"I forget," the President said. "There was some adequate explanation given at the time. It was the sort of thing often done by the landed gentry of that period. In any event," he went on, a trifle testily, "it was not relevant to the case."

"Oh."

"What *was* relevant, however, was that at some time during the night it began to snow."

"Snow," old Simpson repeated attentively.

"The next morning he was discovered. Dead. By the parlourmaid who had gone to change the sheets."

"Change the sheets?"

"The sheets of his bed," the President explained, a shade impatiently, "were changed daily. Whether he slept in the summer-house or the main house."

"Ah."

"There were two sets of footprints in the snow."

"Two sets of footprints." Old Simpson enumerated them on his first two fingers.

"One set leading to the summer-house, and other back to the main house."

"What about hers?"

"Hers?"

"The parlourmaid's?"

The President drew a deep breath.

"Hers do not count."

"Oh."

"The parlourmaid is of no importance"

"Ah."

"The important fact is—*there was only one pair of feet large enough to have made those two sets of footprints.*"

With no change of expression on his round imperturbable countenance, the President regarded the polished black toe of one of his size-12 shoes.

Old Simpson leaned forward. "What happened?"

"The local bobby was about to take me off to the station house when a gentleman whom my master had invited to spend the weekend arrived in a small sports car. He was, he said in an aristocratic voice, an amateur detective who had had some success in America with apparently insoluble cases of this sort."

"Insoluble?"

"Precisely the question raised by the local bobby, who then outlined the evidence of the footprints in the snow. But the gentleman glanced at me and inquired whether I was concerned about getting my feet wet."

"Were you?"

"Certainly, I told him, but in the flurry of being arrested that morning I had been unable to find my galoshes. Whereupon he turned to the bobby and suggested in an amused, sardonic manner that it might be a mistake to arrest the most obvious suspect."

"Why?"

"Cases of this sort, the gentleman implied, were never obvious. It took a superior brain like his to solve a classic puzzle like this. He referred to the bobby as 'old thing.' Persuaded him to wait until Monday, pointing out that communications in this part of England were already paralysed by the two-inch snowfall. And after a day and a half of whistling snatches of operatic music and quoting bits of Latin and looking at the feet of the neighbours, the local clergy, and the tramps of the vicinity, the gentleman announced that he'd found the guilty party."

"And it wasn't you?"

"All I stood to gain, he explained, was a small pension. And a few bottles from the wine cellar. It was the person who'd been overlooked from the beginning—my mistress."

"But how could she have made those footprints?"

"By borrowing my galoshes."

"Whew." Old Simpson sat back, as relieved at the outcome as he had been the first time he had heard it, 33 years ago.

Old Bates shook his bobbing head in wonder. "Amazing piece of reasoning."

"Did she ever give them back?" old Simpson asked. "Your galoshes, I mean?"

"Claimed she never had them. Lucky for me the gentleman had been invited."

"Who was he?"

"Vance was his name," the President said gravely. "Philo Vance."

There was a respectful pause.

"Reminds me of the chap who solved my case," old Phillips said from his wheelchair. "Thorndyke. Dr. Thorndyke."

"Ah, yes," the President said, relighting his cigar. Now that he had finished his own narrative, he could afford to be a polite interlocutor.

"Scientific investigation was his line," old Phillips went on in his rich, bass voice, like a large invalided bullfrog. He took a sip of brandy. "No personality to speak of. Practically no first name. But a wonderful mind. Thorough. Methodical. Always picking up things, putting them in little envelopes, and looking at them through a microscope."

"And he played a part in your case?"

"Fortunately. For me." Old Phillips pointed dramatically at the floor. He made up for the immobility of his lower half by oratorical gestures.

"There," he said vibrantly, "was my master's body. Shot, in the library, with the fatal revolver lying beside him on the Oriental rug. And there"—he pointed in the opposite direction, which happened to be the ceiling—"was a house full of guests. Including his first wife, his daughter by his second wife, his aunt by his mother's third marriage, his niece by his sister's first marriage to his fourth cousin, and his son-in-law, a nervous chain smoker."

"A whole crowd of suspects, eh?"

"Too many for Scotland Yard. Call in Dr. Thorndyke, they agreed. And the first thing he said, when he made his inconspicuous appearance was, 'We can eliminate the servants.'"

"Reassuring."

"I don't mind telling you I was glad to hear it. 'They are only receiving a few insignificant bequests,' he said 'in the form of old family portraits.' Then he said he was going to examine the revolver in his laboratory, to see if there were any fingerprints." Old Phillips paused rhetorically. "Sure enough, there were."

"Whose?" asked the President, who knew quite well.

"Mine."

"A disturbing development."

"Bit of a facer for Dr. Thorndyke, too. 'Have you recently mailed a bulky parcel?' he asked me. 'As a matter of fact,' I answered, 'yesterday I posted my master's stuffed rhinoceros head to a dry-cleaning firm.' 'Was it possible to wrap it adequately with string?' 'No,' I said, 'it wasn't. I had to use a roll of sticky tape.' 'How did you know that?' the Scotland Yard man asked, perplexed. 'I fear,' Dr. Thorndyke replied, 'that this case is less simple than it may have at first appeared.'

"The industrious fellow spent the next three days with his finger-print powder and magnifying glass before he turned to the son-in-law and said quietly, 'When did you ask Phillips the butler to light your cigarette with your silver cigarette lighter?' Baffled looks on the faces of the other guests, assembled in the library. On mine, as well. 'Why,' stammered the son-in-law, 'I may have done so on the day I sprained my wrist while getting out of the bathtub, making it inconvenient for me to operate my cigarette lighter myself, a few hours before my father-in-law was shot.' Bewildered gasps.

"'If indeed you did suffer such an improbable accident,' Dr. Thorndyke said. 'If, instead, it was not part of your carefully con-ceived plan to gain control of the family fortune by shooting your father-in-law with a revolver to which you then *transferred Phillips the butler's fingerprints from your cigarette lighter by means of adhesive package-sealing tape.*'"

Old Simpson whistled.

Old Bates drew an admiring breath.

"Astounding bit of deduction," the President said.

Old Phillips, sitting back in his wheelchair, observed with grati-
fication the effect he had created in his audience.

"Almost as good as my case," old Murgatroyd said irritably.

"Almost?" Old Phillips raised his eyebrows good-naturedly.

But old Murgatroyd was too engrossed to notice. "Imagine," he
began, clenching his bony hands on the arms of his leather chair,
"my master and me, alone in the billiard room. With the door open.
And with the sworn testimony of three independent witnesses, guests
at the house party, that no one else had passed through that door."

"Locked room, as it were, eh?" old Phillips said agreeably. "But
with an open door?"

"Imagine the sound of an agitated cry. Of a body falling. Imagine,
immediately thereafter, my master's twin brother, recently returned
from a visit to Australia to take charge of the family's flourishing
umbrella-stand factory, rushing into the room to discover my master
dead on the floor, of a gaping wound. While I stood over him clasp-
ing the hilt of the angular medieval knife that ordinarily hung on
the wall."

Old Bates peered up and sideways.

"Good heavens," old Phillips said.

Old Murgatroyd nodded grimly. "A difficult situation."

Old Simpson, who had been sitting with his mouth open, closed
it. And opened it again. "What did you say?"

"On the spur of the moment I could not think of anything suitable to say."

Old Phillips clicked his tongue. "Open-and-shut case."

"So it appeared. Until Lord Peter entered it."

"*The* Lord Peter?"

"The Lord Peter." Old Murgatroyd's bony face softened. "Charming man. Made one conscious that one belonged to the lower orders, but that one *liked* it. 'Oh, no,' he said to the Inspector, when he'd assembled us all in the billiard room to reconstruct the crime. 'it's not the butler.' 'Not the butler, Wimsey?' the Inspector said disbelievingly. 'Standing over the body? With the knife in his hand?' 'I fancy you'll find,' Lord Peter said, in his kind, boyish, impulsive way, 'that young what's-his-name—'

"'Murgatroyd?' the Inspector supplied. 'That young Murgatroyd,' Lord Peter went on, 'who, by the way, is only gettin' a modest annuity and two or three acres of the family estate, was simply pullin' the knife out of the wound to see what could be done for his master.' To which I gratefully agreed. And my master's attractive daughter, whom I'd known since she was a baby, gave my hand a little squeeze.

"The Inspector looked dumfounded. 'But this *is* the knife that made the wound?' 'Oh, yes,' Lord Peter said, 'no doubt about that.' 'And nothing went through that door, according to three independent witnesses who were sitting within six feet of it?' 'Nothing,' Lord Peter said, 'human.' The Inspector turned pale. 'Good God. Something—supernatural?' 'More interestin' than that,' Lord Peter said, and turned carelessly to face my master's twin brother.

"'Delightful summer we've been havin',' isn't it?' 'Unusually pleasant,' the twin brother agreed, at a loss. 'Not for someone though, who's borrowed heavily in the City,' Lord Peter went on remorselessly, 'on the strength of an increased demand for umbrella stands.' 'But—' the twin brother began. 'I suppose as soon as you saw this curiously shaped knife you knew it could be used in a rather special way.' 'Special way?' 'Thrown around a corner—through an open door—past three independent witnesses—as *an Australian boomerang*.'

"The others exclaimed with mingled horror and relief, while the twin brother stood there speechless, and the Inspector clapped the handcuffs on his wrists. 'But how could you be so sure,' the Inspector said, 'that it wasn't Murgatroyd?' 'Who?' Lord Peter asked, with that endearing forgetfulness of his. 'Murgatroyd,' the Inspector said, 'the butler.' 'Oh, the butler. It always looks as if it's the butler.' There was a mischievous twinkle in Lord Peter's eye. 'It looks as if it *must* be the butler, on Friday, when the body's discovered. But by Sunday night it always turns out it isn't.'

"Then he stopped, and grew serious. 'Wouldn't be fair, really would it, if it was? If you couldn't count on spendin' the weekend explorin' the case? And analysin' the problem? And usin' your intelligence? And findin' someone else?'"

This time no one spoke. Old Simpson stared into the dying fire. The President drew on what was left of his cigar, looked at it, and stubbed it out. Old Phillips sighed.

"Reggie Fortune was the one who solved my case," old Simpson said tremulously. "Plump chap. Relied on his intuition. Kept saying, 'Oh, my aunt!'"

"They brought Max Carrados into my case," old Bates said wistfully. "Blind fellow. Used his other phenomenally developed senses."

"Remember Trent?" the President asked. "Father Brown? Inspector French? Albert Campion, obscurely related to royalty?" He surveyed the room, as if searching in the deepening shadows for a sixth chair, and a seventh, and an eighth, which were no longer there. "All the others?"

One nostalgic old voice followed another.

"Working out their timetables?"

"Drawing their diagrams of the bedrooms?"

"Interrogating the guests?"

"Hypothesising?"

"Investigating?"

"Reasoning?"

"Never resting until they'd proved it wasn't the butler?"

"The obvious suspect?"

· "But someone else?"

"Until they'd discarded the simple solution?"

"And thought up another?"

"That was *really complicated?*"

Old Phillips snorted. Old Simpson emitted a quavering guffaw. Old Bates, his head bobbing faster, began to chuckle. The President allowed his round cherubic face to break into a very slow, very broad smile.

"Silly asses," he said.

Old Murgatroyd was the only one who sat with a preoccupied expression on his bony, ill-natured features. "I say," he remarked peevishly, "do any of you chaps think there was something odd about the meat loaf?"

Three-quarters of an hour later, young Morgan testified that he found, when he entered the room to ask if anything more was required of him, that the last five members of the Butlers Club had gone to their rewards. To judge from their attitudes, they had passed their final moments endeavouring to reach either the bell or—for both were located on the same sideboard—the brandy bottle.

Whatever contribution they could have made to our knowledge of the wave of weekend country-house murders that swept over England in the '20's and '30's has gone with them. The mystifying circumstances of their own deaths, however, may soon be solved. Young Morgan was the first to come under suspicion, when it was discovered that a quart of liquid drain cleaner had been mixed into the meat loaf. But that explanation was quickly dismissed.

Scotland Yard, with the help of a number of amateur experts, is now working on the theory that the drain cleaner was frozen into tiny ice pellets, which, during one of his absences from the kitchen, were shot through the bars of the basement window, perhaps by a South American blowpipe, and which then melted, leaving no trace of the ingenious murder method, while the empty bottle of drain cleaner was tossed into the kitchen waste receptacle to confuse the authorities.

A distant cousin of old Bates, they point out, has just returned from a trip to the Amazon. And young Morgan stands to gain nothing from the evening's extraordinary events, according to the Club's constitution, but a few wine bottles, cuff links, paintings, stock shares, and real-estate holdings.

AS IF BY MAGIC

Julian Symons

I mentioned in the introduction to this book that Julian Symons (1912–94) is often regarded as a scourge of the classic detective story. This is because his history of the genre, *Bloody Murder* aka *Mortal Consequences*, the first edition of which appeared in 1972, sought to argue that the detective story had evolved into the crime novel; his book amounted in effect to an obituary for Golden Age fiction. Nevertheless, Symons' early (and avowedly commercial) fiction showed a considerable interest in the tricks and trappings of the puzzle mystery and his deft way of handling them. Even the most sophisticated of his later crime novels display touches of ingenuity worthy of Golden Age greats such as Agatha Christie and Anthony Berkeley, both of whom he knew and admired. But as the success of the British Library's Crime Classics and the current popularity of puzzle mysteries have demonstrated over the past eleven years or so, reports of the death of the craftily plotted detective story were exaggerated.

Symons wrote a long series of short stories featuring the private investigator Francis Quarles, most of them turning on a single plot twist. Like Michael Gilbert, he won the CWA Diamond Dagger and was a Grand Master of the Mystery Writers of America, but I suspect he'd never have dreamed that one of his Quarles stories would appear in an anthology of locked room mysteries in the second quarter of the twenty-first century. This little tale can be found in the collection *Murder! Murder!* (1961) as "The Hiding Place"; the present title was used when the story was reprinted in *Ellery Queen's Mystery Magazine*.

THEY SAY THAT A MURDER IS MOST EASILY COMMITTED IN A crowd, and that was the way it almost proved, for there was a big enough crowd that Bank Holiday Monday at the end of Brightsand Pier.

On the windy side of the pier people streamed into the Amusement Arcade to play on the Kentucky Derby or the Great Brooklands Speedway, to see What the Butler Saw or to lose pennies on little machines. The Brightsand Concert Party had given their afternoon performance and gone home. The Punch and Judy stand was silent. In the onion-domed tea pavilion in the middle of the pier worn-out parents refreshed themselves with nice cups of tea while their clamorous children ate rich fruit cake and ice creams. On the sheltered side of the pier people sat in deckchairs sunning themselves, sleeping with newspapers over their faces, or looking out at the toy-like boats on the sea.

It was in this cheerful, busy, unobservant Bank Holiday crowd that the murderer saw his chance. His name doesn't matter—he was an inoffensive-looking supremely ordinary little man. His victim, whose name is also unimportant, was a dark bulky man sleeping in one of the deckchairs, with his feet on the railing. The deckchairs on either side of the bulky man were vacant.

The inoffensive-looking little man stood over the deckchair, like a man greeting a friend. He pulled a heavy clasp knife from his belt and stabbed downwards, once, twice, three times. The bulky man gave a kind of grunt. The little man flung the knife, now gleaming red. It curved in a wide parabola into the blue sea. The little man walked quickly but calmly away round the end of the pier. The murder did not take more than thirty seconds.

This was, as afterwards appeared, a quite unpremeditated crime. The murderer simply saw his enemy, back to him, at his mercy, remembered his clasp knife and acted almost without thought. The motive? It proved to be grinding, agonising jealousy. The bulky man had taken away the little man's wife and was living with her. All that was discovered in the succeeding day and weeks by the slow machinery of the law. What happened now was quicker.

The murder had been seen. Miss Slater, a capable middle-aged schoolmistress down on a day trip to Brightsand, actually saw the knife rise and fall. She saw a vivid spurt of red splash up on to a brown jacket. For a few moments her mind refused to take in what her senses had recorded. Then she pointed, and she screamed...

At once the scene was changed to one of frantic, slightly purposeless action. People in deck chairs stood up, fishermen abandoned their lines, one of the waitresses ran out of the tea pavilion. There were confused questions and answers.

"It's a thief... lady's fainted... running this way... a little man she said... a boy's fallen in... no, somebody's been murdered."

The confusion lasted only a couple of minutes. Then the body was discovered, and two plainclothes policemen stationed on the pier to watch for pickpockets had cordoned off the top end of it and begun investigations. But in that time the little man with the bloodstain on his brown jacket had vanished.

Francis Quarles had been on the pier for half an hour before the murder, acting as companion to his small nephew Roger. They had been on the Dodgem Cars, played Skeeball, and spent several shillings in the Amusement Arcade. Roger had eaten an extraordinary amount of ice cream and candy floss, and had watched the Punch and Judy show, which he characterised as smashing, though really for kids. With some interest Quarles saw the cordoning off at the end of the pier, and the arrival of the local Inspector Garrity. He accepted with pleasure the Inspector's suggestion that he might like to see what went on.

Miss Slater's evidence was simple. Yes, she had seen the murderer, but she had not seen his face. He had been standing over the deckchair. She was quite sure she had seen the blood spurt on to the right sleeve of his jacket. He had been wearing grey flannel trousers, he was of less than medium height, she thought he had brown hair. He had walked away from her, towards the entrance to the tea pavilion. She repeated this evidence again and again, and could not be shaken from it.

Had he gone in the tea pavilion? No, said the waitress who had been standing at the door and had then run out, quite positively not. Nobody had come in just before or after she heard the scream.

Had he entered the Amusement Arcade next door? The attendant said no. The changing-room behind the concert party stage was locked and padlocked. The Punch and Judy man, who was still in his box, had seen no little man in a bloodstained brown jacket hurry past.

Had he got off the pier, then? The two plainclothes men, who had been stationed at the point where the bulbous end of the pier narrowed into an ordinary promenade, were ready to swear that no such little man had passed them just before or after Miss Slater's scream. Quarles, who had been standing near them, was ready to swear it too.

The police proceeded methodically. Either the murderer had changed his jacket, which meant that he must have had a spare jacket and a place to change in without being noticed. Or he had got rid of his jacket in some way. Or he was still wearing it.

You couldn't evade those conclusions. But somehow the murderer did evade them. There were more than three hundred people on the end of the pier, rather less than half of them men. Only six of these were jacketless, for there was a nip in the air, and these six were vouched for by friends or relatives. There were a good many brown jackets, but none with blood on. For good measure Inspector Garrity checked on the people in the tea pavilion and the Amusement Arcade. At the end of an hour he had got precisely nowhere, and the people who had been kept on the end of the pier were extremely restive.

"It's no use," he said. "The man had no place to hide, no place where he might have changed his coat. He passed you somehow, and he's off the pier."

"On the contrary," Quarles said. "The murderer was the only person on this part of the pier who had a hiding place, and a good reason for being in it. He walked quickly round to his hiding place, entered it, changed into the old jacket he uses for his performances and put his bloodstained jacket into the case in which he carries his professional paraphernalia." Quarles put his hand upon the shoulder of the inoffensive-looking little man who ran the Punch and Judy show. "What better hiding place and changing-room could you want than the inside of a Punch and Judy box?"

THE HOUSE IN GOBLIN WOOD

Carter Dickson

Carter Dickson was the principal pen-name utilised by John Dickson Carr and is particularly associated with his stories about Sir Henry Merrivale, a rumbustious character whom some fans admire even more than Dr. Gideon Fell. This is the only short story to feature Merrivale and was written for Carr's friend Fred Dannay, the editor of *Ellery Queen's Mystery Magazine*. The writing process, begun in August 1946, proved challenging and eventually took three months. Carr's biographer Douglas Greene says that Carr tore up one draft because it was only "all right". He explained to Dannay that: "The best way to arrange the punch-ending was what gave me trouble." Dannay was so pleased with the result of Carr's labours that he awarded the story "a special award of merit" in the magazine's second annual short story competition, although Greene observes that "most readers thought it deserved first prize in the contest".

This is such a fine example of the detective short story that I don't want to say too much about it, for fear of spoilers. But I think it's well worth rereading to see just how skilfully Carr sets about hoodwinking his readers. The story's first appearance in *EQMM* was in November 1947; it was published in the *Strand Magazine* in the same month.

I N PALL MALL, THAT HOT JULY AFTERNOON THREE YEARS BEFORE
the war, an open saloon car was drawn up to the kerb just opposite
the Senior Conservatives' Club.

And in the car sat two conspirators.

It was the drowsy post-lunch hour among the clubs, where only
the sun remained brilliant. The Rag lay somnolent; the Athenæum
slept outright. But these two conspirators, a dark-haired young man
in his early thirties and a fair-haired girl perhaps half a dozen years
younger, never moved. They stared intently at the Gothic-like front
of the Senior Conservatives'.

"Look here, Eve," muttered the young man, and punched at the
steering-wheel. "Do you think this is going to work?"

"I don't know," the fair-haired girl confessed. "He absolutely
loathes picnics."

"Anyway, we've probably missed him."

"Why so?"

"He can't have taken as long over lunch as that!" her companion
protested, looking at a wrist-watch. The young man was rather
shocked. "It's a quarter to four! Even if…"

"Bill! There! Look there!"

Their patience was rewarded by an inspiring sight.

Out of the portals of the Senior Conservatives' Club, in awful
majesty, marched a large, stout, barrel-shaped gentleman in a white
linen suit.

His corporation preceded him like the figure-head of a man-of-
war. His shell-rimmed spectacles were pulled down on a broad nose,

all being shaded by a Panama hat. At the top of the stone steps he surveyed the street with a lordly sneer.

"Sir Henry!" called the girl.

"Hey?" said Sir Henry Merrivale.

"I'm Eve Drayton. Don't you remember me? You knew my father!"

"Oh, ah," said the great man.

"We've been waiting here a terribly long time," Eve pleaded. "Couldn't you see us for five minutes?—The thing to do," she whispered to her companion, "is to keep him in a good humour. Just keep him in a good humour!"

As a matter of fact, H.M. was in a good humour, having just triumphed over the Home Secretary in an argument. But not even his own mother could have guessed it. Majestically, with the same lordly sneer, he began in grandeur to descend the steps of the Senior Conservatives'. He did this, in fact, until his foot encountered an unnoticed object lying some three feet from the bottom.

It was a banana skin.

"Oh, dear!" said the girl.

Now it must be stated with regret that in the old days certain urchins, of what were then called the "lower orders", had a habit of placing such objects on the steps in the hope that some eminent statesman would take a toss on his way to Whitehall. This was a venial but deplorable practice, probably accounting for what Mr. Gladstone said in 1882.

In any case, it accounted for what Sir Henry Merrivale said now.

From the pavement, where H.M. landed in a seated position, arose in H.M.'s bellowing voice such a torrent of profanity, such a flood of invective and vile obscenities, as has seldom before blasted the holy calm of Pall Mall. It brought the hall porter hurrying down the steps, and Eve Drayton flying out of the car.

Heads were now appearing at the windows of the Athenæum across the street.

"Is it all right?" cried the girl, with concern in her blue eyes. "Are you hurt?"

H.M. merely looked at her. His hat had fallen off, disclosing a large bald head; and he merely sat on the pavement and looked at her.

"Anyway, H.M., get up! Please get up!"

"Yes, sir," begged the hall porter, "for heaven's sake get up!"

"Get up?" bellowed H.M., in a voice audible as far as St. James's Street. "Burn it all, how *can* I get up?"

"But why not?"

"My behind's out of joint," said H.M. simply. "I'm hurt awful bad. I'm probably goin' to have spinal dislocation for the rest of my life."

"But, sir, people are looking!"

H.M. explained what these people could do. He eyed Eve Drayton with a glare of indescribable malignancy over his spectacles.

"I suppose, my wench, *you're* responsible for this?"

Eve regarded him in consternation.

"You don't mean the banana skin?" she cried.

"Oh, yes, I do," said H.M., folding his arms like a prosecuting counsel.

"But we—we only wanted to invite you to a picnic!"

H.M. closed his eyes.

"That's fine," he said in a hollow voice. "All the same, don't you think it'd have been a subtler kind of hint just to pour mayonnaise over my head or shove ants down the back of my neck? Oh, lord love a duck!"

"I didn't mean that! I meant…"

"Let me help you up, sir," interposed the calm, reassuring voice of the dark-haired and blue-chinned young man who had been with Eve in the car.

"So you want to help too, hey? And who are *you*?"

"I'm awfully sorry!" said Eve. "I should have introduced you! This is my fiancé, Dr. William Sage."

H.M.'s face turned purple.

"I'm glad to see," he observed, "you had the uncommon decency to bring along a doctor. I appreciate that, I do. And the car's there, I suppose, to assist with the examination when I take off my pants?"

The hall porter uttered a cry of horror.

Bill Sage, either from jumpiness and nerves or from sheer inability to keep a straight face, laughed loudly.

"I keep telling Eve a dozen times a day," he said, "that I'm not to be called 'doctor'. I happen to be a surgeon—"

(Here H.M. really did look alarmed.)

"—but I don't think we need operate. Nor, in my opinion," Bill gravely addressed the hall porter, "will it be necessary to remove Sir Henry's trousers in front of the Senior Conservatives' Club."

"Thank you very much, sir."

"We had an infernal nerve to come here," the young man confessed to H.M. "But I honestly think, Sir Henry, you'd be more comfortable in the car. What about it? Let me give you a hand up?"

Yet even ten minutes later, when H.M. sat glowering in the back of the car and two heads were craned round toward him, peace was not restored.

"All right!" said Eve. Her pretty, rather stolid face was flushed; her mouth looked miserable. "If you won't come to the picnic, you won't. But I did believe you might do it to oblige me."

"Well... now!" muttered the great man uncomfortably.

"And I did think, too, you'd be interested in the other person who was coming with us. But Vicky's—difficult. She won't come either, if you don't."

"Oh? And who's this other guest?"

"Vicky Adams."

H.M.'s hand, which had been lifted for an oratorical gesture, dropped to his side.

"Vicky Adams? That's not the gal who…?"

"Yes!" Eve nodded. "They say it was one of the great mysteries, twenty years ago, that the police failed to solve."

"It was, my wench," H.M. agreed sombrely. "It was."

"And now Vicky's grown up. And we thought if you of all people went along, and spoke to her nicely, she'd tell us what really happened on that night."

H.M.'s small, sharp eyes fixed disconcertingly on Eve.

"I say, my wench. What's your interest in all this?"

"Oh, reasons." Eve glanced quickly at Bill Sage, who was again punching moodily at the steering-wheel, and checked herself. "Anyway, what difference does it make now? If you won't go with us…"

H.M. assumed a martyred air.

"I never said I *wasn't* goin' with you, did I?" he demanded. (This was inaccurate, but no matter.) "Even after you practically made a cripple of me, I never said I *wasn't* goin'?" His manner grew flurried and hasty. "But I got to leave now," he added apologetically. "I got to get back to my office."

"We'll drive you there, H.M."

"No, no, no," said the practical cripple, getting out of the car with surprising celerity. "Walkin' is good for my stomach if it's not so good for my behind. I'm a forgivin' man. You pick me up at my house tomorrow morning. G'bye."

And he lumbered off in the direction of the Haymarket.

It needed no close observer to see that H.M. was deeply abstracted. He remained so abstracted, indeed, as to be nearly murdered by a taxi at the Admiralty Arch; and he was halfway down Whitehall before a familiar voice stopped him.

"Afternoon, Sir Henry!"

Burly, urbane, buttoned up in blue serge, with his bowler hat and his boiled blue eye, stood Chief Inspector Masters.

"Bit odd," the Chief Inspector remarked affably, "to see you taking a constitutional on a day like this. And how are you, sir?"

"Awful," said H.M. instantly. "But that's not the point. Masters, you crawlin' snake! You're the very man I wanted to see."

Few things startled the Chief Inspector. This one did.

"You," he repeated, "wanted to see *me*?"

"Uh-huh."

"And what about?"

"Masters, do you remember the Victoria Adams case about twenty years ago?"

The Chief Inspector's manner suddenly changed and grew wary.

"Victoria Adams case?" he ruminated. "No, sir, I can't say I do."

"Son, you're lyin'! You were sergeant to old Chief Inspector Rutherford in those days, and well remember it!"

Masters stood on his dignity.

"That's as may be, sir. But twenty years ago..."

"A little girl of twelve or thirteen, the child of very wealthy parents, disappeared one night out of a country cottage with all the doors and windows locked on the inside. A week later, while everybody was havin' screaming hysterics, the child reappeared again: through the locks and bolts, tucked up in her bed as usual. And to this day nobody's ever known what really happened."

There was a silence, while Masters shut his jaws hard.

"This family, the Adamses," persisted H.M., "owned the cottage, down Aylesbury way, on the edge of Goblin Wood, opposite the lake. Or was it?"

"Oh, ah," growled Masters. "It was."

H.M. looked at him curiously.

"They used the cottage as a base for bathin' in summer, and ice skatin' in winter. It was black winter when the child vanished, and the place was all locked up inside against draughts. They say her old man nearly went loopy when he found her there a week later, lying asleep under the lamp. But all she'd say, when they asked her where she'd been, was, '*I don't know*'."

Again there was a silence, while red buses thundered through the traffic press of Whitehall.

"You've got to admit, Masters, there was a flaming public rumpus. I say: did you ever read Barrie's *Mary Rose*?"

"No."

"Well, it was a situation straight out of Barrie. Some people, y'see, said that Vicky Adams was a child of faërie who'd been spirited away by the pixies..."

Whereupon Masters exploded.

He removed his bowler hat and made remarks about pixies, in detail, which could not have been bettered by H.M. himself.

"I know, son, I know." H.M. was soothing. Then his big voice sharpened. "Now tell me. Was all this talk strictly true?"

"What talk?"

"Locked windows? Bolted doors? No attic trap? No cellar? Solid walls and floor?"

"Yes, sir," answered Masters, regaining his dignity with a powerful effort, "I'm bound to admit it *was* true."

"Then there wasn't any jiggery-pokery about the cottage?"

"In your eye there wasn't," said Masters.

"How d'ye mean?"

"Listen, sir." Masters lowered his voice. "Before the Adamses took over that place, it was a hideout for Chuck Randall. At that time he was the swellest of the swell mob; we lagged him a couple of years later. Do you think Chuck wouldn't have rigged up some gadget for a getaway? Just so! Only..."

"Well? Hey?"

"We couldn't find it," grunted Masters.

"And I'll bet that pleased old Chief Inspector Rutherford?"

"I tell you straight: he was fair up the pole. Especially as the kid herself was a pretty kid, all big eyes and dark hair. You couldn't help trusting her story."

"Yes," said H.M. "That's what worries me."

"Worries you?"

"Oh, my son!" said H.M. dismally. "Here's Vicky Adams, the spoiled daughter of dotin' parents. She's supposed to be 'odd' and 'fey'. She's even encouraged to be. During her adolescence, the most impressionable time of her life, she gets wrapped round with the gauze of mystery that people talk about even yet. What's that woman like now, Masters? What's that woman like now?"

"Dear Sir Henry!" murmured Miss Vicky Adams in her softest voice.

She said this just as William Sage's car, with Bill and Eve Drayton in the front seat, and Vicky and H.M. in the back seat, turned off the main road. Behind them lay the smoky-red roofs of Aylesbury, against a brightness of late afternoon. The car turned down a side road, a damp tunnel of greenery, and into another road which was little more than a lane between hedgerows.

H.M.—though cheered by three good-sized picnic hampers from Fortnum & Mason, their wickerwork lids bulging with a feast—did not seem happy. Nobody in that car was happy, with the possible exception of Miss Adams herself.

Vicky, unlike Eve, was small and dark and vivacious. Her large light-brown eyes, with very black lashes, could be arch and coy; or they could be dreamily intense. The late Sir James Barrie might have called her a sprite. Those of more sober views would have recognised a different quality: she had an inordinate sex appeal, which was as palpable as a physical touch to any male within yards. And despite her smallness, Vicky had a full voice like Eve's. All these qualities she used even in so simple a matter as giving traffic directions.

"First right," she would say, leaning forward to put her hands on Bill Sage's shoulders. "Then straight on until the next traffic light. Ah, clever boy!"

"Not at all, not at all!" Bill would disclaim, with red ears and rather an erratic style of driving.

"Oh, yes, you are!" And Vicky would twist the lobe of his ear, playfully, before sitting back again.

(Eve Drayton did not say anything. She did not even turn round. Yet the atmosphere, even of that quiet English picnic party, had already become a trifle hysterical.)

"Dear Sir Henry!" murmured Vicky, as they turned down into the deep lane between the hedgerows. "I do wish you wouldn't be so materialistic! I do, really. Haven't you the tiniest bit of spirituality in your nature?"

"Me?" said H.M. in astonishment. "I got a very lofty spiritual nature. But what I want just now, my wench, is grub.—Oi!"

Bill Sage glanced round.

"By that speedometer," H.M. pointed, "we've now come forty-six miles and a bit. We didn't even leave town until people of decency and sanity were having their tea. Where are we *going*?"

"But didn't you know?" asked Vicky, with wide-open eyes. "We're going to the cottage where I had such a dreadful experience when I was a child."

"Was it such a dreadful experience, Vicky dear?" inquired Eve.

Vicky's eyes seemed far away.

"I don't remember, really. I was only a child, you see. I didn't understand. I hadn't developed the power for myself then."

"What power?" H.M. asked sharply.

"To dematerialise," said Vicky. "Of course."

In that warm sun-dusted lane, between the hawthorn hedges, the car jolted over a rut. Crockery rattled.

"Uh-huh. I see," observed H.M. without inflexion. "And where do you go, my wench, when you dematerialise?"

"Into a strange country. Through a little door. You wouldn't understand. Oh, you *are* such Philistines!" moaned Vicky. Then, with a sudden change of mood, she leaned forward and her whole physical allurement flowed again toward Bill Sage. "*You* wouldn't like me to disappear, would you, Bill?"

(Easy! Easy!)

"Only," said Bill, with a sort of wild gallantry, "if you promised to reappear again straightaway."

"Oh, I should have to do that." Vicky sat back. She was trembling. "The power wouldn't be strong enough. But even a poor little thing like me might be able to teach you a lesson. Look there!"

And she pointed ahead.

On their left, as the lane widened, stretched the ten-acre gloom of what is fancifully known as Goblin Wood. On their right lay a small lake, on private property and therefore deserted.

The cottage—set well back into a clearing of the wood so as to face the road, screened from it by a line of beeches—was in fact a bungalow of rough-hewn stone, with a slate roof. Across the front of it ran a wooden porch. It had a seedy air, like the long yellow-green grass of its front lawn. Bill parked the car at the side of the road, since there was no driveway.

"It's a bit lonely, ain't it?" demanded H.M. His voice boomed out against that utter stillness, under the hot sun.

"Oh, yes!" breathed Vicky. She jumped out of the car in a whirl of skirts. "That's why *they* were able to come and take me. When I was a child."

"They?"

"Dear Sir Henry! Do I need to explain?"

Then Vicky looked at Bill.

"I must apologise," she said, "for the state the house is in. I haven't been out here for months and months. There's a modern bathroom, I'm glad to say. Only kerosene lamps, of course. But then," a dreamy smile flashed across her face, "you won't need lamps, will you? Unless…"

"You mean," said Bill, who was taking a black case out of the car, "unless you disappear again?"

"Yes, Bill. And promise me you won't be frightened when I do."

The young man uttered a ringing oath which was shushed by Sir Henry Merrivale, who austerely said he disapproved of profanity. Eve Drayton was very quiet.

"But in the meantime," Vicky said wistfully, "let's forget it all, shall we? Let's laugh and dance and sing and pretend we're children! And surely your guest must be even more hungry by this time?"

It was in this emotional state that they sat down to their picnic.

H.M., if the truth must be told, did not fare too badly. Instead of sitting on some hummock of ground, they dragged a table and chairs to the shaded porch. All spoke in strained voices. But no word of controversy was said. It was only afterward, when the cloth was cleared, the furniture and hampers pushed indoors, the empty bottles flung away, that danger tapped a warning.

From under the porch Vicky fished out two half-rotted deckchairs, which she set up in the long grass of the lawn. These were to be occupied by Eve and H.M., while Vicky took Bill Sage to inspect a plum tree of some remarkable quality she did not specify.

Eve sat down without comment. H.M., who was smoking a black cigar opposite her, waited some time before he spoke.

"Y'know," he said, taking the cigar out of his mouth, "you're behaving remarkably well."

"Yes." Eve laughed. "Aren't I?"

"Are you pretty well acquainted with this Adams gal?"

"I'm her first cousin," Eve answered simply. "Now that her parents are dead, I'm the only relative she's got. I know *all* about her."

From across the lawn floated two voices saying something about wild strawberries. Eve, her fair hair and fair complexion vivid against the dark line of Goblin Wood, clenched her hands on her knees.

"You see, H.M.," she hesitated, "there was another reason why I invited you here. I—I don't quite know how to approach it."

"I'm the old man," said H.M., tapping himself impressively on the chest. "You tell me."

"Eve, darling!" interposed Vicky's voice, crying across the ragged lawn. "Coo-ee! Eve!"

"Yes, dear?"

"I've just remembered," cried Vicky, "that I haven't shown Bill over the cottage! You don't mind if I steal him away from you for a little while?"

"No, dear! Of course not!"

It was H.M., sitting so as to face the bungalow, who saw Vicky and Bill go in. He saw Vicky's wistful smile as she closed the door after them. Eve did not even look round. The sun was declining, making fiery chinks through the thickness of Goblin Wood behind the cottage.

"I won't let her have him," Eve suddenly cried. "I won't! I won't! I won't!"

"Does she want him, my wench? Or, which is more to the point, does he want her?"

"He never has," Eve said with emphasis. "Not really. And he never will."

H.M., motionless, puffed out cigar smoke.

"Vicky's a faker," said Eve. "Does that sound catty?"

"Not necessarily. I was just thinkin' the same thing myself."

"I'm patient," said Eve. Her blue eyes were fixed. "I'm terribly, terribly patient. I can wait years for what I want. Bill's not making much money now, and I haven't got a bean. But Bill's got great talent under that easygoing manner of his. He *must* have the right girl to help him. If only…"

"If only the elfin sprite would let him alone. Hey?"

"Vicky acts like that," said Eve, "toward practically every man she ever meets. That's why she never married. She says it leaves her soul free to commune with other souls. This occultism—"

Then it all poured out, the family story of the Adamses. This repressed girl spoke at length, spoke as perhaps she had never spoken before. Vicky Adams, the child who wanted to attract attention, her father Uncle Fred and her mother Aunt Margaret seemed to walk in vividness as the shadows gathered.

"I was too young to know her at the time of the 'disappearance', of course. But, oh, I knew her afterward! And I thought…"

"Well?"

"If I could get *you* here," said Eve, "I thought she'd try to show off with some game. And then you'd expose her. And Bill would see what an awful faker she is. But it's hopeless! It's hopeless!"

"Looky here," observed H.M., who was smoking his third cigar. He sat up. "Doesn't it strike you those two are being a rummy-awful long time just in lookin' through a little bungalow?"

Eve, roused out of a dream, stared back at him. She sprang to her feet. She was not now, you could guess, thinking of any disappearance.

"Excuse me a moment," she said curtly.

Eve hurried across to the cottage, went up on the porch, and opened the front door. H.M. heard her heels rap down the length of the small passage inside. She marched straight back again, closed the front door, and rejoined H.M.

"All the doors of the rooms are shut," she announced in a high voice. "I really don't think I ought to disturb them."

"Easy, my wench!"

"I have absolutely no interest," declared Eve, with the tears coming into her eyes, "in what happens to either of them now. Shall we take the car and go back to town without them?"

H.M. threw away his cigar, got up, and seized her by the shoulders.

"I'm the old man," he said, leering like an ogre. "Will you listen to me?"

"No!"

"If I'm any reader of the human dial," persisted H.M., "that young feller's no more gone on Vicky Adams than I am. He was scared, my wench. Scared." Doubt, indecision crossed H.M.'s face. "I dunno what he's scared of. Burn me, I don't! But..."

"Hoy!" called the voice of Bill Sage.

It did not come from the direction of the cottage.

They were surrounded on three sides by Goblin Wood, now blurred with twilight. From the north side the voice bawled at them, followed by crackling in dry undergrowth. Bill, his hair and sports coat and flannels more than a little dirty, regarded them with a face of bitterness.

"Here are her blasted wild strawberries," he announced, extending his hand. "Three of 'em. The fruitful (excuse me) result of three-quarters of an hour's hard labour. I absolutely refuse to chase 'em in the dark."

For a moment Eve Drayton's mouth moved without speech.

"Then you weren't… in the cottage all this time?"

"In the cottage?" Bill glanced at it. "I was in that cottage," he said, "about five minutes. Vicky had a woman's whim. She wanted some wild strawberries out of what she called the 'forest'."

"Wait a minute, son!" said H.M. very sharply. "You didn't come out that front door. Nobody did."

"No! I went out the back door! It opens straight on the wood."

"Yes. And what happened then?"

"Well, I went to look for these damned…"

"No, no! What did *she* do!"

"Vicky? She locked and bolted the back door on the inside. I remember her grinning at me through the glass panel. She—"

Bill stopped short. His eyes widened, and then narrowed, as though at the impact of an idea. All three of them turned to look at the rough stone cottage.

"By the way," said Bill. He cleared his throat vigorously. "By the way, have you seen Vicky since then?"

"No."

"This couldn't be…?"

"It could be, son," said H.M. "We'd all better go in there and have a look."

They hesitated for a moment on the porch. A warm, moist fragrance breathed up from the ground after sunset. In half an hour it would be completely dark.

Bill Sage threw open the front door and shouted Vicky's name. That sound seemed to penetrate, reverberating, through every room. The intense heat and stuffiness of the cottage, where no window had been raised for months, blew out at them. But nobody answered.

"Get inside," snapped H.M. "And stop yowlin'." The old maestro was nervous. "I'm dead sure she didn't get out by the front door; but we'll just make certain there's no slippin' out now."

Stumbling over the table and chairs they had used on the porch, he fastened the front door. They were in a narrow passage, once handsome with a parquet floor and pine-panelled walls, leading to a door with a glass panel at the rear. H.M. lumbered forward to inspect this door and found it locked and bolted, as Bill had said.

Goblin Wood grew darker.

Keeping well together, they searched the cottage. It was not large, having two good-sized rooms on one side of the passage, and two small rooms on the other side, so as to make space for bathroom and kitchenette. H.M., raising fogs of dust, ransacked every inch where a person could possibly hide.

And all the windows were locked on the inside. And the chimney flues were too narrow to admit anybody.

And Vicky Adams wasn't there.

"Oh, my eye!" breathed Sir Henry Merrivale.

They had gathered, by what idiotic impulse not even H.M. could have said, just outside the open door of the bathroom. A bath tap dripped monotonously. The last light through a frosted-glass window showed three faces hung there as though disembodied.

"Bill," said Eve in an unsteady voice, "this is a trick. Oh, I've longed for her to be exposed! This is a trick!"

"Then where is she?"

"H.M. can tell us! Can't you, H.M.?"

"Well... now," muttered the great man.

Across H.M.'s Panama hat was a large black handprint, made there when he had pressed down the hat after investigating a chimney. He glowered under it.

"Son," he said to Bill, "there's just one question I want you to answer in all this hokey-pokey. When you went out pickin' wild strawberries, will you swear Vicky Adams didn't go with you?"

"As God is my judge, she didn't," returned Bill, with fervency and obvious truth. "Besides, how the devil could she? Look at the lock and bolt on the back door!"

H.M. made two more violent black handprints on his hat.

He lumbered forward, his head down, two or three paces in the narrow passage. His foot half-skidded on something that had been lying there unnoticed, and he picked it up. It was a large, square section of thin, waterproof oilskin, jagged at one corner.

"Have you found anything?" demanded Bill in a strained voice.

"No. Not to make any sense, that is. But just a minute!"

At the rear of the passage, on the left-hand side, was the bedroom from which Vicky Adams had vanished as a child. Though H.M. had searched this room before, he opened the door again.

It was now almost dark in Goblin Wood.

He saw dimly a room of twenty years before: a room of flounces, of lace curtains, of once-polished mahogany, its mirrors glimmering against white-papered walls. H.M. seemed especially interested in the windows.

He ran his hands carefully round the frame of each, even climbing laboriously up on a chair to examine the tops. He borrowed a box of matches from Bill; and the little spurts of light, following the rasp of the match, rasped against nerves as well. The hope died in his face, and his companions saw it.

"H.M.," Bill said for the dozenth time, "where is she?"

"Son," replied H.M. despondently, "I don't know."

"Let's get out of here," Eve said abruptly. Her voice was a small scream. "I kn-know it's all a trick! I know Vicky's a faker! But let's get out of here. For God's sake let's get out of here!"

"As a matter of fact," Bill cleared his throat, "I agree. Anyway, we won't hear from Vicky until tomorrow morning."

"*Oh, yes, you will,*" whispered Vicky's voice out of the darkness.

Eve screamed.

They lighted a lamp.

But there was nobody there.

Their retreat from the cottage, it must be admitted, was not very dignified.

How they stumbled down that ragged lawn in the dark, how they piled rugs and picnic hampers into the car, how they eventually found the main road again, is best left undescribed.

Sir Henry Merrivale has since sneered at this—"a bit of a goosy feeling; nothin' much"—and it is true that he has no nerves to speak of. But he can be worried, badly worried; and that he was worried on this occasion may be deduced from what happened later.

H.M., after dropping in at Claridge's for a modest late supper of lobster and *pêche Melba*, returned to his house in Brook Street and slept a hideous sleep. It was three o'clock in the morning, even before the summer dawn, when the ringing of the bedside telephone roused him.

What he heard sent his blood pressure soaring.

"Dear Sir Henry!" crooned a familiar and sprite-like voice.

H.M. was himself again, full of gall and bile. He switched on the bedside lamp and put on his spectacles with care, so as adequately to address the phone.

"Have I got the honour," he said with dangerous politeness, "of addressin' Miss Vicky Adams?"

"Oh, yes!"

"I sincerely trust," said H.M., "you've been havin' a good time? Are you materialised yet?"

"Oh, yes!"

"Where are you now?"

"I'm afraid," there was coy laughter in the voice, "that must be a little secret for a day or two. I want to teach you a really *good* lesson. Blessings, dear."

And she hung up the receiver.

H.M. did not say anything. He climbed out of bed. He stalked up and down the room, his corporation majestic under an old-fashioned nightshirt stretching to his heels. Then, since he himself had been waked up at three o'clock in the morning, the obvious course was to wake up somebody else; so he dialled the home number of Chief Inspector Masters.

"No, sir," retorted Masters grimly, after coughing the frog out of his throat. "I do *not* mind you ringing up. Not a bit of it!" He spoke with a certain pleasure. "Because I've got a bit of news for you."

H.M. eyed the phone suspiciously.

"Masters, are you trying to do me in the eye again?"

"It's what you always try to do to me, isn't it?"

"All right, all right!" growled H.M. "What's the news?"

"Do you remember mentioning the Vicky Adams case yesterday?"

"Sort of. Yes."

"Oh, ah! Well, I had a word or two round among our people. I was tipped the wink to go and see a certain solicitor. He was old Mr. Fred Adams's solicitor before Mr. Adams died about six or seven years ago."

Here Masters's voice grew triumphant.

"I always said, Sir Henry, that Chuck Randall had planted some gadget in that cottage for a quick getaway. And I was right. The gadget was..."

"You were quite right, Masters. The gadget was a trick window."

The telephone, so to speak, gave a start.

"What's that?"

"A trick window." H.M. spoke patiently. "You press a spring. And the whole frame of the window, two leaves locked together, slides down between the wall far enough so you can climb over. Then you push it back up again."

"How in lum's name do you know that?"

"Oh, my son! They used to build windows like it in country houses during the persecution of Catholic priests. It was a good enough *second* guess. Only... it won't work."

Masters seemed annoyed. "It won't work now," Masters agreed. "And do you know why?"

"I can guess. Tell me."

"Because, just before Mr. Adams died, he discovered how his darling daughter had flummoxed him. He never told anybody except his lawyer. He took a handful of four-inch nails, and sealed up the top of that frame so tight an orangutan couldn't move it, and painted 'em over so they wouldn't be noticed."

"Uh-huh. You can notice 'em now."

"I doubt if the young lady herself ever knew. But, by George!" Masters said savagely. "I'd like to see anybody try the same game now!"

"You would, hey? Then will it interest you to know that the same gal has just disappeared out of the same house *again?*"

H.M. began a long narrative of the facts, but he had to break off because the telephone was raving.

"Honest, Masters," H.M. said seriously, "I'm not joking. She didn't get out through that window. But she did get out. You'd better meet me," he gave directions, "tomorrow morning. In the meantime, son, sleep well."

It was, therefore, a worn-faced Masters who went into the Visitors' Room at the Senior Conservatives' Club just before lunch on the following day.

The Visitors' Room is a dark sepulchral place, opening on an air-well, where the visitor is surrounded by pictures of dyspeptic-looking gentlemen with beards. It has a pervading mustiness of wood and leather. Though whisky and soda stood on the table, H.M. sat in a leather chair far away from it, ruffling his hands across his bald head.

"Now, Masters, keep your shirt on!" he warned. "This business may be rummy. But it's not a police matter—yet."

"I know it's not a police matter," Masters said grimly. "All the same, I've had a word with the Superintendent at Aylesbury."

"Fowler?"

"You know him?"

"Sure. I know everybody. Is he goin' to keep an eye out?"

"He's going to have a look at that ruddy cottage. I've asked for any telephone calls to be put through here. In the meantime, sir—"

It was at this point, as though diabolically inspired, that the telephone rang. H.M. reached it before Masters.

"It's the old man," he said, unconsciously assuming a stance of grandeur. "Yes, yes! Masters is here, but he's drunk. You tell me first. What's that?"

The telephone talked thinly.

"Sure I looked in the kitchen cupboard," bellowed H.M. "Though I didn't honestly expect to find Vicky Adams hidin' there. What's that? Say it again! Plates? Cups that had been..."

An almost frightening change had come over H.M.'s expression. He stood motionless. All the posturing went out of him. He was not even listening to the voice that still talked thinly, while his eyes and his brain moved to put together facts. At length (though the voice still talked) he hung up the receiver.

H.M. blundered back to the centre table, where he drew out a chair and sat down.

"Masters," he said very quietly, "I've come close to makin' the silliest mistake of my life."

Here he cleared his throat.

"I shouldn't have made it, son. I really shouldn't. But don't yell at me for cuttin' off Fowler. I can tell you now how Vicky Adams disappeared. And she said one true thing when she said she was going into a strange country."

"How do you mean?"

"She's dead," answered H.M.

The word fell with heavy weight into that dingy room, where the bearded faces looked down.

"Y'see," H.M. went on blankly, "a lot of us were right when we thought Vicky Adams was a faker. She was. To attract attention to herself, she played that trick on her family with the hocused window. She's lived and traded on it ever since. That's what sent me straight in the wrong direction. I was on the alert for some *trick* Vicky Adams might play. So it never occurred to me that this elegant pair of beauties, Miss Eve Drayton and Mr. William Sage, were deliberately conspirin' to murder *her*."

Masters got slowly to his feet.

"Did you say... murder?"

"Oh, yes."

Again H.M. cleared his throat.

"It was all arranged beforehand for me to be a witness. They knew Vicky Adams couldn't resist a challenge to disappear, especially as Vicky always believed she could get out by the trick window. They wanted Vicky to say she was goin' to disappear. They never knew anything about the trick window, Masters. But they knew their own plan very well.

"Eve Drayton even told me the motive. She hated Vicky, of course. But that wasn't the main point. She was Vicky Adams's only relative; she'd inherit an awful big scoopful of money. Eve said she could be patient. (And, burn me, how her eyes meant it when she said that!) Rather than risk any slightest suspicion of murder, she was willing to wait seven years until a disappeared person can be presumed dead.

"Our Eve, I think, was the fiery drivin' force of that conspiracy. She was only scared part of the time. Sage was scared all of the time. But it was Sage who did the real dirty work. He lured Vicky Adams into that cottage, while Eve kept me in close conversation on the lawn…"

H.M. paused.

Intolerably vivid in the mind of Chief Inspector Masters, who had seen it years before, rose the picture of the rough-stone bungalow against the darkling wood.

"Masters," said H.M., "why should a bath tap be dripping in a house that hadn't been occupied for months?"

"Well?"

"Sage, y'see, is a surgeon. I saw him take his black case of instruments out of the car. He took Vicky Adams into that house. In the bathroom he stabbed her, he stripped her, and *he dismembered her body in the bathtub.*—Easy, son!"

"Go on," said Masters without moving.

"The head, the torso, the folded arms and legs, were wrapped up in three large square pieces of thin transparent oilskin. Each was sewed up with coarse thread so the blood wouldn't drip. Last night I found one of the oilskin pieces he'd ruined when his needle slipped at the corner. Then he walked out of the house, with the back door still standin' unlocked, to get his wild-strawberry alibi."

"Sage went out of there," shouted Masters, "leaving the body in the house?"

"Oh, yes," agreed H.M.

"But where did he leave it?"

H.M. ignored this.

"In the meantime, son, what about Eve Drayton? At the end of the arranged three-quarters of an hour, she indicated there was hanky-panky between her fiancé and Vicky Adams. She flew into the house. But what did she do?

"She walked to the back of the passage. I heard her. *There she simply locked and bolted the back door.* And then she marched out to join me with tears in her eyes. And these two beauties were ready for investigation."

"Investigation?" said Masters. *"With that body still in the house?"*

"Oh, yes."

Masters lifted both fists.

"It must have given young Sage a shock," said H.M., "when I found that piece of waterproof oilskin he'd washed but dropped. Anyway, these two had only two more bits of hokey-pokey. The 'vanished' gal had to speak—to show she was still alive. If you'd been there, son, you'd have noticed that Eve Drayton's got a voice just like Vicky Adams's. If somebody speaks in a dark room, carefully imitatin' a coy tone she never uses herself, the illusion's goin' to be pretty good. The same goes for a telephone.

"It was finished, Masters. All that had to be done was remove the body from the house, and get it far away from there…"

"But that's just what I'm asking you, sir! Where was the body all this time? And who in blazes *did* remove the body from the house?"

"All of us did," answered H.M.

"What's that?"

"Masters," said H.M., "aren't you forgettin' the picnic hampers?"

And now, the Chief Inspector saw, H.M. was as white as a ghost. His next words took Masters like a blow between the eyes.

"Three good-sized wickerwork hampers, with lids. After our big meal on the porch, those hampers were shoved inside the house where Sage could get at 'em. He had to leave most of the used crockery behind, in the kitchen cupboard. But three wickerwork hampers from a picnic, and three butcher's parcels to go inside 'em. I carried one down to the car myself. It felt a bit funny..."

H.M. stretched out his hand, not steadily, toward the whisky.

"Y'know," he said, "I'll always wonder if I was carrying the—head."

ALSO AVAILABLE

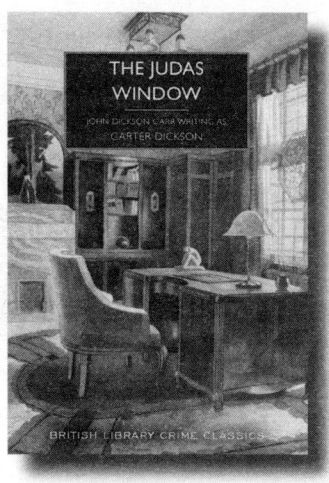

James Answell is paying a visit to his future father-in-law, the champion archer Avory Hume, at his Grosvenor Street townhouse. Invited into the study and offered a drink, Answell suddenly swoons—and awakes to find the door and windows locked from the inside. His host is dead, skewered with an arrow, and Answell is prime suspect. The devilish puzzle constructed, Carter Dickson unravels an ingenious courtroom thriller, in which the razor-sharp amateur detective Sir Henry Merrivale argues for the defence in all of his outlandish glory—and the mystery of the "Judas Window" is unveiled.

First published in 1938, this landmark novel remains one of the greatest locked-room murder mysteries of all time, and a dazzling showcase of the author's unsurpassed flair for narrative legerdemain and jaw-dropping twists.

ALSO AVAILABLE

A cold case of poisonings heats up at a quaint guest house. A string of suspicious murders follows a crime writer's tour bus. Two seedy stowaways uncover an infamous smuggling ring.

Everyone needs a break now and then, but sometimes getting away can be murder. In this new anthology, Martin Edwards presents a jam-packed travel-case of eighteen classic mysteries, featuring short stories from crime fiction legends such as Christianna Brand, Anthony Berkeley and Celia Fremlin, alongside rare finds revived from the British Library archives. Including intriguing notes on the stories and their authors, this volume is your ticket to a thrilling journey from 1920s seaside skulduggery through to calamity in 1980s suburbia—perfect for armchair travelling or your own summer getaway.

ALSO AVAILABLE
IN THE BRITISH LIBRARY
CRIME CLASSICS SERIES

Big Ben Strikes Eleven	DAVID MAGARSHACK
Death of an Author	E. C. R. LORAC
The Black Spectacles	JOHN DICKSON CARR
Death of a Bookseller	BERNARD J. FARMER
The Wheel Spins	ETHEL LINA WHITE
Someone from the Past	MARGOT BENNETT
Who Killed Father Christmas?	ED. MARTIN EDWARDS
Twice Round the Clock	BILLIE HOUSTON
The White Priory Murders	CARTER DICKSON
The Port of London Murders	JOSEPHINE BELL
Murder in the Basement	ANTHONY BERKELEY
Fear Stalks the Village	ETHEL LINA WHITE
The Cornish Coast Murder	JOHN BUDE
Suddenly at His Residence	CHRISTIANNA BRAND
The Edinburgh Mystery	ED. MARTIN EDWARDS
Checkmate to Murder	E. C. R. LORAC
The Spoilt Kill	MARY KELLY
Smallbone Deceased	MICHAEL GILBERT
The Story of Classic Crime in 100 Books	MARTIN EDWARDS
The Pocket Detective: 100+ Puzzles	KATE JACKSON
The Pocket Detective 2: 100+ More Puzzles	KATE JACKSON

Many of our titles are also available
in eBook, large print and audio editions